DEATH

BY

FUGUE

The Jimmu Files – 1

A Novel by

Mr. Cagey Magee

DEATH BY FUGUE
The Jimmu Files – Book 1
Copyright © 2024 by Cagey Magee

FIRST EDITION SOFTCOVER
ISBN: 162253588X
ISBN-13: 978-1-62253-588-0

Editor: Lane Diamond
Cover Artist: Kris Norris
Interior Designer: Lane Diamond

EVOLVED PUBLISHING™

www.EvolvedPub.com
Evolved Publishing LLC
Butler, Wisconsin, USA

Death by Fugue is a work of fiction. All names, characters, places, and incidents are the product of the author's imagination, or are used fictitiously. Any resemblance to actual events or persons, living or dead, is entirely coincidental.

Printed in Book Antiqua font.

Books by Cagey Magee

NORTHWATCH
Book 1: *Cass and Wat*
Book 2: *Cass and Logan*
Book 3: *Cass and Nat*
Book 4: *Cass and Keith*

THE JIMMU FILES
Book 1: *Death by Fugue*
Book 2: *Death by Cathedral*
Book 3: *Death by Quantum*

Find more from this author at the link below.
www.EvolvedPub.com/CMagee

Dedication

For Judith A. Thomas,
My friend and partner in virtuosity.

Author's Note

I recommend *The Jimmu Files* series of mystery thrillers, for adults and especially for age 13- to 110-year-old young adults. If you are a chimpanzee or an Artificial, you are exempt from these age recommendations unless your keepers, parents, teachers, or Artificial Intelligence consultants choose otherwise.

In *Death by Fugue*, NYPD Inspector Rex Caine suffers from a "fugue state." If you have not encountered this term in TV, movies, or your own nightmares, a fugue state occurs when a person has amnesia, cannot find his own life, and adopts or creates another. In the case of Inspector Caine, he ceases to know which side of the law he is on. Therein lies the tale.

Please enjoy the book but know that the author will not take responsibility for nightmares, sleepwalking, bed wetting, tantrums, or misbehavior in any age or intellectual group.

Cordially,
Cagey Magee, Author, Editor, Virtuoso, Curmudgeon

DAY ONE
---2038---

Chapter 1 - Spring Ball

Dale had never seen a naked girl outside of swim class.

—1—

Saratoga, NY. Tate Prep School. The Spring Ball. Midnight. Dale Summers.

"Cow, this dance was great," Dale said.

"It took a long time to get the decorations up," Fred said. His real name was Wang Lei Lóng. He was a Chinese immigrant, fourteen like Dale but short, very short. "This is the end of the school year, Dale, and we needed to get it right. I think we succeeded. Everybody seems happy. Now it's time to take the decorations down and clean up." Fred headed the cleanup committee.

"You really did get it right, Fred." The Tate Prep School kids had stuffed and exhausted themselves by gluttony, dancing, and other teen stuff. Gradually, they were now disappearing to their dorm suites.

"Hey, look at little Mark Kershaw," Fred said. Mark was eight, holding on to eleven-year-old Martha Sweeney, and kind of humping her leg to hug her. He often did junk like that.

"I think he's asleep," Dale said.

"Nothing new there. Gotta go, Dale. See you after cleanup." Fred ran over to a group forming at the other side of the dining room.

Dale and Fred were roomies and were in the Tate Special Service program. Their service at the moment was to mentor little Mark Kershaw. They were very careful about that. Mark was super lively and possessed a vocabulary that would make a sea urchin turn to slime. On top of that, his dad and two uncles, Mannie, Marion, and Marvin were NYPD cops, just like Dale's future father, Inspector Rex Caine.

Dale joined the last kids drifting back out. He lived on the top floor. Close to his room, a door stood open with Mary Margaret Pinkham standing there looking straight at him. It was 2038, and separating boys from girls had ended eons ago, replaced by education, common sense, and machines overflowing with condoms and morning-after pills.

Mary Margaret was fourteen too and was in a couple of Dale's classes but had never even spoken to him, much less danced with him. She had danced with a bunch of other boys tonight, though, and was standing there smiling up a heat wave, not easy to do in a Saratoga, New York, boarding school.

"Hi, Dale, sorry I missed you at the dance." She was the daughter of rich Cindy McGraw, who gave the great balls over at the Canfield Casino. "Let's talk." She motioned him into her suite, one of the really elegant singles.

Dale thought about her invitation for a fraction of a second, then went straight for Mary Margaret's door. Everybody knew she was active.

She closed and locked the door, and he found himself in her bedroom. "I'm so sorry that I missed dancing with you tonight. I want to make up for it." She clicked a remote. The lights went down and slow dance music came on.

Dale was a good dancer and was suddenly doing it with Mary Margaret herself, every Tate boy's romantic fantasy.

"Oh, my," she groaned. "You're a great dancer."

"Fred taught me."

"No surprise there. Fred's small but does everything really great."

They glided around the room pressed against each other. Dale had danced with a number of girls tonight but none like Cindy. She floated when she danced and even when she pressed Dale's back toward her and kissed him.

He used to kiss his mom too, but on the mouth, not in it. Being on Cindy's dance card was like going to Wet Heaven.

Somehow, they danced their way to his shirt and belt being open and Cindy being naked. Dale had never seen a naked girl before outside of swim class. She stretched out on the bed and pulled him along. By then, he was wearing as much as she was.

"Dale, I'm so glad you gave up being the Class Evangelist."

—2—

Tate School. Dale and Fred's Suite. 7:00 AM. Dale.

The next morning, Dale and Fred locked their room and headed for breakfast as usual. They were both a little tired from staying up late and everything.

When they made it to the first floor, Cindy ran up, gave Dale a peck on the cheek, whispered, "Dale, I'm so sorry," and took off for the dining room.

Less than a minute later, they met Tom Mallard going the other way. He grabbed his crotch, looked straight at Dale, and said in a low, sexy voice, "Hallelujah, Deacon."

—3—

Long Island, NY. North Shore Medical Center. 3:00 PM. Angie Summers.

"So much blood." Angie knew this day could not be worse but would be.

This afternoon, embraced by the reds, purples, and grays of the Belmont Racetrack flower beds, Angie had sat on the pavement and held Rex's head in her lap. Filaments of blood from his forehead crocheted her white blouse. Blood splotched the asphalt. Blood pooled under the man Rex had killed. Blood even spattered the dusty miller. As much as Rex disapproved of Angie playing detective without him, she needed to learn the truth, and no one would stop her.

Now, Angie sat in the Intensive Care waiting room.

"So much blood. Please let Rex live." Half prayer, half demand. "Please let him live, no matter how far past the line he's gone." There had been so much Belmont Park blood on his head and chest as he lay there during the ninth race.

"*Buck up, Kid,*" Mary Helen Mack said in Angie's mind. "*Rex will make it.*"

"*I wish I could believe you, Mary Helen.*"

Mary Helen Mack was Angie's detective in many of her novels but had somehow come alive in Angie's mind. They spoke often.

Alone in the Intensive Care waiting room of the Northshore Medical Center, Angie Summers slumped into the chair and clawed at the armrests. Some crucial bit of truth lay hidden in the pulpy blue vinyl, something she could not quite reach. Three buzzing flies landed in a splotch of sunlight on the faded blue sill of the ICU waiting room window.

Once, that window looked into the nursery. Now, it revealed the hall that led to Intensive Care, Emergency, and Surgery. Fourteen years ago, Angie gave birth to sweet, befuddled Dale in this hospital, a surprise landing during a Long Island vacation. Someone killed his father, Bernie, two months before his birth. Inspector Rex Caine investigated the murder and ultimately took Bernie's place at the nursery window.

Now, as Angie was considering Rex's third marriage proposal, he lay in the ICU, connected to the entire room.

Dale had moved to Tate Prep, up near Saratoga, NY, to escape his mother's hectic writing schedule, book signings, and talk shows. He was a wise child occasionally and even helped her with her books, but he was best off in Saratoga for now. She had called him about Rex before he could hear it on the news. Dale worshipped Rex. Angie could think of no way to tell him that the man he wanted for a father participated in something illegal.

Down the corridor, monitors lined the nursing station. A dumpy nurse named Judy would be watching the screens intently. Angie had met her when Rex reached ICU. Judy doubtless changed her hair color daily, ran over squirrels for sport, and asked the staff to call her Madam Death. She would not make a good friend but did appear well-focused and capable, a good character for one of Angie's highly profitable Literary Crime Thrillers.

ICU held a dense urgency and silent chaos even when no one moved, spoke, or breathed. In Emergency, a siren neared the distant end of the corridor. Doors swished open and men ran in pushing a gurney. Behind them, a wailing woman's diamond necklace shot light onto the ceiling as she ran close behind. Her screams wet the long corridor.

Angie created many grim and enchanted worlds for her novels. Fans relished the suspense, mystery, gore, guts, and sex, all impregnated by the dim light of magic, but nothing she had written could compare with this place.

This afternoon, Angie and Rex left Belmont after the Eighth Race. They often left early to beat the crowd. Cloud puffs dotted the sky, and a tangy breeze inspired their intention to drive to Freeport for swordfish.

A nervous-looking man, short and dark, was standing by the last tear-shaped flower bed before the parking lot. Rex shoved Angie with his left hand, drew his Beretta M9 with his right and fired twice, simultaneously with the man's three shots. A haze of blood showered a nearby boy, about six years old, with red hair and freckles. He had been playing with a Gorgi model on the walk. The blood that blurred the red-brown stripes on his Garfield T-shirt and splashed his face and pants included some of his own.

"So much blood."

The man's bullets struck Rex's temple and chest. Rex spun and crashed forehead-first onto the asphalt. Angie heard the shots and the scuff of Rex's heel on the walk. She felt the bullet wind and heard the blood-drenched child's screams.

In the quiet of the ICU, Angie still heard the echoes of horror weaving into the din of the ninth race.

"So much blood."

Down in Emergency, the diamond lady's wailing dwindled. The waiting and terrifying speculation were subduing her as they had Angie. Rex's assailant lay in the morgue, and Rex lay in ICU.

In the NYPD, Rex had worked Homicide but now specialized in drug homicides and substance traffic curtailment. Mega dangerous. Angie had begged him to quit. Nearly a year ago, someone assassinated his brother Emery, who had been working Narcotics.

Angie thought for a moment and pulled out her Pear Superphone. When she had told Dale about the shooting, she also told him to stay in Saratoga for Summer School because there was nothing he could do here. He loved Rex and needed support from the school and his special roommate, just as Angie needed support from her best friends, Gretta and Maddie. Hopefully, they would be as mature about this as Dale.

Angie smiled and stared at her phone, then whispered to herself, "No. They are both publishing CEOs. They couldn't possibly be that grown up." If only Rex lay down the hall as innocently as newborn Dale once had.

"Face it, Angie," Mary Helen said. *"Rex drew first."*

"I know, Mary Helen. I know."

—**4**—

New York City. Spencer and Sons Publishing Group. 3:30 PM. Gretta Braun, CEO.

Gretta Braun sat at her desk, forked a blob of key lime cheesecake garnished with sliced kiwi and black currents into her mouth, and used the plate to push the desk lamp closer to her super-excellent Sceptre Monitor. The Excel spreadsheet glared back at her. The company numbers were excellent, and even the trends gave her the damp twiddles, an extra good thing.

Dark curtains cloaked her office, so only Gretta, the desk, the on-screen spreadsheet, and the cheesecake remained visible. She kept her drapes closed to hide the passage of time because her workload never fit comfortably into the clock.

Time lack could impair passion. In Gretta's case, her passion for profit never wavered. She persevered and smiled as she ate, partly at the super scrumptious cheesecake, mostly at the equally delicious numbers on the spreadsheet. Gretta's greediest board members, all Japanese, would find much to please them. Of course, they also owned a chain of obscene knick-knack stores that pleased them.

Angie Summers's latest book, *Sister Mary Margaret — Dead,* was selling better than the Bible and possessed more readers. Angie had found the secret of writing successful commercial fiction bordering on the literary: Literary Crime Thrillers. The casual fifth grader could read them during recess for the sex, dirty words, or whatever else kids did these days behind their adults' backs. A college professor could ponder, ruminate, and never be disappointed — much lay tucked into Angie's prose.

Gretta propelled the fork toward her mouth, then paused and looked at the chunk of cheesecake waiting to stroke her atavistic longings with its smooth richness and piquant tang, then slip straight down to her hips, where it would expand to obscenely bulging luxury.

Reluctantly, she allowed the fork to drift back to the plate but snatched one last piece of kiwi and tossed it into her mouth. If propriety demanded that she forgo the last third of the cake, she at least could have the fruit. The dementedly healthy kiwi, with 0.3 percent fat and low sodium, now sticky with the afterglow of burnt-butter icing, slipped down her throat guiltlessly.

The antique Bakelite Ma-Bell rang, probably God calling to observe that Gretta Braun was a glutinous ass or possessed one. God could entertain whatever opinion She wished as long as She never published it. If She did, Gretta would sue.

$-5-$

New York City. PMS Center. Centered Women. 4:30 PM. Madeleine Franck CEO.

"Oh, my Christ. That frigging snot!" Maddie snatched up a crystal ashtray that intended to suggest an apple but resembled a shrunken nostril instead. "Snot!" With the full fury of her celebrated rage, she hurled it across the width of her office, against the amber wall, just below William Randolph Hearst in the Dali frame. "How dare that insufferably obsequious little dingus—not you, Billy—write such crap?" One dared not insult precious dead old Willy. He haunted those who offended him, as did Orson Welles.

The snot in question, Webb Drake, routinely provided Maddie's high-class hag-rag, *Centered Women*, with superb book reviews. Maddie had hired the little prick for his gorgeous God-damned reviews—but for him to accuse Angelica Summers of authoring superficial novels? "Snot!"

And Maddie could not stop the little puke's review—the damned Postal Service was already delivering it to 100,000 peerless ladies who fancied themselves the non-cookie-bakers of the generation or some such crap, not to mention the ten million who paid for the digital.

"I'll fire that pebble-balled little prick!" She would not, of course. If she did, some other women's magazine would snatch him up with a hairy snatch, or one of Maddie's part-time sometimes friends, enemies, rivals, or allies would turn him into a cause célèbre so they could use his experiences at *Centered Women* for a piece called *Ditched by the Bitch* or some other suitable euphemism. Besides, firing the devious little dick-drip would hurt circulation.

Too exhausted to let loose another shriek, she said, "Oh, my Christ, my life is nothing but a prolonged tantrum." Maddie growled like a Siamese pussy, flopped into the high-back chair at her desk, and gulped in a huge breath. The fur felt good on her thigh bottoms. Of all the CEO-fems in New York, only Madeleine Franck, the Chief Executive Officer and absolute monarch of *Centered Women* owned a sable chair and could hear the little bastards shriek with delight as she wiggled it in their furry faces. Not even Gretta owned a sable chair. "Of course, she did wear custom-made silk underwear." Maddie tried it but got jock itch.

"Oh, my Christ, Gretta!" It struck her like a Larry Sanders climbing axe. "Wait until Gretta hears about Webb's damned review! GeeGodOhFat! Vengeance, thy name is Braun. Close friend or not, she'll wreck me." Maddie grabbed the flowered porcelain phone from its brass cradle, paused to contemplate her options, apologies and promises, then dialed.

One did not cross Gretta Braun this way without discussing it with her first and asking for permission. She squeezed every penny from every book she ever published and, if she wished, could squeeze your body until your soul bled in tandem with your bank account.

"Spencer and Sons," a squat voice pronounced from the earpiece.

"Gretta?"

"I'm sorry, Ms. Braun is out. May I take a message?"

"Gretta never goes out during working hours—she's too paranoid. So where is she?"

"Oh, hi, Ms. Franck. This is Leslie, Gretta's Executive Assistant."

Maddie didn't know Leslie's last name. Gretta always said that secretaries and executive assistants should not have last names.

"I was just about to call you, Ms. Franck. Ms. Braun is en route to the North Shore Medical Center on Long Island to see Angelica Summers. There's been a shooting. I believe it concerns Inspector Rex. Gretta took a WhisperChop from the roof."

"Oh, my Christ!" Maddie owned a rooftop WhisperChop pad too.

Chapter 2 - The Call

Blood on the Wimple.

Saratoga, NY. Tate Preparatory School. 9:00 PM. Dale.

Dale Summers was having trouble going to sleep after his mother's call and after the day of heckling he'd just endured, who could blame him? If one more kid grabbed its crotch, boy or girl, and said, "Hallelujah," he might just whip it out and grope right back at them. Seemingly, the entire school knew that he'd lost his virginity to Mary Margaret Pinkham last night. On top of that, the man he desperately wanted as the father he'd never had lay dying in New York.

The sheet felt cold against his chest in the dim, air-conditioned room. He never wore tops to bed. In the case of the dark red silky PJs Aunt Gretta had given him, he'd donated the top to Fred Styles as a nightshirt. It was part of Dale's campaign to help minorities, especially a minority kid like Fred, who was Dale's best friend and roommate. Fred was a shrimp and his seduction by the silky red top cut down on his embarrassing habit of going to bed stark naked. Fortunately, he still used his good-smelling wintergreen junk after his evening weight-lift and exercise campaign. He was getting stronger, just not taller, but he smelled good.

When Dale's mom's call came, he was relaxing on his bed, only to go heavy shook — that meant shocked in Old English, old people dialect. Terrible things should not happen to good people, especially Uncle Rex, whom Dale wanted as a father. If only his mom could get her butt off the back burner and marry the guy! Rex was a cop, something to do with drugs. Cops and bullets went together, just not like this. You were not supposed to ambush Inspector-level cops in broad daylight at the Belmont races and knock them into comas.

Now, Dale lay here depressed, hoping sleep would help if he could find some. His bath-powder scent merged with Fred's wintergreen liniment and drifted in layers through their dorm room. Both Fred and Dale loved that delicious, clean, and simple smell. Dale would like his body to always smell like this despite puberty. If you were going to be a wholesome pink dweeb, why not smell like one?

"Cow, Summers, your mother is such a brilliant writer." Fred was lying on the far side of the spacious room on the cowboy bedspread that his Aunt Mirtha had sent him. "I'd give anything if I could learn to write even half as well as your mother—my money, my property, my gonads, my whole body even, what there is of it. Damn!"

How Fred could lie flat on the bed, hold a book above his face, and actually read was incredible, and to say "damn" while he did it was marvelous. Fred said damn often. Dale figured it was one of the things he did to make up for being tiny. Fred also knew all the other four-letter words but used those only in front of receptive audiences.

Dale, of course, told everyone that he couldn't understand what people saw in his mother's books, but usually did it while offering to sell them one. Until recently, he belonged to the YCC, the Young Christian Coalition, DSFJF branch—Drug and Sex Free for Jesus Forever. The other members did not approve of saying "damn" or the "F-word," though most did it behind each other's backs and without parents or teachers present, just like kids did worldwide.

His mom's novels used every four-letter word ever imagined and some she made up. That was perfect for 2038, and what the DSFJF thought was not. Dale's mom's best friends, Maddie and Gretta also knew those words, though Maddie was more apt to use them than Gretta.

Truth to tell, Dale not only read his mom's books but also proofed the virtual galleys, the virgins — if you could have a bastard title page, why not virgin galleys. He also ensured that his mom's books would not offend or disappoint the adults or the tweens and teens who needed to sneak them behind their adult's backs. Fair was fair.

Thus far, all of Angie Summers's novels perfectly met adult, teen, and tween standards, even if they had made school-bound SexEd passé. Dale was not sure how he felt about that. His wump rotated on the fence. He'd learned about Mugwumps in his History of Political Morality Class with Dr. Voncile Fudd.

Best of all, Dale was cleaning up, selling digital copies of his mom's books to his friends and to Tate School professors. He'd heard that his friends' younger siblings, including sisters, also enjoyed them. To prove that point and say the most about little, Fred was lying on the other bed in his candy-cane briefs, obviously getting off on Dale's mom's latest, *Sister Mary Margaret — Dead.* Fred was small but not shy. He constantly let it all hang out or stick up.

Dale's mom always put in a few hot scenes in her novels, usually the same number as the body count. Before her call today, Dale and Fred had showered and were heading out for pizza and a movie to celebrate the break between regular school and summer sessions. The news about Uncle Rex upset them massively, and they decided to stay in and order Chinese from Huang's Feast Port, which offered many styles of excellent Chinese cuisine. Dale and Fred loved the Hunan Scallops, Spicy Bitter Melon Soup, and lots more.

Food eaten, Fred was reading again, and Dale was funking out on the way to Dozeville.

"Wake up, Summers!" Freddy called in his soprano "Land Ho" voice—it occasionally cracked, which was a good sign for his height. Dale and Fred were both fourteen, so the end was near.

"I'm not asleep, Fred."

"I just wanted to tell you that this book is definitely her best. Thanks for gifting me with a signed hardback."

"My mom will be really pleased that you like it, Fred. She always asks about you. And I will keep my promise to introduce you to her the first chance I get. She'll be interested that you want to be a writer and may offer to mentor you, but you better have something ready for her to read."

"Oh crap, yeah! I'll really cream lean if I can meet your mother, Summers. Does she have a dog named Stud like Mary Helen Mack does?" Fred said crap lots in addition to a few F-word, s-word, and c-word blasts—in appropriate situations, of course.

Dale's mom's books probably affected many people like they did Fred, if not between the legs, then in the head. Dale could attest to that but would not. "Naw, I think she made Stud up, but I don't know much about Mom's little-girl days in Saratoga. We did have a Sheltie named Sheep. He got hit by a diaper truck that tried to miss him and turned over into Mrs. Fenley's rose bed while she was pruning. Everything spilled. Sheep survived but never got rid of the dirty diaper smell. Neither did Mrs. Fenley."

Dale's mom authored big sexy Literary Crime Thriller novels. Her favorite detective character, Mary Helen

Mack, was a tough lady detective who didn't care which sex she bedded, wore leather, and held several black belts in different disciplines. Mary Helen loved Stud, her Doberman, who was the size of an elephantine rhinoceros and could jump tall people in a single bound if she needed to pee, which she did on anything she wanted to.

Somehow or other, everyone seemed to love MHM and all his mom's other characters. The critics loved her use of sex and gore to elevate crime thriller detective fiction to actual literature.

"She does sleuth, doesn't she, Summers? Your mom just has to sleuth. I've read about her sleuthing in the PostNews. It's gotta be true."

"Yeah, I guess, but only with my Uncle Rex's help and protection." Lying to your best friend didn't count. In the call, Dale sensed that his mom was again diving into detective mode.

"Inspector Rex Caine is a great detective for real. I sure hope he survives," Fred said. "He's solved so many drug murders that made the front pages of The TimesGuardian and PostNews."

"Yeah," Dale said, "but press people don't mention his name much. If Mom calls the cops to help her with a hangnail, it makes a front page somewhere, usually with a picture."

"Well, that's okay. As long as your mom sleuths sometimes." Unlike Dale's, Fred's brain tended to stick to the point. "She does, doesn't she?"

"I guess. Mom will really like you. She handles horror exceptionally well."

"What did you say your mom wanted to call this book?"

Dale stretched and yawned, really wanting to go to sleep. They played squash for two hours this afternoon. It hadn't pooped them, of course, but had made them more meditative. "My Aunt Gretta, not my real aunt but

Mom's publisher and editor, the CEO of Spencer and Sons, made her change it. Mom wanted to call it *Blood on the Wimple,* but Gretta insisted on *Sister Mary Margaret — Dead* because she thought Catholics and other fundamentalists would tolerate a dead nun more easily than a bloody wimple. Aunt Gretta also made Mom shorten the disemboweling scene."

"Your mom does write violence and horror great, Summers, but her rape and love scenes are even better. She should use asbestos paper."

"So what's this one about?" Dale said it automatically and instantly knew he shouldn't have.

Fred froze, slowly tented the book over his middle, pushed himself onto his elbows, and looked across the room to Dale. "Are you still claiming you haven't read it? This afternoon while we caught our squash breaths, you admitted to enjoying the cozy disembowelment scene in *Mary Margaret*. It is, incidentally."

"It slipped out. I do not usually admit that I read Mom, at least not to other kids. I'm enough of a dweeb without admitting to reading Angie Summers novels just because she's my mother. I can trust you, can't I, Fred?"

"Yes, of course, but I'm seriously ashamed of you, Summers! You should own up that you love them." Fred's eyes got huge on his little face when he decided to go aghast — they were terrifically bright dark blue and stuck out against the white wall — something you didn't see in Asian kids much.

"You've got to be loyal to your own mom, Dale. You should be pushing them instead of offering them, and maybe should even give readings here at Tate or convince your mom to. She used to read to us street kids in Manhattan libraries."

"Hey, I give a student discount and even offer signed paperbacks. I just don't admit to reading them."

"My Aunt Mirtha is nice and very literate," Fred said, "but I'd give anything to have a real mother to be loyal to instead of a dead one I can barely remember. When my family came to this country, I did have one and even a father, but you have at least got to admit reading her books, Summers. You've got to! And, of course, you can trust me. Why would you even ask? We have so many secrets between us that we need to trust each other so we can relax as roommates."

Fred was great at being a bigger-than-life best friend, and then some — that was a special talent. He was such a good friend that he'd even tell you that you were a jerk and should reconsider your jerkhood and the jerkdom you jerked it off of.

At the start of the second semester this past year, Dale did reconsider his jerkhood when Fred became his roommate. Fred's and Dale's original roommates both got kicked out for doing unspeakable junk together — smoking. In the eyes of the administration, smoking was way worse than the carnal knowledging that everyone except Dale did. Well, once.

As hard as it was at first, Dale had gotten lots happier after taking Fred's advice. Who wanted to admit that you were mean to your mother, whom you loved dearly, or that you had made a first-class ass of yourself with everybody else you knew? Dale's friends, like Aunt Maddie and Aunt Gretta and selected young people, were too polite to tell him, but Fred told him.

Fred seemed to like Dale plenty but got fed up and told him that he was preaching to everyone in sight in a way that would give Jimmy Swaggart, God, Jesus, James, Mary Magdalene, and Billy Graham heat rashes. That was a real friendship. So Dale paid him back by dropping the preaching and resigning from The Coalition, which did seem to believe mostly in itself. Dale also decided to move away from his father's brand of religion. As Fred said, religious or not, you didn't need to let it all fall out of your mouth like bad diarrhea."

"Look, Fred, all the kids know who Mom is, and the books are great and exciting. It's just that sometimes she writes some pretty embarrassing stuff. You know what I mean. She describes activities in detail and names actual body parts and things."

"What? Words like penis, vagina, and anus turn you off? They are not expletives, and even if they were, every kid in Tate, boys and girls, uses expletives. Even you and I do occasionally. Crap!" Fred shook his head in genuine disgust. "And none of your mom's writing is dirty the way she does it. It used to be taboo in polite conversation, but that's not true anymore and has not been for years. It's 2038. Civilization has grown up."

"I don't know, Fred."

"She's just being real, Summers. Her books grab you and yours and don't let go. They are real. They do sometimes stimulate, but embarrass? No, they couldn't embarrass anyone with standard body parts and a desire to set goals. You and I live together and sometimes shower together. I know you lug around a complete set of body parts that work like everyone else's. I thought you'd dropped the Hallelujah Hal shtick. Goodnight." With that, he turned the light out.

"Okay, I'll loosen up about Mom. I promise." He half swallowed it. Fred was wise and not allergic to poison ivy, either. "I hope you're right."

"Of course, I'm right. After all, I'm me."

"You like being right, don't you, Fred?" Dale said.

"Sure I do. That's why I always make a point of being right."

"I wish I was or were, if you want to be subjunctive about it."

Fred groaned. He was great at English and would be a great writer someday, exactly as he planned. "I have a suggestion, Summers."

"What suggestion?"

"You can start being right by shoving your subjunctive up your anus and going to sleep so I can get some."

Dale chuckled. "Get some what?"

"Beauty sleep, Summers. So I don't stunt my growth."

Dale chuckled again, despite himself this time.

"Okay, Summers, don't say it. I've already stunted it."

"Stunted what?"

"Jeez. A best friend like you and short too? Maybe it's a family curse. Now, will you please rotate off to Dreamland? In other words, perch and twirl."

Dale giggled again. "You're trying to cheer me up because of Rex, aren't you."

"I'm trying to get some frigging sleep, Summers." Five seconds later, he began pretend-snoring.

"Okay. And thanks, Fred." Upset with the call or not, Fred was great. He supported Dale and kept him from going off the deep end and racing home to Mommy. "Goodnight, Fred."

"Goodnight, Dale. Mary Helen Mack be praised."

"She does that herself, Fred, but ditto."

"Say it. Mary Helen Mack be praised."

"*Say it, sprout*," Mary Helen whispered to Dale, which she did now and then.

"Okay. Mary Helen Mack be praised."

DAY TWO

Chapter 3 - Chuck

A pig in the head.

New York City. Greenwich Village. 1:00 AM. Maddie.

That night—really 1:00 AM the morning after that night—Maddie Franck began to develop the uneasy feeling that old, old friend Angie Summers had cracked her stopper, and the feeling grew as they climbed the steps of 1778 Perry Street in Greenwich Village, where Rex lived when he was not in a coma. Even more than usual, the Village smelled of damp underwear—no place for ladies. The place reeked of malevolent danger and imminent demise, but in the life of Angie Summers, one disaster spawned another.

This afternoon, when Maddie reached the hospital—it lay in a splotch of the Long Island urban wilderness—Angie was drying her tear-wet face and preparing to faint onto the ICU waiting room floor while Gretta was preparing to puke into her amply enhanced cleavage. Each reacted to stress differently.

Maddie had yet to decide on an aberrant habit that would justify the expense of her therapist, preferably none of the above. Mostly though, the three of them, two eight-figure CEOs and a world-famous, multi-seven-figure author, had just stood in the waiting room, hugged, and bawled. Rex was important to them all, to Gretta because he helped Angie write bestsellers, to Angie because she loved him, and to Maddie because he helped with the research for her article and possible book about The Snow Queens, which she now feared publishing.

Once the doctors pronounced Rex sufficiently stable, they shipped him to Columbia Presbyterian Hospital in the city, and Maddie sent Gretta home in the Gretta-mobile, a Robinson WhisperChop named Caruso. Maddie then gathered Angie up and flew her to Central Park South for a quasi-pajama party at Maddie's condo. Maddie intended it as a shoulder-to-cry-on-within-limits get-together, more than a party.

Angie could not visit Rex until tomorrow, and Maddie could not allow the needy little author to spend the night alone in her East 64th Street, thirty-million-dollar slum. In her simple-minded way, Angie loved Rex deeply. Why she had not accepted one of his frequent marriage proposals, Maddie could not fathom.

Angie's tears vanished when they reached Maddie's place, and her beady little brain sped into hyperdrive. That usually preceded the queen of Literary Crime Thrillers doing something off-plum, such as this God-damned midnight ride to Greenwich Village to save a cat.

Regrettably, Rex owned a cat, a detail Angie remembered an hour ago after they sloshed down three Black Russians each and poured themselves into bed between Maddie's red satin sheets. GeeGodOhFat, that felt good after a horrible day, but the feeling lasted only fifteen minutes.

So now Maddie trudged behind Angie up the steps to Rex's apartment at 1:00 AM in the God-damned morning so that Rex's cat would not go hungry.

Angie fished in her udder-sized purse until she found a slim set of keys, and they finally got through the front door of this ancient brownstone. The first floor housed only Rex and his cat. They walked down a narrow hall to the apartment's back entrance. Angie fumbled with the lock and eventually unlocked it. Mechanical contrivances were not Angie's thing except for guns — she knew everything about guns and was an excellent shot, thanks to Rex. They all spent time at the range, really.

"Maddie, I am sorry to get you up in the middle of the night, but she is such a sweet thing that I couldn't sleep if I let her go hungry. You're sure you don't mind if we take her back to your place?"

"I suppose." Maddie did not loathe pussies, just this cat at this moment. "What's her name?"

"Chuck." With that astounding revelation, Angie pushed open the white metal door. "It's short for Charlene."

"Is it really." The door open, a whiff of socks ran through the doorway and down the hall, odd considering Rex's elegant hygiene and precise dress. He even wore sexy dapper vests.

Maddie could not understand why a darling man like Rex had not years ago abandoned Greenwich Village for civilization. No one considered it chic to live down here anymore.

Angie flipped the switch by the door. The stained-glass ceiling-lantern spread green and yellow light over the room. "Oh, Maddie."

The apartment was chic before someone pulled books off shelves, turned over and cut open furniture, pulled up carpet, and emptied all drawers onto the floor in one gross heap. Rex was anything but gross. He even wore a vest and an under-arm horizontal holster.

"Angie, someone tossed the frigging place."

"Oh, Maddie!" Angie's voice sounded saturated with horror, but a special brand of horror that chilled Maddie's implants. That tone reeked with wide-eyed inquisitiveness, suggesting Angie Summers would shortly run to the nearest telephone booth to don her M-emblazoned satin tights and turn into Mary Helen Mack, female sleuth without peer, fear, shame, or shred of cerebellar discontinuity.

Since Rex got himself shot, Angie had remained strangely quiet. She put forth no theories, no plans, and none of the furious mental activity that one would expect from a famed Literary Crime Thriller author after a shootout. Even when she discovered that Rex's deceased assailant was Jake Slag Lessix, a suspended and about to be de-frocked cop, Angie held her peace. That would not last forever.

"Oh, my Christ," Maddie repeated. "Crap. Who would do this?"

That summarized the situation and would doubtless start Angie's engines. Mary Helen would appear shortly. She led eight of Angie's most successful novels, made tons of money for Angie and Spencer and Sons Publishing, and caused peerless inconvenience for Gretta and Maddie, whom ThePress inevitably interviewed about why a sweet little woman authored books about a bisexual female detective who fed on sex, crime solving, and beating up men. Little did they know that sweet little Angie loved to play detective and often meddled in Rex's cases.

"Oh, Maddie!" Angie repeated, as saucer-eyed and raring to go as Little Orphan Annie exploring an old-growth forest of redwood dildos.

The mess in this apartment clearly concerned Rex's current mindless state and gorgeous body that would have made a superb stand-in for Leonardo DiCaprio's corpse. "Obviously, someone tossed the place, Angie. What were they frigging looking for?"

"I don't know. Rex could have nothing to hide," Angie replied, a guileless gamine lying through her teeth.

She always knew more than she admitted and clearly suspected Rex of hiding something—she had for a while. Of course, Maddie had asked about that, and Angie had denied it but let fly with eyes, bod, and silent tongue.

"Angie, all cops have things to hide, no pun intended, and Rex too had something to hide, or whoever was looking for it would not have gone to this much trouble."

"If they did find it," Angie said barely audibly.

That thought certainly warmed Maddie's heart. "They better have found it. I'd hate for them to come back and search me the way they searched this God-damned apartment."

"Not to fret," Angie said, pulling a Walther PPK from her purse. She owned a variety of pistols back at her slum. "Close the door and lock it. I want to look around. Use the deadbolt." Beaming and scary.

"You're crazy."

"Merely determined. Now, close it," dear little Angie repeated with sheer pig-headed determination. Nothing new. Someday, Angie would get them killed, raped, or insulted. If a time existed for Mary Helen to appear in the flesh, this was it.

Maddie closed, locked, and dead-locked the door but planted her butt firmly against it, determined to keep her assets as close to a sane escape as possible.

Angie began prowling the destroyed apartment, turning lights on as she went, peering into chair bottoms, using her toe to move drawers, including some of Rex's thin, brief, neatly pressed ones.

Then, without a shred of warning, something behind a beige door to the right crashed with enough decibels to fry flies, and Maddie shoved her rear harder against the egress and whispered, "Quick, Angie, call the fuzz, the mayor, the pope, Mike Wallace, anybody!"

"Shhhh." Angie tiptoed toward the door with nerveless abandon. Either she knew something she did not care to share, or she had lost what judgment she possessed, a small loss given her history of risky meddling. She opened the door, reached in, snapped the light on, grinned, and beckoned Maddie with a finger.

Maddie crept down the living room and looked over Angie's shoulder. Chuck, an immense orange cat, had knocked an entire food shelf down to capture a five-pound plastic bucket of peanut butter she was now busily consuming.

"Chuck is always doing that." Angie sounded beside herself with smug glee. "I recognized the sound."

Maddie almost howled with relief, but, being the scared-crapless CEO of a major hag-rag, merely giggled with dignity. Unfortunately, while her mouth was giggling, her eyes glanced to the left, into the bathroom, and her giggle committed harikari. The light from the kitchen splashed onto a nude gray man on the toilet. He was not moving or breathing. Maddie nearly crapped off into her Gucci briefs but instead pointed to the john and said, "For Christ's sake, can we call the police now?"

Angie hurried into the bathroom, pulled a pen out of her bun, and used it to snap the light on. The long narrow room glowed a lovely hot-pink color.

The nude corpse did not have an erection—Maddie always wondered about that in dead men. Blood had dripped from nose to penis before drying.

"Don't worry, Maddie," Angie said, "he can't hurt you." She leaned down to better see the stiff's hanging face. "Oh, my goodness! I know this man. He's police brass."

"It figures—I've never known police brass with a big one."

"Be serious. This is John Leech, the Deputy Police Commissioner. He was Rex's partner in Homicide. Rex still works for him on special assignments. I wondered why he did not show up at the hospital. A bullet hole in the forehead is an adequate excuse, though."

"Yes, death is an acceptable excuse for being late — my Grandmother Effie always said that."

Angie edged even closer to the corpse.

"For God's sake, Angie, you're almost in his lap, what there is of it."

"Don't be dirty," Angie corrected as she reached out a hand and touched the side of the man's neck. "He's cold as a fish."

"For God's sake! He's dead! Don't touch it."

"And he's limp."

"I can see that. So what, Ange?"

"He's cold. Rigor mortis has passed, but livor mortis says that he died on the toilet, or someone put him here immediately after they shot him."

"A late call of nature. Call the police, Angie."

"And where are his clothes? They could be in the living-room mess, but why should they be? Why would John Leech be naked in Rex's apartment?"

Maddie hesitated to mention it, but her burgeoning hysteria made her braver than she really could be. "Forget his clothes. Where's his pubic hair?"

"Oooh." Angie looked down and found her Little Orphan Annie impression again. "You're right. I didn't notice that."

"Of course, you didn't, Mary Helen. You didn't notice this either." Maddie reached out and flicked the brass's toupee off his head and across the bathroom. "There! He's missing hair everywhere. Smooth as a baby's derriere, devoid of hirsute adornment, bottle bald, alopecia by name. Now that we've settled the mystery of the hairless corpse on the toilet, can we please send forth a sooey for the constabulary before I lose bladder control?" Maddie heard her voice rise into a shrill scream, which was nothing compared to her svelte body's desperate desire to run.

Quasi-lady publishing Chief Executive Officers like Maddie, who slept her way to the top and lived on a leaf of lettuce and the fantasy of lard-based soft ice cream, did not have the emotional stamina for this nonsense. "Please, Angie!" Maddie graduated from nursing school before snagging a scholarship to Smith, but that would not help here.

"Oh, all right, but I still wonder what happened to his clothes."

***

It being deceased police brass, a fact that Angie duly explained on her Pear Superphone, the cops required only forty minutes to show up, an excellent first response time, considering that the mayor shredded their budget to buy condoms for racially mixed pregnant dwarf-teens related to President Watson or some such crap. After all, toilet-perched deceased law officers could not croak further.

Forty minutes or not, when Detective Kossick rang the front door, Maddie breathed for the first time since she saw the corpse. Something about this situation troubled her, not so much the immediate reality but something about Angie's reaction that would have scared anyone who knew her.

To add orange zest to the Evian, Kossick announced that they were late because someone bumped off billionaire real estate man Paul Michael Senna, owner of PMS Plaza. It happened this afternoon, but his corpse surfaced only a few hours ago, apt terminology since someone murdered the man in his Lake Mead-size whirlpool bath in the building next door to Maddie, who had enjoyed it many times. Senna owned Maddie's building, PMS Plaza, across from CNN at Columbus Circle, as well as half the real estate bordering Central Park.

The second corpse shook Maddie so badly that when she called *Centered Women* to tell them to get up and get busy on PMS coverage, she failed to mention she had just been in the john with a stiff dick, so to speak. To Maddie, Paul Michael Senna was way more than just another billionaire.

"You're sure you didn't change his position, ma'am?" Kossick asked again. "You just pulled the toup?"

"Of course, I'm sure, and I flicked, not pulled," Maddie snapped. "I'm a CEO. I don't touch stiffs."

"Yes ma'am," Kossick said.

"At least, never on Tuesdays, and I'm not a ma'am."

Kossick possessed the same capacity to smile that Senna and Leech currently did—he was a true police putz with untamed nose hairs that made his nostrils look huge. His feet stunk through his brown shoes.

"Yes ma'am." He scribbled diligently on a pad stuck in a black imitation leatherette case, which milkmen once carried back when men delivered milk. Kossick's questionable charm lay in his classic cop monotone, a sound that Maddie always thought existed only in black-and-white TV shows. "Sorry to be disheveled, ma'am. The blood on my shirt is from two forty-five slugs to the sternum five minutes ago. Just routine, ma'am."

Angie had taken her cop friend, Mannie Kershaw, into the bathroom, doubtless to show him something in the immediate neighborhood of the dearly deleted Leech, an area Angie appeared to gravitate to.

Kossick's interrogation of Maddie lasted for fifty minutes, forty-nine longer than necessary. After all, Maddie and Angie had not discovered the treasure of the Sierra Madre — they had stumbled onto a pig in the head with a round in his. Maddie and Angie would both be home in the sheets if it were not for Chuck.

Angie appeared from the head, followed by Big Mannie. "I know," she said over her shoulder. She even used her patented Annie inflection, a wide-eyed sound that men seemed to find appealing, probably because of the insufferable tendency of males to equate masculinity with innocence-defilement.

"You're very observant, ma'am." Mannie maintained the stony demeanor of most Homicide detectives and frequently said "ma'am." African American men that size always heated Maddie's knees. He also frequently scratched his broad nose as though an invisible wart sat twitching there, itching. "I thank you for all your help." Then to Kossick, "I think we can let the ladies go on home now, Matt." That made Mannie Kershaw, Kossick's superior.

Kossick nodded, stuffed his notebook into his back pocket, and walked back into the john.

"Do you ladies have a car?" Mannie asked.

"In Manhattan?" Maddie asked. "You're kidding."

He obviously never checked garage prices, pavement conditions, or stationary traffic.

The big dick smiled gently — Mannie was the size of a small building. "We'll call you a cab."

"Ooooh," Angie said, exceeding her Little Orphan Annie self, "we almost forgot Chuck."

"Oh, for Christ's sake," Maddie said, "let's not forget Chuck."

Chapter 4 - PMS

Angie Outhouse.

—1—

New York City. Central Park South. 3:30 AM. Maddie.

In the corridor outside Maddie's penthouse, Angie read *The TimesGuardian* while Maddie struggled to hold Chuck's motel in her left hand while her right wrestled the exotic lock she had installed on her penthouse door.

"Senna," Maddie said. "Someone killed Paul Michael Senna and John Leech, and Rex killed Slag Lessix. What a frigging day."

"I thought we already covered that, and it is now tomorrow. But you are right," Angie said as she perused *The TimesGuardian.* "Senna's wife and children returned from Eight Flags Great Escape and found him garroted in his gigantic whirlpool bath, the one with the antique gold fixtures."

"Yeah. You really needed to watch where you leaned in that tub." Maddie was so tired that she did not care who killed whom, including the super-bald pig on the pot. Senna's death surprised her. It would take an expert hitman to off that careful a man, especially with his armed bodyguard in the next room. PMS knew his enemies and always took precautions."

"His wife gave the servants the day off," Angie continued, "and this afternoon no one wished to bathe with him. Ergo, he bathed alone and died."

"I can understand that. Good old PMS tended to get frisky in the tub no matter who or what you were. In the absence of like-minded recipients, he often bathed alone. I told you about it back at Rex's place. I do feel sorry for the quintet of kids — they're modestly spoiled but adequately normal."

"I knew him slightly," Angie said. "He threw a cocktail party for me when I released my second novel, *Who Killed Princess Porn*. Even President Watson and First Lady Nips came."

"I remember, Angie. I was there. Did you know Senna personally?"

"Of course not, silly. I have much better taste in men. I wouldn't turn down a night with President Watson, though, except that Nips would shoot me." Angie had not removed her eyes from *The TimesGuardian*. "Besides, Senna only knew his money personally."

"You're right about that!" Maddie confirmed. "Boy did PMS ever get ticked about the homeless, druggies, and predators taking over Central Park. He owned half the park perimeter, and his property values were sinking fast."

"*The TimesGuardian* says a druggie may have offed him. I doubt they based that on empirical data, though. Too soon."

"*The TimesGuardian* says that about any crime that they don't have a clue about. It's an easy direction to aim."

Finally, Maddie unlocked the door. "Crap! Such a darling man. As far as Senna was concerned, you could get shot, mugged, or raped, and you could shoot, shoot up, mug, rape, or get AIDS, TB, Ebola, or flesh-eating fasciitis anywhere in New York, as long as it did not impair his property values. Ergo, if you must do any of the above in or about Central Park, do it inconspicuously and without depositing bodies, needles, or condoms behind shrubs or in the polar bear cage of the Central Park Zoo. I approve of Senna joining his victims."

"Maddie, you're terrible."

"Yes, and no empirical proof necessary." Maddie snapped the light on in the foyer. Her sanitary support person, Jill, obviously cleaned today. Everything appeared tidy, if not absent altogether. "I readily confess I'm terrible. And I'm also a great CEO. I even earned a substantial cut in *Centered Women's* rent, courtesy of Paul Michael Senna."

Once Angie finally made it in, Maddie closed the door with a back kick, released Chuck from his traveling palace, and tossed her keys onto one of the Shaker chairs in the foyer. "Senna owns PMS Center, where *Centered Women* leases the five top floors and a wonderful view of CNN."

"I know that, Mad. I have visited you there roughly twice weekly for the past twenty years."

"Do me a favor, Angie. Do not ever repeat that — the world and my facial upkeep man have clearly established that I am definitely thirty-five. And I knew PMS more than slightly. He was brash and brazen and reeked of tacky taste, a trashy mind, no scruples, and an insatiable desire to control everyone he knew and then some. Everything he touched, no matter where he touched it, turned to gold. And he was terrible in bed and would probably have become president. I know his wife, Vera-Lamar, too, and suspect she hired Pauly's departure. Incidentally, you can get from this building to his condo by the roof. I could have killed him if I wanted to."

"What?" Predictably, Little Orphan Annie promptly reemerged. "Maddie, how well did you know him, exactly?" Her green eyes glowed in the gloomy foyer.

"Well enough to know I didn't care to know him any better." Maddie marched on into the apartment while she confessed over her left shoulder. "I hated the air that wafted about his full golden hair plugs, attractive though they were. My relationship with him consisted of numerous business meetings and a one-night stand, really a one-night lay. Well, to be honest, I had a ten-night stand with him while the wife and kids visited Venice, but never more than one stand a night."

"You're terrible. I love it. Can I use it in a book?"

"Maybe. First, I want to know who killed Senna." After laying PMS, Maddie had decided that money could not save the world from flaccidity, but she also knew how many dangerous people he dealt with. She did not hate him, although "intensely loathed" would have covered the subject. "Trust this soldier from the trenches, Angie. Senna is better off dead. We're all better off with him dead, the arrogant sow."

"Did you mean what you said about his not caring about anyone unless it affected his property values?"

"You want a snack? I have some Gouda and Perrier left, maybe even some lime cheesecake I bought for Gretta's last visit." Maddie paused and eased a sidelong glance back in Angie's direction.

Angie looked mildly disgusted for a moment, then yawned. "Let's go to bed. This day was awful. I'll hear the details about Senna some other time."

"This is the second time we've tried bed tonight," Maddie grumped.

"Yes."

— 2 —

New York City. Central Park South. 4:00 AM. Angie.

Angie's body appreciated Maddie's soft mattress.

"Don't get too comfortable, Kid," Mary Helen said.

"I plan to do exactly that. All my sleeps are turning into power naps."

"There's another anvil about to drop, isn't there?"

"Always, Mary Helen."

Angie's mind spun. This affair resembled the expositions of Angie's best books. She always tried to barrage readers with surprises to soften them for the hinted-at red herrings to come and catch them off-guard with the truth, fictional or social. That plus creative sex and a ton of advertising money could give you a best-selling novel, and then, if you added some social insight and a few hundred thousand dollars more of carefully placed non-review publicity, you could have a Literary Crime Thriller blockbuster.

Despite Maddie's condo being CEO big, they had climbed together back into the big king-sized bed they had left to rescue Chuck. This time was for sleep. Maddie groaned sleepily. Chuck climbed in bed, too, with her peanut butter breath and rattling purr. Angie hoped that a little togetherness would help soothe her. Maddie and Angie had known each other for years.

"Did Senna spend the night in this bed?"

Maddie had published some of Angie's stories long before Gretta decided to publish her first novel and help Angie write it—former senior editors did that sort of thing if they thought they could increase profits.

"No. We did it on the fridge." Maddie's voice sounded sleepy and rumpled.

"I can picture that." Angie could picture Maddie doing it anywhere, except maybe in the Tevi fountain—the Polizia di Stato would get you for that.

"Any perennial innocent could picture that. How do they do it back in Kansas, Dorothy?"

Angie yawned. "In silver slippers on a bed of wheat chaff, in a hot-air balloon floating above a cornfield being burned by Quantrill. And I am not innocent. I was born in Saratoga, New York, one of the least innocent areas in upstate New York." Chuck kneaded Angie's left foot. Rex would have done it far better.

"Was your maiden name really Angie Outhouse?"

"Of course. Everyone knows that. It's a fine old family." Angie was glad that Maddie invited her to spend the night. Her house back on East 64th Street would have seemed beastly empty. And those dreams last week when Rex awoke screaming about the rats again but refused to explain—that was when this story really began.

Angie wondered if she had done the right thing tonight.

***

"Sorry, Mannie," she told her longtime friend last night in the Village. "It's right here." Angie used her pen to pick the toupee up and hold it out to him in the bathroom. "It looks like somebody ripped something off the safety pin, leaving only a tiny scrap. Hey, Mannie, I think that's a fragment of microfilm."

"You ladies found the toupee on his head, Angie?"

"Well, yes. Where else would Deputy Commissioner Leech wear it?" Maddie flicked it off with one finger to prove that John possessed no hair on his head or, apparently, elsewhere. "He had alopecia."

"He tried to keep that quiet, but we all knew." Mannie, gloved, examined the toupee carefully, especially the inside. He struck Angie as a little frantic. "I see. Other than that, neither of you touched the remains?"

"Of course not. I know better than that. Maddie shouldn't have touched the toupee, even though she only flicked it onto the floor."

"Well, we appreciate your being so observant, Angie." Mannie's eyes darted nervously around the bathroom. "I wish we could find the Deputy Commish's clothes, but we've kept you long enough. It doesn't bother you to be in here, with you being a lovely, sophisticated lady and all?"

"Why, of course, it bothers me. Doesn't it bother you, Mannie?" Angie chuckled an evil chuckle, the kind she often gave to Mary Helen. "I may write about this sort of thing, but I'm certainly not used to being around it, especially without Rex standing guard." Sometimes you needed to play the role, even with an old friend like Mannie. Angie knew all the Kershaw boys. "I suggest you have your men look through the heaps of clothing and junk on the floor for his clothes." Angie had removed the microfilm without touching the toup.

***

In Maddie's delicious bed, the memory drifted away like the microfilm had.

"Mary Helen, are you there?"

"Of course, I'm here, my drab little dolly, Angelica."

"Stick around. I'm going to need you."

"*Are you sure you want to go on with this? You've already committed a crime by stealing the film.*"

"*Wouldn't you have done the same, Mary Helen?*"

"*Yes, of course. I would also have laid Mannie.*"

"*Rex wouldn't want me to proceed without him, but I must. He is a potential father for Dale and husband for me, a decent one this time.*"

"*I know, Kid.*"

Maddie's great bed began to launch Angie into sleep. She would not worry about anything now. First thing tomorrow, she would need to find a privately situated microfilm reader.

"*You see it then grab it,*" Mary Helen quipped. "*Angie and I have a case.*"

Chapter 5 - Jimmu

Lean and mean will get you upstream.

—1—

New York City. Central Park South. 8:00 AM. Maddie.

"Oh, Christ, I overslept." Maddie had decided not to tell Gretta about Webb Drake's review. Gretta could not possibly read all that junk. Besides, it was not too late for her to pull Maddie's new book, *Climbing Up the Ladder in Bed — A HowTo Book with Legs Selectively Spread*.

Maddie could not be certain that she had returned to life. She stared at the other side of the bed. Something was missing. "Angie?" The bathroom door stood open. "Ange?" Realization hit. "Oh, my Christ, Ange is at it already. I know she is. Crap!"

Maddie grabbed her Pear Superphone, pushed "Gretta" on the call list, and listened to the thing ring until a weary voice answered. "Hello."

"Do you know who this is?"

"Unfortunately, I do. It's Madeleine Franck as in César. And this is Gretta Braun, as in Eva. What's happened now that I don't want to know about, Maddie?"

"We need to talk. I'm coming over."

"I've got to get to work. I'm late already," Gretta countered.

"CEOs can't be late. 'On time' is whenever they arrive. Anyway, screw our companies. We need to talk. Stay where you are until I get there."

"I'm on the toilet."

"Whatever. Wherever. However. Do not move. I'm coming. We need to talk about Angie."

"I'm way ahead of you," Gretta said.

—2—

New York City. Spencer and Sons. 8:10 AM. Angie.

Angie rode Gretta's favorite elevator, the gold one, up to the penthouse of Spencer and Sons Publishing Group. Someone had dropped a Reese's Peanut Butter Cup wrapper in the elevator. Gretta would not like that. She would not pick it up, but she would not like it.

"What makes you think she could bend that far, Ange?"

"That's not nice, Mary Helen!"

"When have I ever bothered with nice?"

Angie figured she would get good cooperation here, considering her friendship with Gretta Braun and her status among the company's authors. Angie's books made huge profits for Spencer and Sons, and everyone here knew it. When the elevator doors opened, she paused long enough to snatch the candy wrapper off the red carpeted floor of the elegant Otis Flash, then walked straight through the carved oak doors of the executive suite.

Leslie was spreading cream cheese on her bagel. Leslie—Angie could not recall the girl's last name—always began the day with cream cheese and bagels. So did Gretta. Her office's Spanish oak wall cabinet hid hyperwave and toaster ovens. Angie wanted to know where they hid the microfilm readers.

"Oh, hi, Ms. Summers. Gretta is not in yet. Would you like a bagel?"

"No, thank you."

"Good girl, Ange. Lean and mean will get you upstream."

"Shut up, Mary Helen."

Angie explained what she wanted.

"Well, we must have a microfilm reader somewhere," Leslie replied. Small-busted and hippie, Leslie always appeared neat, elegant, efficient, and beholden to silicone. Gretta preferred hippie employees, and thin ones never lasted. "I'm not sure where. Probably down in the basement, in the research lad, but I'll find out." Between bites, she poked a button on her mini switchboard. "Jimmu will know. He knows everything or can find it out very quickly."

"Ah, yes. Jimmu. I've met him."

"Sounds like a useful fellow, Ange. I wonder how he is in bed," Mary Helen said.

"Shut up, Mary Helen. He's just out of high school, and you already know he's useful after the night of the rats."

"Indeed."

Gretta had not arrived. Unusual. She was the most compulsive workaholic Angie knew.

"So maybe you didn't delight her soul yesterday, Ange," Mary Helen said. *"Grett can only take so much before she pukes."*

"Maybe, but she should be used to me by now," Angie said.

"I'm not." Mary Helen was correct, of course. By now, Gretta and Maddie would be comparing notes on what crazy thing Angie might do next. They should know Angie was doing it, whatever it was.

Apparently, Jimmu, "who knew everything," was taking some tracking down. Leslie had tried three extensions so far. Publishers did not use public address systems — too paranoid. Angie's previous encounter with Jimmu and in the following days had been very trying. She flopped herself into one of Gretta's squishy Naugahyde chairs to wait. Gretta loved Naugahyde. According to Maddie, she probably used Naugahyde undies as a break from her silky ones and, if able, would buy herself a Naugahyde husband. She had tried every other kind.

"*So why not, Ange? Men go out and buy latex ladies these days.*"

"*Shut up, Mary Helen.*"

True, though. Angie had found some really gross faux ladies when she researched *Who Killed Princess Porn*. It only sold fifty-five thousand copies.

"*You should have sent a lates lady to Dale. I think he needs help figuring out what to do.*"

"*Shut up, Mary Helen. He's only fourteen and would not be thinking about such things yet.*"

"Oh, thank you, Jimmu. I'll send her right down," Leslie said. "And yes, I am sure she will give you her autograph. By all means, get her to sign a book for you — it may be worth something someday."

"It's worth something now, Leslie."

"Go to the basement, Ms. Summers. Jimmu will be waiting for you."

— 3 —

Saratoga. Tate School. Dining Room. 8:10 AM. Dale.

Breakfast suddenly became awkward when Mary Margaret came over and sat between Dale and Fred. The conversation dragged for a while. She kept talking about puffed rice, but Dale's mind kept seeing her naked. They really did need to discuss what had happened, especially after Fred found out that it was all a setup, a prank, and that Mary Margaret had been in on it. He had intimidated almost everyone to stop the crotch grabbing, but it still hurt.

"I'm going home today, Dale," Mary Margaret said," but I'll be back for the summer session. It's mom's ball time, and she won't have time for me anyway."

"You live in Saratoga," Fred said. "Why not go day student."

"Because mom is getting ready for her grand ball at the Canfield Casino, in a few days. It's a really hectic time at our house, big though it is. The only reason I'm going home at all is to remind Mom I exist.

"Oh," Dale said. If she wanted him to feel sorry for her, she had succeeded, despite Dale being in a similar boat. Fred was better off than either of them. Dale had met his brother but not his Aunt Mirtha—she sounded like a real peach. "You were in on it."

"Yes. I have a mean streak sometimes, and I'm a little loose. Everybody knows it, but I didn't know you were such a sweet guy and considerate lover, Dale. I'm really sorry. Please accept my apology."

Dale paused, then said, "Okay."

Before he knew it, Mary leaned over and kissed him on the cheek.

"What about me, MM. We've been on and off friends for a while."

She swung around and kissed his cheek too.

— 4 —

New York City. Spencer and Sons Basement. 8:20 AM. Angie.

Jimmu, a handsome, slightly hyper Asian teenager, met Angie at the elevator with a pad, pen, and book in his quivering hands. He looked so much better than when Angie met him the first time. She knew about his family from Gretta, who frequently described him as her rare and valuable bird.

"Gracious, Ms. Summers, I really, really did wonder if I would ever have the opportunity to see you again and press, press your flesh, and I would be forever ever grateful if you would sign *Mary Margret – Dead* with your precious autograph, although not as grateful as the first time we met. I love your books, you know, and own all of them. Oh please, do, do give me your autograph. I'm such a huge, huge fan."

Angie shook his firm hand, then boldly signed the bastard title page, "With huge gratitude. The absolute best of excellent luck always and forever in your search for the ideal and for the security of your family. Love, Angelica Summers, your fan always."

"Oh, how, how could you know, Ms. Summers? I'm so, so filled with gratitude to you, as is my brother, I'm sure."

"How is he?"

"Doing wonderfully thanks to you and Ms. Gretta."

"Wonderful." Angie wondered if there had been a place on Noah's ark for Jimmus, but it was wonderful to see him again, and she felt relieved. He appeared to be doing well. "I'm so happy you're happy, Jimmu. Leslie said you have a microfilm reader somewhere down here in the tombs?"

"Oh, undeniably. If you will but follow me." He floated toward the far end of the mailroom with grace. "We have all sorts of readers down here, mainly because of the reference materials we did before Mother Gretta added blockbuster sex-and-violence fiction and salacious celebrity bios to our repertoire. Many of our current fiction writers research here even now."

"It feeds us well, Ange," Mary Helen said.

"In Mary Helen Mack's case, though," Jimmu added, "it's such nice sex-and-violence."

"Thanks, sonny — maybe," Mary Helen quipped. *"There is more to Jimmu than meets the eye, Ange."*

The boy could easily grow on Angie. With a flourish, he escorted her through Gretta Braun's underworld, then stopped at a metal door with bolts. He reached to his belt and lifted a set of keys that would have put Mrs. Danvers to shame.

Jimmu opened it smoothly, snapped the inside light on, and bowed, his left arm extended to the interior of a large, well-lit, surprisingly cheerful white block room filled with carpet-walled cubicles, each containing a computer or some other electronic equipment. "Now, just follow me," he added.

Angie did, to a tarp-covered machine in the far-left cubicle. "Does all this stuff still work?"

"Oh yes! And this is the cubicle you want. There's a copier on your right. Thanks to you and your desire for correct forensics, our staff and some of our authors have come down here to research the universe. When Ferenc O'Hara was planning to threaten the world in his next novel, he spent ever so much time here researching the possibility of fusion-powered submarine implosion. As for me — research is my life when I'm not running the mail room. I need to know! I need to feeee! I need to dooooo!"

Angie's mind whirled. She may just have found a whole new character to complement Mary Helen. She did wonder if this were the real Jimmu or just a performance.

"You're kidding, Ange. Well, I guess I could use a sidekick."

"Shut up, Mary Helen, but you probably could use a dog walker to care for Stud while you roll in the hay with the local constabulary."

"Stud takes care of himself, though I can't remember him ever being walked. As far as the brainy kid goes, I like him. I have a special place in my heart for built and intelligent Asians."

Jimmu dropped to his hands and knees on the concrete floor. For a moment, Angie feared that he planned to escalate his worship of her, but then realized he was unplugging and plugging. He finally stood, jerked the heavy plastic cover off the machine before her, and flicked a red switch.

"It lives!" Mary Helen said.

"Would you like me to load it for you, Ms. Summers?"

"No, thank you. This is very confidential." She winked at him. "But please stay close in case I have trouble. I'm not great with machines."

"Except for guns," Jimmu said.

"Yes. Except for guns. That is a product of our times."

"Ah ha, Mary Helen Mack rides again. I can't wait. I almost died dead when Stud, lurking in Mary Helen's hospital room, grabbed the assassin's throat in *Withered Bodies, Righteous Souls.*"

Angie had always regretted giving Mary Helen Mack a Doberman named Stud. It had been a convenient deus ex machina at the time, but Stud, with even scant mention, ultimately stole the show in novel after novel. "I'll send you an autographed advance copy of Mary Helen and Stud's next adventure, Jimmu."

Jimmu clapped both long-fingered hands over his mouth—she noticed calluses on his knuckles. "Oh, would you, would you?" In stunned delight, he backed from the room and gently closed the door, as though he feared he would disturb the spell of this precious, precious moment.

"Apart from a possible role in my ego-maintenance program, that young man could prove usefully useful, Mary Helen. I must remember to get his number."

Angie knew from Gretta that Jimmu, just out of high school, possessed formidable research and fighting skills, a tragic background, and an inventive, industrious, and fearless nature. When he turned twenty, Gretta planned to promote him to an editorial assistant in his spare time when he was not attending Columbia University.

Angie reached into her blouse and pulled out a small canvas bra bag containing the microfilm she had snipped out of the toupee last night. It probably contained much she did not want to know, but which could advance her investigation.

"Yeah, it could also start you on your way to a jail cell, Dummy," Mary Helen said. *"You tampered with evidence in a murder investigation."*

"I certainly did. You would have too, Mary Helen."

"So, who could toss me into the can, Ange?"

"I could."

"You have. Several effin times."

"Watch your language."

"Why? You never watch my language."

"True. Fans have told me that your foul mouth is part of your charm, that and your blond crewcut, Beretta M9, violent hip action during intimacy, and, of course, Stud."

"I've got so much charm, Ange, that it's impossible to tell where it comes from."

Angie believed that if Jake Slag Lessix were a lone gunman targeting Rex, Leech's death would be too much of a coincidence. She could accept that Senna was a coincidence despite Rex's moonlighting as security at some of his parties. PMS paid well.

"Everything's connected, Ange. Face it."

An intriguing, gossamer net was settling over this affair. If it had not been for Rex, Angie would be enjoying herself. She positioned the film on the block and clamped it in place. She knew about microfilm and microfiche readers from her library research. Here no one could read over her shoulder except Mary Helen. At the New York Public Library, confidentiality could be a problem, despite the lovely lions.

The first frame contained an unlabeled but numbered list of fourteen names, mostly men but with two women. Several names interested Angie: Mannie Kershaw, her huge Homicide detective friend, Marvin, his huger baby brother, and Marion Kershaw, the oldest and hugest brother who often worked undercover. All three Kershaws were cops whom Rex liked and trusted. Mark, Mannie's adorable eight-year-old son, who attended Tate, was also on the list. Angie always sent him Christmas and birthday presents. Dale and Fred mentored him.

"Mannie Kershaw is your friend, isn't he, Ange?" Mary Helen said.

"Indeed, he is. The Kershaws are all my friends and are all on the list. Matt Kossick is on the list too, the detective who questioned Maddie."

"If turds could turn to stone, then talk – "

"Be nice, Mary Helen."

"Get real, Ange. Kossick is a caricature of himself and of all B-movie mystery detectives. At least Poirot had style."

The last name on the list was "Inspector Rex Caine." The second frame contained a list labeled "Snow Queens" —no identifiers except locations.

Emmanuel Rodriguez, Paraguay
Ferenc Bartok, Geneva, Switzerland
Jacob Bush, New York City
Jesus Velazquez, Cúcuta, Columbia
Leslie Sanders, Pompano Beach, Florida
Lester Tozzi, Chicago
Marsha Lessix, New York
Motel Yudin, Israel
Paul Michael Senna, New York
Rego Zazak, Baghdad
Sakzen, Polish Entertainer
Vera-Lamar Senna, New York
Frank Suskeeze, New York
Jerome McMurray, New York

Little of this meant much to Angie. If only Rex were able to help.

The third frame contained another list of names, mostly cops, including Rex Caine, the Kershaw boys, Matt Kossick, and Mark Kershaw.

"Crap, Ange, that really complicates things. Little Mark can't be involved in a crime. But if he were kidnapped, it could affect his father's and uncles' participation in this case or the racket."

"Yes, Mary Helen, and I suspect all our perps may be willing to kidnap or kill, including Frank Suskeeze and Jerome McMurray. The problem with these lists is distinguishing between perps and targets. That's deliberate, I think."

Suskeeze was a lawyer turned president of Schwanda, an international commercial bank. McMurray, a lawyer and financier, was president of McMurray, Langdon, and Jeffers, a major Wall Street investment house. The third was Senna, the late great white shoe divorce attorney turned real estate mogul and former visitor of Madeleine Franck's bed.

This group comprised the richest men in Manhattan. Except for Senna, all possessed reputations for being public-spirited, ivory-pillar stable, and exceedingly generous to charitable causes. He was the kind of rich who could be incredibly kind but from whom you would never consider buying a car. PMS's dirty side was covertly known but never mentioned. He specialized in profitable trickery, was proud of it, and loved plastering his name everywhere — in magazines, on buildings, wherever. The others doubtless profited by supporting him, and the press helped because they invariably covered his outrageous lies.

The fourth, fifth, and sixth microfilm frames contained five maps. They looked familiar, but Angie could not place them. One map showed a city with what appeared to be two large parks or fields at the edge of a town, with a much smaller park in the middle. Two maps showed rural areas with roads, a few houses, and open spaces. One map held the floor plans of two buildings, one a large house, the other a big I-shaped building with many rooms, possibly a hotel. No labels or dimensions clarified the floor plans.

One contained a list of crossed-out names, including Jake Lessix, Washington Heights.

"Crap, Ange."

"Exactly."

The seventh frame contained some kind of plan. Angie read it, gasped, and flicked the machine off.

"I saw that, Ange. Are you trying to get us killed from both sides?"

"Shut up, Mary Helen."

Chapter 6 - Keys

Rex shot first.

— 1 —

New York City. 9:25 AM. Angie Summers.

Having no explanation of why she needed a microfilm reader, Angie avoided Gretta, hurried out of Spencer and Sons and onto Madison Avenue. Jimmu had helped her blow up and print several lists and floor plans. Somehow she did not care if he saw them now. Jimmu was so Asian, so interesting, and so much fun. Angie was counting on his integrity and intelligence.

Gretta and Maddie tended to be overprotective and very sharp. Angie knew that they periodically harbored deep fears about her life. Of course, Angie had gotten the three of them shot at, once or twice.

"You're right about Jimmu, Ange," Mary Helen quipped. *"He could be really useful. There ain't nothing quite like a super-bright, eerily handsome Asian. You know he's following you, don't you."*

"I know. I still trust him."

Gretta had obviously primed him, which was fine.

"Somebody else is following you too, closer than Jimmu."

"That's not fine."

The morning Madison Avenue traffic seemed particularly thunderous today, mostly from delivery trucks, cabs, limos, and Grand Central Station traffic. Angie stopped dead at 43rd Street and Madison Avenue, turned, and studied the sidewalk behind her.

"I think I see him, Mary Helen. I don't recognize him, though."

"Just a feeling, Ange. I tingle below when I should pay attention to something on top."

"Not sure this is dangerous. The guy may just be going my way."

Angie thought about it momentarily, then walked on and turned right onto 42nd Street. This was not her first tail, but before, it was usually Rex trying to ensure she did not get into trouble again. She headed for the New York Public Library. This day would include a trip to *The TimesGuardian Index* to look into Suskeeze, McMurray, and Senna, three supposed community pillars. Following that, she would visit Rex and attend a meeting of Excess Anonymous with Gretta and Maddie before the three of them dined at Michael's European on 52nd Street, a fattening post-meeting ritual that the triumvirate waited for weekly.

"It's a full day, Mary Helen."

"You're going to be tired and really fat," Mary Helen whispered.

"You would work in even more today, wouldn't you, Mary Helen?"

"Sure would, Ange. And let us not forget Washington Heights."

"Yes. Good old Slag. His wife is still in Florida."

"And you're right, I'd probably work in a roll in the hay with the boys in blue if it were me."

Angie's friends probably would not have believed her rolls in the hay with Rex Caine. What was private was private.

"Oh, Angie. Jimmu and the tail just disappeared."

−2−

New York City. Columbia Presbyterian Hospital. 4:00 PM. Angie.

Once Angie identified herself and showed her Power of Attorney for Rex—they had executed mutual Powers of Attorney and Health Care Proxies a short time ago—she received excellent cooperation from the Columbia Presbyterian Hospital staff, but Rex's new Living Will threw her. After much befuddlement and second thinking, she signed the papers for his transfer. Last, she collected his personal effects, packed them into a shopping bag, then went up to his floor.

"Why the new Living Will, Ange?" Mary Helen asked. *"You're the detective."*

"Naw, I'm just the muscle. Why would Rex specify that in case of incapacitation, he must be transferred to a nursing home as soon as stable, within hours if possible? And why to that particular nursing home?"

"Why, indeed, Mary Helen. Of course, it is next door to Tate School and Dale. They have always been father-son close."

"Maybe because he wanted—"

"He's in a coma," Dr. Prat said.

They stood outside Rex's room on the presumption that, in a coma or not, Rex could hear and understand, a reasonable possibility according to the doctor. An enormously obese woman with pendulous breasts and no feet rolled by in an extra-wide wheelchair, and Angie thought of Gretta's distant future if she continued eating raspberry-swirl cheesecakes as though they were Saltines. Of course, being the CEO of one of the big five publishing houses could make one a nervous eater.

James Prat seemed an unlikely physician—five feet tall, acne, froggish voice, stunted look, black frame glasses, and a retarded but developing personality more like a weird teenager than a brilliant young resident. "I'm sorry, Ms. Summers. No reliable treatment exists for TBI — traumatic brain injury — other than surgery in some cases, but not at all in Inspector Caine's. The prognosis for his coma of unknown origins is, at best, an uncertain guess. A general rule is that the sooner he comes out of it, the better his chances of regaining normality will be."

"*What the eff was that?*" Mary Helen asked.

"He looks so good, Doctor," Angie said, "apart from the small bandage on his chest and the four-by-four on his temple."

"The two bullets nicked vessels and produced a large quantity of blood, undoubtedly making a minor injury appear severe. Inspector Caine's fall head-first onto the asphalt path caused the more serious injury and likely the coma. It appeared a bullet graze but was definitely from the fall."

"And there's no way of determining how long he'll be like this, Doctor, or what shape he'll be in when he awakens?"

"We see no cerebral edema, bleeding, or voltage abnormalities. Inspector Caine's vitals, cardio and cerebral PETs and MRIs are all fine. His swallowing appears unimpaired. We inserted a nasogastric tube for feeding but will change it to a G-tube before he leaves. Odd as it sounds, Inspector Caine is in excellent health except for the fact that he's in a coma. Essentially, he is suffering from a bump on the head. If it weren't for that, I would have considered the possibility of some sort of psychotic break, a psychiatric matter."

"It's fortunate that his attacker was a bad shot."

"*You shouldn't have said that, Ange,*" Mary Helen said emphatically.

"Given the upward trajectory of the bullet, we know that Mr. Lessix was falling when he fired."

"See what I mean, Ange?"

"Yes, I do."

"I beg your pardon, Ms. Summers?" Dr. Prat asked.

She had spoken to Mary Helen aloud. "Thinking aloud, Doctor. Thank you for your honesty and thoroughness." She said to her alter ego, *"And I do, Mary Helen."*

"Dr. Prat is a dick."

Once the dick finished depressing Angie and left, she crept into the room. Rex was lying on his back in a silly-looking hospital gown with small blue geese, his hands at his sides, his eyes closed, his breathing smooth, his magnificent body relaxed, as he often lay beside her, exhausted after making love.

"If only you fell on the flower bed rather than the sidewalk, Rex. You are definitely a great cop and have been hit on the head and have gotten shot before without ending up like this. If only you did not insist that we go to the track yesterday." She bent down and kissed his sleeping lips just as she so often did when he slept a less troubled sleep. Angie loved this man no matter what had happened, would stick by him no matter what she unearthed, and would marry him if they both survived.

"Rex shot first," Mary Helen whispered.

"I know, Mary Helen. I was there."

When Angie finally convinced herself to leave, she lifted the shopping bag by one handle, and it broke. Clothing and two sets of keys fell to the floor, one set Rex's.

"There you go, Ange."

Angie stared at the three keys on the unfamiliar ring, two for cars, one probably for a house or apartment. "Yes indeed, Mary Helen. Here we go."

Chapter 7 - Michael's

Veal Prince Orloff.

—1—

New York City. West 52nd Street. 10:00 PM. Maddie.

The Fat Foundry, Michael's European Dining by its proper name, constituted the ideal cuisine establishment to visit after a heated meeting of Excess Anonymous. Michael's served nothing not grossly fattening, and Maddie always needed to be on-alert or her svelte figure would become less enticing to visiting firemen. Even walking into the place felt like breathing butter. At their favorite table in the left back corner of the small private dining room, the one with the mahogany woodwork and gold filigree wallpaper, Maddie felt more at home than she would have back at her Park South condo.

"Oh, my God, I just don't know what to try tonight, Carl," Gretta said, probably because she wanted to try everything on the menu and pastry cart but wanted someone else to decide. It amazed Maddie that Gretta kept her figure as well as she did — being six feet one doubtless helped.

At Gretta's elbow, Carl, the Fat Foundry manager who always took their order, waited patiently — he was intimately familiar with the problems Gretta presented.

"I'm sure you'll be able to decide on something, dear," Maddie said. "Carl, what will happen to the restaurant with the passing of PMS."

"Hopefully, nothing, Ms. Franck. Mr. Senna set up all his businesses to be financially independent. When he founded or purchased them, he supported them for five years. At that point, they would need to be self-sufficient as judged by his percentage, sold off, or shut down. We have been here for eighteen years. The board chairpersonship will now go to his wife and children. I have heard that his wife, Ms. Vera-Lamar Senna, will become our El Supremo. She dines here often and sometimes even brings the children — that's where our children's menu came from."

"Wonderful." Sometimes, Maddie could not decide whether her sarcasm snarled, smirked, or meowed. There were also sometimes drawbacks to being the other woman. "What looks great, Grett?"

Gretta would eat anything, and in business, anyone. To the weak, the weary, and the ingenuous, publishing often became a voracious world, but Gretta regarded it as a huge playpen. The woman reveled in success and excluded all other priorities. No wonder two of her six husbands dropped into oblivion while the other four dropped into the ground.

"The duck looks good, Gretta," Angie said. She loved the duck here, Spicy Duck Alfredo. Despite her petite look and only slightly plump hips, Angie did not usually stint. With a few notable exceptions, writers possessed much more efficient metabolisms than CEOs, hence, Gretta's ample figure and the current New York shortage of raspberry-swirl cheesecake with kiwi.

The meetings of Excess Anonymous attracted the filthy rich and near rich, the famous and would-be famous, the fat and thin, and anyone who could make a major donation somewhere, sometime, including charitable donations for something in return. All who attended possessed positive or negative obsessions with food, pathological self-involvement with a need for self-justification, a business or social need to meet others of their ilk, or a social addiction to self-help meetings, the fashionable neurosis of the day. Spending could be cathartic.

Maddie beat the odds with self-discipline, her only area of such, and kept her little ass skinny even if she needed to cut down to one-half lettuce leaf between gorging and evacuating. She planned to prevent the fat body stored in her thin one from escaping and growing a dimpled rear the size of a centenarian hippo's. She did not actually need Excess Anonymous to do that, but she met such interesting people there. Besides, Maddie, Angie, and good old Gretta had been an elegant trio there for so long that they would not know what else to do with their Tuesday nights.

Afterward, came Michael's European, the Fat Foundry, where pastry grew from every aperture and protrusion, thick sauces covered 75 percent of the visible earth, and rich female thighs could not ambulate without masturbating. There were men and children too.

The current problem, of course, was how much longer pencil-thin Carl could stand there in his tux and smile like a frigging woodchuck in heat, waiting for—

"I'll have the Veal Prince Orloff, Carl," Gretta finally said. Veal seemed less fatty than some meats. Besides, Maddie and friends would snack on NatuFiber tonight, and Maddie would return to lettuce tomorrow.

You needed to live sometimes, so why not do it with old, symbiotic friends?

"I'll second that," Maddie said, "and bring Dom Perignon all-around."

"I'm a third," Angie said. "So, we'll all have Prince Orloff and champaign, please." She sighed to her friends as she handed her menu to Carl, who was enormous on the bulge scale from the looks of the thing—Maddie could enjoy that.

"The hospital can do nothing more for Rex," Angie said, "but perhaps he'll come out of it soon." Tonight, Rex would be the main course, of course. Anything that delicious should be.

"Have you selected a nursing home yet, Angie?" Gretta asked.

"It's not my choice, Gretta. Without my knowing, Rex executed a Living Will just two weeks ago. I guess he did not want to burden me with problematic decisions. You have no idea how sweet my Rex is. We executed mutual powers of attorney when Emery died, but he must have wanted something more detailed, and his Living Will is quite detailed."

"You two were lovers, weren't you." Maddie read their relationship in Angie's tone.

Gretta tightened. She disapproved of such directness.

Angie smiled and watched the graceful bubbling of the Dom in her glass. "Thought you two would never notice. We were even talking about marriage. He has proposed three times, and Dale loves him like mad and is dying for us to tie the knot. Rex is really the only father Dale has known. Now, I don't know what will happen." Her tears began.

Maddie and Gretta both let loose tears too. It was astounding how rich women could so often cry in unison.

Maddie gulped. "Did you girls know that Smith Girls often menstruate in unison? Now ladies, we are past the need for a good cry. We took care of that yesterday at the hospital out on the island. What we need now is intelligent support planning."

"Yes, indeed," Gretta said, putting her hand over Angie's.

At that point, they turned to business. Angie's new book, *From the Mouths of Assassins*, would be out in August. They discussed Gretta's phenomenal luck with the bestseller list and Maddie's soaring circulation.

"Luck has nothing to do with it," Gretta said. "You simply need a consummate knowledge of what must go where, how, when, for how much, and how *The TimesGuardian* currently generates the list. It used to be bookstores, but that had changed of course."

When the food finally arrived, they propelled themselves into the frenetic anticipation of orgasmic satiation. To better appreciate their food, they ate with little conversation. Maddie loved it, even though no serious planning to support Angie and Rex took place.

Gretta marked the end of dinner by delicately blotting her lips with the end of her napkin and asking, "Where is Rex going to be, Angie?" Quietly. Only female CEOs could come across as that mildly concerned.

"The Golden Arms. It's in Saratoga Springs and close to Tate School, where Dale is," Angie said.

"We should visit." Maddie loved Saratoga, but not for the racing season.

Gretta beamed. "I know the place, and we can all go together when we go. As you girls know, I own a house there next to Congress Park and know the community very well. Besides, Angie and I are from Saratoga."

"I was definitely born there," Angie said. "Oh, my, that's it. The address was right there in the book." Since Angie loved non sequiturs, Maddie and Gretta usually ignored her until details emerged.

"We should visit up a Saratoga storm," Gretta said. "Your both invited for the summer. Now I want dessert. I definitely want dessert." An appropriate sentiment. The dessert cart stood eighteen inches from her left elbow.

Angie looked up at the pastry waitress. "Helga, I would like a Cherry and Zabaglione Cream Tart."

Gretta took Les Réligieuses, and Maddie had her favorite, a stewed prune with cognac, a trickle of vanilla syrup and soupçon of lemon zest.

When they finished dessert and were still holding their farts in, Angie announced, "I hope you two are free tonight."

Maddie and Gretta stared at her, dumbstruck and too terrified to ask. Finally, Gretta broke the emotional impasse by motioning to Helga. "Dear, would you please bring the pastry cart again?"

−2−

New York City. Columbia Presbyterian Hospital. 11:00 PM. Inspector Rex Caine.

Rats with owl eyes sat there, perched on bare black limbs, their shadows looming against the gray horizon.

They sat there, and they stared at him.

He tried to remember but found no memories.

He tried to move but could not move sufficiently to feel it.

Death? No. He heard distant murmurs about blood pressure, vital signs, pupil response, nothing. He could feel nothing, but in a way, that actually was feeling.

He sensed his breath.

He sensed his body.

He sensed his blood.

He sensed his life.

He could smell, though, and knew well the smell of the rats, a cheddary reek of blood and bowel. They would not leave. They would wait there on the gray horizon, wait for him as they had waited for the boy.

Chapter 8 - A Stormy Night

Guts of stainless steel.

New York City. West 77th Street. Midnight. Angie.

"*It's a dark and stormy night,*" Mary Helen whispered into Angie's mind.

"*Good grief.*" Angie almost laughed. "*Shush, Mary Helen. It's just a thunderstorm.*"

The wind howled down Columbus Avenue as though it wanted to stop their cab. Thunder rolled through the streets like airborne subways. Streetlights flickered as Manhattan grit scoured the air.

Angie could feel her two friends' tension as the cab turned into West 77th Street. She had told them where they were going but not why. She could not imagine why they would be nervous. This block could not be any more dangerous than any other in Manhattan. Semi-elegant townhouses and duplexes lined the street. Granted, a school and playground from hell sat on the corner, but you could not have everything, not in Manhattan.

For safety, Angie stopped the cab directly in front of 1368 West 77th Street. No one was following them. Hard to tell, though. The NYPD, private dicks, and head hoods all used un-lit medallion cabs for surveillance. In Manhattan, they blended better than private cars, and there were more. Who wanted a car in Manhattan?

Angie wondered if Jimmu really had followed someone following her when she left Spencer's this morning, then again when she headed to the Excess Anonymous meeting. Lightning illuminated the entire block and transformed the brownstones into eerie sepia negatives.

"Crap, this really is a dark and stormy night," Mary Helen whispered.

Angie ignored her, paid the driver, and got out. "Here we are, girls."

Maddie and Gretta followed dutifully but looked ready to mess their knickers when the cab pulled away. The rain had not started yet, but from the thunder, lightning, and wind, it would soon.

"So, Ange, old friend." Maddie raised her voice to fight the wind but still tried to sound nonchalant. She failed. "Would you mind telling us why we're here?"

"Dumb, aren't they, Ange," Mary Helen said.

"Angie?" Gretta looked terribly pale under the streetlight. "This is not a great neighborhood for a midnight stroll, a have-block surrounded by have-not blocks."

"Please, Grett," Maddie said. "Cool it. On the Manhattan streets after dark, you always look like you fear being raped on horseback by a band of marauding Vikings from Knopf Doubleday."

"She's sure as hell got that right, Ange."

"Quiet, Mary Helen."

"It isn't good, and it isn't bad, Gretta," Angie said. "It just is. No city composed of haves and have-nots contains any truly safe neighborhoods. It's going to rain. We better get in." Of course, Angie did not really know the key would fit. She just believed it would.

"I second that," Maddie said. "Let's get inside, wherever we are."

"Sure thing." Angie led.

Gretta and Maddie followed.

"You just have a feeling that the key will fit, but you're certain?" Mary Helen said.

"I just have a feeling. That's right. My writer's gut is gurgling."

The doorbell and mailbox bore no name, just the number — not unusual for Manhattan. The key fit.

"Always trust your instincts, Mary Helen."

"Always have, Ange."

The heavy oak and glass door swung open. A small lamp on the remember-me table cast a circle of yellow light on the oriental carpet and a long hall, endless in the dim light. A dusty, acrid smell drifted through the silent air.

"I thought so." Angie reached in, felt around, and snapped on the hall lights, two simple brass sconces and a chandelier with brass poles supporting fake crystal stars. "Anybody home?"

"Good money, bad taste. And I don't think anybody is at home," Mary Helen quipped.

"I agree. Good money, bad taste, huh, ladies."

Maddie and Gretta looked at Angie as though she just belched her dentures across the room. A blast of thunder set the townhouse trembling. The roar of rain followed.

Gretta led the way back to the front door and peered out. Angie and Maddie followed. The storm roared and threatened to break the glass.

"You can't even see to the street." That seemed to disappoint Gretta.

"So why does Chubs want to see the street?" Mary Helen asked.

"Don't be disrespectful. Chubs is our publisher."

Angie knew exactly what Gretta meant. Being alone and uninvited in a strange house made one feel isolated.

"Gretta, have I ever begun a novel with, 'It was a dark and stormy night?'"

"No, and you had best not. On the other hand, if it's a horny story and contains an adequate racial mix, controversial social commentary, and your name, it might sell."

"Okay, you two," Maddie said. "Let's look around and get out." Maddie was apparently beginning to relax.

An archway on the left opened into the living room. Someone looking for something had destroyed the place. Upholstery was ripped, chairs overturned and gutted, books off shelves, cabinets opened, emptied, and overturned to expose their backs. It resembled Rex's apartment.

Gretta: "Let's get out of here."

Mary Helen: *"Chicken."*

Maddie: "Déjà vu."

Angie: "Not to fret. I'm reasonably sure that we're alone, girls."

"Angie, if there's a stiff in the john, I'm leaving." Maddie sounded as though she meant that sincerely. "Whose house is this?"

"Don't worry," Angie said with a smile. "The owner is dead."

"Dear God." Gretta ran to the brass umbrella bucket by the front door.

"Oh, Jeez," Mary Helen said, *"she's going to puke the bucket."*

Gretta did appear ready to take one of her patented CEO regurgitations. She did not, though. No surprise to Angie. Gretta would cling to her Les Réligieuses with guts of stainless steel. A true lady could not abandon some pleasures, even in the face of nauseating fear.

Angie giggled. "Relax, ladies. This is John Leech's house. The key was in Rex's jacket, and so was John's address book. I made a lucky guess."

Gretta shakily abandoned the umbrella stand. "Breaking and entering with a key is still breaking and entering, more so with the owner being dead police brass."

"It's not illegal entry," Angie said. "John Leech sent me, so it's okay. That he got killed since he sent me is unfortunate, but who will ask him?" Angie smiled, tilted her head to the right, and raised her hands, fingertips up and out.

Silent, Maddie and Gretta looked at each other.

"Are you okay, Gretta?" Angie asked.

"I suppose. Let's get moving." Gretta's color was improving. "This place makes me nervous." But she was relaxing.

A sheet of lightning filled the house. The chandeliers and remember-me table lamp flickered in unison as thunder shook the windows. Surprisingly, Maddie and Gretta ignored it and continued snooping like good little sleuths.

Maddie lifted a book from the floor, read the spine and dropped it. "Hey, Ange, isn't this an expensive place for a cop?"

"She's right there, Ange," Mary Helen said. *"This joker was either independently wealthy or taking or doing something on the side."*

"Maybe he was a civic-minded millionaire who yearned to be a cop." Angie always tried to be positive.

"Maybe twats grow feathers," Mary Helen said.

"Go gander a goose, Mary Helen," Angie replied. "And yes, girls. Isn't it amazing how far the Deputy Commissioner's salary went? Follow me." She led the way into the dining room.

"Why haven't the police sealed the place off?" Gretta said. "It's obviously a crime scene."

"They may have searched it and created the chaos for fun." Maddie was relaxing, too.

Angie dove into her purse and pulled out gloves for everyone.

"Good thinking, Ange. I'm proud of you," Mary Helen said. *"Don't ever forget gloves."*

"Thank you."

"Here, put these on, girls." Angie handed Maddie and Gretta each a pair of black latex gloves. "It wouldn't do to leave fingerprints."

"So, let's get out of here before they show up and find our fingers, much less our prints." Maddie remained pragmatic.

"So, what are we looking for?" Gretta had obviously caught the bug.

"We'll leave soon, ladies," Angie said. "And we're looking for John Leech's clothes."

Gretta said, "Oh," and returned to the umbrella stand.

"Oh crap, she's really going to ralph randy this time," Mary Helen said.

But Gretta reached into the pressed-metal gold stand and began flinging clothes over her shoulder. If she had not been wearing a $2600 bespoke suit, she would have looked like one of those ladies who ran laundromats. The clothes landed in the hall.

"Oh, crap," Maddie said. She and Mary Helen had lots in common.

Angie hurried over to Gretta and found a man's sports jacket, a blue shirt, pants, and the most absurd rainbow bikini briefs with a bisecting brown stripe she had ever seen. Someone had carefully dissected each seam of everything. Red-brown spots had dried stiff.

"Those are what Leech was wearing when someone shot him," Mary Helen offered.

"You've got it, Mary Helen. Whoever killed Leech left Rex's apartment in such a hurry that he took Leech's clothes to search them and this place later."

Angie lifted the jacket higher, studied it, then let it drop.

"These are the brass cop's clothes?" Gretta was really getting into this.

"Deputy Commissioner Leech's clothes, Dummy," Mary Helen said. *"The pig on the pot. The dick without much."*

"Deputy Commissioner Leech's, Gretta," Angie corrected.

"How did he get to Rex Caine's apartment naked?" Gretta asked.

Angie chuckled. "No, silly, whoever tossed Rex's place and killed the Deputy Commish brought his clothes over here to search the clothes and the house. For some reason, 'whoever' needed to hurry. The question we need to answer is where 'whoever' went from here."

"Thank you for not being sexist," Maddie said. "But what were they looking for?"

"They were looking," Gretta answered, "for what our dear Angie needed a microfilm reader for this morning." She was pretty sharp for a CEO.

Maddie wandered down the main hall.

Angie did not comment on Gretta's bit of truth but she smiled beatifically.

Gretta rolled her eyes. "For the microfilm you lifted from his toupee."

"I see Jimmu talked." Angie grinned.

"He's mine. He had no choice," Gretta said.

"I know. I expected that."

Maddie shrieked from deeper in the house.

Angie and Gretta raced down the hall and into the study.

Maddie still had her gloved hand on the doorknob of the open closet. Light from the study filled the small closet and illuminated the man's body hanging from a clothes hook, his hands tied behind his back, his bare feet on the floor, his ankles tied with strips of ripped pajamas, his knees bent, his black tongue protruding, his naked body a dead blue-gray color, a thin cord knotted firmly around his neck. Gray hair. Layers of wrinkles. Sixty or seventy years old. These days, maybe eighty or ninety.

Gretta gasped, then gagged.

Maddie stood there frozen for a moment more, then gasped, "Christ! Who's that, the Police Commissioner? No!" She corrected herself after staring further. "The Police Commissioner is Jewish."

"I've been to parties here with Rex," Angie said. "That's Leon, Leech's butler. He must have awakened at the wrong time."

"*Someone snuffed his wick*," Mary Helen put in.

Angie cringed. Absently: "Someone definitely snuffed him."

Maddie and Gretta looked at Angie as though she had donned a deerstalker and Calabash pipe.

"Oh, my God. He's naked," Gretta whispered. She pressed both hands to her mouth and looked ready to finally release her Les Réligieuses. She did not.

Maddie stared, gulped, and said haughtily, "Well, he looks livelier than some of the servants I've hired lately." She gulped again. "Angie, I think I'm getting used to this. Do you think the seen-one-seen-all thing applies to corpses?"

"*It applies to everything.*" Mary Helen was getting cynical in her middle age.

Lightning glared into the windows and closet and lit the body like a stripper in a klieg light.

Thunder shook the place again, and the lights went out. A few minutes later, red lights appeared in the hall.

"Follow me, girls." Angie pulled a bright flashlight out of somewhere and led the way. When she reached the hall, she turned it off. She got them into this and would get them out of it. Gretta grabbed the back of Angie's coat, Maddie grabbed her arm, and they felt their way back to the foyer, where the only light clearly came from a police car in front of the house.

"And just remember, girls, it's still raining like mad outside," Maddie said, "and pigs can't swim."

The grandfather clock in the hall struck one. Learning quickly on the job, Gretta broke from the huddle, eased to the front door, and peered out without disturbing the curtain.

"Do you know what's black and white and has fuzz inside," Maddie whispered, staring at the flashing lights.

"Shush," Gretta whispered. "There's a police car out in the street."

"Obviously," Maddie whispered.

Angie and Maddie crept up to join Gretta at the front door.

"Don't move the curtains." Angie hadn't anticipated this, not in the middle of the night.

Outside, directly in front of John Leech's house, an NYPD patrol car sat in the driving rain, light bar blazing. The spotlight flashed on, focused down the block toward Amsterdam, then on the house next door.

"Duck, girls. We are next," Angie whispered.

The light hesitated on John Leech's house, then disappeared.

"Stay put." Angie eased up and looked out.

A man, not in uniform, got out and started toward Leech's steps. A gray Hyundai Elantra pulled up next to the patrol car, and the passenger-side windows eased down. The driver leaned over and spoke to the officer still in the patrol car. The officer called his partner back to the car, and they took off like bats out of hell. The Elantra drove on into the rain.

"We're safe if we get out of here fast."

"*Quite a coincidence, Ange,*" Mary Helen said.

"*Wasn't it.*"

The lights came on. Angie ran back inside, quickly snapped off every light, then returned to the foyer where the only light again came from the streetlights on 77th Street.

"Let's get out of here." Gretta was sitting flat on the floor, her back against the foyer wall. "Let's get the hell out of here."

"Yes, we should leave," Angie said. "It's too difficult to thoroughly search an already searched house and is probably a waste of time." Besides, Angie had begun to feel ill-at-ease now. She missed having Rex with her for protection. He had always gotten her out of anything she ever got herself into.

The thought stopped her mind.

"Ditto to leaving." Maddie sounded done in. "And the rain has mostly stopped."

"Praise the Lord." Gretta pushed herself up into a squat.

Angie opened the door as quietly as she could, eased out, and peeked down the street toward

Columbus and then Amsterdam. Nothing. No one. Streetlights dripped rain. Distant lightning flickered. "It's safe, girls."

They eased out onto the stoop behind her. Their collective breathing became deeper and smoother.

"This has been a hectic night. Thank you for humoring me. Take your gloves off but keep them." Angie would have searched more, but the police could return.

"Of course, they'll come back. And at this hour, they likely weren't on the up and up," Mary Helen said. *"The lights were out already, or they would have busted us."*

"I know."

"I want you girls to stay at East 64th Street tonight," Angie said. "I could use some company." It occurred to Angie that her request resembled a command.

"I can't imagine why," Gretta said.

"Nor I, Angie dear." Maddie crossed her eyes and stretched her tongue nearly to the tip of her nose. "I can't imagine why at all."

"Unique," Mary Helen snarled. *"I've always liked Maddie."*

"Well, Mary Helen, it takes uniqueness to deal with centered women."

"I've never known one, but if it sells, it sells."

The Elantra that had sent the police off pulled up and stopped.

Gretta said, "Thank God," and opened the passenger door. "Just in time, Jimmu."

DAY THREE

Chapter 9 - Memories

Rat path.

—1—

New York City. Columbia Presbyterian Hospital. 1:30 AM. Inspector Rex Caine.

He was beginning to remember. He knew he might have been a cop, but what was his name? He had to think hard. "My name is Rex." The memory returned slowly.

Cat-sized rats, New York's enhanced species, squatted on the edge of his bed, waiting for him to die so they could snack. They might not wait. They might eat his intestines before he died as they ate the boy's. Rats relished hurting you, especially if you were young and tender.

The interiors of their mouths glowed blood-red. Pine-green mucus dripped from their chins. Christmas rats, he thought. If Rex was a cop, he didn't want to be one anymore. He didn't really want to know who he was or what he had done in the past. He knew rats, especially those who lived in the abandoned tenements he used for stakeouts. Those rats came from Brooklyn or the Bronx. They strolled into Manhattan for bright lights and superior dining. The dead ones remained in Brooklyn. "Only the dead know Brooklyn." Tom Wolfe wrote that.

Rex saw a jigsaw puzzle, like the ones he used to do with some woman and her kid. Once again, he had to force it forward in his mind. Her name was —? The rats knew more about him than he did. Memories eased back but without connections. Maybe they lied.

A little kid eased into his head, a good kid, except for the drugs taped to his lower abdomen.

Then his walk to Brooklyn popped up.

John Leech and Rex strolled on the Brooklyn Bridge from Manhattan to Brooklyn — light to dark, joyous to joyless. Only the dead knew Brooklyn.

Rex sensed that this walk would bring him no joy, as something in Leech's expression and the quiet tenseness of his tone gave him away. Rex's ability to read people had saved his life more than once.

"Justice stays out of reach for most of us, Rex." Leech glanced down at the East River as though it might be eavesdropping. He sounded nervous. "But not for all of us." Lights glimmered in the river, distorted by wet whimsy. "Some of us reach out and take justice by the snout. We make it happen despite the crap that clogs the system. They're jellyfish. We're Man o' Wars."

Rex glanced at John Leech and recognized tension. He looked brittle. He would prevail or shatter. Leech obviously feared Rex's response. "Where are you going with this, John?" Rex caught a whiff of East River garbage drifting down through the soft summer night and wondered if his vest would absorb the stink.

"You don't know?" Leech asked.

Half the force knew the rumors. So far, Rex had ignored them. "You and The Candy Troops, John?" Not Rex's old friend. Not the Assistant Commish.

For a time, Leech and Rex clung to silence as if to sanity. A scow crept beneath the bridge, bearing its gifts to the sea.

Drugsters and pushers and users, beware.
The Candy Troops will soon be there.
You'll suck the lollipop and go punk-plop-plop.
God-damned drugsters must go quite stone dead.

Some genius penned that on the wall of a precinct men's room. Rex wished the weirdos would get their graffiti to scan properly.

I chewed off her buttocks,
I chewed up her rump,
I sucked out her guts in hot, fragrant lumps.

That scanned better, but still no Pulitzer.

"You, John? The Candy Troops?" Rex wanted to reject the notion.

Leech nodded as they left the bridge. They leaned side-by-side on the rail at the overlook plaza and watched Manhattan burn in the writhing East River.

"Don't go further, John. Do not ask me to join you. I'm a cop. I know the frustrations. But I hate hit men, even when they're cops targeting drugsters."

"It's the only way, Rex. The courts won't do it or can't. Even if the judge wants to throw the key away, there's no room at the inn, and the drugsters don't kill each other off fast enough to matter. Our way is the only way."

Many times, like all cops, Rex had wanted to take a drug dealer up to the roof of a deserted building, jam an S&W thirty-eight up his ass and blow his guts out his nose. He dreamed about it. Rex specialized in drug trafficking and drug homicides, which included everything related. Politicians were worse than cops, though. Their actions mostly concerned election or reelection, and truth died.

"Maybe I can't tolerate the only way, John." He did not and would not. That mattered.

For a time, they stared at the fire in the water. Caine wondered if Leech, having made the approach, would feel compromised. That could be dangerous, but Rex had survived worse threats than The Candy Troops targeting him. He had offended druggies, drug lords, politicians, courts, cops, and what remained of organized crime — a potent brew.

John continued his pitch. "Drugs have surpassed sex as recreation. No matter social status, economic status, educational status, age, or gender, drugs cross all boundaries. The piles of Coke grow. Heroin flies. Bodies rot. Kids and adults methocate. Men, women, and children kill or are killed or are court executed. Drugged guns kill masses. Crack crystals hang on the Christmas tree. There is no room at the inn without two clips of bullets. Our way is the one true path, the one true way. We are the light."

As far as Rex was concerned, John's light occurred only at the end of his cigar. If drug killings mattered, they would have led to something more important from lawmakers, politicians, cops, clergy, or someone — this was the United States of America.

John Leech went on and on, then stopped, and they stood together without speaking. Finally, he broke the tension with, "I'll see you tomorrow, Rex. We can talk more."

"Okay, John, we can talk more."

Leech sunk into Brooklyn though he lived in Manhattan. Caine recrossed the bridge, back toward his beloved Island of Lights.

Rex and John, NYPD veterans. If men like them contemplated short-circuiting the legal process, what would inexperienced cops on the street contemplate because of their passions, prejudices, and bigotry? What must The Candy Troops be doing now? What would the future hold for a legal system that freed crooks and protected bad cops, a legal system with irrationally bound hands?

Rex could believe that. Some cops would protect the system. Some would nurture it. Society would discover its errors and doom Leech's way. Otherwise, what kind of world would survive for Rex's intended son, Dale?

—2—

Columbia Presbyterian Hospital. Rex.

The dark expanded into flashing sparks.

Rex trembled.

Rats sniffed his nostrils.

His limbs stiffened.

His trembling became shaky and effervescent.

His body split into quarters, each flying away toward the four poles of the universe.

Sparks burned his brain.

Crystal light blinded him.

"Give him the injection. Seizure damage is all this poor bastard needs," said a man's voice from somewhere, commanding and intense. "He's going to have no brain left."

"Here, Doctor," an out-of-breath woman said.

The sparks dwindled. The fire faded to black.

"There, that's better. I hope that damned nursing home can manage him."

"They specialize in long-term care but accept head-injury patients, Doctor."

"We don't know if this is long-term, short-term, or no-term. We don't even know if it's really a head injury.

There's no evidence of it except the damned coma. What's his name?"

"Rex Caine. Inspector Rex Caine, NYPD."

"Poor bastard."

"His Living Will specifies his immediate transfer. He drew it up two weeks ago."

He'd executed a proxy, POA, and Last Will and Testament a few weeks before.

"Well, his vitals are good. He might not need acute care. He's stable despite the one seizure, poor bastard. I just hope to God that they know what they're doing at that nursing home. I've never seen a head injury go through here this fast and without more diagnostics. Jesus. This bastard may actually have a chance. What's that place called again?"

"The Golden Arms. It used to be The Golden Arms of God. Just outside Saratoga. Very well-staffed. They even have respiratory therapists. I covered there occasionally before I moved to New York. Dr. Little signed Inspector Caine's order. He's sent patients there before. It's better than Bellevue. The first thing you learn as a nurse at Bellevue is how not to put your feet in the rat path under the desk."

"I don't think Little was with this guy more than two minutes, if that," the doctor said. "It's in his Living Will, huh? That very place?"

"That's what I hear. The Department arranged for private pay. In case of incapacitation, Caine is to go to The Golden Arms immediately."

"The only gold in those places is in the owner's pocket. I hope to God they know what they're doing."

"The ambulance will pick him up early tomorrow morning."

"Poor bastard."

Chapter 10 - Saratoga

Bogeyman rat virus.

New York City. East 64th Street. 1:35 AM. Angie.

Angie awoke sitting up in bed, her chest moist, her breath fast and raspy. For a moment, she could not remember who she was or where she was.

"You're Angelica," Mary Helen whispered, *"and you're okay. You're fine."*

"I wish I could believe you, Mary Helen."

The ceiling light came on. Angie never heard the door open or saw the light from the hall.

"Angie, you screamed." Maddie, in one of Angie's pale blue nightgowns, stood in the doorway with Gretta just behind in a silk, designer number. "And who were you talking to?"

"I thought I might have screamed, but I didn't know I was talking to anyone."

"You screamed like the Devil, Hon. And you were talking to me aloud."

"I'm not surprised." The rats came again, doubtless for unfinished business, but what unfinished business?

Angie had sensed that Maddie and Gretta had accepted her invitation to spend the night more for her than for themselves—perhaps they were correct. They had picked Chuck up from Central Park South, retrieved some of Gretta's precious silk lingerie from

East 82nd Street, and bedded down at Angie's house for a weird pajama party.

Now, Maddie and Gretta entered Angie's bedroom and sat on the left side of the bed. It was the middle of the night.

"Was it the rats, kid?" Gretta asked. Angie had told Maddie about the dreams, and Maddie had told Gretta. They had even discussed it at Michael's European.

"Yes." Angie began having Rex's rat dreams a few weeks ago.

"I still think it's just the power of suggestion," Maddie said.

"I agree," Gretta said.

"I agree too. What else could it be?" Angie loved animals. As a young girl, she even allowed her pet indigo snake to sleep with her, and apart from the pragmatic fear of getting bitten, she liked rats until the nightmares began to torment Rex. He talked in his sleep, then would awaken shaking but would never elaborate past admitting that the rats had come on some kind of retributive mission. He had evidently passed his rats to Angie like a virus, a bogeyman rat virus.

"Come on," Gretta said, pulling Angie out of bed with one hand and Maddie off it with the other, "time for a nightcap." Gretta wore rings on her carrot-shaped fingers every day, then switched them every morning. She deposited Maddie and Angie in the living room on the long blue sofa and walked over to the black-and-white bar. "Brandy Alexanders for everyone! You have plenty of heavy cream, I presume, Angie." Gretta enjoyed taking charge.

"In the bar fridge. I keep that and the raspberry-swirl cheesecake just for you," Angie said.

"Wise woman," Gretta replied. "Staying on the right side of your publisher is tremendously important."

"Very wise woman," Maddie added.

"Crap. Who needs this crap," Mary Helen whispered in Angie's ear.

Gretta pulled a bowl from under the bar and set to work. No one made Brandy Alexanders like Gretta Braun made them. From the fridge, she pulled cream and a bowl of sliced kiwi. "Excellent. We shouldn't drink on empty stomachs."

"Your stomach is never empty." Maddie yawned, stretched, and slumped onto the plush green velvet throw pillows at the far end of the couch.

"Neither is your bed, Maddie darling," Gretta replied sweetly.

"Don't fight," Angie managed. They did seem evenly matched. "I can't stand it when you two fight."

"We won't," Gretta said. "At least we won't until we're too drunk to remember doing it."

"The behemoth and the bitch." Maddie chuckled with her mouth closed. "We could be a tag team, Grett."

They all giggled at that one until Gretta snarled, "Shut up, you two! I'm creating the elixir of the gods, at least of the God Bacchus."

"I wish she'd stick to single malt scotch," Mary Helen said.

"Variety is the spice, Mary Helen. Try a little elegance," Angie replied.

"Crap on elegance."

Ten minutes later, Gretta arrived at the sofa with an eggnog bowl of Brandy Alexanders and a plate of cold sliced kiwi garnished with strawberries. She then plopped herself onto the floor between Angie and Maddie, her back against the front of the sofa, balanced the bowl between her legs, and ladled the Alexanders into cups. "There you go, kid, now we'll all sleep better." She served them over her shoulders, then flipped a strawberry to Maddie. "I'm sorry that it can't be a cherry, dear."

Maddie caught the strawberry, popped it into her mouth, and smiled with Mother Theresa-like radiance. "Gretta, why don't you give up publishing. You could write a bestseller. *Stomachs I Have Known*, or *Stomachs I Have Grown*."

They all giggled. With friends like Maddie and Gretta, how could Angie ever need *Saturday Night Live*? Twenty minutes later, she had mellowed substantially. Thirty minutes later, they all needed to go to the bathroom simultaneously. No problem. Angie's East 64th Street palace boasted many bathrooms.

When they regrouped at the sofa, Maddie asked, "So what was on the microfilm? And don't ignore me this time."

Angie looked from Maddie to Gretta and back. She had decided to trust Jimmu, so she should probably trust her best friends. She had even worked out an arrangement with Jim for future research and tasks. He expressed delighted delight at the lengthy length of the arrangement. Gretta agreed too. Jim would attend Columbia University this fall, so he would be around for a while.

Angie handed the envelope to Maddie. "You figure it out." She then flopped onto the sofa, drained her cup, and bent down to refill it directly from the bowl. The ladle seemed too far away.

Gretta moved onto the sofa to help with the ongoing investigation. She would know less than Maddie. Book people invariably paid less attention to reality than magazine people, unless the selected reality promised increased profit.

"Oh, crap!" When Maddie began to read the lists, instant horror blanketed her face.

"What's that supposed to mean?" Angie hated sloppy sentiment.

"Oh crap, oh crap, oh crap," Maddie repeated. "Except for Rex, Kossick, the Kershaws, and Dale, I don't know anybody on the one list, but I do know The Snow Queens. They are international drug thugs! Biggies. Known but never busted. *Centered Women* did a piece on them not long ago. These folks are major international crooks. We got threats, bad threats, and dropped the exposé."

"So what." Angie got drunk faster than her friends. "If they bother me, I'll just get my good friend, Gretta, to puke on them." She belched.

"Don't get gross, Ange. I admire it in most people but not in you." Mary Helen sounded offended, like a nun after a non-immaculate conception, stigmata, or some damned thing.

"I recognize these maps." Gretta never got smashed, no matter how much she drank. Either it was a CEO thing, or she offered the alcohol more space to store itself in. She did tend to get high when she ate. "I recognize the area. I own properties there, including Crumb House, across from Congress Park. You two should both recognize these maps. You have visited there often enough. It's Saratoga!"

"Saratoga, New York?" Angie drained her cup again. "Horse racing? Where I was born and raised, though not in a stable." Angie drained the cup again, and reality finally reached her. "Then those are not parks. They are racetracks. Crap! The flat track and the harness track. Crap! I knew I had seen 'em. Crap!"

Angie admitted to herself that she was a bit intoxicated, what with her ballooning tongue and cotton lips. She over-imbibed infrequently but thoroughly.

"You're smashed, Hon." Mary Helen held her liquor much better than Angie.

Of course, why create a fictional hero if she couldn't do everything you had always wanted to do?

When Gretta picked up the manilla envelope to put the documents away, a folded piece of paper fell onto the blue carpet. "What's this?" She bent down and picked it up.

Angie forced her eyes to focus, and finally said, "That's Rex's Living Will from the hospital."

Miraculously, without moving off the sofa—not that Angie would have noticed anyway—Gretta and Maddie were abruptly standing at Angie's feet, looking down at her as though they disapproved of something. The behemoth and the bitch seemed unwilling to believe Angie or what they had just learned. That, or they did not care to believe the state of absolute drunkenosity Angie had thrown herself into, whereto, thento, etc.

Then Angie doubtless made their day or night or whatever time it was. "Saratoga is where Rex is going tomorrow, and where Dale is today, which is after yesterday but before tomorrow, I think, thereto, whyto, whereto, thento, crapto."

Gretta studied the page and frowned. At that point, Angie's light darkened, and Maddie and Gretta left the room, or maybe it was the room that left.

Through the fumes of delight, Gretta's distant voice said, "John Leech witnessed this."

Chapter 11 - Zelda

The Gold-Coast Penthouse.

—1—

The Golden Arms. 3:00 AM. Zelda McCauley, RN.

Zelda sat at the nursing station on Skilled Seven and tried to finish her charting without nodding off. She had not possessed the foresight to sleep before she came in at 3:00 PM yesterday or to anticipate that Agatha Lichtman, the Associate Nursing Director, would bounce her big ass over here at 7:00 last night and ask Zel to do a double. She would have enjoyed saying no because she loved seeing Agatha beg, grovel, and whine, but Zel needed the money.

Money or not, her mind shut down when the call light went off for the seventeenth time this shift. "Mrs. Markley always figures that her call light won't be answered unless she puts it on five minutes after her last pee. Anticipatory bladder distress. Dear thing, the bitch."

Zel lifted her eyes and stared at the elegantly flowered wallpaper opposite the desk. "If they spent as much money for staff and supplies as they do for salesmanship fru-fru around here, things would be much easier." You wouldn't find any Medicaid here, and because of that, you needed to keep the beds full of private pay clients. No bed night went empty except for the Gold Coast—few could afford it.

Decent nursing care and healthy food attracted no one. Restaurant-style dining rooms, wet-look floors, waiters in faux tuxedos, chandeliers, wallpaper, and the illusion of gracious living, did.

The staff's first priority was to supply anything that would make families feel less guilty about dumping Mama, who fell on her head, or Aunt Matilda, who was not right in hers, into the tender mercies of The Golden Arms. You also needed to market the hell out of the place to prevent Medicaid admissions — that was what social workers did.

At some point, the nursing home business had morphed into show-and-don't-tell. Here, a special team even removed the decubiti sheets from the charts whenever The State pulled into the parking lot. Because of all the finagling, The Golden Arms paid way more than the competition, and here sat Zel, well into the second of two exceptionally well-paying shifts, so tired she couldn't care less if the whole floor fell off a cliff. Life didn't exist here, only the appearance of life, including Zel's. She ran her right hand through her hair, short, frosted, stiff ringlets on top, like wet clippings taken off the barber shop floor, then bleached, shellacked, and glued on. The cognitively intact patients hated it, but that didn't bother her.

— 2 —

Saratoga. Tate Prep School. 7:30. Dale.
Dale and Fred walked down to the dining room. Most of the kids had taken off for summer vaca. Fred would be leaving probably tomorrow to spend time with his Aunt. Dale was waiting for his mom to appear. Uncle Rex should arrive sometime today too.

The breakfast buffet was in place when they reached the dining room. It had the usual food, but also the stuff they never served any other time, like Pop Tarts, sugary cereal, chocolate cokes, and other junk. The two of them dove in for an end-of-school-year pig out.

"So are you going to keep seeing Mary Margaret, Dale?"

"If she'll have me?"

"You know that there's more to being with a girl than sex, don't you?"

"Yeah, but sex is sure nice. What do you want to do today? Squash?"

"Yeah, I guess. How about a swim too."

"You're on."

"You're mom's coming today?"

"In Saratoga, yeah, but she said she probably wouldn't pick me up until tomorrow."

"I think my Aunt Mirtha will be here tomorrow. She usually just calls and tells me to get ready, then picks me up in a half hour or something. If it works out, I'll introduce you to her."

"Me too. You said you wanted to meet my mom, didn't you?"

"Meet Angie Summers? I'm dying to meet her. She's a great writer."

"With a dirty mind."

"This is 2038. Her writing wouldn't be great without a dirty mind."

"Yeah, I guess."

— 3 —

New York State Thruway. 10:00 AM. Maddie.
Maddie, Gretta, and the hungover remains of dear sweet old friend Angie reached Albany at 10:00 AM.

Gretta had rented the WatStretchEV for the entire summer. It had all the comforts of home: space, comfort, fridge, drink, and lots of Grettaesque food. To top the Stretch, she had rented a chauffeur who looked like Arnold Schwarzenegger, a big, handsome, inscrutable young man with a profile that suggested a crotch to reckon with. Maddie was all too happy to admire the young man dear Gretta had rented for the rest of the summer as a house boy, chauffeur, security man, and hopefully for whatever else you could talk the gorgeous brute into.

And what a name! Mr. Gorgeous went by the moniker of Adonis Woods, phony, of course, but scrumptious. According to Gretta, he aspired to be a model. He could easily be, with his muscles on muscles, perfect skin, beautiful face, graceful catlike movements, and smooth Viennese accent.

With a little help from his future friends he might succeed at anything he desired. Maddie suspected that he was about to get the help he needed. Both Gretta and Maddie used models. Sometimes Maddie even used models as models. Even Angie seemed remotely impressed with the triumvirate's catch for the summer.

"Hey, Gretta," Maddie said, "I like your taste in chauffeurs."

"Oh, Adonis is ever so much more than that." Gretta smiled beatifically, as though she just ate Philadelphia, and it was cheesecake. "He could prove especially useful. He knows how to protect his friends — and since we may shortly involve ourselves in something risky, having a useful man around the house seems wise. Hands off!"

For some reason, Gretta winked at Maddie. Was she suggesting that Adonis could adequately defend himself against Maddie? If so, Gretta could sally forth and seek carnal knowledge of herself. On the other hand, if he was a bodyguard for the three of them, he might very well prove useful. Communing with Angelica Summers sometimes cause Maddie and Gretta worrisome episodes, like being shot at.

At their little tête-à-tête yesterday morning, Gretta and Maddie discussed hiring a detective agency to keep an eye on Angie. With Adonis around, who cared? In fact, with Adonis around, who wanted anyone watching?

Angie took the cold cloth off her forehead and stared at the back of Adonis's gorgeous head. "I agree. We could easily develop a need for someone who can lift a car."

Adonis was wearing a T-shirt, probably because he appreciated admiration. As for Little Orphan Annie of the high-proof head over there, Maddie doubted that Adonis had ever encountered anyone like her. Ditto on the rest of them.

Back on East 64th Street, when Maddie saw the list of drugthugs, this affair began to excite her to the max. She even began to think of the article about The Snow Troops lying unpublished in her briefcase that sat next to her left calf. Maybe Angie could turn it into a limited serial that Gretta could sell to Maddie for *Centered Women*, and which would then become an Angie Summers novel for Spencer and Sons. Angie's name was valuable.

And Saratoga? What could be more convenient? Gretta and Maddie always worked off-site in summer. Gretta owned a beautiful house that overlooked Congress Park, and even knew Cindy Ellen McGraw of the Scottish McGraws, who owned Saratoga during the racing season and gave the most marvelous balls at the

Canfield Casino whenever she wanted to. She was also shopping her first novel to publishers, Gretta among them. Cindy Ellen hoped to be the new Truman Capote. She even looked like him.

Angie let her head fall back on the seat. "Girls, I have decided that I may die shortly."

To the best of Maddie's memory, Angie had never before tied one on quite as she had last night or this morning, whenever it was. Her hangover would be a brute. "So what's our plan of action, Angie? You must have a plan."

"It's there. I just can't remember it." Angie carefully arranged the cloth back over her face. "Where's Chuck?"

"Up front with Adonis," Gretta said. "They like petting each other. He told me that he'd been pussy-prone since he was nine."

Maddie wondered what or whom he'd had between his legs at nine but let the matter pass.

"What time is Rex due at The Golden Arms?" Gretta asked.

"One." Under the cloth, Angie's voice sounded like it came from some new circle of hell.

"The cleaning crew should have finished at my place the day before yesterday," Gretta said, "but the paintings and silver are still in the vault. Unfortunately, burglars and jewel thieves invariably target Saratoga houses during the racing season and before, when everybody tries to impress everybody else. You soon learn to keep your valuables only in a safe under responsible supervision and with twice the adequate insurance."

Gretta loved to flaunt it. God knew she had it. God and everyone else also knew that she loved to control it and everyone else. Adonis needed to watch her, or he would end up in a vault under responsible supervision.

"We'll make do." Maddie did not mind roughing it. "Nova and Beluga taste better off the fingers, anyway."

"Try not to be gross, Maddie dear," Gretta said, "and salt is essential, just not too much of it." She reached down and opened the fridge. "Anyone want a snack?" She reverently lifted out a white box bearing Erda Stevens's fattening imprint, then a green bottle bearing Dom's delightful one.

When Gretta opened the box, Maddie gagged. "Champagne with raspberry cheesecake?"

"I brought some carrots and lettuce for the rabbits among us, Maddie," Gretta said, "and two cases of Chuck's cat food from Cat.com."

Angie pressed down on her face cloth with both hands. Apparently, she did not care to hear about the calories du jour.

— 4 —

An Ambulance. Inspector Rex Caine.

The hum of tires on pavement made Rex want to scream.

With each hour, chaos grew closer, but he couldn't remember why. He just somehow knew he caused it, started it, or planned it.

He lay in some sort of moving vehicle.

No voices except murmurs above his head. He sensed no presence of any kind, only motion and murmurs.

He should know where he was going. He sort of remembered arranging it. But when, where, how, and why?"

He was going somewhere.

For some reason.
For —

— 5 —

The Golden Arms. Fourth Floor. 11:10 AM. Suki.

Beth Elsuk — her friends called her Suki — was on the Skilled Seven. Most of her patients were female. Men tended not to make it to nursing homes or to survive long if they did. Women simply lasted longer. She was tired but fortunately was working with Martha Bartlett, a nursing assistant who had worked here for years. She possessed the patience of a saint, the body of a bull, and the mind of a goat — the ideal Certified Nursing Assistant. You aimed her in the right direction, said a few words, and she did the job.

"Do you know about your new admission, Suki?"

Suki looked up into the gray eyes of Agatha Lichtman, who had appeared from nowhere as usual. Dirty blond hair, humorless, configured in middle-aged gaunt, Agatha had risen from nurse to Associate Director of Nursing. Her stone face reeked of medical competence, paranoid secrecy, and willingness to ignore ethical considerations to support the company's bottom line. She would have admitted Jack the Ripper for butt warts if he had money.

"What new admission?" It would be nice if Agatha would provide some staff to go with some of the new admits.

"Oh, I'm sorry, Suki. 1:00 PM. From Columbia Presbyterian in New York."

"I know where it is."

"A New York Police Department Inspector. Fresh head injury. Coma. Uncertain prognosis."

"Where's his file?"

"Medical Records is making it up. Columbia Presbyterian didn't fax us that much, but Social Service arranged the whole thing in an hour or so. There was already a plan for his placement here if he ever needed one. Just in time, from what I've heard."

"So, what's his name?"

"He doesn't have one until Medical Records gives him one. We just know that he's coming and that he's paid up. He'll be in Private Suite Seven."

"A cop is going into The Gold-Coast Penthouse?"

"You got it."

That explained it. The company rarely rented those suites and then only to short-term head injury or geriatric rehab cases, some of whom appeared strangely healthy. Of course, at $3000 per diem for room and board, you could recover quickly or, if rich, lounge indefinitely. "In other words, we're getting a VIP cop."

"Correct."

"We haven't used Suite Seven in months." It was the best suite in the place. "Private-duty nurse?"

Agatha hesitated. "I'm not sure. I have not heard yet. Housekeeping's already dusted, etcetera-etcetera-plus." Agatha hesitated again, which had never been part of her makeup. "And Suki, this one gets the full treatment. Claude hinted that the patient had a connection with his father, Gregory Rue, who, as you know, owns the place."

"Claude Rue should know." One year after Claude became an RN, he became the administrator here. Suki had never laid eyes on the owner, Gregory Rue, and had often wondered if he existed. "Rue, the mysterious?" How many Peruvians owned nursing homes in Saratoga?

"Don't kid the product, Suki." With that, Agatha strode off toward Skilled Eight. God knew what bomb she intended to drop over there.

Suki walked down the hall and around the corner toward Suite Seven. She sensed that this cop admission made Agatha nervous. It was better to play it safe.

The Golden Arms building formed a huge I-shape. Each cross-wing held a gold-coast suite, eight in all. Private Suite Seven sat nearest to Suki's charge desk. She pulled her keys out, unlocked the door of Suite P7, and went in. The door closed behind her. The suite could have been in a luxury hotel. The bed had all the utility of the most advanced hospital beds, but in its lowest position became a king-sized luxury bed with all medical equipment hidden. It could even split into two singles.

Plush red carpet covered the floor, and soft blue filaments swirled through the gold wallpaper. Two easy chairs sat close to the bed, both high-end Howorth recliners. An eighty-inch Mitsubishi TV sat on a movable platform next to the wall opposite the foot of the bed. Built-in controls could move the TV up and down and around the room.

Suki walked to the door across from the bed and snapped the light on. The recessed whirlpool dominated a large bathroom with a separate shower and normal tub. The only handicapped adaptation visible here was a hydraulic chair to lower the patient into either tub, if necessary. Occupants of the private suites often preferred complete privacy—a surprising number belonged to the Smith family.

The private-duty nurse's mini-suite sat down the inside hall to the patient's left. The suite appeared clean and orderly. A door to the patient's right led to a short outside hall and private fire stairs that exited The Arms' north end. The patient or Nursing could lock all entrances remotely.

The designer of P7 had placed the nurse's room at the farthest point from the patient's bed, a pain for a good nurse but a requirement for control-freak patients. Occasionally, the facility would turn on the full electronic monitoring system for extremely sick patients, what few had ever occupied the suites. No one had yet ordered that for this admission. No one had yet ordered anything.

Suki walked across the sitting room and opened the door to the auxiliary hall. All was clean and sparkling.

Satisfied that the place appeared in good shape, Suki closed the hall door, returned to the bedroom and opened the double patio doors. She stepped out onto the patio that ran around the corner of the building. Fresh summer air filled her lungs. The view consumed her.

The Golden Arms sat perched halfway up the long slope of a four-mile-long ridge. To the right, an ancient stone well sat in a vast pasture. The John Appleseed Cottage sat on the far side of the road, the original sections in stone, the massive addons in roughhewn clapboard. Down the road to the left sat Tate School, far enough away to conceal the screams of preteens and moans of horny adolescents. In the distance, the city of Saratoga and the thoroughbred track gleamed.

A green and white ambulance climbed the main driveway to The Arms. Suki yawned. "Right on time. I had best go see if Medical Records has given him a name yet."

Chapter 12 - Crumb House

I love Victorian ugly.

— 1 —

Saratoga, NY. Crumb House. Noon. Maddie.

When Adonis, the gorgeous one, eased the limo into the gravel drive of old friend Gretta's old homestead, Crumb House, Maddie saw dear, sweet, naive, old friend Angie lift the cold hangover cloth from her childlike face. Maddie looked bleary-eyed at the fat tan house, and said, "Didn't this house used to be green, Gretta, or am I more hungover than I thought."

"Yes, you are," Gretta said, "and yes, it did. I decided to restore the house to its eighteenth-century tan elegance. Do you like the candles?"

Glimmering electric candles burned in every window, a Christmas of white lights. The place would be exactly what you would look for in the middle of the night if you were Paul Revere or Jack the Ripper and needed to make a pit stop.

Gretta ran three fingers around the edge of the empty cheesecake plate and licked them delicately. "The original color of the Crumb Homestead was tan. And they supposedly burned real candles in the windows at all times." The place even had a thick tower tacked onto the back left corner, rising to a fourth, tower-only floor.

"I love Victorian ugly," Maddie smiled haughtily, "but I didn't know you were a Crumb, Gretta." She was determined to avenge herself on Gretta for providing the excruciating temptation of cheesecake all the way up from New York. "You strike me as more the whole cake."

"Please," Gretta huffed, "the past social fabric of Saratoga regarded the Crumb family highly. Money begets money no matter where it came from."

"Good pedigree, huh," Maddie said. "Like the horses over at the track?"

"Yes. Let's just say that in the good old days when gambling instead of balls flourished in the Canfield Casino, and booze came in under hay, the clan of Elias Crumb, my grandfather, flourished with multiple dollar signs and to the delight and sexual satisfaction of the assembled gentility."

"Don't brag, darling—I already know your granddaddy was a bootlegger/pimp to the upper crust. Was Grandpa's house for living in or for business."

"Both."

"Will you two stop it!" Angie used a bottle of Evian to wet her cloth, then slapped it back onto her head. "My head is hung."

"And you hung it, dear." Maddie could not feel too sympathetic to Angie's plight. "You are what you drank, and you knew better."

Gretta smiled, and a devilish glint crept into her eye that Maddie had never noticed. "Bootlegger Gramps or not, Maddie, flourishing is flourishing. And I am the one with the old homestead in Saratoga who can afford a limo and driver/bodyguard. And, of course, you can use his services, dear. I've known him for quite a while. He's very reliable."

The WatStretchEV door opened, and there stood the gorgeous Adonis with Rex's pussy tucked into a hugely attractive left armpit. "We've arrived here." His voice sounded smooth, and his gentle Viennese accent forced Maddie's internal personals to twitch. "May I assist you and your friends into the house, Fräu Braun?"

Maddie climbed stiffly out of the WatStretchEV and followed Adonis-with-cat toward the broad front porch. Next came Angie, washcloth on top of her head. Gretta brought up the rear, struggling to support all the cheesecake she had consumed.

Heady group. Maddie had proved correct about Adonis's basket they, and they would all need to protect the dear boy constantly to prevent him from being put out to stud with the rest of the stallions at the Saratoga Thoroughbred Track.

"Your house overlooks Congress Park," Maddie said, "and is in spitting distance of the Canfield Casino. During prohibition, customers came up from New York on the Night Boat to gamble. In such proximity, how did Grandpa get away with it?"

"Nobody cared. Everybody enjoyed," Gretta said wisely, as though she would like to return to that time.

Traffic whisked up and down Circular Street, making it anything but the pleasant place it had doubtless been when last Elias Crumb parked his horse and flourished from his business. Gretta had just admitted the scope of her grandfather's activities, "booze and broads" to be specific. With Gretta a Crumb, Angie an Outhouse, and Maddie a Franck, as in César, their combined closet skeletons could doubtless fill a stadium.

A great house, though. A simply great house. Maddie would, of course, never admit that to

Gretta. Friendship could survive only so much truthfulness, and that included truthful compliments.

When they reached the grand front porch, Gretta unlocked and threw open the door. "Welcome, welcome," she announced.

Adonis put Chuck down and said, "I'll get the bags." His accent smelled of honeyed sex, which Maddie imagined was his major in college.

Angie said, "Gretta, I need a bed," and pressed the cloth onto her head so hard that water squished out and splattered down onto the porch.

Maddie surmised that Gretta had many beds to spare with a house this size, preferably none containing skeletons from the 1920s or 30s.

"And a bed you'll get," Gretta offered genially.

— 2 —

Somewhere. Sometime. Inspector Rex Caine.

"He's Rancho 1," a female voice said.

Rex didn't know what time it was. He was in a bed surrounded by female voices.

Cool air flowed across his body when someone lifted the sheet off.

A dim voice spoke, a warm female voice with a full measure of concern.

Fingers on his face opened his mouth.

Odd skin on the fingers. No. It was latex gloves.

Rex sniffed and listened. He was in a hospital.

"Head good, Suki. Be sure to set up the flushing and feeding schedule for the G-tube. He got it just before he left New York Bedford-Stuy—"

"Columbia Presbyterian, Agatha."

"Of course. Bullet wounds appear to be minor and healing. The bruises aren't bad. It's a pity his head hit the asphalt."

"Do you really think that's what happened, Agatha?"

"I really think that's what happened, but with cops, you never really know." Fingers examined Caine's hair, separating hair from hair to look at his scalp.

"You don't expect a man with a body like this to have lice, do you, Agatha?"

The voices in this new place sounded clearer than the voices Rex heard before. These made more sense, or perhaps Caine could merely understand them better. He obviously lay nude on a hospital bed. Two women, probably nurses, were examining him. One was nurse-like and professional, but the other sounded technically competent but driven by considerations other than care, almost as if she didn't want him here. The fingers lowered his head back to the pillow, then began moving down his body to his neck, shoulders, armpits, breasts, chest, stomach, and abdomen.

"Spread him," the cold voice said.

Two warm cold hands spread his knees. Warm fingers lifted his genitals, examining each centimeter of skin. Fingers gently pulled his foreskin back.

"He retracts well. Make sure the girls don't neglect this, Suki. We'll catheterize him to simplify things, then I'll get the order and date the procedure to match the MD's signature."

"Do we have to?"

"It saves time. We're overworked, so enhancing nursing convenience is always justifiable."

The fingers moved down Rex's thighs, knees, calves, and ankles.

"Call Physical Therapy, Suk. We want to keep him in good shape in case he ever does wake up. That means no contractures and no decubiti."

Fingers examined his feet, between his toes, probably for needle marks.

"Here, Suki, help me turn him on his side."

The hands rolled Caine's body onto its side.

He wondered how he looked in this position.

The fingers examined the back of his head, neck, spine, and lower back. His buttocks separated and then closed. The fingers moved down his legs, then returned to his buttocks and spread them again. Cold grease bathed his anus. Fingers pushed in.

"No stool. No blood. No prostate enlargement." The proficient nurse's cold fingers withdrew. His buttocks closed. The cool grease chilled. "He's in great shape," she said.

"He certainly is, Agatha."

Caine's body returned to its back.

"Give me a new pair of gloves, Suki." Something snapped. He heard a tearing sound, a pop, like someone thupped a plastic container open.

Fingers lifted him, pulled his foreskin down, grasped the corona, and pulled down slightly. He could not move, but he certainly felt the details. The cold grease felt cold. A warm sensation followed, sliding slowly down. The pain burned, then eased. "There. Good. Now for the balloon."

Silence. The fingers released him. "Good flow. Make sure the girls record it."

"Of course, Agatha." Strain in that voice. Suki didn't like Agatha.

The sheet floated up over Rex's body. He felt it covering him.

He felt it! He felt the entire examination. Before, back at the first circle of Hell, he felt nothing. Now he felt each molecule of the fabric, one at a time, settle onto his naked body!

He felt the tube, a slight stretching sensation, a pleasurable pressure. He felt the cold sensation that lingered around his anus, pleasurable also.

Snapping sounds again.

"What a waste," the cold voice said.

"He might come out of it, Agatha."

"You know the probability. Ninety-eight times out of a hundred, the ones who awaken from this level after two weeks or more have impaired levels of function somewhere. If the coma continues too long, he's probably better off not coming out of it because he could not possibly regain full function, physiological or cognitive."

"But his injury is only forty-eight hours old. Nursing homes don't usually get them—"

A distant door closed.

Rex lay in a nursing home? Something or someone hurt him a short time ago. He thought a horse may have done it. He was a Rancho 1 but couldn't remember what that meant? Maybe a horse kicked him in the head.

He couldn't think but was.

He couldn't know but was beginning to remember.

He couldn't move.

Or could he?

— 3 —

Saratoga, NY. The John Appleseed Cottage. 1:00 PM. Jeremy Hooker.

Jeremy Hooker, president and only agent of Hooker Real Estate of Saratoga, stood under the roughhewn beams in the living room of The John Appleseed Cottage and watched Mr. Gregory Rue, a Peruish Jew, nose around the dining room. You could feed fifty in here.

"Fine," Rue said, "this'll be just fine." Queer duck. He wore a yarmulka but spoke with a Spanish accent. "I especially like the red maple paneling and the wide plank floors, Hooker. When will it be available."

About two weeks ago or something, the original renter died. New York fellow. "The owner wants it rented ASAP." According to town-talk, Rue came from Peru, South America. Jeremy guessed that made him a Peruish Jew. "And yeah, the floors are pretty. The owner has always kept the place real well, although I don't know he, she, or it has ever even visited."

"Who is the owner?"

"No idea. New York lawyer, a scabby tight-lipped type, manages it for the owner, a rich female lady of some sort." Before Greg Rue turned up in town five days ago, Jeremy didn't know that Jews came in tortilla flavor, not that Jeremy had the prejudice. If a Jew wanted to eat tamales or catch kosher clap, more power to it. "It" because you weren't supposed to refer to folks as one sex or the other these days, which was likely why they all kept getting mixed up in bed so much. Not that it bothered Jeremy any more than pissing on the rhubarb.

This rental didn't surprise him, neither. Rue owned property all over Saratoga and even down into Ballston. He even owned The Golden Arms of God Nursing Home across the road and up the hill from The John Appleseed. Rue likely wanted to rent, then try to buy. That'd be a dead end. Jeremy knew the owner well, the whole family too. What Rue wanted to buy didn't matter as much as spit on a spindle. However, he could rent The John Appleseed Cottage until the end of the racing season, which would delight the owner.

Whether Johnny Appleseed ever stayed in The John Appleseed Cottage didn't matter, neither, not a crap on a shank. Someone called it The John Appleseed Cottage, and it stuck. Lizzie Outhouse, County Clerk of Saratoga County, and Jeremy, too, doubted that Johnny ever spent the night in any of the places named after him, although there was a strong rumor that George Washington and Thomas Jefferson once did their business here. 'Course, if Johnny Appleseed or George Washington spent a night in all the places named after them, they would have been full-time sleepers.

"So then, Hooker, do we have a deal?" Rue smiled that scented oil smile of his—rose it was, like his vest. He was not the sort that Jeremy would want to buy a used pickup from.

"We do."

"Done." Mr. Rue walked quick as a pinch over to the pine dining room table, sat himself in a high-back oak chair, and pulled out a checkbook. Funny little man, short, brown, polite, thirty or forty years. Real soft voice that stayed so but still grated on a person after a time. "I'll be in Europe for a few weeks. Please have someone clean and send me the bill."

Jeremy noticed that Rue was missing his right hand's third and fourth fingers. That didn't slow him down none, though. He wrote out the check quick as a wink, hopped up—he did everything with a kind of a hop—and handed it to Jeremy. "I hope that this will be satisfactory. I don't like to bother with payments."

"Well, now, that is quite satisfactory. I don't mind a bit. The place will be yours as soon as I notify you that the owner has accepted your offer. You bringin' your family up, are you?"

Rue smiled a little broader than his regular all-the-time smile. "I just like the area. I expect many guests for the meeting, but I'll likely not be able to attend. I do plan to bring my family eventually."

— 4 —

Saratoga. The John Appleseed Cottage. 1:00 PM. Dale.

Lunch was delicious. Dale had eaten three Sloppy Joes, and lost track of how many Fred had put away. He always ate like a big person. Tate didn't serve Sloppy Joes when all the kids were present. It was too sloppy.

Now Dale and Fred were lying in the grass behind a short stone wall behind The John Appleseed Cottage. They had seen Mr. Hooker go in with a Spanish-looking guy, which ended their sneaking in to see what was in there. Hooker was a real estate man from Saratoga, an old timer if ever there was one. He looked like he had lived during prohibition and had participated in the organized crime activity then

"We need to get out of here," Dale whispered.

"Not until they leave. We can't cross the open grassland to get back to The Golden Arms side of the road. We'll just wait. Besides, I not sure I can walk after you landed on me when we jumped the wall."

"I'm sorry about that. I'll let you jump on me to make up for it."

"Then neither of us could walk," Fred said.

Chapter 13 - Memories

A happy, rosy little fellow.

—1—

Saratoga, NY. The Golden Arms. 4:00 PM. Inspector Rex Caine.

Lying motionless, Rex felt the world return and the sheet wrinkles on his back itch. He heard random sounds and smelled faint whiffs of pee easing out of his catheter and dampening the sheets. Random memories trickled back, but whether it was history or fantasy, he couldn't be sure. He knew his name and that he was a cop, but he possessed no idea of what put him here. Vivid splotches of memory splashed his consciousness as flowing wine filled a Bavarian Crystal goblet — good wine containing a decomposed toe.

***

In the Upper West Side of New York City, Caine stood in the shadow of the stoop and watched the boy.

Last year, the call reached Rex just before midnight. A narc bust had gone bad behind 1540 West 72nd Street. Caine's brother Emery worked Narcotics — no better narc, straight as a light beam. Druggies hated him, and druggies blew narcs away from time to time. But for every narc dead, Emery blew ten druggies away into cells, or worse.

Caine pulled into the fan of cruisers and ambulances, jumped out, and hurried toward the crowd.

John Leech appeared from the huddle of uniforms and grabbed Caine by the upper arms. "Rex, I'm sorry. This cannot go unanswered."

Caine hesitated, wondering what Leech was talking about. The Deputy Commissioner rarely showed up at crime scenes.

Then Caine realized. "Dead, John?"

Leech nodded.

Caine shoved past him and ran into the alley. Emery's partner, Lester Hurd, lay face down across two trash cans, his slit throat dripping into a black pool. Another corpse, probably one of the perps, lay farther down the alley, face blown away.

Emery lay face up in a bed of garbage. A floodlight glared at him. His open eyes pointed at Rex. The perps had slit his throat, sliced his stomach horizontally, tossed his guts on the ground, and amputated his genitals. They had even dusted him white — coke, probably.

Blood splatter decorated the alley everywhere.

Caine stared at the savaged shell of his only sibling, Emery, the indestructible, the rough and ready cop who scorned Rex's taste for the good things in life, but they were close anyway.

Caine moved closer to the body. The fetor of blood, urine, and intestines raked his nostrils. He fought puking. From the dark, a white sheet moved into the circle of light and covered Emery's body, the charmed life gone from it. As Caine turned away and walked to his car, he felt Leech's eyes on him. Maybe the son-of-a-bitch had a point, but yearning to kill your brother's killers was primitive and unrealistic. It ranked with wanting to bust the face of whoever said something rude about your mother, but John was right for once — Emery's death could not go unanswered.

Now Caine stood in the shadow of the stoop and watched the boy.

The deserted tenement behind him was boarded up, likely occupied by only rats.

Caine had already loosened the sheet metal that covered the entrance. The place seemed ideal for his purposes.

He now knew that Sam West, who died at the scene, Ted Williams, Harry Griffin, and Helen Shinker, a sixteen-year-old crackhead who enjoyed taking on druggies twice her age and four times her size for DPs, had murdered Emory. Helen had a sad backstory, but who the hell cared? And that boy out there was her little brother Benji.

Benji stood at his favorite corner, under his favorite streetlight, his open-air emporium twenty yards away from where Caine stood. The boy appeared a happy, rosy little fellow for a schoolyard pusher-plus. Asian, barely four feet, black hair, air of intelligence, Benji looked cute, clean, and combed with a slight body, clean jeans, and white T-shirt with a picture of Albert Einstein.

He had earned his own record for petty theft, but nothing compared to Helen's. They had locked him up a few times, but not for long. He started pushing at twelve, a year ago, but, as far as anyone knew, had not used — his blood and urine samples always came back clean when they picked him up. A smart kid, he made excellent grades in school and apparently good money at his favorite lamppost. He would know where his sister and her crew were.

As Caine watched, Benji made four sales out of his underwear. Now, apparently out of customers or product, Benji looked around to make sure no one lay in wait for him. Satisfied, he moved down the block, likely toward home, definitely toward Caine. The kid was getting careless in his old age.

Actually, Benji didn't need to fear. Street muggers avoided problems with kid pushers. Stealing drug money off a little kid could prove fatal, thanks to the kid's ruthless suppliers. The kid's family might burn you, the kid might, his supplier might. Not long ago, an eleven-year-old bit through his attacker's jugular because he'd forgotten to bring his gun but had great teeth. Child pushers survived and thrived until they crossed a supplier's invisible line or encroached on foreign territory. Then the kid would end up floating in a river or decomposing in a deserted tenement.

When Benji passed the stoop, Caine stepped from the shadows, grabbed him by the mouth and the back of the neck, lifted him off the ground and squeezed his neck until the serious kicking stopped, and carried him onto the stoop and into the entrance hall of the decaying building.

Before Benji knew what hit him, Caine stripped him to underwear, rammed him face-first against the wall, and held him there with a knee. The kid's pants pockets contained two wads of cash. The right sock contained a six-inch switchblade, the left sock, a small skinning knife in a sheath, and the back pocket, a mini can of pepper spray. Inside the belt, Caine found two long hat pins, but no gun. A kid who did not carry a gun in this neighborhood might be retrievable if he was also not part of a major gang.

Benji didn't cry or yell. He doubtless knew better and figured whoever snatched him would want his money, drugs, body, or all three. He would live through it if he didn't put up a fuss, but yelling could get his guts ripped. A kid pusher who didn't know that would not still be here.

Caine dropped the clothes, grabbed the neck, ground the forehead harder against the wall, and stuck his hand down the back of the kid's briefs. Nothing. The kid cringed. The possibility of sexual assault obviously scared him. Nothing in his record suggested that he sold himself, but he'd visited Youth House three times and likely knew the score. He would not have had his weapons there and would have been a target because of his size and appearance, but he seemed a clever kid who would persevere.

Caine stuck his mini flash in his mouth. Benji struggled as Caine slid his hand around the skinny hip to the front of the briefs. A harder neck squeeze and rougher ram against the wall to steady him for the search succeeded — smooth skin, smell of baby powder. Benji took care of himself, or someone else did. Rubberized electrical tape held four vials to Benji's lower abdomen.

Benji finally spoke. "Aw, man, that's my reserve." Quietly. A murmur. When Caine ripped the vials free, the kid finally complained. "Ow! Okay. Take it easy, man. You got it all. I don't suppose yelling stranger danger will do anything for me."

Caine dropped the flash into his right hand and fought a smile. "You already know the answer to that." He held the kid against the wall with his knee again and shined his light on the vials of crack-cocaine, then stuck them into his inside coat pocket.

Quietly, as far from his own voice as he could, he said, "I know all about you and your sister. Wanta buy your way out of dying, Benji?" Money, death, betrayal — the kid would understand the language. "You've got no choice."

"What do you want, mister?"

"Not your goods. Not your money. Not your body. If you cooperate, not your life. I want your sister. Where is she?"

"I don't know, man." His voice went up — he was lying.

"Where'd you get the crack?"

"I found it."

"Bullcrap. You sell for Williams and West. I already know that." A guess, but they appeared the only drug dealers among Benji's known associates.

"If you know that, why'd you ask?" A whimper eased its way into his voice. He would cry soon.

Caine ignored the question. "Simply put, you sell drugs. Williams and West sell to sellers like you and hang with your sister. Your sister and her friends, where are they?" Caine pulled Benji out and slammed him back against the wall harder. The decaying sheetrock caved in under his forehead. The stench of rot and rat crap sprayed out, and Benji sobbed now. Caine drew the line at hurting children, but Benji didn't qualify, not if he sold drugs. "Tell me. Otherwise, you're dead meat, cocksucker."

"You're a cop." Not a question.

"Would a cop splatter your guts all over this hallway and leave what's left for the rats?"

"I guess not." Benji sounded unsure.

Caine needed to stop talking so much. He could not risk Benji recognizing his voice. They knew each other from the street and Juvie. "I would without a second thought, Benji." He rammed the kid's head into the wall again.

"Fuck, man. You'll burn me if I don't tell. Half a dozen friends and business associates will burn me if I do. Where am I supposed to go with that?"

"You know the answer. You need to manage the nearest threat—me. The others will not know you snitched if I don't tell them, but if I find your sister and her friends without your help, I will let it slip to your friends that it was you. If I find their location from you, I won't." Street kids appreciated realism. "Your choice, cocksucker."

"Don't call me that, please, because I don't do it. I'm not my sister!"

"No?"

"And Helen's dead already, the others too. Sam bought the pit when they killed that narc for no good reason except that he called Helen the c-word."

"Too bad. That really makes me want to bawl. Where are your sister and her friends, dead or alive? That's the last time I ask." Caine rammed Benji's head against the wall again. Soon he'd be inside the wall with the rats.

"If I tell you, what will you do to me?"

"If you lie, you'll visit West. If not, I'll give back your money, spank you, take you home, and forget about where your income came from."

"Okay, I went up this morning and found them dead. I didn't report it because times being what they are, somebody would think I did it. Helen and them are down the block at 1610 West 110th Street, Saint Teresa Residence Hotel, Room 714. The key was in my back pocket. You probably have it by now. Room 714 is where I used to pick up product and divvy up the money. All three are there, and I was not part of it. What they were doing made me puke, especially since they're dead. Who could enjoy that crap? Also, you should not off cops because of a true insult, and I do good in school and everything, and I'm hardly ever disgusting like Helen was all the time. There's just no point in turning people off."

The current moment in life was usually what mattered to street kids. Rex wouldn't have hurt him no matter what, but a spanking and taking him home sounded reasonable. Kid pushers would be 98 percent out of business were it not for the adults around them.

"Okay, boy." Rex tied a rag around the kid's eyes, helped him dress, used Tac loops on his wrists, ankles, and thighs, then lifted him onto a pallet of rags and discarded clothes on the floor. "I'll check out what you told me. If you're telling the truth, I'll come back, give you your money, and let you go. If not, I won't bother."

Rex didn't mean that. He'd hassled the kid more than enough and felt guilty. Benji was the best street hoodlum he'd ever met.

***

The night attendant at the Saint Theresa Residence Hotel sat slouched and asleep against the bars. Caine reached through with his thirty-eight and thumped the man's head. Everyone needed a good night's sleep.

The tiny elevator would have accommodated four thin men. It creaked upward, in no hurry to arrive anywhere in particular. When it stopped on the seventh floor, the car bounced slightly.

Rex eased down to Room 714. Light slipped under the door. He pulled the Saturday nighter from the small of his back, mounted the silencer, quietly unlocked the door, and eased it open—smoothly, silently. Good cops knew all aspects of their business, including how to do what crooks and murderers did.

All three lay in bed shot, Helen sandwiched between the two men. She had glued her lips to the man in front. The three scum-buckets' death spasms had clawed them together. "What the hell." He fired three times just for pleasure. The Department, the Medical Examiner, and the street would regard it as refried beans. "Sorry about your sister, kid," Rex said to himself.

−2−

Saratoga. The Golden Arms Nursing Center. P7. 6:00 PM. Rex.

He wished he'd somehow refused this damned leaking catheter. His bed felt wet, and he hated that. He'd been drowsing.

"He looks so natural," a woman's voice said, a familiar voice.

"He's not dead, Grett." Cutting and playful, the voice belonged to a fun flaky fruitcake who lacked the viciousness of most aggressive New York businesswomen.

Grett, the first voice, loved raspberry-swirl cheesecake with kiwi. He recognized all three voices but couldn't quite remember the names that went with them.

"Oh, Rex, you've got to come back." Closer than the others, next to his ear. Close in another way. So wonderfully close. The voice dimmed to a whisper. "Please, Rex." Familiar. Loving. Close. Gone then.

— 3 —

Saratoga, NY. The Golden Arms. Suite P7. 6:10 PM. Maddie.

Angie, tears in her eyes, bent close to Rex's ear and whispered to him. They deserved to be alone.

Maddie tapped Gretta's arm and they went outside to the patio. The fresh air felt grand. "God, look at that." The view astonished Maddie. The green slope swept into the valley with a glorious grace Maddie last saw when she visited Switzerland. In the distance, Saratoga and its racetracks lay like diamonds. Closer, a few small houses dotted the valley.

"Great place for a hotel," Gretta said. "Wonder why no one thought of it before The Golden Arms of God turned up."

"Well, Gretta, I suppose The Golden Arms is actually a little like a hotel."

"Long ago, it was a monastery," Gretta said.

Maddie giggled. "What happened to the brothers?"

"Guess. Monasteries get lonely. Some brothers became sisters, and others turned into papas. When they left, the place became the County Poor House, then The Golden Arms of God, where you went to die. They have improved their rehab extraordinarily since then."

"For Angie's sake," Maddie said, "I hope Rex hasn't come here to die."

"If it's a choice of that or his current state, I hope he dies for Angie's sake." Gretta's face turned to stone.

DAY FOUR

Chapter 14 - Grandeur

Leech needed killing.

— 1 —

Saratoga, NY. Tate Preparatory School. 6:30 AM. Dale.

"Fred, wake up."

He didn't.

Dale grabbed and shook. "Fred."

"The place is on fire?"

"No." Dale wondered if Fred was drunk.

"There's a tornado?"

"No, but almost. The hospital moved Uncle Rex up here to The Golden Arms. That was the ambulance we saw when we were hot-footing it away from John Appleseed."

"The Green Foot?"

"The Golden Arms. And Mom will be here to get me."

"Crap!"

"I thought you wanted to meet her."

"I do—big-time—but I won't be here. I need to pack and rev up my cutes to spend time with Aunt Mirtha."

"Crap. Well, I'll see Rex and tell you all about it."

"Cow!"

"Fiddle."

— 2 —

Saratoga, NY. Crumb House. 7:00 AM. Angie.

Angie lay in bed and enjoyed the heady scent of roses after she called Dale. He sounded happy. He would be doubly happy later. The fresh sun roared into the room through gold-tinged sheers framed by roped-back gold drapes. Grandpa Elias Crumb obviously favored loud grandeur over elegance.

This bedroom resembled a page from *Early American Homes*. The pegged, wide plank floors gleamed. Hand-painted wildflowers bordered the ceiling. And when Angie turned in last night, the walnut four-poster creaked, a true antique — or Angie was.

"You should — "

"Shut up, Mary Helen."

The early American furniture fit the room so perfectly that Angie wondered if Gretta had dug up an early American to supervise the restoration. One could easily imagine that George Washington had slept here for the gift of comfort and might still be sleeping here on occasion.

"That's crazy, Ange," Mary Helen said.

"I don't care a fig for what's crazy, Mary Helen, so just enjoy it."

Gretta never half-did anything. When she ate, she ate globally. When she dieted, she dieted assiduously, transforming heft into the rich voluptuousness that cushioned her when she walked with pride up Broadway, arm in arm with the best writers of the day. When she spent, she spent lavishly. When she stinted, God herself could not wrest a nickel from Gretta's fist. When Gretta restored, she restored fully.

"I wish she could restore Rex, MH."

"Little you probably can restore him," Mary Helen said.

"I don't know about that. I may be able to solve the how, why, and who of this affair, but that won't bring Rex back."

Angie's helping to solve this mess would please Rex because she was doing what he would if he could. He would not approve at first but would eventually.

She stretched. Chuck purred in fat-cat ecstasy on the folded blue and white quilt at the bottom of the bed. In the soothing sun, the black memory of Angie's hangover faded, but the pain of seeing Rex at The Golden Arms remained vivid. She had avoided Dale until she stopped hanging.

"So, what's our plan of action, Kid?" Mary Helen asked. *"You must have a plan."*

"I have a plan, but it's dormant at present — like the rest of me." Angie rolled onto her stomach, stretched, then onto her back, and stretched again, but Mary Helen was correct. They should not waste time. *"Okay, I'm not dormant anymore."*

She reached to the walnut bedside table and lifted the phone from its cradle. "First, let's see what Jimmu has unearthed." She had asked him to do what she didn't have time to do before Columbia Presbyterian transferred Rex: find Mrs. Jake Slag Lessix.

— 3 —

Saratoga, NY. The Golden Arms. 7:30 AM. Zelda, RN.

Night Charge Nurse Zelda stood at the bedside of Inspector Rex Caine and wondered what the hell was going on. The bullet had barely grazed this man's head. The bullet to his chest had missed everything important. Basically, he fell and hit his head. He'd thrown a seizure at Columbia Presbyterian, but just one, and had ended up here all in the space of fewer than two days due to a previous care plan of his own making. Everything about him appeared normal except for grazes, bruises, two four-by-four bandages, and a coma. Zel had treated worse injuries on ten-year-old flag-football players.

Still, Caine hadn't moved. He apparently couldn't see, hear, or think, even though, for all anyone knew, he got up and danced when no one was watching. No test could detect what a man did privately, but Zel wished one did — she would have dumped her husband, Finn, way earlier. The bastard was regularly humping three different waitresses, one jockey, and probably the horse the jockey rode. No wonder the son-of-a-bitch had nothing left for Zel.

Rex Caine was healthy! No one would think he was sick if he weren't lying here in The Golden Arms of Hell with a G-tube in his belly and one of Agatha's precious catheters stuck up him so he could piss in a fashion convenient to the Nursing Department. Otherwise, Caine appeared in peak pink with perfect vitals, good reflexes, normal MRI, EKG, EEG, and PETs. He also possessed a beautiful, gorgeous, desirable body, something nurses appreciated but never spoke of.

What Zel wanted to do shocked even her. That was why she'd never done it. This time, though. "How sick can you be with your medical readings, Inspector Caine?"

Zel had scheduled a two-week vacation to have started tomorrow, but Agatha needed a private-duty RN for this man. That meant sleeping in. The regular staff would have taken care of him if Zel had gone on vacation, but she didn't want that. Time and a half for the duration of his stay was no small matter. No one seemed to know how long he'd be here. Besides, handsome Rex here intrigued Zel no end.

With Finn six months gone, Zel still didn't have so much as a cat to keep her company at home. Besides, she knew no place to go for a vacation and, with her Flynn-related debts, no money to spend going there. Her life had emptied itself of everything other than nursing, so why not nurse a gorgeous guy and make a few bucks? "You've got a deal, Agatha," she had the bitch. "I'll take care of Inspector Rex, and Suk can run the floor."

— 4 —

Saratoga, NY. The Golden Arms. 7:40 AM. Inspector Rex Caine.

Caine sensed somebody by the bed. Didn't matter. He could do nothing about it. His own spluttery little world mattered more, or at least the shards of it that appeared to come from his world from time to time — come and go, really. Sometimes a black void sucked up his glimpses of reality without warning. Sometimes, when he thought he was getting a handle on the truth, everything would go black or disappear in a blast of white light. Sometimes, whole chunks of the past would return. Reality. He thought it was real but could accept that it was all make-believe. His biggest problem? He didn't trust himself to tell himself the truth about himself.

Chapter 15 - Angie and Dale

Go, Mom. Go!

— 1 —

Saratoga, NY. 1:00 PM. Angie Summers.

North of Saratoga, Angie turned off and headed up toward Tate Road. Her red Maserati Hydro-Quad convertible gave her that special freedom that successful writers should always have. She had decided that recently but with gusto.

"Thumbs up to that, Ange. I love the wheels, girl."

"I agree. Now for Dale."

"Hallelujah. I love that kid."

"Shut up, or I'll tell him the truth about you, Mary Helen."

"You wouldn't dare. I'm you, or else the detective you want to be."

Crumb House's backside had become a parking lot. Gretta kept the WatStretchEV for the summer but would use her Saratoga EscaladeLectro as a runaround and leased a Mercedes EQE 1000 for Maddie. Not to let her friends outdo her, Angie bought her Rat. She worshipped the Maserati Company and hoped they did not mind her calling her new Maserati Hydro-Quad Convertible a Rat.

She couldn't reach Jimmu this morning. Gretta's receptionist, Fran, said he took an emergency vacation yesterday. Either he threw himself into Mary Helen's enterprises, lock, stock, and swish, or he crossed his legs and ran, ran. Angie would give him a few days to complete her project and then write him off. He knew the Crumb House number and address.

"But you're so damned alluring, Angie girl. Jimmu wouldn't dump you. Besides, you are responsible for me, bat, gun, and Doberman. He won't write you off."

"Sure, Mary Helen. I'm about as alluring as a flaccid beach ball, a puce and chartreuse flowered flaccid beach ball. Remind me to put those colors on your bat."

"Bull! And the same from Stud."

"Bull, yourself, Mary Helen. And the same to your vicious puppy."

"Hallelujah, Ange. I knew you had it in you."

"I told you to shut up about Dale and his hallelujahs. He didn't blow a single H-word when I talked to him about Rex's condition."

"So maybe he's decided to join us heathens."

"I wouldn't object."

Tate School's school year ended two days ago. The first term of Summer School would begin shortly. Dale always opted to attend Summer School and usually stayed at Tate for all breaks except Christmas. Yesterday, Gretta suggested that he spend his break at Crumb House. In the past, Dale called Mary Helen and Stud "despicable heathens" and loathed Angie's books. They embarrassed him, and so did Angie, apparently, but Dale miraculously accepted Gretta's invitation.

Not that Angie disapproved of God or allowed Him no part in her life. Bernie Schwartz, her late husband, was devout, to say the least, and Dale's similar notion that God focused on sin and not on humanity troubled her.

"I think he'll outgrow it, don't you, Mary Helen?"

"Why not. He outgrew pissing the bed. So did you, for that matter."

In the IRS and with a penchant for ruthlessly thorough audits, Angie's dead husband, Bernie, got so moral that he eventually blew the whistle on someone who played rough. When his Chevy wagon fell into a lake near a children's camp in Bear Mountain State Park, his body contained enough lead to sink the Titanic without the benefit of an iceberg. Someone had wanted him gone.

Though Dale was born after Bernie's murder, the boy had somehow ferreted out his father's religious fervor from left-over books, tracts, and probably from the nightmares his older twin brothers, Marcus and Mather, recounted to him. They despised Bernie and his don't-spare-the-rod fundamentalism and had insisted on taking Angie's book-pseud — she, at least, had that one connection with them now.

When they wanted to change their names to distance themselves from "Schwartz," she had offered them her maiden name, but they feared "Outhouse" would not flush well in Hollywood and became Marcus and Mather Summers. Unfortunately, they lumped Angie in with Bernie's philosophy and moved to California to live with their agent when they were thirteen. They finished school there, earned acting chops, and were doing well. She rarely saw them anymore and should probably have confessed to them that she was considering murdering their father — maybe they would have stayed and helped. Once she stopped being angry, she would author that book.

"You should have written it already, then married Inspector Rex," Mary Helen said.

"Maybe." Rex was there when Angie gave birth to Dale, and the two developed a positive father/son relationship. *"You're right, Mary Helen. I should have married him. How do you do it?"*

"The same way you do it, Ange."

To add to the family joy, Angie's scholastically perfect and spiritually smug youngest child, Dale, found it intensely humiliating that Angie Summer's "smut" paid for his tuition at one of the best prep schools in the Northeast, even though he helped her proof and edit them. Appreciate her books or not, Dale had learned to live with them for the family's sake, and for the extraordinary income.

"Mary Helen, do you think Dale realizes that without me and my profession, he would be going to a New York City Public School and probably be dead by now?"

"And he wouldn't have me, Ange."

"True. Too true."

Angie's extended family, Gretta, Maddie, and Rex, adored Dale no matter what he said, believed, or did. Rex did occasionally take him to task and persuade him to focus. *"Hey, Mary Helen, maybe he needs someone to come right out and tell him that at this point in his fourteen years and one month of life, he's sometimes an obnoxious little snot."*

"But Angie, he didn't shout hallelujah even once when you called him."

"He will, Mary Helen. He will." As Angie turned onto the long driveway to Tate Prep, she hoped for the best.

The central building of Tate School stood tall, huge, and Victorian at the head of an impeccably landscaped horseshoe drive. The campus spread like a village and resembled every photo Angie had ever seen of the elite British boarding schools they visited before deciding on Tate, which combined scholastic excellence with a relaxed joy of life in which taking responsibility for one's actions was crucial. Angie regarded that an enormously important feature, considering that Tate shepherded the lives of boys and girls during their most perilously inquisitive, raisin-lobed years.

"Bravo, Angie. Hallelujah."

Tate offered elective courses in historical theology but shunned religious indoctrination. Dale never knew Bernie but had obviously researched him fervently and enthusiastically.

"Don't worry, Ange. Maybe the kid will become a televangelist and make good money for a few years before he falls into disgrace for sexual misconduct, fraud, or insanity."

"Shut up, Mary Helen."

When Angie pulled up in front of the school, Dale stood posed at the curb in front of the main entrance. He looked clean-cut in his well-scrubbed tidiness, with his cashmere cardigan tied around his neck, a suitcase and briefcase at his sneakered feet, and baggy, wrinkled, powder-blue denim pants. He was the perfect picture of a preppie religious fanatic, except for Sigmund Freud smirking out from his pink polo shirt.

"Hey, Ange, something's wrong with this picture."

"Oh, my stars, he doesn't have a Bible in his left hand." Angie gasped.

For a while, she had feared that his white leather Bible had merged with his—

"Mom!" He ran to the car, tossed his luggage into the back seat, hopped in over the passenger door, caught his heel on her windshield and damn near took it out, then landed with his butt in the air and his head against the steering wheel and Angie's stomach. He would never be a wide receiver for the Jets, but he recovered quickly, scrambled himself upright, and gave Angie a huge wet kiss on the mouth. "How's Uncle Rex? Stilled vegged?"

"The same." Angie's astonishment surpassed her joy. Dale had never been this effusive, energetic, or handsome. "How is my youngest son?"

"Ask him if he's lost his mind," Mary Helen said. *"More to the point, ask him if he's lost his virginity."*

"Don't be disgusting, Mary Helen. He's only fourteen."

Dale's black hair looked even blacker today and exceptionally clean. His hazel eyes glowed in concert with his ruddy complexion. He vibrated with energy. His neck and behind his ears looked clean, and he smelled fresh and minty, no small thing for a teenager.

"I want to go see him, Mom."

"Now?"

"Now! It's not far to The Armpit. We could actually walk there through the woods."

"What?" Teenagers could be very informative once you figured out what they were saying.

"The Armpit, Mom. The Green Armpit of Rue. That is what the locals call The Golden Arms. I'll tell you later. Right now, I want to see Uncle Rex. I waited for you because they probably wouldn't let me in without you, especially since he's vegged out."

"Gregory Rue owns The Golden Arms?" Angie asked.

"Yeah. Everybody knows that. Claude Rue, his son, is the administrator. Please, I must see Uncle Rex right now."

"Okay, but I have another stop before going back to Gretta's house. She and Maddie are expecting us for dinner. Gretta's cooking, which is always a treat."

"Oh, my gosh, it is, Mommy, but they'll understand if we're a little late. And we won't be late if we dash like mad! Go, Mom. Go!" And he leaned over and planted another wet one on her mouth.

"I may vomit, Ange."

At times, Mary Helen deserved no answer, so Angie threw the Rat into gear and dashed.

As they pulled out, Dale turned in the seat and waved to a small boy exiting the building with a suitcase. "That's Fred, my roommate."

"I thought your roommate was Tom," she lied.

"He was. The Headmaster threw Tom out for doing unspeakable things with Harry."

"Unspeakable things?"

"Smoking. The honor code does not tolerate third smoking chances unless The Student Court intervenes. It didn't. Smoking is unforgivably disgusting unless you really like the person doing it. Tom also farted too much."

The administrator had promised Ange that Dale and Fred could eventually be roommates, and she knew all about Harry's and Tom's departures. Tate was all about its honor code.

***

Angie and Dale had reached the top of The Golden Arms driveway without a "Praise the Lord!" She wondered if the excitement of seeing her had driven the holy-spirit mouth-offs from her kid's mind like an exorcism.

"You're kidding, Angie."

"Okay, I'm kidding."

After she killed the Rat, Dale stared at Angie for a long time before he asked, "Mom, could I spend more time with you?"

"Of course. I have always given you that choice. You're the one who wanted to go to Tate and stay there for most holidays."

"I know. I do love Tate — the place, the teachers, and Fred, of course — and I effusively thank you because I know it's terribly expensive." He leaned forward and looked into Angie's eyes. "I also know that without you, your books, and Aunty Mary Helen Mack, I wouldn't be here—I don't mean born, I mean at Tate School. I have been totally wrong about all that. Fred clued me in, and I've started pushing your books to everyone and am even admitting that you are my mom. Some of our teachers are fans and have even asked me to do readings, but I think they would rather hear you, and I've hinted that you might be willing. You used to do readings in New York for the filthy-poor kids in the libraries and community centers, so why not us."

Aunty Mary Helen made a gross gagging sound. *"Don't forget Uncle Stud, Dale."*

"I especially love Aunt Mary Helen's dog, Uncle Stud, Mom, and I know you've given me choices about almost everything."

"You don't like choices?"

"I like choices fine, but I would love to spend more time with you before you're totally over the hill. No offense, of course. I just mean I want to spend more time with you while you're alive and still fun. Oh, my hell, I don't know how to say what I'm trying to say, but maybe a kid can have too many choices." He leaned over and kissed her again, on the cheek this time. "I know all about the frontal lobe thing that causes part of the bad judgment that teens use once in a great while. We studied it in life sciences." He kissed her cheek again.

Dale had turned into quite a kisser, and Angie wondered where he'd been practicing.

"He told you he loved Fred, and he actually said, 'Hell.' Would you mind telling me how an early teen kid could get this unobnoxious this fast, Ange?"

"I thought you wanted to puke."

"I'll hold off on that. This child interests me. He confuses me, but he interests me."

"He's a teenager. Of course, he confuses you."

When they exited the Rat, the lush green of rural Saratoga engulfed them. Angie noticed the stone house across the road. It looked familiar. "What's that, Dale?"

"Oh, that's The John Appleseed Cottage. Not Johnny, mind you, Mom. John! No one knows why."

"It's a little big for a cottage, isn't it? It looks like a museum."

"It's privately owned but rented most summers for the racing season. Companies have meetings there sometimes in the off-season. It used to be a tavern back in the olden days. Once, George Washington stopped there for brew, bed, and companionship. Thomas Jefferson too. I don't know if they were together."

"That was back in the old days," Mary Helen put in, *"when you were a crazy teenager and not over the hill, Ange."*

"Everything in Saratoga stays rented during summer, especially during the racing season, Dale. Do you ever go to the races?"

He held the front door open for her. "No. I thought betting was sacrilegious because soldiers gambled at the cross, but I don't anymore and would like to attend this year. And—"

"And what?"

"And I don't fudding know. I just thought that—"

"Fudding?"

"It's a substitute for the other F-word," Mary Mack said.

"You thought what, Dale?"

"I kind of maybe want your possible permission to skip Summer School altogether and stay with you, Aunt Gretta, and Aunt Maddie this summer, and Aunt Mary Helen too, and Uncle Stud, of course." Mega seriously, he said, "And have I ever told you about Fred?"

"You love Fred, Kid. Like you love your mother and me and your Uncle Stud. Wow, Angie."

Dale had always called Rex "Uncle" but had never bestowed a similar complement to anybody else, though he had known Gretta and Maddie his entire life and had always seemed to enjoy them. And he had never talked about his roommate when it was Tom or about Harry, whoever he was.

"Of course, he hasn't, Ange. Fred isn't Tom, who got caught doing it with Harry. Smoking is really sick."

"Have I mentioned Fred, Mom?"

"You've mentioned him, Dale. Are you in trouble?" He had never been in trouble at school, any school he ever attended, not even during the treacherous nines and tens when lovely dependent seven- and eight-year-olds turned into miniature sociopaths until their elevens, when they started to become real people.

"No, of course, I'm not in trouble. I don't think I know how to get into trouble!" he said miserably.

"So, what about Fred?"

"Oh, I love Fred. He gets in trouble lots, and I bail him out when I can. I seem to mind his getting into trouble more than he does."

"Oops, Ange."

"He's like my brother. I love everybody, but old Fred is my best friend. My real brothers, M&M, would be like Fred if they were closer to my age and were not in Hollywood. At least they always write to me and sometimes send pictures—no dirty ones, even though I think I might like one once."

"The boys are doing well in Hollywood," Angie said, "and are getting small but frequent and increasingly significant parts. I think we'd better talk about this some more, Dale."

"Way to go, Ange. If you find a problem, short-sheet the crap out of it."

Dale pursed his lips and nodded. Light hair had begun to show on his upper lip. "Me too. I agree. We need to talk lots more."

"Something's gnawing at him, Mary Helen. I'm his mother, but I can't read him anymore."

"Dale?" Angie said softly.

"Yeah, Mom." He stared at the red dashboard.

"I would love for you to spend the rest of the summer with me, but I may need to stay here in Saratoga, and we may not be able to take a trip or anything. Tate does offer wonderful trips in the summer."

"Yes, I know. I can't wait to see Uncle Rex." Dale pecked her cheek, then hopped out of the Rat and rammed the door into a Blue Escalade in the next slot. He ran around to open Angie's door for her. "I'm not dumb, Mom. I know exactly what you're planning to do, and I love you for it. You bet I want to stay with you and Aunts Gretta, Maddie, Mary Helen, and Uncle Stud at Crumb House." He leaned back into the car and planted a huge wet one on Angie's mouth again. A Maserati Hydro-Quad was good for that. "You're really swell, Mom. Mary Helen be praised!"

"Oh, crap! Ange, he knows we're getting involved in the Rex affair and wants to take part."

—2—

Saratoga, NY. The Golden Arms. Suite P7. Noon. Inspector Rex Caine.

"Mom, why did this have to happen?"

Two voices had entered the room minutes ago. Caine had felt two kisses, one on each cheek. The female voice had visited before. The male voice had an adolescent crack to it and sounded familiar.

"He's a cop, Dale."

Rex remembered a puppy of a little boy called Dale who sat on his knee once upon a time—big eyes, eager to please, enthusiastic, frequently fell down.

"I always knew Uncle Rex might get hurt, but why this, Mom? Some son-of-a-bitch has fudding vegged him out."

"Did you hear that, Angie? 'Son-of-a-bitch,'" Mary Helen whispered.

Angie ignored Mary Helen. "Shhhh, Dale. He might be listening."

Uncle. Mom. Rex wished he could remember.

"I hope he is 'cause I want him to know I'm really mad about what happened to him. I'm damned mad!" Tears colored the boy's voice, then choked it off altogether.

"It's okay, Dale. Rex will return to us. I feel it in my bones."

Rex somehow knew that voice, that wonderfully gentle voice, and wondered what had happened. The images fought one another—the bodies, the blood, the rats. Did he really do all that? The kid with the taped vials. When Rex returned, the rats had attacked Benji. The voice of the kid next to him grasped Rex's brain and twisted, but the feelings of warmth and closeness bathed him.

— 3 —

The Maserati Hydro-Quad. New Saratoga. 1:30 PM. Angie.

Slumped in the passenger seat as they headed down the hill from The Golden Arms, Dale had become a bereft little boy. Angie had not seen him cry in years.

Rex's condition had crushed him, not as a strapping young man, but as a little boy.

"Dale? Dale?"

"Yes, Mom."

"Do you still want to spend the rest of the summer with me?"

"More than ever. Have I told you about Fred?"

"A little. You've really guessed why I'm here in Saratoga, right?"

Dale turned his head and studied her carefully. The tears had streaked his cheeks, but devilish life sparkled back into his eyes. "It's not just to be close to Uncle Rex, is it, Mom? You have lots more on your mind than that. You're playing detective again, aren't you, like Angela Lansbury or Miss Marple or Robert Downey Jr.?"

"We're a damned site better than those, sonny," Mary Helen said.

Angie smiled. She did not need to say more.

"Invite Fred for him, Ange."

"Would you like to invite Fred over for a visit, Dale?

"Sure, but Fred was leaving to visit his Aunt Mirtha. He didn't say how long he'd be there or where it was."

Angie smiled. Surprises could be fudding great.

— 4 —

Saratoga, NY. Philadelphia Street. Hooker Real Estate. 2:15 PM. Jeremy Hooker.

Jeremy looked up from his desk and could not believe what he caught himself looking onto, a familiar face and a few steps behind it, the youngish face of a right handsome young boy that Hooker had also seen somewheres before. The attractive woman with the long blond hair couldn't be the picture on the backs of the

Literary Crime Thrillers he loved, the ones with the hot parts.

"Miss Angelica Summers? Is that you, standing there in the doorway of Hooker Real Estate?"

She looked startled. "Why, yes. How did you—"

"I'll show you, ma'am." Suiting his hands to his mouth, he opened his desk and jerked out a tattered copy of *The Speaker of the House Burns in Hell*. He'd read it four times. It was about the mindless zombies in Congress pretending to be holier than thou but then sexing behind podiums in front of everybody. Jeremy got a rise just from thinking about it. And then came Mary Helen and Stud. And oh God damn, it was like ketchup on his skivvies.

Ms. Summers walked to the desk and looked down at the book that had given Jeremy many a horny and intellectual minute. "I'm flattered, Mr. Hooker." The boy followed her. "Oh, this is my boy, Dale. He attends Tate Prep."

"Ahh, that's where I've seen him. They're always willing to buy adjacent property when it comes up, and the Tate boys and girls come into town all the time." Hooker stood and stuck his hand out.

The boy trotted around the desk, took Jeremy's hand, and squeezed it real good. "I'm very pleased to meet you, sir." Once done, he trotted back to the back of his mom and stood there, all pointy-eared and attentive.

The Tate kids had manners.

"Could I ask you to sign it, Ms. Summers?" It didn't matter that she might be here to rent half the county. He really wanted her autograph.

"Of course, Mr. Hooker." She took a big blue pen from her tiny purse, opened the front cover, and wrote,

"To Jeremy Hooker, one of my most treasured fans. Love, Angelica Summers."

Jeremy almost came off in his rupture strap and dropped a load to his boxers all at the same time. He had to stop and clutch the book to his chest and think about who he was for a minute before he could get out, "What can I do for you, ma'am? I have some fine places I could show you."

"Oh no, I'm sorry," Angie said, "I'm staying at Crumb House now but may buy a place up here later this summer. I was born here, you know. Just now, I need some information about the Saratoga area. I plan to make it the setting for my new book and am trying to identify an old house's floor plan and get a look inside if I can. I've heard that you know more about the houses in Saratoga than anyone in the history of real estate."

"I'm blushing, Miss Summers, but yes, that's true. Let me see it, and ten times out of nine, I'll know it if it's one of the old ones like I am."

Miss Summers drew a folded paper from her purse, spread it onto the desktop, and smoothed the wrinkles out some. The floorplan looked well-nigh as tattered as the speaker coming out from the podium.

Jeremy didn't need to look twice.

"I do know. It's The John Appleseed Cottage, out across from The Golden Arms of God. I rented it this morning. It's not usually available this late, but the original renter passed on."

Miss Summers took in a tremendous breath as if Jeremy had lifted a stone off her mind. "Oh, thank you. Would you mind telling me who rented it and who died?"

That would be telling a confidence, which Jeremy never did before now, but when Ms. Summers perched on the desk edge and battered her eyes, he didn't give a crap on a capon about staying confidential. "Not 'tall, ma'am. Mr. Paul Michael Senna used to rent her every summer but recently went to meet his maker. Mr. Gregory Rue, the owner of The Golden Arms, rented it this year, but if you would like to see it, I think it'd be okay. Mr. Rue won't be back for a few weeks."

"I should have started here." She gathered up her floor plan and tucked it away into her purse. "I can't thank you enough, Mr. Hooker. Would 10:00 AM tomorrow be convenient? I will gladly pay you for your time. I could also look over your listed properties then."

"My pleasure, ma'am. No payment necessary, not for Angelica Summers." Jeremy couldn't believe he'd just said that. Of course, he couldn't believe that Ms. Angelica Summers was standing here in front of him, either.

Miss Summers leaned over the desk and kissed Jeremy on his old cheek, and he went thunderstruck and started wishing he'd shaved today and used his Right Guard Sport.

Ms. Summers was halfway to the door when she turned around and asked, "By the way, who is the owner?"

"Some kind of a trust in New York City. I don't know the details. Think it might be a shell."

"Yes. Thank you so."

The youngster ran around the desk again, squeezed Jeremy's hand, and said, "Thank you so much, sir."

And Shazam! Summers and son disappeared as fast as they had appeared.

Jeremy opened his copy of *The Speaker* and looked down at his life's one and only autograph. "She was really here."

Chapter 16 - Tongue

It's in the Kid Charter.

—1—

Saratoga, NY. Crumb House. 5:00 PM. Dale.

Maddie opened the door. "Ah, my best friend and her precious progeny, Dale!" She stepped onto the porch, grabbed Dale into a clutch hug worthy of Duane Johnson, then leaned down and kissed him squarely on the mouth with even a bit of tongue.

Dale had only experienced tongue once before, and it was more of a rape. At least he'd gotten rid of three of his virginities. "Aunt Maddie, it's great seeing you and—"

"You called me 'Aunt!' Oh, you dear sweet boy!" And she repeated the whole greeting but this time for a longer time. When she finished, they had somehow reached the entrance hall. She may have carried him there.

"Aunt Maddie, it's really great seeing you. No one's hugged me like that in a long time, except Mom, and that doesn't count because she has to—it's in the Kid Charter."

"So do you want another one, boy," Gretta said, approaching grandly through the central hall.

"Of course, I do, Aunt Gretta."

Gretta hugged him until it hurt but only kissed his forehead—she was bigger than Maddie. "I'll bet you're tired of your mother dragging you all over Saratoga. Thank you so much for accepting my invitation."

"Thank you for inviting me," Dale said, trying to catch his breath. I would like to change my clothes. Do I have a room or something?"

"End of the central hall to the left and then the very end of that hall. You will share. I've only had a few rooms cleaned, but I suspect you'll like the young man."

Dale noticed Aunt Gretta smile at his mother, who, for some reason, looked a little worried, as if she doubted Dale could behave himself. "That's fine, Aunt Gretta. I'm used to a roommate and love company." Dale grabbed his bag, but as he started down the hall noticed Maddie, Gretta, and his mom huddling for a play. He grinned back at them. "Want a cauldron, ladies?"

Dale raced down the hall that seemed to go ahead forever before it forked in both directions. He turned left. All doors were closed and had embroidered dropdowns, except the door at the end of the hall, which stood wide open and aimed straight down the hall toward him.

Dale heard music, Beethoven's *Ode to Joy*. He loved *Clockwork Orange*, the movie and the book. When he stepped into the room, he saw no one, but then, a toilet flushed and the bathroom door opened. "Oh, my God!"

Fred stood outside the bathroom, looking shocked in his black, blue, and chartreuse brief-briefs.

"Fred?"

Fred looked down at himself. "I know I'm easy to miss, but I think so."

Dale dropped his bags, said, "I know so," and got a boy hug, his fourth hug of the day. No kiss, of course, although Fred did say, "Kiss my ass," once in a while.

"I knew your mother was coming, just not you. Is she here yet?"

"Right here," Dale's mom said from the doorway, with Gretta and Maddie behind her. "Did you two enjoy our surprise?"

Fred looked down at his trademark briefs, then at the triumvirate in the doorway and calmly said, "Do you ladies mind?"

Aunt Maddie slipped past Dale's mom, hugged Fred, bent, and kissed him on the top of his head. "We don't mind yet, dear," she whispered.

Dale wondered what that meant—he'd need to ask Fred.

"And for your information, Dale," Gretta said, "we just decided to declare ourselves, The Fellowship of the Cauldron."

"Great," Fred said, "like in *The Lord of the Rings*."

"Yeah!" Dale had discovered HRR Tolkien just a week ago. Fred introduced it to him.

— 2 —

Saratoga, NY. Crumb House. 8:00 PM. Maddie.

The evening meal astounded Maddie. If things kept going like this, she would need to break down and compliment Grett on her chef abilities and thank her again for her hospitality.

"Gosh, Aunt Gretta," Dale said, "you make the absolute best chicken pot pie I've ever tasted."

"I agree, Aunt Mirtha!" Fred dressed in a suit for dinner, and Dale followed his example, as usual. They flooded the place with cute and handsome.

Maddie suspected that if they grew up looking like this, someone would arrest them for unfair competition.

"Please pick one name, gentlemen. Gretta is my first name, and Mirtha is my middle name."

Simultaneously, Dale said, "Aunt Gretta," and Fred said, "Aunt Mirtha." Then they looked at each other.

Dale pointed to Fred and said, "You decide. She's yours, after all."

"I wish my brother were here. He's good at diplomacy." Fred looked at Dale, then at Aunt Whatever, thought for a moment, and proudly announced, "Aunt Mirthretta!"

"Okay, I'll make the best of it," Aunt Gretta said. "Aunt Mirthretta, it is. And Dale, I make the best poularde en soutien-gorge you have ever eaten. Pot pie contains different herbs."

Dale and Fred grinned at each other and said not a word. Maddie had a feeling that they had both caught the double meaning. Poularde en soutien-gorge also meant chicken in a bra. The boys appeared not only to be best friends but also to read each other's minds. That was good since, to Maddie's knowledge, Gretta had no real nephews, although she had married six times and had dropped numerous suckers. Possibly, she had never noticed her nephews in the crowd.

"Oh yes, Aunt Mirthretta, you do a great job of making it delicious," Fred said.

He sounded so sincere that Maddie wanted to render a terse remark about how no one could be that sincere without choking. She also had not gotten used to suddenly being Dale's aunt, much less part of an aunt harem.

"Whatever it is, I love it," Dale said. "Please give Tate and Mom the recipe."

A huge appetite had infected Dale and Fred. Maddie supposed it was one of those puberty things, except that Fred showed no signs of plumping except below the belt—his underwear back in the bedroom proved that. Regrettably, cute boys usually grew up into common-faced whatevers.

"It really is delicious, Gretta." Angie had remained curiously silent throughout this meal. That was ominous.

"But it's so fattening, Mirthretta," Maddie said.

"We won't do it often. Dale and Fred's arrival deserved something extra special, and God knows they can both stand some bulk on their bones, even though we girls will need to go to the Merry Fountains Spa tomorrow."

"The Hairy Mary?" Maddie blurted. "There is one up here too? Dale and Fred hardly need a trip to the fat spa."

"They can swim," Gretta said beneficently, "or work out in the exercise room, try the steam, or go girl watching—you remember when boys watched you, don't you, Maddie dear?"

"Of course, darling," Maddie returned. I had to fight them off with a birch club on the wagon train. And girl watching is a marvelous pastime for rapidly growing boys."

"I can think of worse, dear." Gretta smiled broadly. She obviously had warm feelings for both boys.

Maddie adored Gretta and heartily approved of how her sporadically heavy old friend had restored this house. The dining room gleamed with different woods, all of which seemed to blend with the aromas from the kitchen while the delicious food slobbed you. Maddie wished Gretta would bestow as much loving care on her plump body. She would soon pass from ample to overstocked, which was to say from pulchritude to flabulation.

Maddie had seen Gretta on the brink before. Usually, her business saved her. A conference, a negotiation: both were mandatory reasons to thin down to social acceptability and logistic superiority. She wore a foundation garment, of course — high-tech, but a girdle just the same. They had made a comeback with civilization's obesity pandemic, but no longer used whalebone.

Dale and Fred's arrival had delighted Maddie no end. The boys could refresh a corpse, and Dale's sudden public closeness to his mother and ersatz aunts was intriguing. He had even managed to coax a smile from Adonis, who, despite his gorgeous package, had turned out to have the personality of a sturdy tree, and Maddie was eager to acquire direct knowledge of what that tree had in its crotch.

Dale had brightened Crumb House no end and did it with nary a Bible in sight. And Fred? How could anyone not love that little guy?

"Aunt Mirthretta, where's Adonis tonight?" Fred asked. "Dale, Adonis, and I were going to play chess tonight. Adonis is a master."

"Yes, he was at twelve. I don't really know where he is, Fred," Gretta said. "He works for me, but I don't own him. More broccoli sautés à la niçoise, Dale?" Aunt Gretta had obviously vowed to put a few pounds on the boys — they could use it. She had sautéed the broccoli in butter with bacon and onions and had added fried garlic as a garnish.

"No, thank you, Aunt Gretta," Dale said. "As astonishingly succulent as your amazing culinary performance has been this evening, I don't think I could suck down another nibble. Besides, it's time to play chess with Fred, I think."

Mirthretta snickered. "Oh, no, no, no. Do not say that, Dale. We have dessert." Gretta bounced out of her chair and into the kitchen and, in five minutes, returned bearing a big orange thing with a side of sauce. "Mousse d'oranges à l'ananas!"

"Oh, my goodness," Angie said, "you're going to put a few elegant ounces on us." She could understate so well.

"Tonight, we eat, for tomorrow we go to the spa," Gretta said.

That made as much sense to Maddie as sending a steer to stud. But this house belonged to Gretta, who had cooked this magnificent meal. When in Rome, you did the Romans because tomorrow you would die at the Hairy Mary.

— 3 —

Saratoga, NY. Crumb House. The Gazebo. 9:00 PM. Angie.

Climbing roses scented the air. Angie and Dale sat in the gently floating gazebo swing. "Up there," she said, "where the dark half and the light half meet, astronomers call that the Terminator Line."

"It must be gorgeous and super dope to be just at the edge of the dark looking into the light." Dale cuddled close. He had not cuddled in years. "It's so beautiful."

Back in those wonderful frequent-cuddle years, Angie had read thousands of stories to Dale and his brothers. It had always been their best time together. Dale's wonder about the moon suggested that at least part of him had not changed. "Like you're escaping the gravitational pull of puberty and looking forward to an adult orbit?"

"Hey, Mom, it's a little early for that. I've barely learned to grow face fuzz. I've read the books on adolescence, though." His voice trailed off into embarrassment but then snapped back with, "I'll bet that if you were up there in the dark part, it would be like looking into another world."

"Or getting ready to be born and go out into this beautiful world," she said.

"Shadows would be longest near the Terminator Line. Cheer up, Mom. Uncle Rex is going to be okay."

"How about you?"

Dale hesitated. "What do you mean?"

"Well, I mean that the last time I saw you, you were giving a fair imitation of an evangelist after seven fourteen-ounce zombies topped with 110-proof rum. Now you are not. That is a substantial change, the kind that makes parents worry. Is there anything you wish to talk about?"

"No. With me, there's never much to talk about. There's never been."

"You have not mentioned God."

"Hey, Mom, God is there whether I mention him or not. I was really turning people off, wasn't I?"

"Some people, but it would take more than loud preaching to turn me off."

"Oh, I knew that you'd put up with me."

"There were some people who were not willing?" Angie asked.

"Lots. Maybe most."

"Did you do it because of your father?"

"A little. I heard about him from Marcus and Mather, not much of it good. More than that—"

"Preaching gave you an identity? Maybe you were just being your own special self, not to be confused with your friends' special selves."

"Yeah, I guess. It made me different in what I thought would be a safe way. I mean, who would want to argue with God?"

"You would be surprised. So, what changed?"

"Fred. That's why I love Fred."

"Oops," Mary Helen put in.

"Tell me about Fred," Angie said.

"Steady, Ange. It's not what you think."

"Well, Fred is more than my roommate. He's my best friend — I already told you that. We hit it off at first sight. He's Chinese and I think Buddhist, but he keeps it to himself. He flat-out told me that I was making a disgusting ass of myself and of God. He said I was turning everybody off, to say the least about the most, and that Jesus would have been ashamed of me, not to mention royally pissed off because I had turned religion into something like a hairstyle or a way of dressing or wearing weird makeup or doing crack-cocaine or something."

"I see." She really didn't but wanted to be supportive.

"And Fred said that he loved living with me but didn't much want to hang in public with me anymore because my rep might rub off onto him, and kids would think he was weird too, more than they did for reasons like being Asian and seriously short. He's only the twenty-third in the history of Tate. Asian, I mean — I don't know about short. And even little eight-year-old Mark Kershaw next door, whom we are mentoring, gave me the COD and addressed all his questions to Fred instead of me. Why didn't you tell me I was being a back-vent, Mom?"

"COD?"

"Certificate of Disapproval."

"Back-vent?"

"That's polite for 'asshole,' Ange," Mary Helen said. *"But keep going. You're doing great, Kid."*

"Butt," Dale said.

"I don't know, Dale. I think I didn't talk to you about it because I figured that if water finds its own level, a good kid like you would, and you did. How are you and Fred getting along now?"

"Oh, we never stopped being absolute best friends. Fred was making a point when he said all that, and I'm happy I took his advice."

"So, they're absolute best friends?" Mary Helen said. *"What's wrong with that, Ange?"*

"Fred is really your best friend, isn't he," Angie said.

"Among kids? Sure, and he's wise and sociable. So's his big brother, who comes to visit him occasionally, he's a rich orphan like—

"He has no parents?" Angie knew why but did not want Dale to know she knew.

"His father died in Desert Storm, and his mother died on her own. He's been in boarding school most of his life, and he just beat me at chess, for which I'll get him. I'm much more organized at chess than when I jump into a Maserati."

"Fred was lying to him, Ange. Desert Storm was ages ago. His immigrant parents died in an auto accident and were highly educated but dirt poor, and their own may have killed them. Unlike our own, Chinese organized crime is alive and well. Drop it, Ange. Don't be a back-vent."

"Mind your own business, Mary Helen. I already know exactly how Fred became an orphan."

"Would you like to invite Fred to visit us in New York sometime?"

"Sure, Mom!"

"But there's more, isn't there?" Angie asked.

"You're doing really great, Kid. I'm proud."

"I guess there is, but I'm not sure I'm ready to—"

"That's okay. You should wait until you're ready."

"Thanks." Softly, he leaned over and kissed her on the cheek. His eyes smiled in the moonlight.

"Remember the Terminator Line, Dale. Shadows may be longest there, but if you point your nose in the right direction, you'll always see light." Angie did not quite know what she was saying but hoped it was helpful to at least one of them.

"Thanks, Mom." He stuck a fat one onto her cheek again. "You are truly a gracious goat, and those metaphors about the Terminator Line came from *Mary Margaret—Dead*, didn't they?"

"Oh yuk. Your little boy got you that time, Kid."

— 4 —

Saratoga, NY. Philadelphia Street. Hooker Real Estate. 10:30 PM. Jeremy Hooker.

Jeremy had stayed late to play catch up. Papers seemed to breed.

When the door opened, the sight purely shook his guts. Well-dressed and refined looking, the man looked well-built and broad, like a cop or one of them body-building freaks.

"What can I do for you, friend?"

Then Jeremy saw the gun.

DAY FIVE

Chapter 17 - Mrs. Letz

Do we lift?

Saratoga, NY. Crumb House. 4:00 AM. Maddie.

"Great Red Balls of Christ." Maddie flipped over and tried to pretend that no one was pounding on the front door. She could not imagine what time it must be and could not see the face of her Tiffany Ben anywhere. How the hell could she go to bed and lose her clock? And who the hell would be out on the streets of New York City this late. When a few more of her little gray cells turned on, she remembered. "Oh yes. I am in Saratoga, in the Palace of the Crumbs. Christ."

Maddie tossed the quilt back. She vaguely remembered it was powder blue but couldn't see that in the dark, and who the hell cared? The night had gone chilly. No one had installed climate control in this place because George Washington had laid the sandstone foundation, and Maddie had left the windows open. In Saratoga, without climate control, you got naked because of the heat, then cold thanks to Mother Nature, and whatever else that bitch decided to fling at you.

She threw on the beige robe Grett had loaned her. The grooved plank floor felt like fingers on Maddie's bare feet and smelled outrageously wholesome and pure. When she opened the door of her room — she had made the mistake of taking the downstairs guest room — Adonis was just passing her door.

"It's okay, Ms. Franck. I'll get it." The dim amber light in the hallway reflected on his white Adidas, and the white stripe across the nylon jacket stretched across his delicious broad male shoulders.

Not to be left out, Mad slunk after Hunk-Baby from a discreet distance and stopped in the shadows of the grand staircase while Adonis opened the double oak and beveled glass front doors of Crumb House.

An attractive, tall, young Asian woman stood in the doorway. Just behind her stood an older, less attractive white woman studying Adonis. Of course, what woman who could still breathe would not study Stud-Wonderful.

"Well, my gracious, is this the famous Crumb House, the summer residence of Ms. Gretta Braun, Chief Executive Officer of the Spencer and Sons Publishing Group?" For an Asian, she had quite the southern accent.

"Yes, it is. Who are you?" Adonis stammered.

"I'm Ms. Letz, and this is Mrs. Slag. Ms. Summers is expecting. She said anytime would be fine, even this silly old time. We are terribly, terribly sorry to disturb your rest, although I see you were up, unless you sleep in your clothes, which you obviously would not because you look terribly tidy and powerful. And my, don't we cut a marvelous figure. Do we lift?"

"Yes. Of course, we do. Miss Letz, is it?" Adonis's voice remained flat and Viennese.

"Yes, I am Miss Letz. As I said just before, Ms. Summers is anxious to see us. Trust me on that, darling." The accent vanished.

Angie had a talent for collecting strange people to help her investigations. Maddie pulled her robe tighter and stepped farther back into the shadows.

Adonis admitted the weird couple. "Wait in the library. I'll tell her you're here."

"I already know, Adonis," Angie said from the top of the grand staircase that would have put Tara to shame. "Go on into the library, please, Ms. Letz." She motioned to the door on Ms. Letz's left, pulled her flowered flannel robe tight, and started down.

Miss Letz gently urged an apparently terrified Mrs. Slag into the library.

Angie reached the bottom of the staircase, hurried into the library, and softly closed the curtained glass doors behind her. She apparently wanted to allow the other inmates of Crumb House to remain in sleepy-bye land.

That didn't work. Dale appeared in his New Jersey Jets pajama bottoms and bare feet a half-minute later. Just behind him, Fred, in purple, green, and pink briefs and an open maroon robe, frowned as though he did not appreciate early rising. The two of them looked younger than Maddie had ever believed boys got. In true kid fashion, they went straight to the library door, stopped, and listened for a moment before they slipped in without saying a word.

Ten minutes of unbearable silence passed, and then, at the head of the grand stairs, an immensity loomed in a bulky black velour robe, a sort of CEO Victorian greatcoat. Wire curlers peaked out of torrents of henna hair held in place with a thick net. The ghostish white paste on Gretta's face had stained her black gloves.

Maddie finally knew why Gretta took so long to appear in the morning.

One semester ahead of Maddie, Gretta had attended Smith as a matter of family tradition. Maddie had just finished her RN when she got in on a help-the-poor full scholarship. Back then, money desperately mattered to Maddie. For affluent young ladies like Gretta, domination and success had become the final frontier. To them, money mattered little, and scruples, not at all. Maddie learned the rules quickly. She had even learned to walk like a real Smith Girl: as if goosed or otherwise impaled.

When Gretta reached the library door, she shook her head to loosen her brain, pushed her shoulders back, regained an amazing amount of her regal bearing, strode into the library, and shrieked like a drunken moose.

"That rips it." Maddie and Adonis bolted for the library, barged in, and froze. Inside, Gretta stood there, hand over mouth, eyes stretched. She was staring at the young Asian woman. Dale had grabbed Gretta's arm as though he thought she would faint and he could catch her.

"Christ, I do know who that is," Maddie said. "Oh, come on, Grett, haven't you ever seen your mailroom boy in drag before? I have one whose gender I couldn't identify, no matter what it wore."

Gretta's scream had turned Jimmu frantic. He listened to Maddie in shock, then turned to Gretta. "I'm not really this way, Ms. Braun. Please don't disown me." He was obviously terrified that his high jinks would lose him his job. "I was supposed to only talk to her and then report back to Ms. Summers, but then the hoods came, and Mrs. Lessix and I escaped by the skin of our teeth, the very skin of them. I wasn't the only one looking for her. I disguised us to confuse them—I'm not really this way, even though it's comfortable—and I was right. On the Thruway, we had several flashlight drive-bys. I think even the police may be involved in this thing."

"Did you report all this to anyone?" Adonis's stony glare matched his straightforward man-into-the-breach focus.

"He's not really that way, Aunt Mirtha," Fred said. "You and I know that better than anyone."

At that, Dale's eyes nearly crossed, and his ability to focus fled his face in bits and pieces of lost reality. "I don't know what's happening, people," he said.

"Jake Slag Lessix is the man who shot Rex. This must be his wife," Maddie said. "Any chance someone followed you, Jimmu?"

He shook his head. "I don't think so, but I don't really know."

"Adonis," Gretta gasped, "move his car behind the house into one of the outbuildings. It's the Elantra."

"Right away, ma'am."

Maddie noticed Adonis carried heat in a horizontal holster on his right hip. That made him left-handed.

Gretta dropped her hand from her mouth and allowed Dale to ease her into a dangerously slim Shaker chair. He grabbed a copy of *Sister Mary Margaret — Dead* off the desk and began fanning.

"It's okay, Jimmu," Gretta gasped. "I just didn't expect —"

"He was working for me, Gretta," Angie apologized. "I did get your approval. I asked him to find Mrs. Lessix, interrogate her, and then call me."

"Apparently, he was successful." Maddie gestured toward Mrs. Lessix, a mousy little lady with brown hair and far too much makeup.

"Please sit down, Aunt Mirtha," Jimmu insisted.

She was already sitting and had attached Dale to her as an appendage of abject solicitude. Gretta's hairnet undulated in the library-fan breeze.

"Jimmu's a good boy." Gretta sounded befuddled. "I'm sure he had a good reason for whatever he did or became. And we may as well get it all out in the open: Jimmu and Fred are brothers, Fred and James Styles, and Braun eventually, if they wish. I am their guardian. Their Chinese names still confuse me, something about turning them upside down or backward."

"It's family names first, Aunt Mirthretta," Fred said, "but that's just in Chinese."

Mrs. Lessix removed her hair and shifted into a modestly attractive middle-aged tart. Apparently, the room contained more disguises than Jimmu's lovely polyester sheath. Maddie wondered if Adonis was wearing anything phony. She hoped not.

"I want to thank you all." Mrs. Lessix's voice sounded younger than her face appeared. "If Jimmu hadn't helped me, I don't know what I would have done. That was the first time anyone ever shot at me."

"Shot at you!" Gretta leaned back, threw her chest out, and Dale fanned faster.

With his hips wagging in frantic little jabs, Jimmu trotted over to Grett and used his smart hot-pink purse to help Dale fan. "Yes, Mom, I am afraid that we picked up a few holes in the Elantra. I'm sorry."

"Oh cow, Fred!" Dale said. "Didn't you teach your brother any better than getting himself shot at?" He fanned Mary Margaret faster, apparently trying to outdo Jimmu.

Gretta joined them, fanning the front of her face with her hand.

"I doubt that he requested getting shot at," Fred said.

"That's what you get for not buying American, Grett." Maddie felt a strong need for a bit of levity. At the same time, she walked casually to the window to try to spot a gleaming gun barrel in the sunrise or an Indian scouting party ready to kick butt on the butte. "Are you sure they didn't follow you?"

Adonis returned from the back of the house and joined Maddie at the window. His body behind her sweated her loins. She would have him, though not just now. It would be unseemly while looking out the window with a room full of people behind you.

"I don't see anything," Adonis whispered. "We're probably okay for the moment."

Without turning, Maddie whispered, "Did you know you smell fabulous."

Adonis whispered, "Yes, Fräulein Franck, as in César. You, also."

"I'm sure they're looking for us," Jimmu said. "But I don't think they figured out who I was or where we were going."

"Oh cow, Jimmu! Everything will be super, Mom Mirthretta," Fred said.

This affair worried Maddie more than finding the stiff on Rex's pot had. Somehow, when it sat there in front of you, it seemed less threatening than when you visualized one in every bush.

"When I spotted them watching Mrs. Lessix's building," Jimmu said, "I went home, changed, and collected some things to disguise her. When I returned, I pretended I was visiting Jeremy Schekle, whoever that was. I read his name off the buttons and pushed all of them. He let me in without asking. Then I explained myself by whispering through Mrs. Lessix's door and telling her that thugs were watching her, who I was, and why we needed to make tracks. She believed me, thank God, and we went. Gracious, gracious, I nearly wet my pantyhose going up the West Side Highway — there's just no place to hide along there."

"Keep watch, Ms. Maddie. I'll look around." Adonis patted Maddie's shoulder, then slipped out of the room. He moved like a cat but talked like a cop and smelled like heaven.

Maddie had let pass why Jimmu had something to change into at home, much less why he had something to use to disguise Mrs. Lessix. "You make a very attractive girl, Jimmu." She could not resist.

"Thank you so much, Ms. Franck." Jimmu bowed. "So do you."

Maddie found herself admiring Jimmu. She had no trouble understanding why he had won the Lessix woman's trust so easily, not to mention the intense admiration of his guardian Gretta Braun, who generally admired no one unless they could improve her sales.

Gretta groaned. Angie cast a weak smile into the tension. Mrs. Lessix trembled. Dale and Jimmu fanned.

"I gather that Mrs. Lessix has been able to shed some light on this matter," Maddie said.

With that, Angie, quiet, standing apart from them next to the towering bookcase by the fireplace, began to cry and ran out of the room.

Chapter 18 - Memories

An obnoxious weasel.

—1—

Saratoga, NY. The Golden Arms Nursing Center. 3:30 AM. Zelda.

Zelda had dozed in the Barcalounger at the end of the room. Several times in her lengthy career, she'd wanted to take the chance but never had the guts. This time though, she might.

Rex Caine had turned out to be the easiest private-duty patient she'd ever accepted. This morning, she talked Agatha into yanking the catheter. Agatha could be a stubborn pig, but when Zel pointed out that Caine's catheter put the facility count over the norm and could trigger a careful look during the upcoming state survey, Agatha became a reasonable stubborn pig. The cath disappeared together with the doctor's order and the nursing notes. Sometimes, the biggest backstabbing bitches could become wimps when you called them on their game.

Now, Zelda's path was clear.

—2—

Saratoga, NY. The Golden Arms. 3:31 AM. Inspector Rex Caine.

Rex was aware that the nurse had just tended him, but now he followed Benny the Butt up the Upper West Side, and there he was in his fancy coat, lying in the gutter of Manhattan's West 115th Street. No one out. The man sprawled there on his back looked surprised though dead.

"No." Rex could not believe what he saw. Who was this man? It should have been Benny Shapiro, a.k.a., Benny the Butt, a slimy teen weasel who ran a string of juvie pushers. Rex had picked Benny up leaving his mother's apartment on Amsterdam Avenue and had been following him for twenty minutes. Alone on the street, in the shadow of the boarded-up brownstones at the end of the block, Rex had just rendered the little bastard.

He thought he had.

Had he killed the wrong person, or was this guy lying here shot to begin with? Older. Same size. Same baggy clothes. Same coat! Rex drew his penlight out and shined it in the man's face, which was dirty and had a half-grown beard, and ketchup-stained egg on his hairy upper lip.

The corpse reeked of sweat, alcohol, and piss as Rex opened the man's coat. The $1600 vicuña coat didn't match the man's filthy multiple shirts and pants. Benny the Butt, Shapiro always wore that coat like a coronation robe, but he gave it to a bum somewhere along the line? That meant that Benny had known Rex was following him and was scared, and that meant Rex might be the target now.

He glanced swiftly around the street—nothing but shadows. In many ways, his life with The Candy Troops had become nothing but shadows. Lightning rattled the windows and split the glassine rain that fled down the street. A trash can lid flew off and clanged down toward Columbus Avenue. No light came on that had not been on before. No shadow appeared at any lit window. No one cared. No one knew except Rex, Benny, and the poor bastard in the gutter. The wet wind blew Rex's nostrils open. In the last lightning blast, he'd spotted footsteps approaching the stoop.

Wet shadows slithered around his neck like intestines. Another sound of metal. Trash can? No. More musical, deeper, vibrating, like a symphony orchestra's storm battery during Richard Strauss's Alpine Symphony. Sheet metal. Close. He hopped lightly down into the basement entrance of the building. Sheet metal covered many doors and windows along this block.

Rex suspected that Benny the Butt had slipped in there. He wouldn't have the guts to attack Caine in the open and would not be stupid enough to try to flee with Rex on the street. For Benny, his way out would be oozing up through one of the deserted houses and trying to cross through the gardens and courts, or across the roofs.

Rex quickly left the basement entry and ran up the front steps to the door of the derelict house. The edge of the rain-slick steel clawed his hand as he pulled the loose entrance cap back and flashed his light in — wet footprints led up the stairs inside. Squatters abounded in these deserted houses: druggies had parties, homeless souls clung to existence, and felons hid. Adults and teens and younger screwed for money, food, drugs, or fun. Rapes, murders, and searches happened. Even love likely happened amid the frolicking rats feasting.

The footprints to the stoop might not have been Benny's, but they were the only guides Rexs saw.

Soundlessly, he slipped in and stood for a few moments in the entrance hall to let his clothing drip as his eyes adjusted. He started up the stairs, the frantic fists of rain beating on the metal barricades of the house, and climbed carefully, using lightning to see. He fastened his flash to his gun.

On the top floor, the air hung with sweat, foreign to the damp storm smells.

A sound.

Again.

Rex moved quietly to the side of the open doorway on the right and waited. Lightning came and the room blazed for a second, then again for two. On the carpet remains, buttocks moved violently between spread legs. Sex sounds squished against the roar of the storm and the panting groans of connected bodies.

Lightning came again, a lick of light that flicked away the building's shadow. Rex sensed, more than glimpsed, the shadow at the top of the stairs, just inside the door to the roof. Benny the Butt was crouching up there, aiming.

Rex fired. The silenced shot popped like a champagne bottle uncorked in a well.

The roof door flew open, and rain sped down the steps and flicked against Rex's face. He took the steps three at a time. A bullet hit the metal door as he dove through onto the roof.

Benny was stumbling across the roof toward the next building.

Rex had known Benny the Butt since the kid was ten or eleven, an obnoxious weasel then, a dangerous reptile now. Benny had never evolved enough to deserve anyone calling him human. Rex watched him scramble and smiled.

When Benny reached the roof's edge, he realized his mistake—the building next door had already been demolished. He turned back toward Rex, a shadow with his hands stretched out, the gun in his right, his ass smashed against the three-foot wall surrounding the roof.

Rex terrified scummy animals like Benny. "Drop it," he growled.

Benny flung his gun backward into the excavation below. "Don't end me. Please, Caine. I'll go away. Newark, or somewhere like that. You'll never see me again. Oh God, Caine. Please! Come on, man. We go way back. Oh, Jesus. It's true." He was sobbing now. Rex had never seen the kid cry before.

"What's true, Benny?"

"You're one of them." In dimming lightning, terror burned on the kid's face.

"One of who, Benny?"

"The Candy Troops. The guys call you Candy Caine."

Rex shined his light in Benny's eyes. "Turn around. Over the wall."

Benny turned, leaned over the wall, and pointed his hands and teen-weasel face toward the ground.

Candy Caine moved up behind him, shoved the barrel of his silenced thirty-eight firmly against the leaning neck, frisked and found an eight-inch knife strapped to the leg and a second gun under the left pit. Candy Caine, indeed. He reached around, unbuckled Benny's belt, and ripped open the pants. They fell to the roof—no underwear, no modesty among scum like Benny. Caine once found a switchblade poking out of an ass.

He ripped off the glassine packets taped above Benny's coccyx, as Benji's had been on his abdomen.

"Please don't kill me, Caine. Please, man. I ain't done nothin' more wrong than anyone else."

"You've pushed."

"Everybody pushes. It's a living."

"You've raped your mini-slave pushers until they can't walk."

"They can walk, man. I do 'em a little to keep 'em in line. I always tip 'em. That crap works, dude, and they get the biggest cut in the hood. Nobody cares about it, man."

Rex grabbed Benny's ankles and flipped him over the wall into the dark. "How's that for a tip?"

"I didn't just do that. I couldn't do that!" Rex yelled in anguish.

There had been no scream, no impact sound. Benny had merely disappeared into the dark where he belonged. Rex stood waiting for some sign that Benny had really slithered off to meet his maker, that he had really been here. Nothing—no sound but the rain plunging onto the black roof.

Rex could sense no sign that Benny the Butt had ever been here. Had he been? Rex could not have done that. He hated The Candy Troops, had never joined. He wanted to destroy them.

The lightning calmed to glimmers as he looked out into the rain. He didn't want to leave. He couldn't mourn. He couldn't regret. The poor bastard was better off dead. Leech would be better off dead, too.

Rex retraced his way to the roof door and down to the top floor. Near the door where he'd heard the humping thumping, he now heard a muffled whimper. Perhaps he could turn back into a cop and help. He turned his light on and shined it into the room.

She stood there naked, young, and vulnerable. "He heard something and took off," she said through sobs. "I can't find my clothes. Please don't hurt me."

"Don't move, or I'll kill you." He killed the flash, slipped it into his pocket, stripped off his leather gloves and opened his pants. "Don't move."

"Please, mister, you can, but you're not the first tonight. It hurts so. Please."

"Quiet." He moved to her in the dark room. His lips ran down her forehead. Her mouth opened and he tongue-raped her mouth until he knew every tooth, every fleshy bump. He pushed her to the floor.

"No, mister, please. It hurts." She sobbed.

— 3 —

Saratoga. The Golden Arms. Suite P7. Zelda

"Continue!" Rex's hands pulled her down on himself until he reached her soul. "If you scream, I shall kill you."

Zelda continued riding him, bit her lip and looked down into the open, well-focused eyes of Inspector Rex Caine.

He had returned.

DAY SIX

Chapter 19 - Meddling

Nobody thrives in Florida.

—1—

Saratoga, NY. Crumb House. 7:00 AM. Maddie.

"We need to talk to her." Maddie did a decent thing this morning and allowed Gretta to assemble herself for thirty minutes before knocking on her bedroom door and confronting her with confronting Angie. "We can't just let her stew in her own plot, Grett. Something she discovered last night crushed her, and we've got to help."

"You mean we need to meddle." Gretta sat in her huge velvet recliner and stared through the second-floor bay window. The beauty mask and curlers had disappeared. A silk house coat had replaced the Victorian greatcoat. She looked ready for anything. "Angie didn't tell us, so maybe she doesn't want us to know, Mad."

"But we're here because we decided to protect her — that includes knowing what's going on and preventing missteps." Maddie walked over and perched on the window seat. "For God's sake, Grett, Angie ran out of the room crying last night and didn't tell anybody anything. And when I went to her room later, she wouldn't even let me in, much less talk to me."

Gretta looked Maddie straight in the eye and found the interminable gall to say, "Maybe just now I should not have let you in. I smell trouble."

Maddie remained sufficiently a lady to let that pass. "Gretta, how are we—"

"Do we want to? Do we really want to be part of this, Mad? Angie has gotten us into embarrassing predicaments and even more danger in the past. This seems worse than anything before."

"Like the bomb in the toilet of Spencer and Son's executive bathroom that time?"

"That's right. The bomb that fell off the bottom of the seat into the toilet and almost gave Jude Hopkins heart failure. She thought she'd had a miscarriage without realizing she was pregnant, a shock since she was a lesbian. Fortunately, the bomb was homemade and had a detonator that succumbed to pee. That made Jude a hero. Our adventures with Angie have always been near misses at worst or just whacky at best, but before, Inspector Caine was always around the corner to help us if she went too far. Now he's—"

"Broccoli, I know," Maddie said. "Gretta, we both know that she'll try with us or without us. Angie Summers is our friend, and we need to help her, damn it! Also, she has left no unresolved cases in her wake. You know that, and I know it."

"But there's more danger this time, Maddie. Don't you sense it?"

"Of course, I sense it. It was sitting on Rex's toilet. Three bodies—Angie's already topped herself. And who knows how many stiffs are sitting around on New York City toilets that we haven't noticed yet?"

"Four."

"What?"

"Not on the toilet, but there have been four bodies in one week. There was a murder in Saratoga last night!" She tossed a copy of *The Times Union* onto the window table.

SARATOGA REAL ESTATE MAN SLAIN

Before Maddie finished reading the article about the late-night shooting of Jeremy Hooker, Gretta interjected, "And our little Angie, Dale in tow, saw Hooker just before dinner last night."

"How do you know?"

"We agreed on what to do, Mad, and I did it. I've never before hired anyone to watch Angie, but I did this time — two watchers, in fact. Although with Dale and Fred on the scene, she won't be the only one who needs watching. At the very least, I must hire extra guards and watchers, and there's something else different too."

Maddie assumed that Adonis was one of the watchers and wondered if Jimmu might be.

"Also, because of Rex, Ange is emotionally involved this time," Gretta said. "We all are. More than that, I'm hungry."

"Fine. Now I know you're okay. First, we see Angie, then you can cook, then we can all go to the Hairy Mary Pudge Pub."

"I assume that you are referring to the Merry Fountains Spa," Grett corrected.

"Whatever the hell, wherever," Maddie said. "The fat may also just slip off if we soap our saddles enough."

Gretta sneered. "You have no fat, and Angie has little. Don't bother to say it — I have enough for all three of us."

"You can never be too thin. It's like you can never have too much money. Nelson Rockefeller said that about money. I don't know if he said anything about fat."

"Spoken like a true CEO. Now let's talk to Angie."

–2–

Saratoga, NY. Crumb House. Angie's Room. 7:30 AM. Angie.

"They're here, Ange," Mary Helen said.

"I can hear them, Mary Helen."

A knock came.

Angie asked, "Who is it?" to the door.

"Us," Gretta answered.

"Come on in, girls," Angie replied.

The door opened. Gretta in a silk housecoat entered first, then Maddie in a white silk pantsuit.

"They dressed up, Ange," Mary Helen said.

Angie, in her sweats, was standing by the windows, watching the goings on down in the backyard. "I suppose you two want to know what I found out, don't you," she said without turning. She felt neither willing nor reluctant to tell them, just careful.

Adonis, Jimmu, Dale, and Fred were all down there on the steps of the backyard gazebo. Dale was doing most of the talking.

"Well, yes, of course, we want to know what happened last night," Maddie admitted.

Angie turned to talk to them.

A silent "No!" radiated from Gretta's face, but she said, "Well, yes, we're concerned about you, Rex, and, by extension, Dale, Fred, and Jimmu."

Angie smiled but felt the tears returning and turned back to the yard, where Adonis stood before the boys, now explaining something very carefully. "Gretta, where did everyone sleep last night?"

"Jimmu slept with Dale and Fred. Fred's room has two double beds and the boys invited him. He does have his own room a few doors down the hall. I put Mrs. Lessix in the Tower Suite for safety."

"*Hey, Ange, you aren't thinking what I think you're thinking, are you?*" Mary Helen asked.

"*I don't know.*"

"*Well, don't. I know Dale,*" Mary Helen replied. "*He's your kid and naturally a little weird, but he likely isn't gay. And even if he is or will be, it's no disgrace. This is the twenty-first century, Kid. No matter who or what you are, accepting it and trying to not go backward is essential to thriving, except in Florida. Nobody thrives in Florida.*"

Angie sat down on the window seat and studied her two friends. She would need to be careful about what she told them. Protective friends could easily get in the way. "When Lessix and Leech hatched the plot, they didn't know that Mrs. Lessix was in the house. They planned the shooting carefully. No one was supposed to be injured. And when John Leech came to the Lessix apartment the second time, Rex was with him. Mrs. Lessix still didn't know what the plot was supposed to accomplish. The point is that something went wrong, and that Rex was in on it."

"*You already suspected that, Ange,*" Mary Helen said.

"*Shut up, Mary Helen. I only guessed it.*"

"Oh, my God," Gretta said.

"*We have such an eloquent publisher, don't we, Ange?*"

"So, Rex was in on it," Maddie said, "and something unexpected happened that vegged him and killed Leech, Lessix, and PMS? He knew them all. It's obvious." She perched herself on the foot of the big bed.

"I think so," Angie admitted. "I have been going over and over it and cannot escape it. At the track that day, Rex drew his gun first. As hard as it is for me to understand, I think Rex may have thought Lessix wanted to kill him, and Slag did have his gun out in a blink. Rex may also have been there to assassinate Slag. Rex is an excellent shot, and he's quick. Lessix fired three times, then fell. Rex's head injury was a fluke and was what put him in a coma. That suggests that the plot hatched at the Lessix house the second time may have been illegal and aimed at soon-to-be-ex-cop Lessix. Internal Affairs had suspended him from the force, pending an investigation."

"Investigation of what?" Gretta asked.

"According to his wife, the NYPD suspected Jake Lessix of murdering a teen drug pusher, some kid named Benny. A state cop saw it." Angie extended her right hand toward them, palm up, and slowly opened it. In the palm of her hand lay a large red-brown capsule, roughly the size of a horse suppository. "I knew that I had forgotten something. It nagged me in the waiting room." She stopped and pressed her lips together for a moment. "After the Belmont shooting, I held Rex's head in my lap, his hand in my hand. His hand held this. I slipped it into my purse and forgot it until Mrs. Lessix entered the picture last night."

Gretta walked over to Angie and looked at it. "So, what is it?"

"I used one of those in the annual Smith production of the Euripides Medea," Maddie said. "It's a Grimas blood capsule. Squeeze twice for fatal hemorrhage."

"Exactly." Angie slipped the capsule back into her purse.

Maddie and Gretta walked straight over to Angie and hugged her in a two-plus-one, and they all looked into the backyard together at what Angie had been staring at.

Adonis had stripped to his black bikinis and was posing as if vying for the Mr. Universe title. Dale, Fred, and Jimmu were oohing and aahing as Adonis swelled first one muscle, then another. Angie could see what the muscle fuss was about.

Maddie drooled but wiped it away.

Gretta just looked astonished. "I've known him for years but never realized how huge his muscles had gotten."

"Now, there's a sight," Maddie said in a breath. "He's built all over."

"*I repeat, Ange,*" Mary Helen said. *"Don't sweat it."*

"You're right, Mary Helen, but Dale's my baby just as Fred and Jimmu are Gretta's."

"Gretta," Angie said quietly. "We need to get Mrs. Lessix out of here. Now."

"I can hide her at my club," Gretta said. "But there's something else." She handed Angie *The Times Union.*

Angie looked at the front-page article about Hooker, frowned, and tossed the paper on the bed. The window was already open. She called, "Jimmu, Adonis, Dale, Fred, we need you." Then to Maddie, "This doesn't add up, and that woman is hiding something. Let's confront her in the Tower Suite before going further."

— 3 —

Saratoga, NY. The Golden Arms. Inspector Rex Caine

Rex studied the tan ceiling and wondered who else had lain here before him, in what condition, and why. The ceiling looked ordinary except for the fly walking across it. It seemed odd that the New York State Department of Health would allow a fly on a nursing home ceiling.

He was Inspector Rex Caine. Yes, he was certain now. This was who lay here: Inspector Rex Caine of the NYPD. Zel had confirmed it after they finished a wonderful roll in bed. She was needy. He was horny. It worked.

"Please don't turn me in," Zel had begged.

Of course, he wouldn't consider turning her in, just on. They had enjoyed each other immensely. Almost as good, she told him everything she knew about where he was and how he came to be here. That helped but left many unanswered questions.

Rex's recent past and intended future lay a jumbled mess in his head, and he could not imagine having done some of what he remembered—awful things. Evil fantasies hooked to real events in his life? Dr. Stephen Fry, a shrink, had told Zelda that he could be in a fugue state or awaken in one. Rex needed Zel's help in sorting it all out. He would keep her molesting-a-patient secret, which he massively enjoyed, and she would support his now fake coma, which he would greatly appreciate. But did he work for the NYPD or Leech? He could remember both but didn't know where his loyalties lay. The even greater question was why.

Death in alleys, children selling drugs, corpses in gutters—he knew that to be a true part of New York City that apparently included assassinating miscreants and leaving children to be eaten by rats. He could not imagine that being true where he was concerned. According to what Dr. Fry told Zelda, dissociative fugue states could come and go as if he were participating in two separate lives.

Random shards of disconnected memory moved across the ceiling like barely perceptible blocks of light, but the shards were multiplying and beginning to rearrange themselves—sheet metal, vials of drugs. He couldn't discern whether his memories were true, and he was laying a hot nurse. He loved sex, but someone important was missing from his sex life.

"An assassin shot you, and you have a traumatic brain injury, but not from the bullet, from falling on your head. You've been in a coma," Zelda had explained. "Your Living Will specified that the hospital should transfer you here right away, way faster than usual. No one here knows why."

He claimed to Zelda that he was on special assignment and had been injured unexpectedly. It was the best story he could come up with, which could be true but probably was not. He told her he could not reveal the assignment, which was definitely true because he couldn't remember it.

Rats, rats and apples, block parties at night, rats, blood drives, alone but not alone, rats watched, rendering lard, rats, traitors, rats in empty tenements— it all encircled his mind in rapid rotation. Rex pressed the palms of his hands against his temples. What had happened to him? What was supposed to have happened?

"Have no direct contact with anyone until 'Go.'" Who told him that?

He'd awakened last night. Zelda, nude, was walking toward him, climbing onto him. When he grabbed her hips and pulled her down hard, pretty little Nurse Zelda got the surprise of her life, right up to her pretty neck, the one that he later offered to squeeze the life out of if she let anyone know that he had returned.

He didn't understand why he would threaten her. He knew his presence here must remain a secret, but why? He was supposed to do something that needed to remain confidential, which it would if he could never remember it.

His first orgasm had blown Zelda to the ceiling, and the next two, into orbit. He'd had shakily slipped off the bed, then pushed Zel to the floor. Orgasm number four for both of them came on the floor. His knees felt stiff, but his body felt well fuc —

Rex never used that language, but his memory had returned only partially, and his sense of self. Who or what he had been, had not returned. What other distortions remained. What parts of his dreams and recollections were true? This nursing home must be his cover. A shiver eased down his body. He remembered Benji's rats, poor little kid. Was that fantasy or reality?

He had enlisted Zel's cooperation and made her part of his unknown assignment, his arms, legs, and eyes in the outside world. He had professed his instant love, which was a lie. She couldn't refuse to help. She would not refuse. He had her by the short hair and loved her for the moment.

He never thought of women that way.

He began to weep. "I'll kill you for this, Leech." But he couldn't remember who Leech was.

"Hey, I did kill you!"

Chapter 20 - Riding the Rails

Hidden exits for emergencies.

Saratoga, NY. Crumb House. 8:15 AM. Angie.

Just inside the Tower Suite, Angie said, "Gone."

"Gone," Maddie and Gretta said together. Behind them, Adonis, Jimmu, Fred, and Dale stood, trying to see into the empty Tower Suite Elias Crumb once used when he did not wish to stay downstairs with his comfort employees.

"From the looks of the place, Mrs. Lessix did not sleep here," Angie said.

"She could have used the recliner," Dale said.

"We do that sometimes at Tate," Fred added.

Angie should have foreseen this, but how could the bitch escape? There was only one exit from the fourth-floor tower, and after they made Mrs. Lessix comfortable last night, they locked her in for safety.

"Crap," Maddie said.

"Come on, gang." Angie led the way into the suite.

"You can't know it all ahead of time, Ange," Mary Helen pointed out.

"No, but I am in a slump and need to escape from it."

The sun gleamed on the polished pine plank floor. Rag rugs lay about. An undisturbed rust and brown quilt lay unwrinkled on the bed.

Jimmu went over to the back window and opened it. "There's a trellis that runs down to the ground. I suppose you could crawl down if you had strong arms, courage, and a death wish. But Mrs. Lessix?" He leaned out farther, then returned with a black-and-white silky fabric scrap.

Adonis came to life and said, "She was wearing that."

"I know," Jimmu said, "It's mine, part of the disguise I created for her."

Maddie joined them at the window.

"She wouldn't have taken the trellis," Mary Helen said. *"She was dumb and scared, not crazy."*

"She must have left as soon as we returned to bed." Angie walked over and looked out the window with Jimmu, Adonis, and Maddie.

"There's no sign of a struggle," Adonis said. "If she didn't use the trellis or stairs, how did she do it, and how did a scrap of her blouse end up on the trellis?"

"So maybe the broad got stuffed, snuffed, and discarded, Kid." Mary Helen loved dark fiction.

"Maybe she waited until we were all asleep and actually did use the trellis," Adonis said.

"Adonis and Lessix have lots in common except that Adonis is prettier and sounds like a wannabe cop," Mary Helen said.

"She went down a four-floor trellis?" Jimmu wondered again. "It looks strong, with rough-cut 1 x 3s screwed on with braces every few feet, but four floors? She couldn't have gone down it—she's a girl!" Then he whispered, "Is the triumvirate looking at me, Dale."

"With daggers," Fred whispered. Then louder he said, "No sign of a struggle. I love it up here. I come here to read sometimes. When the windows are open, it's like riding the cloud you save stuff to."

Dale went over and looked down the trellis. "Wait a second, Jimmu. If you got the scrap, it was within reach of the window, and I don't see any others below."

"Obvious, sport." Jimmu looked at Dale like his brain was leaking.

"Dale's right. She planted it, then left some other way," Fred said. "Aunt Mirthretta, did Grandpa or his ancestors ever use this place for anything?"

"I don't know for sure, Fred," Gretta said. "People accepted having a high-class pleasure and entertainment house close to the thriving Canfield Casino. There could be all kinds of hidden exits for emergencies. Gangsters proliferated here during prohibition. I have an archive of pictures, notes, autographs, and requests."

"A pleasure and entertainment house?" Fred sounded horrified.

"A top-end whorehouse, dear," Gretta explained, "but your bed is new." She was not that good at soothing.

Fred said, "Top-end? What about the other — "

"Do you wish to experience a six-month allowance sabbatical, young man?"

Fred cringed. "No, Aunt Mirthretta."

"Fine. Let's return to seriousness," Gretta grumped. "There is an ancient story that the underground railroad stopped here. That usually means a secret hiding area with multiple external access, but no one has found physical evidence. It could be only a legend. This place abounds with legends."

"I think we should let that mystery rest," Angie said. "Lessix got out. It's a mystery but is a done deal and probably not important. We have already heard what she had to say, and I question whether she was telling the truth. You girls and boys go on to the Merry Fountains. I need to drop by Hooker's place first."

"We're coming with you," Gretta proclaimed. "I can prune later, and Maddie might disappear if she gets any thinner."

Angie felt Maddie and Gretta's bare-naked glance at each other. "You two don't need to come. I'm quite safe."

"No way," Maddie said. "We're coming."

"You may be safe," Gretta said, "but I worry about Saratoga. It's my hometown."

"I'd like to come too if no one minds." Jimmu seemed much more serious than before.

"I think I like him, Kid," Mary Helen said.

That was no surprise to Angie. If Mary Helen detected working male glands, her libido erupted into merry-fountain floods.

"I have liked him from the moment I met him, Mary Helen, along with a bit of suspicion."

"I want to come too, Mom," Dale said, "and Fritz and Fred want to come." He ignored that they were standing next to him.

Angie had almost forgotten that her son was standing beside her, backed by his curious crew. For the past few years, he had never been anywhere but boarding school or on vacation with Rex and her in one exotic resort or another.

"Who's Fritz?" Maddie whispered, still staring at the empty room.

"Adonis is Fritz," Jimmu whispered back, reviving his swish. "It's his real name. I know he's pretty, but let's give him an even break and at least use his real name occasionally. We should be non-sexist here, shouldn't we?"

Dale giggled. So did Angie.

"Yes, dear," Gretta said sweetly to Jimmu. "Of course, you've been non-sexist from the get-go."

Angie wanted to put Gretta in her next book. Clever tongues that sharp didn't grow on trees.

Chapter 21 - Cops

I'm a common-law cop.

—1—

Saratoga, NY. The Golden Arms. 8:30 AM. Inspector Rex Caine.

Rex awoke from his doze.

"Something," he murmured. "Someone."

Keys lay on the bedside table.

"Zel? No, she would not have come back yet. It would attract suspicion." They had discussed how Rex could pull off pretending to still be comatose until—

"Until what?"

Rex reached over and picked up the keys and the note under them. "Keys for the blue Marquis parked close to the foot of your entrance. I suggest you reach the cottage on foot."

The handwriting was not Zelda's. Rex examined the keys. Two were car keys. One was a double-blade Superlock key, and three others were probably house keys.

While Zel was out shopping for him, a nurse came in every two hours to check. She had been here about twenty minutes ago to ensure that Rex was alive and out of it. She would freak out if she knew the truth. Zel had turned off telemetry and visual supervision.

He slipped out of bed, walked to the sitting room, and looked down the driveway. A dark blue Mercury

Marquis with black windows sat in the yard, close to the bottom of the private exit path.

Zel had shown him the suite exit early this morning after they could walk again.

Rex walked to the windows to the left of his bed and looked down over the sloping lawn. A sprawling one-story part-stone house sat at the bottom of the hill across the road. Rex stared at the house for a long time. It should mean something to him. It didn't. Neither did "The Snow Queens," which kept echoing through his mind.

—2—

Saratoga, NY. Philadelphia Street. Hooker Real Estate 9:00 AM. Angie.

"Pigs to the right of us. Pigs to the left of us," Mary Helen intoned.

"Shut up, Mary Helen. You were a cop once."

"Still am. No badge, though. I'm a common-law cop."

"Park in Lena's lot." Maddie had suggested that they approach from the lower end of the street. She had been correct. Police cars had filled Philadelphia Street. The lot served Lena's Coffee House, across from Hookers, and a couple of restaurants, one with excellent southern fried chicken.

Before anyone could object, Angie slipped out and headed up the street. A small crowd of onlookers stood around watching the police. They would have removed the body by now, but that did not bother Angie. The paper said Hooker died from a single shot to the forehead while sitting at his desk. The gunman fired from just inside the front door.

"How are we going to get past the police line this time, Ange," Mary Helen asked.

"Not to fret."

Angie had already spotted her target. When she slipped under the yellow crime-scene line, a burly Sheriff's deputy hurried toward her. His broad cheeks and thick neck were sunburned. He needed a shave but had probably been up all night.

He held his hand up and said, "Sorry, ma'am, you can't come in here. That's the reason for the tape you just went under."

Angie ignored the man but did not move. "Mannie," she called into the building.

Mannie looked. His eyebrows rose. "Let her in, McEnaney." Then to the detective next to him. "She's close to Caine."

Angie glanced at a silent McEnaney and walked on into the little building. "I'm surprised to see you, Mannie."

He nodded. "I'm surprised to see you, Angie."

Rex and Mannie were close friends. "I didn't know Mr. Hooker worked for Paul Michael Senna."

Mannie smiled. "I didn't say he did."

Angie smiled. "Why else would the NYPD be up here? Certainly not for nice old Mr. Hooker's homicide."

This time Mannie just nodded. "I was in the area, visiting my son, Mark, but I'm still on the Senna case. And you, why would you be here, Ms. Angelica?" He smiled. Mannie and his brothers had been Angie's friends for years.

"Oh, I came up for the racing, Mannie, and also because I'm interested in property in the area. I was born here. Mr. Hooker was searching for real estate I might like."

"Liar, liar, panty shields on fire."

"Shut up, Mary Helen."

"I'm really devastated that he's dead, Mannie. He was such a nice old man and had a house he was dying to show me."

"I'm sorry he's dead too, ma'am." Mannie's eyes turned away from Angie and looked through the store-front window to the other side of the street where her six musketeers stood: Gretta, Maddie, Adonis, Jimmu, Fred, and Dale. "Your posse?" His gaze focused on them intently.

"Yes. The taller of the two younger boys is my son. The shorter is his roommate at Tate. I believe you know them."

Mannie squinted and seemed to focus on Adonis, "I certainly do," then smiled.

"Has there been a break in the Leech case or Rex's?" Angie asked.

"The boys are mentoring my son, Mark, who lives in the next suite, and I'm incredibly grateful. Thank you for the part you played in that."

"My pleasure."

His smile vanished. "And no, we've hit brick walls in the PMS, Leech, and Slag cases. We are relatively certain that they're related."

Angie nodded. Then, remembering the microfilm list, "How are your brothers, Marion and Marvin, and how is Detective Kossick?"

"Fine, ma'am, as far as I know. My brothers and I are here for a couple of weeks. Mark is also doing fine. Dale and Fred are doing a great job with him, and he's not the easiest eight-year-old to manage. He figures he'll grow up to be a cop the size of my brothers and myself and has started practicing intimidating people. It doesn't really work. Have you seen Kossick around?"

"I don't believe so. Did you misplace him?"

"I believe so, Angie. I do believe so."

—3—

Saratoga, NY. Merry Fountains Spa. Men's Steam Room. 10:00 AM. Dale.

Sweat rolled off Dale like he was melting. Fortunately, Fred was sitting next to him to drip onto.

"Master Dale, what happened to Adonis?" Jimmu asked. "I was looking forward to practicing T'ai Chi Chuan with him."

Adonis had dropped them off, then left.

"Aunt Mirtha sent him on an errand of some kind," Fred said.

"I was looking forward to working out with him too." Dale shrugged. "He seems like a nice guy, maybe not the easiest to get to know, but kind and tough."

"Hey, Dale, you've got me to work out with," Fred said.

"That's for sure. Fred and I work out all the time, Jimmu."

"Germanic weightlifters are always stuck unto themselves a bit," Jimmu said. "Adonis will come out eventually. His body reminds me of a young Arnie Schwarzenegger. Yummy."

Dale shivered a bit at that—he knew what his mother suspected, but they slept together in the same room and showered one after the other. The worst thing Jimmu did was snore. He didn't even swear.

The steamed sweat still flowed so fast that Dale felt like the Wicked Witch of the West melting. "Damn. Is this what they call a Saratoga Steamer?" The steam in here was wilting Dale's trunk. Three tiers of wood slat benches lined the tile-walled steam room. They were sitting on the top row, where the steam was the thickest and freshest.

"Yes, I suppose you could call it that." Jimmu wiped his forehead. "And here is little me with little you two, just like we were last night. I admit that I'm looking forward to another shower and swim."

"Us too, Big Brother," Fred said.

Jimmu, Fred, and Dale were the only ones in the steam room. Early morning was a weird time to go to the spa, but Aunt Gretta wanted to come and twisted everyone's arm to do the crime scene first, then the spa. It seemed that busy people did things at unconventional times.

Dale enjoyed this place, especially Jimmu, who was refined, intelligent, full of sparky fun, and scarily adept at martial arts — he was teaching Dale and Fred Chinese floor fighting. His ability to go from fem-fem to tough-tough amazed Dale. Fred amazed him too. Though tiny, he could seriously kick ass. No bully tried anything with him at school anymore, and it had rubbed off on Dale.

Of course, in the past half year, Dale went completely over the top with his mindless praise-the-Lord patter. He'd turned into a Gilbert and Sullivan prophet but had learned better and had regained his sanity and classmate standing.

"Oh, gracious, gracious," Jimmu upped and said to nothing and nobody.

"Will you knock it off, please?" Dale said.

"Why, whatever do you mean, Master Dale?" Judging by the wiseass smile beaming through the steam, Jimmu knew exactly what Dale meant.

"I mean the swishy-gay Asian American act." Dale didn't understand how he knew it was an act. He just did. "What would you do if you saw Fred or me getting destroyed by bullies?"

"I'd break their arms and any other appropriate parts I could reach, but that has nothing to do with gay or straight, Master Dale. It has to do with practice and skill."

"Thank you for that, but after you saved us, you would put on a gay swish-act that surpassed all put-on artists. You know exactly what I mean—you're about as gay as J. Edgar Hoover."

Jimmu howled at that one for some reason, then whispered, "You're right, Dale. I mostly like girls, but there's a time and place for everything."

"Jimmu!" Dale snarled.

Fred was laughing his little head off. He obviously knew his brother better than anyone else on Earth.

Jimmu quieted down then and said confidentially, "Well, look at it this way, Master Dale, it's better to be a front-and-center clown than a member of the hairy Cro-Magnons hiding in condemned buildings. Also, you live longer because you're no apparent threat to anyone."

Now Dale giggled, but he still felt a little ill-at-ease talking about this with a super-excellent guy he really enjoyed. "I suppose, but if we meet any of my school friends in town, would you do me a favor and cool your fem-frequency a little?" Sheepishly.

"I promise. I'll turn into Rock Hudson for you."

"Thanks."

Fred had been giggling since the beginning of this conversation and now burst into a roar. "Summers, you're a trip and a half. I'll never forget you."

Dale laughed despite himself. "Okay, you guys, so I'm a snot-nosed little rich kid who says all the wrong stuff, probably believes lots of it, and gets embarrassed for all the wrong reasons. But before you condemn me for not knowing much about the dark side of the moon, please remember that my mom and Mary Helen make their living by creating dangerous worlds and that I help. I just keep it a secret."

Jimmu stopped laughing, reached over, and picked Dale's head up until they were staring eye to eye through the steam. "Are you ashamed of your mother, boy?" His hand felt like iron on Dale's chin.

"No, of course not. It's just that all those wild, sexy scenes with Mary Helen and Stud embarrass me. I love my mom big-time, but the guys at school sometimes say and do things."

"He's telling the truth about that," Fred said. "Sometimes, it's not good-natured teasing either."

"What happened?" Jimmu's voice became calm, a concerned friend and confidant.

"Well," Dale said, trying to frown and pout simultaneously. "Well, they had this big discussion in the locker room about whether Mary Helen had ever made it with Stud and took bets on whether mine was as big as Stud's, then checked in the shower and decided it wasn't. They are my friends and all, and I know they're just kidding, but it bothers me. I don't know. It's hard as hell being the kid of a famous writer, even though I help with her books. That's all."

"In other words, your friends sometimes think you're one of your mother's characters and belong in one of her stories?" Jimmu asked.

"Something like that." Dale let his head sag back down between his knees.

"I admire your mother, Dale," Jimmu said. After your father died, she ended up with a few thousand dollars, your two brothers, baby-you, and her imagination. She supported you and hoisted herself and you into a considerably higher tax bracket. She also gave many great reads to hundreds of poor little street kids at the local libraries and social-intercourse centers, kids like Fred. She also collected tons of sophisticated and educated folks, including me, into her fan base."

"Yeah, I guess. I never know what to ask for at Christmas because she's already bought me everything I ever wanted and well past that, and I love to read her stuff, if only while proofing. But I'm prejudiced — she's my mom. Do other people think her writing is any good?"

"Of course, they do, and of course it is." Fred sounded furious. "It's excellent."

"But what do Mom's books say about her?"

"They say," Fred continued, "that she's a bright, bright lady who came up with an amazingly effective method of making ends meet. And it says that she's stuck on you so much that she allows you a super-expensive school to spare you the turmoil and dangers of living with a best-selling author in a city like New York, where everyone carries a grudge. Never forget that your mom grieves because you're not with her but believes you are in the right place. She's a goddess. Isn't she any good in the mother department?"

That hurt. "Of course, she is, Fred!" No one had asked Dale that question! And to tell the truth, he never spent much time thinking about it. "With all her traveling, she always has time for me on vacations and emergencies like my appendectomy — she canceled a London trip for that. She can read me great, too, and always knows when to push ahead or pull back. I couldn't ask for —"

"Dale," Jimmu whispered. "You don't know how lucky you are. And, aw shucks, how do you know I'm not gay."

"I don't," Dale said.

"You don't?" Jimmu sounded sincerely astonished.

"I don't know either, Jim," Fred said, "and I'm your brother."

"I figure you might be," Dale said, "but I don't care. Nobody does anymore, not anybody intelligent and not an ideologue. I like you, and that's that." Dale figured that this was honesty time. "Are you?"

"Well, dear, that's for me to know."

"And me to find out?" Dale finished for him.

"Not on your life. Now, what's good for the goose—are you?"

"Am I what?" Dale asked.

"Are you gay?" Jimmu shrugged.

"I don't think so. Do I look gay?" Dale asked.

"You look clean, intelligent, and proper to a fault, but most gay folks don't have a look."

"But back at Crumb House," Dale said, "I saw my mom watching us out the window. She may be worried about you, me, Adonis, and even Fred. I don't know why. All Adonis did was strip in the garden and pose to let us see his muscles."

"Does it worry you that she watched?" Jimmu sounded concerned. "He does have impressive muscles."

Dale regretted bringing it up. "I guess not, but Mom's a great detective, and maybe she wanted to see his muscles too. If she's worried about me, I'm sure she'll arrive at the right conclusion." Dale wanted to end this conversation.

"I agree," Jimmu said.

Fred nodded.

Dale didn't quite know what all that meant but guessed everything would turn out okay.

"You ready for a swim yet, guys?" Jimmu asked.

"Sure," Dale said. "There's just one thing."

"And what might that be, Master Dale?"

"Do you swish when you swim?"

"Gracious no, Master Dale. I might pop my water wings."

Jim and Fred laughed and laughed, and Dale felt himself turning redder than the steam could make him.

They left the steam room for the cool locker room, showered, pulled on their suits, and headed to the pool. There was no one there except the lifeguard, so Dale, Fred, and Jimmu eased themselves into the water and began swimming quietly down the length of the long pool. The sun blazed through the domed glass roof, casting crystal cubes into the water.

"How old are you, Master Dale?"

"Fifteen almost, but not all the way. I will be in eleven months. I'm two months younger than Fred. He never lets me forget it, either."

"That's what I like about you, Dale. You get right to the point." Jimmu swam with long steady strokes. His tall body seemed all muscle.

"Hey, Jim, you swim good for an old man," Fred piped.

"Thank you, Little Brother," Jimmu replied courteously before he stopped swimming to dunk Fred. "So do you."

—4—

Saratoga, NY. Merry Fountains Spa. Women's Steam Room. 10:30 AM. Maddie.

For Maddie, this day was awful already. Thus far today, they had misplaced a key witness, investigated a murder scene — sort of — and watched Mrs. Lessix's warning actually happen — senseless murders, cops out of their jurisdiction, and generally weird crap. In addition, Angie and Maddie experienced a front-row seat to Gretta Braun, as in Eva, losing her cheesecake residual, an Academy Award performance. She'd even asked about a full-body tuck.

This was the worst, though. Even in the middle of all this therapeutic steam, which was no doubt piped in from hell, Maddie could hear the slaps, creaks, and screams of agony in the massage room next door. "What Gretta goes through in the name of cheesecake exceeds the superb Stevie King's most horrific moments."

"A compulsive eater and her cheesecake are not easily parted." Angie's philosophizing seemed disinterested. She had fallen into herself since their trip to Hooker's and was clearly holding something back.

"Indeed, they are not," Maddie said, sitting side-by-side with Angie on the steam slats in the Hairy Mary. "You like Steven King, don't you?"

Angie nodded. "Like most successful writers, I emulate Steven King in all things but would not admit it outside a deserted steam room. Stevie is a grossly underestimated genius with incredible powers of perception, but he would not bother with big stomachs unless they were about to explode or disgorge."

"True, true." Maddie took a huge breath and tried to decide whether she was breathing steam or sweat. It was no wonder that Gretta scheduled a double appointment with the masseuse after their delightful morning of T'ai Chi, Nautilus, Steppercise, and other forms of exceptionally painful punishment, under the direction of Madam Sadie Vicious, S.E.D, Sadistic Exercise Director, a totally bald, physical therapy broad with the build of Sylvester Stallone, and his face too. "Just wait till Gretta picks up another piece of cheesecake."

"Maddie, what on earth should I do?" The steam flew away from Angie's mouth in frantic curls.

"I assumed you decided to lose weight," Mad said, "a pound, maybe. Otherwise, you and Grett would not have put me through this. That is not what you mean, though, is it."

"No."

"You mean Rex, don't you."

"Of course. And Dale. The complexities in my already super-hectic life are burgeoning exponentially. I have not figured out what is happening, but I appear to be drowning in it."

"Are you genuinely in love with Rex, or is he just a good lay?"

"Rex is a superb lover, and I love him."

"Are you multi-orgasmic with him?" Maddie never hung herself onto propriety.

"Multi-multi."

"Then you must resolve the mystery and decide what you want to hold onto most. Dale and writing, certainly. Rex, though, is an unknown at this point." Maddie could feel Angie's eyes widening. "And do not pretend you are shocked. I used to think that nude dogs shocked you, but I have changed my mind."

"That is not what I mean."

"What is not what you mean?" Maddie said. Apart from being brilliant, friend Angie could be massively confusing.

"I mean, of course, that I must solve the mystery, but it is all coming so fast, and I cannot figure out what to do next."

Maddie did not understand that and wondered if Angie, the one person she had never caught in a lie, was telling the truth.

"Rex, Lessix, Hooker, Leech, PMS."

"You always know what to do next. When you and Mary Helen get going, you plow forward with such abandon that you keep Gretta and me quaking in our pantyhose. We look to you for knowing what to do next. Why do you not know what to do next?"

"I think it is because Rex and I are so close and because information is piling up that makes no sense, at least not within a framework where I dare reason. It has given me something like writer's block."

"I did not know that you ever got that. As writers go, you have always been a rabbit among the porcupines — you breed fast."

"Oh, I have gotten blocked, but it has never lasted more than a few hours."

"So maybe this won't." Maddie shrugged.

"It already has," Ange went. "There is something I see that I do not want to see because I do not know what it is."

"I hope you never put that sentence in a book," Gretta boomed from the room's far end.

Maddie didn't know how long Gretta had stood there in her sheet, tall, stately, and Ceasaresq. "Oh Christ, it's the voice of God." Maddie sighed.

Gretta Braun possessed presence, tons of it. Of course, she owned oodles else: buildings, people, money, power, contacts, and contracts. Gretta the Grand walked toward them through swirling steam as Moses probably had the Red Sea. Maddie knew things were about to get moving, if not out of hand.

Gretta perched herself next to Angie, put her arm around her, and squeezed. This morning, Gretta proved adept at all kinds of physical pursuits, including T'ai Chi Chuan. That suggested that with over six feet, a half-ton, and skills, she was not planning to allow anyone to mug her, ever. She had launched their instructor, Uncle Fu, into the air and flung him backward into the padded wall. That was far afield from the Gretta they knew and loved. She also possessed magnificently penetrating chutzpah.

"We need to get organized," Gretta proclaimed. No one could deny that Gretta was grand, albeit a brand of grand that periodically concealed itself between a cheesecake bosom and a hard lard ass. "And if Mary Helen Mack's ingenuity has temporarily shut down, we must stimulate her. Correct, Maddie?" This Gretta Braun was not the Improbable Hulk Maddie saw shakily descend the grand stairs last night. She could not have lost that much weight in a couple of hours, but the effort did wonders for her bearing.

"Right, Grett. I am ready." Maddie stood and pulled Angie up.

Gretta surged up from the bench. "Oh, Maddie darling."

"Yes, Gretta."

"While getting my massage, I read the latest issue of Centered Women. Interesting book review section."

"Oh, GeeGodOhFat! In all the confusion, I forgot to tell you! Oh, Gretta." Horror slammed Maddie in the middle of her tiny gut. Panic followed. She felt heat on her legs and looked down to see if her sheet was turning yellow. She now knew why she paid for a therapist.

"By the way," Angie said, obviously trying to defuse the situation, "you guys need to use regular cars—Grett's WatStretchEV is too obvious."

"You are right. Already done," Gretta said. "I bought an EscaladeLectro for myself and rented a Mercedes EQE 1000 for Maddie."

"The EscaladeLectro was an extravagance, but I have always wanted one."

"News flash, Angie," Maddie said, "a bright red Maserati Hydro-Quad convertible is not inconspicuous. It probably rivals the WatStretchEV in that respect.

"And," Gretta continued, "the dealer will deliver a BMW i9 to my barn this afternoon for Jimmu. His twentieth birthday is tomorrow, but we are celebrating tonight to surprise him. He loves Beamers. I also rented a BroncEV for Adonis and the boys. He will be back in it to pick them up from here."

"A white BroncEV?" Maddie asked, trying to draw the bottom edge of her sheet under with her toes.

"Black and electric, dear, and do not mention the new BMW to Jimmu. He only asked for a rented black car to use as a runaround instead of his bullet-holed Elantra, the one he used to lure the police away from Leech's house for us and to bring Mrs. Lessix up here. White is for flight, but black's where it's at, Mad! And while we have been here, Ange, I had your Rat radio upgraded so we can contact each other without anyone hearing or tracking us."

Angie smiled. "Thank you, Gretta. Now, what are you working up to? I know you almost as well as you know me. You really have started things along. What are you going to tell us next?"

Maddie stepped in. "We want to tell you something dangerous that belongs in your picaresque database."

"We did not want to confuse the issue but have decided this may actually be the issue," Gretta said.

"Have you ever heard of The Candy Troops, Ange?" Maddie asked.

"Of course, I have. It was on the microfilm printout that you two perused. And do you remember reading about The Snow Queens? You seemed to know them well in your unpublished exposé, Mad."

Chapter 22 - Triangles

Teens with Worcestershire Sauce.

−1−

Maddie's Mercedes EQE 1000. 2:00 PM. Maddie.

Gretta had forgiven Maddie for Webb Drake's review of Angie's latest. There would, however, need to be several painfully good-for-Gretta deals on serializations and full-page pre-pub teasers.

Maddie passed the crazy stone shack and guided her Mercedes EQE 1000 into the driveway of the Brass Balls of Jesus or whatever it was. Angie had turned in just ahead of them. "Where did Dale and Fred go after the Hairy Mary?"

"Sightseeing with Adonis and Jimmu." Gretta smiled.

"Angie is worried about Jimmu's safety," Maddie said. "He's only nineteen and has already dodged bullets for her."

"Yes," Gretta said. "I assured her that Jimmu would be quite safe and, like Adonis, would take diligent care of Dale and Fred. And Jim will be twenty in a few hours—that's five years past 'of age.'"

"Dale and Fred are probably much safer with Adonis than we are with Angie. How are we going to keep track of her?"

Gretta smiled, flipped open a panel in the dashboard where the disk player should have been, and typed a password into the control panel. The small screen abruptly showed a diagram of the Saratoga area and a small red triangle close to a building.

"You bugged her car?"

"Of course, I did, the boys' BroncEV too—that's the blue triangle."

Angie had parked at The Golden Arms.

"The technology is targeted GPS." Gretta pushed the blue button. "We can follow one or more specific cars from anywhere. The boys said they were going sightseeing and are apparently doing it around here."

Maddie pulled into the diagonal next to the empty Hydro-Quad.

—2—

Saratoga, NY. Near The Golden Arms. 2:04 PM. Dale.

"There they go, right on schedule," Dale said. Adonis had parked the BroncEV in the woods next to The Golden Arms and slightly cattycorner from The John Appleseed Cottage. "Mom always stays on time, even for book signings. It goes back to when she was poor and actually needed to stay on time. Rich people like my mom, Aunt Gretta, and Aunt Maddie are always on time unless they want to make a point."

"Yes, indeed." Fred yawned. "That's how the cookie crumbles on top of the pile. If you're there, you must look and be better than everyone else."

"Ya." Adonis nodded. He apparently knew Aunt Gretta well.

Dale had noticed them having confidential conversations when they thought no one was looking. He'd always tried to pay attention to his near environment, a trait he likely got from his mom.

Adonis interested Dale, though not in the way his

mother suspected. It seemed that more lurked in that big body than protein and musculature. For starters, Adonis's real name was Fritz Kissinger. He became Adonis when he was trying to make it as a model. That part got Dale suspicious. He'd watched photo sessions for his mom's book covers, and Adonis knew nothing about modeling. He only knew how to make his muscles bulge and twitch, which was no big deal once you built them.

Jimmu and Fred were sitting in the back seat, Adonis and Dale, in the front. Dale would need to watch himself. If his mother caught him sleuthing, she would send him straight back to Tate, where he didn't want to go most. Mary Margaret Pinkham always spent summer at Tate while her mother, Cindy McGraw, concentrated on The Grand Ball at the Canfield Casino later in July. Dale didn't want to see Mary Margaret again for a while. Hooking up with her had been counterproductive. Besides, this was too much fun, especially with Fred — not that Mary Margaret hadn't been fun in a certain kind of way while they were together.

Jimmu and Adonis were fun too. Well, Adonis was not exactly what you would call fun, but according to Jimmu, he could be if they got him to come out and show his real personality. Jimmu, of course, was always keen for a shocking double entendre or an opportunity to demonstrate his physical prowess and martial arts skills. Dale wanted him as a guide to escape vanilla kidhood. Religioning hadn't worked, but he felt sure that Jimmuing would.

Then there were his mom's lists. Jimmu saw them and showed them to Adonis and Fred before Fred showed them to Dale. They needed them to search, of course, had found some list-folks downtown, and were now on the way to look at The John Appleseed Cottage, which Fred insisted on calling "The John." He was lots like his big brother, not with swishes-on-demand, but great in martial arts, gymnastics, and thinking. They could easily be the same person at different ages.

"Nobody home," Adonis said, looking across the road to The John. His speech tended toward the declarative, what Jimmu called Germanic terse.

"See the fieldstone wall along the back of the house?" Jimmu said. "We just need to report about the house, Dale."

"Ya. No one will see us."

"Are you guys sure of this?" Dale had never gone housebreaking before.

"I second that," Fred said. "We've been on some scary adventures, Jim, but never in daylight."

Dale didn't understand how Adonis and Jimmu would report on the place without mentioning Dale, but he hoped for the best. His friends knew about his mom's forbidenation when it came to Dale's imitating her dark-side sleuthing, but Dale had faith because Fred, who knew more about everything than he should, had assured him, and now Jim had.

"You stay in the car, Master Dale."

Jimmu had no call to order Dale around like that. "No. I'm coming with you!"

"But I promised." Jimmu looked so damned serious that Dale wanted to pinch him to get him back into swish mode.

"Promised whom?"

"I can't tell you."

"No matter. There's a limited number of possibilities, particularly one. I'm not staying here. I either go with you, or I follow at a distance. Whichever, we're all going to end up in the same place at the same time."

Dale had decided that no one would leave him out of anything again. That could be a big mistake, but it probably wasn't, not after the silent ostracism that came his way at school during his hallelujah semester and after letting Mary Margaret Pinkham have his virginity.

— 3 —

The Golden Arms. Suite P7. 2:15 PM. Inspector Rex Caine.

Rex lay still. He needed to bring this off. Whoever these ladies were, he could not let them detect he was conscious.

"Christ, he does look life-like and gorgeous." She sounded like a fruitcake.

"He's not dead, Maddie! And he's not going to die."

The voices sounded familiar, especially the last one, but he couldn't quite identify them. One's name was Maddie, but he knew the other one better."

"Have you talked to the doctors?" a sober, deeper female voice asked.

"Of course, Gretta, but they did not shed much light. Rex tests normal."

"He looks as normal as any man I've known well." The fruitcake again. "Of course, at least half of the male gender tests normal, but the ones that don't are more interesting."

He realized that Gretta, Maddie, and the other one were his friends, but he couldn't open his eyes. The mission demanded it.

"Will you two stop it!" the nameless voice said.

He did not dare let them know. It didn't matter who they were.

Nothing did anymore.

Thanks to Rex, the rats killed Benji, a really great little kid.

— 4 —

Saratoga, NY. The John. 2:17 PM. Dale.

Adonis and Jimmu led the way through the trees to the road's edge. Dale and Fred followed.

Dale wondered who Jimmu promised what to. He knew more than Fred, but there was no point in asking. They were both great with secrets. Dale didn't know whether that reassured, annoyed, or scared him. He could take care of himself, sort of, and Adonis, Jimmu, and Fred seemed to have the best intentions toward him. He couldn't get too mad at them for babying him. His mother did it, too, although it was completely unnecessary.

Adonis looked up and down the road to ensure nothing was coming, then raced across the road and vaulted the stone wall to the other side.

Jimmu went next and cleared the wall like an acrobat, which he was.

With Fred close behind, Dale raced across, jumped the wall, and landed on Jimmu and Adonis, a lot on Adonis, whose left eye socket smacked Dale's right knee, and more on Jimmu, whose crotch hit Dale squarely on the foot. Fred, like the gymnast he was, flicked across the wall and landed on no one.

"Oh, crap, crap, crap." That was maybe the most eloquent thing that Dale had heard Adonis say so far. He certainly did say it with feeling, anyway. "I'm gonna have a black eye."

Jimmu, on the other hand, didn't say a word. He just turned Asian pale, bit his lip, and grabbed his pants between his legs with both hands as if trying to keep part of himself from falling off, or because he wanted it to.

"Oh, gee, Adonis, Jimmu, I'm sorry. I'm so sorry. I'm sorry. I really am."

"Enough!" Jimmu said in a funny, squished voice while keeping a solid crotch hold. "It's okay. You didn't mean it. We'll work on your aim. I'll give you Fred to practice on."

"You won't have anything to hold together if you keep that up, Big Brother," Fred said.

Adonis rubbed his eye and looked at Jimmu as though he'd like to cement him to the stone wall. The eye had already started going black and blue green!

Dale couldn't tell whether Jimmu and Adonis were mad. "I really am sorry, you two. Oh, cow! Double cow even!"

"You didn't mean it." Adonis took a big breath. "And I've gotten black eyes before."

"I've never had one," Dale said.

Jimmu smiled a weak polite smile that lay between trying to relax and trying not to puke.

Adonis got things back on track with, "Would one of you comedians mind sticking your head above the wall to see if anyone saw us? I'm a little out of focus. I'm not used to jumping over walls with Jerry Seinfeld."

"Certainly, great white chief." Jimmu, still holding onto his pants for dear life, cautiously eased his left eye up over the wall. They were at an inside corner, hidden from both The John Appleseed Cottage and the road. "It looks clear to little Jimmu."

"Little Jimmu better not err," Adonis said, "or our four little asses will be in a communal sling from more than one direction."

"I'm Buddhist. I don't approve of communism." Jimmu smiled sweetly.

Adonis slapped his forehead with the huge palm of his hand as though he could not believe he was doing this with kids like Dale and Fred. He did, however, remain courteous and respectful. "Let's move along the wall, gentlemen. Don't let anything stick up over it."

The wall led to the rear of The John Appleseed Cottage.

"I hope you two won't hold this against me," Dale said.

"Just move." Adonis led the way.

Jimmu followed him in a crotchy sort of crawl. He looked funny, but Dale didn't laugh because he didn't know whether the crawl-style was a new kind of swish or just something left over from Jim's recent experience as a landing pad.

Fred followed Jimmu, as usual, and Dale brought up the rear.

Adonis lifted his hand when they reached the middle of the back wall, and they all stopped. This time they all eased their heads over the edge of the wall. They were behind The John Appleseed Cottage, completely shielded from the road and from The Golden Arms, where Uncle Rex lay vegged.

The Appleseed Cottage looked much bigger from here than it did from the road. In fact, it looked enormous. "There must be twenty rooms in that place," Fred said.

"Twenty-one," Adonis returned. "I looked at the floor plan."

"Well, gracious," Jimmu said. "I certainly am glad that the house isn't jailbait. I don't approve of breaking into jailbait."

"Jailbait is fourteen and down," Adonis said, "unless the two or more participants are within four years of each other." He sounded like a cop giving a school lecture.

Until now, Dale hadn't considered the possibility of illegal entry. "I don't see any sign of life, Adonis." But he supposed that you needed to get involved in a bit of adventure now and then, especially when your one and only mother had involved herself in the same adventure and, without Rex, might need help.

"Just what we want." Adonis said. A darker green had set into his eye now. Taken as a whole, his eye looked a lot like a round cheese, probably Vermont super-aged cheddar that had molded a little.

"And you're staying out here as a lookout, Master Dale," Adonis said. "Your mother would kill me if I let you break and enter. So would mine."

Before Dale could say, "Hell, no! I'm not going to take it anymore," a car door slammed.

— 5 —

Saratoga, NY. The Golden Arms. 2:25 PM. Maddie.

Maddie heard the soft steps in the hall only a second before the door swished open, and a nurse-type rattled in, her arms filled with packages. Maddie could recognize nurses because she used to be one.

"Oh, I'm sorry," the nurse said. "I didn't expect visitors." She flicked two brief glances at the packages, then carried them over and put them into the closet. She was slightly plump, very sensual, and had an odd look in her big brown eyes, a cross between suspicion, fear, and curiosity.

"Nice big closet." Maddie had already explored the place. Even the extra bedroom with the unmade bed and condoms appeared to have a nice big closet.

"All the private suites have walk-ins. I'm Zelda McCauley, Inspector Caine's private-duty RN."

"I'm Madeleine Franck as in César. This is Gretta Braun, as in Eva, and Angie Summers, as in famous."

"Angie Summers! The writer?"

Angie looked up from Rex, smiled, and nodded. "I'm afraid so."

"The actual Angie Summers?"

For a moment, Maddie could have sworn that Rex's expression changed.

"Yes."

"Ms. Summers, I love your books. I even love your villains. There's not even one that doesn't have some good in him."

"Thank you, Ms. McCauley," Angie said. "How's Rex doing?"

Little Zelda walked over and stood at the bed with Angie. "Well, no problems, except that he should be awake but isn't."

"He's in a coma, for God's sake," Maddie blurted. All this positive crap gnawed at her duodenum like mice up her—

"Well, yes," Zelda said. "But there are no complications, and we're very thankful for that."

"And you are Mr. Caine's private-duty nurse full-time?" Angie asked.

"Yes. It's part of our NYPD contract for Inspector Caine. The staff sometimes relieves me but checks him every two hours if I'm not here. There is also advanced telemetry." Nurse Zelda obviously wanted no trouble. She would tell them Rex needed maternity care if she thought it would flush. "But there are no complications."

The way Zelda looked at Rex, Maddie wondered if there were really no complications here. From her expression, Angie agreed.

— 6 —

Saratoga, NY. The John. 2:26 PM. Dale.

Dale and friends had given up looking over the wall. Each found his own chink. Dale felt ready to muss his shorts as he watched the two men at the back door. One was crouching there, picking the lock like they did in movies. The other one was standing there picking his nose like no one should do in public. Of course, to be fair, the two didn't know they were in public.

"I saw one of those gentlemen in the lobby of the Putnam," Jimmu whispered.

When they were "sightseeing," they checked a half dozen of the biggest hotels in town, looking for matches with the list. They had found a few names who were not traveling incognito. Adonis hadn't said why he thought anyone might need to travel incognito. A Pear Superphone call from Dale's mom had brought them out here.

One of the men looked truly mean, with broad shoulders and a swarthy complexion, like he might be Latin or Italian and might eat teenagers with Worcestershire Sauce for snacks—he was probably just a parent. The lock picker had a long razor blade kind of nose. The nose picker's nose looked more like a sweet potato, which was good because he had fat fingers.

"I think we better get out of here, guys," Fred said.

"Just a minute." Adonis's expression looked frozen. "I want to see what they want." This business didn't even phase him.

Jimmu stayed amazingly quiet with his eye rammed against the wall so hard that Dale wondered if he might not get his own black eye. He'd at least stopped holding onto his pants, which looked kind of wrinkled.

The lock picker got the door open. Both hoods— Dale guessed they were hoods—looked around, went inside, and quietly closed the door behind them. Of course, Dale and his friends were planning to break in, too, weren't they? Did that make them hoods?

"Those gentlemen aren't burglars," Jimmu whispered.

"How do you know that, Jim?" Fred asked.

"Didn't you look at their bulges, Master Dale?" Jimmu said. "They're carrying guns. Burglars don't do that. These guys are checking the joint out for some other reason."

"My eye really sucks." Adonis pulled his face away from the wall. "Does it look bad?"

Jimmu stared.

Dale stared even harder because his knee hurt like mad because Adonis's eye had gone black and yellow faster than any Dale had seen before.

Jimmu raised his arched eyebrows, tilted his head, and twisted his face. "It could be worse."

"Cow!" Dale asked. "How?"

"Don't you guys think it's about time we tip?" Fred said.

"What?" Dale asked. "You want me to fall down?"

Jimmu wrinkled his nose. "It's street talk for leave, flee, make tracks, bug out, blow a Tinkerbell."

"Oh," Dale said. "Oh, yes! Of course."

— 7 —

Saratoga, NY. The Golden Arms. 2:35 PM. Maddie.

On their way out of The Arms, Maddie said, "Christ. Look."

"She's picking and eating it!" a lady in a wheelchair screamed. She was pointing at the same old lady that Maddie had noticed.

"Isn't getting old great?" Maddie said.

"You should know, dear," Gretta said sweetly.

"Will you two stop it!" Angie barked.

"I think that nurse has the hots for Rex." Maddie had seen it in little Nurse Zelda's eyes as clearly as if it dripped down her leg. "She's warm for his form, blazing for his grazing, hot for his hangings, primed for his—"

"Oh, shut up, Maddie." Angie dear was finally showing a titbit of pique. She must have sensed something about Zelda too. "At the moment, my Rex couldn't if he wanted to."

They walked down the parking lot until they stood below Rex's room. Angie was looking up at his windows. She walked past the car to the end of the building, stood looking at the fire exit for a moment, then turned and headed back for the car.

"Gretta, what kind of store is Fred Daniel's?" Angie seemed in a trance.

"Department store, one of the few remaining up here," Gretta answered.

Maddie could feel the air prickle around them. "Why do you want to know, Angie?"

"And Mal's Men?" Angie asked. "That's a men's store, isn't it?"

"Yes indeed. You do not think that Rex is ready for clothes yet, do you," Gretta said in a suspicious tone.

"Angie, he's still in a coma, for God's sake," Maddie reminded her.

"He does seem to be. Maybe Nurse Zelda was shopping for her husband." Angie sounded more thoughtful than convinced. "Gretta, do me a favor. Run into town and find out if Nurse Zelda has a husband and what she bought. I'll be right behind you."

—8—

Maddie's Mercedes EQE 1000. Near Saratoga 2:45 PM. Maddie.

Maddie pulled off the road and stopped. "That snot." She could not believe Angie had lost them so easily, especially in a red Maserati Hydro-Quad.

Gretta giggled, "She's really good, isn't she?" then flipped open her scope. It took maybe five seconds to find her.

"Right back where she started," Maddie bitched, "in the parking lot of the Zink Crotch of Zeus?"

"The same."

"Should we go back, Grett?"

"No. Angie probably just wants some private time with Rex. Let's check the stores, then go on home."

— 9 —

Maserati Hydro-Quad. Near The Golden Arms. 2:50 PM. Angie.

Angie parked farther back in the lot this time so that Gretta's scope would think she had returned to Rex's room, then slipped out of the Maserati Hydro-Quad and into the passenger seat. She had brought black jeans, blue sneakers, and a black T-shirt and bra in her sports bag.

While she was finishing, a man left Rex's fire exit and walked down the hill toward The John Appleseed Cottage, probably staff but possibly not. He stopped and looked back up to the top of The Arms. He looked familiar.

Change of costume complete, Angie slipped along the back of The Golden Arms, into the woods, and toward the road. It took her less than five minutes to find the black BroncEV behind a veil of poplars.

Angie eased down to the BroncEV. Adonis was lying in the backseat, dozing.

"Dozing my butt, Kid," Mary Helen said. *"He can't open his eyes. At least one of them. Look at that shiner!"*

Green, yellow, and black, his eye resembled molded gouda.

Jimmu was sitting in the driver's seat, Fred in the front seat.

"Why is Jimmu holding his balls, Ange?" Mary Helen asked.

The barely audible radio was playing music by the Twisted Pair, Angie's favorite punk rock quartet. "Good evening, gentlemen. I see you did not heed my warning not to take Dale with you."

Adonis, Jimmu, and Fred nearly jumped out of their skins and looked at Angie in terror. All three now wore dark jeans and sneakers, as Angie had suggested when she asked them to watch The John Appleseed Cottage but to leave Dale locked in the car for any excursions.

Angie's blood raced. She felt like a teenager again, like Dale was doubtless feeling.

Jimmu grimaced and shifted in the seat as though sitting on worms. "When we went across the road to get a better look at The Appleseed Cottage as you wished, he insisted. We took him with us rather than have him try to follow us on his own. We really did keep him with us for his own safety."

"I understand." Angie enjoyed being magnanimous, especially where Dale was concerned. "Thank you. I saw you from Rex's suite in The Arms."

"Ya." Adonis gave Angie a silly grin. "We'll take care of him."

"Yes, I believe you will. And exactly where is he?" Angie asked.

Dale appeared from the woods, buckling his belt as if on cue. "Oh. Hi, Mom. I needed to evacuate."

"Does he mean he needed to take a shit, Kid?"

"Of course, it does. Dale's a gentleman. You should try it, Mary Helen."

"I would if you'd let me, Ange."

Angie walked over and met Dale before he reached the BroncEV. She grasped him firmly by his shoulders and looked him straight in the eye. "If you knowingly put yourself in harm's way, it shall be back to school for you, young man, with Fred or without him — no choice."

Dale looked down toward his belly button, as he always did when he was a little boy and Angie had caught him with his hand in the cookie jar, the worst thing he ever did. "I made them take me and threatened to follow them if they didn't. I was safe with Adonis, Jimmu, and Fred. They're even more mother-hens than you are, Mommy. It's just that I want to be part of things. I've never ever been part of anything important before."

"What makes you so sure this is important?"

"Because you're taking the risk of involving yourself without Uncle Rex."

Angie pulled in a sharp little breath. She hadn't anticipated him this time. "Dale?" He wanted to help his family and be part of what was happening.

"He's conning you, Ange."

"He doesn't know how. Good Lord! He wants to follow in my footsteps."

"But we actually are together, Dale, and you actually are part of helping Rex and I solve the case. Just the same, you are not to take risky chances. Understand?" She did not wait for an answer but pulled him close and hugged him. After a bit, they returned to the car, and Adonis, Jimmu, and Dale competed to tell Angie everything that had happened.

"I saw one of the gentlemen who broke into The John Appleseed Cottage in the lobby of the Putnam Hotel," Jimmu said.

"No crap," Mary Helen said. *"The wild bunch is getting useful, but Jimmu and Adonis look battered."*

"Of course, they do. Dale was with them."

Adonis glared at Jimmu.

Angie smiled. She knew that keeping Gretta's secrets and her secrets separate and hidden would flummox them.

"Ya," Adonis said, "we checked the names on your list like Ms. Gretta asked and then came here like you asked."

"Wait," Jimmu said. "Wait just a minute, Ms. Summers. You told us to look at The John Appleseed Cottage and, if possible, to find a way in, which we did. There's a door in back that I think either Fred or I could pick."

"A nose, too." Dale shrugged.

"Ms. Gretta wanted us to find the people on the lists," Jimmu continued. "We were supposed to locate but do nothing else, and Dale probably would have followed us. He's stronger and more able than anybody knows, even maybe you, Ms. Summers."

"Lists?" Mary Helen asked. *"Plural?"*

"Lists. Plural?" Angie may have just discovered what Gretta meant when she mentioned that she had already helped the investigation.

Jimmu glanced at Adonis's one good eye, then pulled out a neat manilla envelope full of papers from under the driver's seat vibrator cushion.

Angie dumped the contents part way out into her hand. On top were the materials for Maddie's unpublished exposé about The Snow Queens. Farther down were copies of the microfilm documents. She remembered showing the copies to Gretta and Maddie at East 64th Street before she puked up her Brandy Alexanders, and also remembered Maddie giving her the exposé material. She had even leafed through it. The copies of all these documents came from her East 64th Street copier — she could tell from the little smudge of White Out she kept meaning to clean off the glass. It all probably happened while she was escaping into a skunk-drunk. In the neat script, Adonis had written in the addresses of the drug thugs they found staying in Saratoga.

"The last page is not there," Jimmu said with a tiny nod.

"Thank you, Jim." Only Jimmu had seen the last page. It contained the plan for the ICE/FBI/NY State operation. He'd copied it for Angie at Spencer and Sons.

From the variety of addresses checked off and the names found, the boys had checked half the hotels in town and had located a third of the people on the list, as Gretta had doubtless requested.

Angie thought for a moment, then returned the documents to Adonis. "Do it the way Gretta told you to, but don't tell her I know that she has all this."

"How thoughtful, Ange. I wouldn't have bothered."

"I know."

In return for the document, Jimmu handed Angie a thumb drive. "It's all in here except the info we added today, even the last section. I think these lists came from Rex, Ms. Angie, but I'm unsure."

— 10 —

Saratoga, NY. The Golden Arms. 3:00 PM. Inspector Rex Caine.

Rex stood at the window and looked down across the road to the stone house. Zelda had run downstairs to check-in. So much of Rex's memory was missing now, but that awful feeling remained. Something somewhere had gone terribly wrong, something directly impacting his mission and some of the people around him. He couldn't ask questions, though. He would need to figure it out on his own.

Then there were the visitors who obviously wanted to involve themselves in his life, who perhaps were already involved. "Angie Summers. I slept with her once. She's special to me. And Gretta. And Maddie. And Mary Helen. Maybe I slept with all of them two at a time. After Zelda, I'd believe anything."

How he could come out of a coma one second and then hump the nurse the next also boggled him. He didn't sex-up in tenements and didn't gun-sodomize teen drugsters then toss them in single flips off buildings. Even his language was wrong. He never used four-letter words or anything resembling it. No cops did. He'd forgotten so much.

John Leech. The name popped again into his mind, like lightning up Rex's besainted butt. "Besainted butt?" Even his own words felt wrong—strange expressions, someone else's expressions. "The rain in Spain corrupts your brain."

Rex knew he needed to go over to that stone house—Appleseed Cottage, The John Appleseed Cottage—but he didn't know why. The Snow Queen lived in The John Appleseed Cottage. "No. The Snow Queens. The John Appleseed Cottage. Angie Summers. Mary Helen Mack. I wonder where old Leech is. And who the hell are The Candy Troops."

Chapter 23 - Therapy

Hey, the cool-whip fairy.

— 1 —

Saratoga, NY. Crumb House. Adonis's Room. 3:45 PM. Dale.

The problem was that it covered Adonis's whole face. Dale hadn't been able to find a good-looking steak down the block at Grimaldi's—the summer people always scarfed them up as fast as the cows grew them— so he bought a nice-looking five-pound pot roast, and now that sucker just about covered all of Adonis's face. Not that he seemed to mind much, lying here in his room, shirt off, arms stretched out, muscles twitching, trying to breathe through his meat.

The bath was running behind the closed door of the bathroom. For some reason, Dale, Fred, and Jimmu had decided to recover in Adonis's room, two doors from Aunt Gretta. They needed to get civil looking before Jimmu's birthday dinner.

Being the son of a mystery writer with flights of fancy into detectivehood was fun but disadvantageous in the doing-what-you're-not-supposed-to-and-getting-away-with-it department. Dale had yet to get away with that or anything really, except once, and he was not about to tell his mom about her. His mom's reaction to their sleuthing was weird, and having Gretta and Maddie sort of in on it was even weirder.

The bathtub was running because Jimmu wanted to take a bath and probably soak stuff. He'd shifted around funny on the seat while driving them back. Dale was truly awfully sorry that he accidentally hurt his friends but had said enough, if not too much, about it, so this time just asked, "Is there anything I can get you?"

Adonis lifted his meat and peered out from under it as if it were the brim of an accountant's eye shield. "You can get lost. No, I don't mean that, and you didn't mean to give me a black eye, but it hurts. I think I can still see, though."

"Please be nice, Adonis. He didn't mean it," Fred said.

"Can we still work together on the case?" Dale asked.

"Yah."

"Oh cow, I'm glad of that," Dale said.

"Yah, but carefully. Very, very carefully." Adonis dropped the roast back onto his face with a meaty slap. His eye had started to open some.

"I really am happy about that. Come on, Fred. Jimmu's your brother." Dale walked over to the bathroom and tapped lightly on the door.

"Who is it?"

"Dale and Fred," Fred said.

"Oh, Tinkerbell and friend," Jimmu answered.

"Can we come in?" Dale asked.

"Sure. Come on in, but prepare yourselves."

"We live in a boarding school." Dale opened the door, unsure whether he got the point across that he wasn't shy, so Jim shouldn't be.

Jimmu was sitting in the bathtub, and he was snow white. That was how much lather he'd spread all over himself.

"Hey, the cool-whip fairy," Fred said. "How are you doing, Big Brother?"

"Do you need a massage?" Dale put in, just to remain in the friendly conversation.

"Watch it, boys, and try not to be such ball-busters in the future. I don't have more than two of anything important except ribs, toes, and fingers."

"I really am sorry," Dale said sadly.

"Me too, Big Brother." Fred mock-wiped his eyes. Jimmu and Fred barbecued each other constantly but obviously loved each other as brothers.

"I am sorry," Dale repeated.

"Dale, you already said that. Down, boy," Jimmu commanded.

"I know, but I am truly awfully sorry." Dale went over and sat on the edge of the tub. "What are we going to tell my mom?"

"That while you were busily kneeing Adonis in the eye," Jimmu said, "you lost your balance and gonzoed my gonads."

"Come on, Jimmu, I feel rotten enough already." Dale really did.

"Not nearly as rotten as you could." Jimmu reached down through the bubbles to his crotch and felt around like he was trying to count. "Now that I think about it, it possibly runs in your family. While I was doing a favor for your mother, I became female, got my car shot, and lost Mrs. Lessix. Then I go out with you and attract a truly remarkable level of agony exactly where I would prefer not to experience it from anyone except—"

"Except whom?" Fred asked.

"You. We used to roughhouse, Fred. Big whoop." Jimmu then studied Dale and said with dark seriousness, "You don't own a pair of black net stockings, do you, Dale?"

"Why would I? And what are they, a bunch of holes tied together by string?"

A scream came from the bedroom!

Dale jumped up and ran. He vaguely heard a heavy thud behind him as he reached the bathroom door. In the bedroom, Aunt Maddie was standing by the bed, her mouth opened wider than Dale ever saw it before—pretty wide. He was also fairly sure that he saw the scrap of a smile on Adonis's face as he lay there, his head up off the pillow, his roast balanced on the upward-turned palm of his left hand. Aunt Maddie must have been the screamer since Dale's mom and Aunt Gretta were each grinning from the opposite sides of the bed.

"Christ on a stick, Adonis," Maddie gasped, "I thought someone ripped your face off."

"Oh, Maddie," Dale's mom said. "He's just bought himself a piece of meat for his black eye. It does work, you know. The enzymes do it."

"But that piece of meat is big enough to block the Hubble's eye," Maddie said, astonished.

Adonis offered, "Dale bought it for me."

"See," Dale's mom said. "I knew there was a logical explanation."

Aunt Gretta ignored all that. "The question is, exactly why and where did he get a black eye."

Dale thought of himself as a pragmatic young gentleman but was scared poopless that his maybe former friend wouldn't cover for him after what he'd done.

"I found the house." Adonis carefully laid the roast on his chest. "While Dale, Fred, and Jimmu went to see the horses across the road at The Golden Arms, I went to see The John Appleseed House firsthand, stood up on a bench to see in better, slipped, and hit my eye. When I met the boys to bring them home, Dale made me stop at Grimaldi's, so he could buy some meat for my eye."

"Well," Dale said, "they were out of steak." Which was true. Dale let out a long low silent breath of ecstatic relief. Apparently, you did get your prayers answered occasionally.

"That was kind of you, Dale," Aunt Gretta said. A tad of suspicion hung in her voice, as if she could tell that Adonis was lying through his meat.

Next, Dale wondered how Jimmu would explain being naked in Adonis's bathroom. It couldn't have been a horse that put him there. The Golden Arms didn't have a stable or a horse. Dale glanced over his left shoulder through the open bathroom door.

When he didn't see Jimmu in the bathroom, he took a few steps backward and, subtly as he could, took a good look. He again did not see Jimmu because Jimmu wasn't there, so Dale strolled forward a couple of steps to force himself to resist the temptation to search the toilet or something. It was a long thin bathroom with no nooks or crannies except the toilet. You couldn't hide much in there, not even a well-built but exceptionally skinny Jimmu.

"So don't keep us in suspense." Dale's mom had a way of getting straight to the point. "Where is this house."

"The John Appleseed Cottage is the partly stone house across from The Golden Arms," Adonis said.

"I knew it," Dale's mom said.

That got everybody's attention, especially Dale's, since she was the one who sent them there to begin with, though just to look, not trespass, maybe.

Dale's Mom knew exactly where The John Appleseed House was—Dale was there when Hooker told her—so what was going on? "I think I'll go shower before dinner," he said. Dale had his own mystery to solve. Where the heck was Jimmu? Dale knew that his mom would not ask much more about The John Appleseed Cottage—she already knew.

Gretta was curiously quiet. With all of her Saratoga roots, she must have known about The John. Adults could really be manipulative, especially Dale's adults.

"Okay, Dale. Shower for me, too," his mom said. "I don't think I'll have time."

Dale did not want to follow up on that, so he walked toward the door.

"And Dale?"

"Yes, Mom?" He moved faster toward the door, with Fred following close.

"Be sure to soak your knee. It's such a delicate joint."

"Yes, ma'am." In the hall, Dale and Fred stopped just out of sight to listen.

"I knew it," Angie muttered behind them.

"You knew what?" Aunt Maddie's voice responded.

"Well, a hunch. Looking down at The John Appleseed Cottage from The Golden Arms, it resembled the floorplan in the microfilm."

Was Dale's own mother covering for him too?

Aunt Gretta got into the act then. "And what about Dale's knee?"

"Well," Dale's mom said wisely. "Dale has weak knees. I noticed him limping slightly. After all that kneeling he did last semester, I think he may have developed Christian Housemaid Knees."

"Bullcrap," Aunt Maddie said. "You know something you're not telling us. Entirely and absolutely bullcrap!"

— 2 —

Saratoga, NY. Crumb House. Jimmu's room. 4:15 PM.
Dale.

"I'm glad to be out of there," Dale whispered as they started down the stairs. Crumb House had three full floors and a fat tower with a smaller fourth, Boss Crumb's Suite. Dale and Fred's room was on the first floor, two doors from Jimmu's. Adonis's room was on the second floor, close to Aunt Mirthretta. The place was huge and must have done a huge business as a lady-of-the-evening emporium.

Dale walked straight to Jimmu's room, figuring that Jimmu had somehow gotten down to it. Besides, it was Jimmu's door that stood open. "No Jimmu," Dale said.

"Let's try our room," Fred said.

They proceeded to their room at the end of the hall and immediately saw wet tracks on the floor coming from their window at the back of the house. Their shower was running full blast without them.

"You're kidding." Dale scrunched his right eye and part of his nose, and they walked over to the bathroom and looked in. There stood Jimmu in the shower, shower door open.

Jimmu watched the last lather disappear down the drain, turned off the shower, and pointed to the towel, which Dale obediently grabbed and tossed it to him. Jimmu carefully dried, then wrapped the towel around his waist, walked over, curled his arms around Dale and Fred, and they all walked down the hall to Jimmu's bedroom.

"Masters Dale and Frederick, do you have any idea of the difficulty of climbing down the outside of a noble old house in broad daylight, wearing only lather. Do you have any idea of the possible hazard of having one's backside spotted crawling down a trellis? I could have become known as the weirdest cat burglar in the history of crime. And do you know the hazard of trellis splinters in such a pursuit and from where I would need to extract them? The night streets of upper Manhattan are dangerous but are nothing compared to this. I'm going out of my mind, young gentlemen. I'm completely certain that I'm going out of my mind."

"So why did you do it?" Fred asked.

It seemed kind of dumb to Dale too. "Why couldn't you have wrapped a towel around yourself and come downstairs the regular way. My mom would have understood."

"Yeah," Fred said.

Jimmu turned his head on his long neck, opened his eyes as wide as their sockets would permit, and looked down at Dale and Fred in frantic disbelief. "Adonis has already needed to explain the half-steer on his black eye. How could I have explained a nearly neutered Asian American in the shower when you two and I were supposed to have been visiting The Golden Arms stable, which, by the way, does not exist. Visiting stables could make one want a shower but would not make one frantic to ease a gonadal catastrophe in which he dropped drawers and dove into the first shower he found, Adonis's! The entire triumvirate of publishing queens would be suspicious about that in ever so many ways."

"Well," Fred said, "maybe you got kicked by a passing horse and got so upset that you crapped your knickers and needed to jump into the nearest shower because you couldn't stand to be filthy and stink like a skunk in a celery field?"

Jimmu looked like he wanted to strangle them but only gave them a little extra squeeze, though a firm one that could lead to strangling.

Dale added, "Besides, the worst Mom would ever do to me is send me back to Tate for the rest of the summer, and maybe have me locked in my room with a guard, and possibly chain me to my bed for a year to subsist on buttered Italian bread and lemonade."

"Ditto, Aunt Mirthretta," Fred said, "but buttered bread and malted milks, because I'm too thin."

"So maybe I didn't want anyone to catch you two," Jimmu said. "You're both fun, like your mother is, Dale, and like Fred's and my volunteer aunt, Gretta Braun, as in Eva, is. Besides, Ms. Summers already knows, and I would bet the other two queens also know by now. I don't think they will say anything, though. If they don't admit they know, they don't need to do anything about it. It's a parent/guardian thing."

"I guess," Fred said, "but is your mom always so laid back, Dale? Even though I've been around her a bit, I don't feel like I know her. Don't misunderstand: I still love her and think she's a great writer with more blood, guts, sex, and wholesome American fun than all of Agatha Christie's novels together."

"And many of Steven King's," Dale said, "and, of course, H. P. Lovecraft's." He assumed an elocution stance in the middle of the bedroom, with his right hand holding onto his shirt like a tux lapel and recited: "We live on a placid island of ignorance in the midst of black seas of infinity, and it was not meant that we should voyage far."

"I'll buy you a horse," Jimmu said.

"Crap," Fred said. "I'll add a boat to that."

Chapter 24 - New York, New York

There's always the vomitorium.

—1—

Saratoga, NY. Crumb House. 7:00 PM. Dale.

"Come on, Jimmu, we'll be late for dinner." Dale was part of the surprise, a positive one this time. His job was to get Jimmu to the dining room on time.

They had all dressed for dinner, as Aunt Gretta preferred. It was time to be good for a while. Besides, this was a surprise party. The dining room was dark when they arrived, but when Jimmu stepped in, the light came on, and Aunts Gretta and Maddie, Dale's mom, Adonis, Dale, and Fred yelled, "Surprise!"

Jimmu acted astonished. "No one has ever given me a birthday party before."

The table was set for a king, or at least for a great Chinese immigrant who had just turned twenty, which was a big one in several ways. Jim was leaving his teens when Dale was just beginning to enjoy his. Gretta had loaded the table with Chinese food plus all the teen delights like hamburgers, fried shrimp, and buttery scallops with spicy Dijon sauce. It was a good sendoff from Jimmu's teen years to adulthood, even though teens became adults at fifteen now. And Jim's gift was a new BMW i9, his favorite car in the world.

At the end of the party, Aunt Maddie, Adonis, and Dale's mom headed to New York for some reason, while Dale, Fred, and Jimmu would use Jimmu's new BMW i9 to do a secret.

— 2 —

New York State Thruway. 11:30 PM. Maddie

"Are you going to tell me what this is about, Angie?"

"We have some unfinished business in New York." Angie sat on her side of the WatStretchEV and watched the cars coming from New York City on the Thruway. Thanks to Dale's lovely pot roast, Adonis was able to drive safely, although he did not look good above the neck.

"I appreciate the convoluted world of your mind, Angelica," Maddie said. "It's always an elucidating trip."

"If she wasn't, how did she tell us as much as she did?" Angie said.

"What?"

"But I don't know who she is or whether what she said was true."

Maddie leaned over and opened Gretta's limo fridge. "Yeah. Want some cheesecake?"

"No. I want to keep my mind clear. You go ahead."

"Okay." Maddie reached in, opened the crisper, pulled out a leaf of lettuce, and shoved the green into her mouth to psychologically counteract Jimmu's magnificent birthday dinner.

"Don't overdo it. You'll get fat, Mad."

"I'll watch that, Angie."

"If you don't, there's always the vomitorium."

"Don't be disgusting."

"When in Rome."

"Don't be disgusting, Angie. Just don't."

"The Romans did have a vomitorium. Maybe you have bulimia," Angie said.

"I don't puke. Gretta pukes from time to time, so maybe she has bulimia. Of course, if that were the case, she wouldn't be puking nearly enough and would be lots thinner." This discussion made Maddie want to puke.

"Be nice, Maddie. Gretta would puke more if she could. That's how she releases stress."

"That's not all she releases."

"Don't be disgusting."

"You started it," Maddie shot back.

"I never start it."

"So, why are we going to New York, Ange?"

"We're going to burgle."

"Why did Gretta stay back in Saratoga?"

"Dale is my son. I know him far better than he thinks. Gretta remained in Saratoga to watch the boys. They're up to something, and it's her house."

— 3 —

Jimmu's BMW i9. Near The Golden Arms. 11:45 PM. Dale.

Jimmu drove his birthday Beamer the last few feet without lights—pretty nervy. Of course, the moon was bright enough to drive by, but Dale still had internal kittens. He needed to work on that but could not quite convince himself that Jimmu could ease his brand-new BMW i9 into the woods without smashing, scratching, or worrying it a couple of hours after Aunt Gretta gave it to him for his twentieth birthday.

Once safely parked and hidden where they'd parked this afternoon, they turned to Fred, sound asleep in the back seat. Jimmu put a blanket over him, and Dale and Jimmu eased out of the car and walked back toward the road. The guys at Tate should see Dale now — they would never dweeb at him again. The lights of The Golden Arms twinkled through the trees.

Jimmu's hand squeezed Dale's left arm. "Now, be careful this time, Master Dale."

"I sure will."

Jimmu flew across the road and hopped the wall like a ballet dancer.

"Gosh, I wish I could do that." Dale drew a bead on the wall way over to the left of where Jimmu disappeared, took a deep breath, ran like a kid fleeing hell, sailed over the wall like a clumsy ballet dancer, and landed in the silver moonlight with his right foot right smack in Jimmu's crotch again — Jimmu had apparently moved the same direction to get out of Dale's way as Dale had moved to not hit Jimmu. They had canceled each other out.

Dale lay there on his side and looked at his foot. Then he looked at Jimmu's face in the moonlight, which hadn't made a sound. Jim was really tough. On top of that, when a cloud moved, Dale saw that he was grinning.

"Oh gosh, Jimmu," Dale whispered. He really hoped this would not end their friendship. "I'm really sorry."

"It's okay, so don't be sorry. I wore a hard cup. It's Adonis's, so it's a little large, but it worked. Come on. Follow me."

Dale exhaled a relief breath, took his foot off Jimmu's cup, and followed. They ran crouched along the wall to the back of The John, where they'd seen the two men break in. A piece of the moon shone down and lit the way, although not well enough that you could see a snake in time to not step on it. With Dale's luck, he'd kill the poor sucker... if it weren't wearing a cup.

Jimmu stoppedH and they looked over the wall to the back door but didn't see a thing. Of course, Dale didn't want to see anything, at least nothing that moved and carried a gun.

"Okay, Master Dale-boy, this is it."

"This is what?"

"This is where we break in, silly."

"The John?"

"Yes, The John. Come on." Jimmu skipped lightly over the wall and carefully headed for the back door.

Dale carefully climbed over behind him. When he landed, he crunched louder than Jimmu — you couldn't be good at this immediately.

When they finally stood on the back porch, Jimmu turned, put his arm around Dale, and squeezed him, which Dale appreciated. Then Jimmu tried the door. "Great," he whispered. "Those bozos left it open. I was afraid I'd have to pick it."

"Where did you learn to pick locks?"

"My roommate at Choate taught me."

"Oh. Jeez, that again. Lose the confabulation, Jim. I want to get to know the real you."

"No, you don't, but okay."

Jimmu carefully pushed the door open, and they went in. The house smelled of cedar, maybe the wood, maybe some kind of cedar-scented disinfectant. Suddenly the room glowed blue, and Dale nearly threw a freak. "Oh, crap." Then he realized that Jimmu just turned on a flashlight covered with a blue plastic filter of some kind.

"Sorry. I forgot to warn you."

"I almost puddled my Adidas."

"That's what you get for not wearing Nikes—you have no swoop. Now follow me. I want to make sure that all the drapes are closed. I think they were this afternoon, but I'd rather not receive a passing visit from the local constabulary, or anyone else."

Dale followed Jimmu into the house. When they found the living room and the front windows, they discovered the place clean and tidied, as if expecting guests. Heavy drapes covered every window.

Once sure that no one could see, Jimmu took the blue filter off his light, and they started exploring in more detail. The John Appleseed Cottage was a hunting lodge sort of a place with knotty pine walls, plank floors, brass fixtures, and lots of expensive-looking early-American stuff. Someone had set up a big table for about fifty in the meeting room.

"It looks like they're going to have a meeting, Jim."

"Who?"

"Whoever Adonis was checking out this afternoon. Oh crap!" Dale said.

"Why oh crap?"

"My mom's lists. There was more on it than the floorplan of this house." Dale vaguely realized that he was acting like a doof.

"Of course."

"I bet those guys were checking the place out for a meeting," Dale said.

"Sounds good. Keep going."

"They wanted to check the place out for safety because they were guarding big cheese criminals like Legs Diamond, Al Capone, Bugsy Siegel, Myer Lansky, Thomas Dewey, or Ma Barker. It's like the Appalachian meeting when all the familiars got together for a summit. We studied it in American History class. Fred helped me."

"That's Apalachin," Jimmu said. "It's a village close to Binghamton, and I think you mean the families, not familiars."

"Okay. Let's check out the rest of the place." Dale felt a little giddy, like he was really getting into this, maybe.

The house was enormous, named for a guy who went around dressed in a burlap bag and wearing a pot on his head. Still, some great houses were named after John Appleseed.

After they searched a few rooms, Jimmu, bold enough to talk out loud now, announced, "Let's try this one." He opened a door near the front of the house, probably another bedroom.

The reflection shattered and flew around the room when the light hit the mirror on the tall antique armoire. Jim's light hesitated, then focused on the bed.

Mrs. Lessix lay there, her dress up around her waist, naked on down, legs spread, face dead like the rest of her. Dale gagged. A pillow with streaks of red and yellow lay beside her head on the blue and white quilt, which would have looked as if it came off George and Martha's marriage bed if it hadn't been for the corpse.

"Oh, God," Dale whispered. "Oh, my God. Oh, my God. Oh, my—"

"Shh." Jimmu killed the light.

"Why shh now?" Dale whispered. "She's not going to hear us." Then he heard it too—breathing, faint, steady, and fast.

Jimmu pressed his fingertips on Dale's chest, easing him back toward the door, and Dale could hear their feet scraping the rug with stumbling I-want-to-panic terror. The breathing came from the armoire.

The door slammed open, and footsteps ran toward Dale.

"Jimmu!"

Jimmu snapped on his light and pointed it into the man's face before he and his light crashed to the floor but stayed lit. The man moved Dale out of the way and ran through the bedroom door and out of the house.

Everything went quiet except the flashlight rocking back and forth on the floor and Dale's and Jimmu's breathing.

"Jimmu? Are you okay?"

"I think he hit my chest with a sledgehammer, but it was probably his hand. I think I'm okay. Are you okay, Dale?"

"Yeah. He kind of picked me up and moved me." But Dale was not okay at all. In that awful flash of light, he recognized the rapist. "I saw his face."

"I recognized him too," Jim said.

DAY SEVEN

Chapter 25 - Housebreaking

This was not a Huckleberry Finn adventure.

– 1 –

New York City. Washington Heights. 1:00 AM. Maddie.

Maddie stood in the hall, wondering what the hell they were doing, and tried to shield Angie from the view of whoever might pass by at one in the morning. Even here in New York, somebody likely considered breaking-in rude. Angie had probably learned to pick from Rex.

The lock clicked. "There," Angie whispered.

"Oh crap," Maddie whispered back, and the door swung open. "Oh, crap." A slightly musty smell drifted down the dark hall to merge with the fried fish aroma.

Angie pulled a little plastic flashlight from her pocket and shined it into the apartment. The last two times they'd done this, they found dead bodies.

"Come on, Maddie."

"Let's not use real names, at least not mine."

"Come on, Medea," Angie corrected.

"Thanks, Sherlock."

Angie knew she was a famous novelist but probably also knew she would need to keep her publishing friends happy if she wanted to stay that way. That was as it should be.

Inside the condo, Angie closed and locked the door behind them, searched the brown tile floor with her flash, found a small oriental throw rug, bunched it, and wedged it against the crack at the bottom of the hall door. Then dear old friend Angie casually snapped on the entrance hall light as if this were in her own flat, and said, "No one will see," as though she did this every day, possibly even for a living. "I don't think that anyone would have anyway, but the rug will see to it."

"Rex taught you?"

"Yes, Rex, my lover and recovering tutor."

"Sometimes," Maddie pontificated, "I think the line between good guys and bad guys is exceptionally thin. They have many of the same talents."

A funny look bathed Angie's otherwise beautiful Orphan Annie countenance — a serious look. "Rex has been talking about that frequently in the past few months. Something was bothering him."

"Belmont was way more than a shooting, wasn't it, Ange?" So much for using false names.

"Yes. It was a starting gun."

Angie moved around the room slowly, carefully, thoroughly, and systematically, as though she had been breaking and entering for most of her life. All she needed was a rope and a pair of sneakers, and she would be a great cat burglar.

"Angie, what the hell are you doing." The apartment living room sported one of those Italian marble fireplaces that seemed to have invaded New York City in past history, especially here in Washington Heights.

Angie stood before the mantle and carefully looked at each photo in the forest of frames.

Maddie recognized Slag Lessix. His picture was on the front of the PostNews when cops arrested him for killing a druggie. Judging by the mantle, Slag really liked getting his picture taken. He apparently received many awards, and his medals hung from the wall above the mantle. The pictures documented award ceremonies, but some were personal, alone or with other people, mostly with his wife, who was not the Mrs. Lessix they'd helped.

Using a wadded latex glove, Angie held his wedding picture up for Maddie. "I thought so. Our Mrs. Lessix is not the real Mrs. Lessix."

"But she had a driver's license. I saw it. And it was her picture and this address."

"That is a problem, and here is another one." Ange held another picture up for Maddie.

"Oh, my Christ. We stole Mrs. Lessix's maid."

$$-2-$$

Saratoga, NY. Crumb House. Jimmu's Room. 1:05 AM. Dale.

An hour or so ago, Jimmu, Fred, and Dale had climbed the trellis to his and Fred's room, which, thank God, contained two double beds. Dale felt safer with Jimmu in the other bed and warmer because he and Fred cuddled together in his.

Not that Dale had gone to sleep, and judging from the breathing in the other bed, Jimmu lay awake too.

Fred was dead to the world next to Dale. He hadn't awakened in the car until they woke him and made him climb the trellis to get into Crumb House. "Jimmu?"

Nothing.

"Jimmu?"

Nothing.

"Jimmu, I know you're awake."

"Is Avon calling?"

"Dale Summers is calling."

"I'm sorry. I just don't care for the ruby blush, dear."

"Thanks for staying over with us," Dale said.

"Never fear—your secret's safe with me, sweets," Jimmu replied.

"What secret? Oh, never mind. Jimmu?"

"Yes, Dale?"

"I'm scared. Multiple bodies connected to Mom, a comatose detective, hoods, probable secret meetings, trespasses, maybe a rape unless someone was looking for gold in a weird place, mysterious maps, my mom and Aunt Maddie dropping everything and going to New York, and last but painfully not least, three broken balls, one of them an eye. All things considered, this was not a Huckleberry Finn adventure."

"It was a wonderful day in our neighborhood, and some of Huck's were worse."

"Jimmu! Will you please get serious?"

"Dale?" Jimmu's voice did a one-hundred-eighty-degree turn into a concerned big brother tone. "I'm scared too, and Aunt Gretta would kill me or toss me back out on the street if she knew what I'd gotten myself into, much less with you and Freddy."

"But that's not what's keeping us both awake, is it?"

"No."

"We're worried about the same thing, aren't we?"

"You betcha. I recognized him too. When we visited Inspector Rex, I suspected he might be regaining consciousness, but I didn't think he could get up and hang out."

"He was going to be my dad."

"Still will be, maybe."

"But he—"

"He killed and possibly raped Mrs. Lessix?"

"Yeah. My Rex wasn't like that. He would never have done that and would have busted anybody who did. He even spanked me once when I was eight and disrespected my mother." Dale sounded self-righteous and naive even to himself this time.

"You were in the room with her, weren't you?" Jimmu asked.

"Yes."

"Did you rape and murder her?"

"Of course not."

"So maybe he, like you, found her that way. He hid when he heard us coming so as not to blow his coma cover."

"I guess. Maybe."

"Maybe." But Jimmu sounded like maybe he hadn't quite convinced himself.

"Jimmu?"

"Yes."

"Promise me that you won't tell anybody just yet?"

"Okay, not just yet."

— 3 —

New York City. Central Park South. Maddie's Condo. 1:45 AM. Maddie.

Maddie put Adonis in the guest room, although God knew she could have found a better place for him. She and Angie collapsed into the king as they always had for sleepovers and their great kitty adventure with Chuck.

Angie sat propped up on the other side of the bed, calmly sipping Benedictine, reading Laurence Sanders's *First Deadly Sin,* and probably waiting for Maddie to stop shaking long enough to tolerate turning the frigging light out.

"God, Ange, you look so sophisticated for a kewpie doll, not to mention calm, cool, and infuriatingly unruffled."

Angie giggled. "If they ever made lower middle-aged Kewpies, I suppose that I would have qualified. I never realized what a really good writer Larry was. And Benedictine makes him even greater. You should try it. He wrote *Days of Our Lives*, too."

"I'd rather stay thin and shaking."

"Do you know Mrs. Senna?"

"Paul Michael Senna's dearly beloved, Vera-Lamar? Yes. When someone killed him, he left the poor dear bereft with five kids, a silver hairbrush, three billion dollars, and uncounted properties in New York, including Michael's European, our favorite eating place."

"Yes, her," Angie said evenly while she continued sipping and reading so placidly that you would have sworn she was making cream of kiwi soup.

"We've met socially," Maddie said, puckering her lips. "She's gooey, sweet, and not nearly aggressive enough to have married PMS. I have never understood how she survived. Of course, she did have five children, all out in the world now except for two, and she does have billions. I doubt that she's exactly suffering."

"Did she know that you slept with her husband?"

"Christ, I hope not. That could possibly rile even sweet little Vera, who, I suspect, has a stone heart and brass bowels lurking beneath her saccharine image. I do not habitually send wives a telegram when I sleep with their husbands. It's not ethical—at least, it isn't if I do not want their husbands, and I never have. I got to the top on my back, which is to say on my appearance, brain, and personal receptors."

"Were the Sennas happily married?"

"With five children, I doubt they found the time to be unhappily married. He never mentioned her to me, and I hope to God he never mentioned me to her. Given his womanizing, I doubt that my face stuck out in the crowd. Incidentally, I hear he also swung on the backside of the pendulum. Apart from frilly frauleins, he liked weightlifters, and teen boys and girls on the cusp."

"Who do you think killed him?"

"It could have been anybody. That behavior did not go over when he did it or ever. Half the world harbored motives. Possibly his wife. Why? Have you decided that dear old PMS has something to do with this apart from being the owner of everything and the screwer of most, one way or another?"

"Yes. There are too many layers of bad here not to suspect everybody involved. This is more a five-thousand-piece puzzle than a five-hundred. Do you think Mrs. PMS would see us?"

"Vera-Lamar? Joycie? Possibly. I have not paid my respects yet, and she will remember me from our social intercourse. I am the head of an international magazine that she has publicly expressed devotion to, and you are a famous and popular writer, though I suspect that Joycie is not heavily into books. She probably likes nasal books, though—if she can put it up her nose, she will be satisfied. She has certainly read no books on birth control. If she doesn't want to see us, I could always tell her I'm one of PMS's other women."

"Good. We're on for tomorrow morning at John F. Kennedy International Airport. We can see Mrs. Senna afterward."

And damned if Ange did not reach over and turn the light off, leaving Maddie staring into the darkness of her own bedroom and wishing that she had put Adonis in here instead of her best friend.

"Oh, Christ," Maddie said, "I really am losing it now. I can feel it all flushing."

"What?"

"Nothing."

Chapter 26 - Pssst

Do it like a bull.

—1—

New York City. Central Park South. 6:00 AM. Maddie.

"Pssst." Then again. "Pssst."

"Is that you pssting, Angie?" Maddie could not bear the thought of opening her eyes so soon after closing them. At least, it felt soon. "Could you really be psssting me after I have slept for only fifteen minutes?"

"Silly, it's 6:00 AM. Rise and shine."

Maddie reluctantly threw the blanket back to wherever and her feet for the floor and did not miss this time. "And I do not want to know what you're talking about, Angelica."

"Don't be silly. We need to get to Kennedy Airport. We have a plane to meet. Two-and-two has been four from the beginning. I'm embarrassed that I did not put them together earlier because they are both on the list. I did last night, though. Come along. I'm going to need you. I have already gotten Adonis up."

"Oh, crap."

—2—

Saratoga, NY. Crumb House. Dale and Fred's Room. 6:05 AM. Dale.

Dale stared at the small square clock by the bed and then at the big round sun ball staring him in the face. The sun brought reality, and Dale wanted no part of it. He'd stumbled stupidly onto a mystery that made anything his mom came up with shrink to the level of finding your underwear under the bed. His mom's books were ideas and fantasies, not nearly as hurtful as having your intended father morph into a murderer, rapist, and fake.

The kids at Tate all read his mom's books, although sometimes only for the spicy parts. Sometimes, of course, they read them for fodder to crucify Dale. He had even slugged Larry Flag, when he wondered if Mary Helen might be Dale's mom and Stud, his father.

Fred had tried to talk him out of slugging kids for insulting Mary Helen, but as good as Fred was at talking Dale in and out of things, he—

"That's it!" Dale said. "Mom arranged the whole thing."

— 3 —

New York. Kennedy Airport. 8:00 AM. Maddie.

Maddie watched Angie study the stream of people coming down the ramp from Flight 286.

"There she is, Maddie," Ange said in her best MHM hoarse whisper.

This Mrs. Lessix looked just like her picture on the mantel.

— 4 —

Saratoga, NY. Crumb House. Fred's Room. 8:15 AM. Dale.

Dale grabbed Fred's sleeping arm and violently shook it, suggesting they should wake up.

Fred stood four feet two inches, naked on a brick, which was what the guys put him on to get him onto the track team. He was also the number one Tate plotter and manipulator. Dale was the official measurer and chose to ignore the brick to let Fireball Fred be last to the finish line. He wanted to be part of everything, regardless of his height, body mass, social status, or brain.

Of course, being best friends and roommates with Fred, Dale also saw the depressed-over-being-a-shrimp side of him. They leaned on each other, and it helped. Jimmu, like Fred, showed great empathy, especially where his brother, Freddy, was concerned, and undoubtedly knew the truth about much that he would never discuss.

"Fred?"

No answer. You couldn't even see the kid breathe, which he was doing because if he weren't, he'd be dead.

"Fred, wake up, will you."

Fred groaned. He slept very soundly and always groaned when he woke. Finally, he eased the sheet down to the tip of his little pointed nose and looked up at Dale with so much disbelief in his sleepy eyes that he probably thought he'd died and manipulated heaven.

He hadn't, of course. "Yeah, it's me, Fred."

"I'm Dale. I need you."

"For what, a footstool?" Like his nose, Fred's ears were a little bit pointy. When you figured in his eyebrows and eyes that went up a little on the outside ends, you could easily have mistaken him for a shrunken Mr. Spock, except that he was 100 percent Chinese. Same for Jimmu. Fred's clear complexion, unlike his lower parts, had not even sprouted peach-fuzz yet, but was he ever smart, which probably didn't require sprouting.

"I just need you, that's all."

Fred squinted his left eye all the way closed and lifted the corner of his left nostril. "So, what if I don't want to be needed?"

"I still need you."

"You want my body?"

"Of course not."

"Yeah. Nobody does. Not even me. Besides, you wouldn't fit in my body, not with your fat ass." Fred sat up and let the sheet fall off his skinny chest—you could count his ribs from twenty feet away. "You know, Summers, I'm beginning to feel really humiliated, crappy, and close to an anxiety-depressive syndrome over people wanting me only for my brain and never for my body, except for a few girl pervs who love my undersized but maturing mini-me. Speaking of which, I need to piss."

He threw the sheet back, hopped out of bed, and trotted to the bathroom nude. The loud burble-splatter had started when he looked back over his shoulder and asked, "What is it this time: your sex life, family problems, calculus classes, mother, Aunts, or Mary Helen Mack?" He finished pissing, laced his fingers behind his head, and shook his bottom back and forth. "By the way, how is your father-in-waiting?"

"I think he may be a murderer and rapist, but I still love him and hope I'm wrong."

Fred turned around and walked back to Dale. "Say that again, Dale. What's going on?"

"I think he may be a murderer. You were asleep. Jimmu and I did it on our own."

"I doubt you meant that the way it sounded, but whatever. Just the frigging same, I'll put on underwear." He often didn't wear any. Outside, Fred was mostly show, of course, but it was not his outside parts that made the two of them friends, it was his brain and apparent past experiences, made up or not. "Now, what's really going on?"

"If you say that again," Dale said, "I'm gonna kick you right where it hurts. And I've had practice."

"Okay, I won't say it again, but I still need your help understanding what I missed while I was zonked out in the back of Jim's new Beamer last night."

"Let's take a walk before breakfast. It looks nice out." Dale really needed some fresh air.

– 5 –

New York City. Triboro Bridge. 8:45 AM. Maddie.

Maddie had experienced much that was rare and wonderful lately, but nothing that matched trailing Mrs. Lessix through the Kennedy Airport crowd and then sitting in the back seat of Gretta's WatStretchEV while they trailed her tan EscaladeLectro.

Angie could not fathom how so many EscaladeLectros could travel between Kennedy Airport and Manhattan and not mate.

"How did you know about her arriving today, Angie?" Maddie asked.

"Her wall pad. I also confirmed Mrs. Blanche Lessix's travel schedules."

"Where was she?"

"Fort Lauderdale. She left the day before Rex shot her husband, returned for the cremation and burial, and then raced straight back to the Fort. She planned from the beginning to come back today."

"Why did – "

"I don't have a clue," Angie said.

"Would you believe me if I said I don't believe you?"

"Yes."

— 6 —

Saratoga, NY. The Golden Arms. 8:49 AM. Dale.

Dale felt it in his bones even before they got there. "Jimmu, are we going where I think we're going?"

"Well, the place does have open visiting hours, which is marvelous," Jim said. "That means you can visit anytime."

"Where?" Fred looked suspicious. Back in bed, he'd probably figured out right away that Dale wanted him for more than a shoulder to cry on.

"We're going to see Uncle Rex, aren't we," Dale said, "at The Armpit of Salvation."

"Definitely," Jimmu affirmed.

"Good. I want to," Dale said, "but I'm possibly almost certain that maybe I can't face it quite yet."

"Well, you're going to," Jim said firmly. "Fred and I will provide support, not to mention protection."

"Uh oh," Fred said. Sometimes, he turned his mouth off, sat back, took it all in, and didn't reassure.

"Jimmu says I need your support and protection, Fred," Dale said just to remind him.

"Uh oh."

"You might as well know, Fred," Jimmu said, "that Uncle Rex may be faking. Jim and I saw him across the road with a raped dead body."

"Uh oh," Fred said.

***

At the front desk of The Golden Arms, Jimmu said, "We're here to visit Inspector Caine."

The nurse looked at Jimmu, Dale, and Fred like she had blown a fuse.

Dale figured they must be a weird-looking trio: a tallish Asian near-man with smart, bright eyes, a skinny Asian short person with the Devil in his, and Dale, who looked like, well, Dale.

The nurse was still sitting there with her mouth open, possibly aghast at the intrusion.

"Visiting hours are open, are they not, madam?" Jimmu turned on his haughty side.

"Yes," the nurse said. She generated a faint whiff of garlic when she spoke. She clearly was not a vampire. "Are you relatives?"

"No, ma'am," Jimmu said, "I'm unfortunately not. I work for Angelica Summers, the significant other of the injured Inspector Caine. This is Ms. Summers's son Master Dale Summers, and my little brother, Fredikins."

Dawn hit: "Oh, of course. You were here before, weren't you, Dale, with your mother, Ms. Summers herself! She signed my copy of *Withered Bodies, Righteous Souls*. I treasure it so."

"Yes, ma'am, I was here, and if you have any of my mother's other books, I'll be glad to get them signed for you. I attend Tate, right next door." Dale learned from Fred and Jimmu how to turn his baby-bottom fresh-and-clean look into super-innocence and precious cooperation. "Fredikins is my best friend. Could we please be allowed to visit my Uncle Rex, miss? I think he's going to be my father after he recovers."

"Yes, of course, you can, dear," the nurse gushed. Being the son of a famous writer came with perks. "You can show your friends the way. I'll call ahead so that no one stops you." She gushed so much that when Dale started off toward the elevator, both Jimmu and Fred stood there paralyzed, probably to see if anything needed mopping up.

"Come along, Fredikins and Jimmy," Dale said, "and I'll share the way with you." Someday, he planned to say "fuck" and shock the dickens out of the whole darn world, but for now, he just politely led the way.

Jimmu, whom Dale didn't know worked for his mom, followed, and Fred brought up the rear. The three of them resembled a dysfunctional family of mismatched but proud partridges.

On the fourth floor, the building top, the elevator door opened, and they stepped out in front of a high desk with nurse types clustered around a tall willowy lady with a flat chest and blonde hair, listening to her read off a clipboard.

A grungy nurse-type in a Hawaiian top made a face and, loud enough for Detroit to hear, said, "Milk of Magnesia? What do you mean, Agatha? Mabel shits like a bull."

Agatha stopped reading, looked horrified and opened her mouth to say something, then spotted Dale and his friends standing there. "Oh yes. You must be Ms. Summers's son and friends."

"Yes, ma'am." Dale wondered if nurses were supposed to say, 'Shits like a bull?'

"Do you know your way?"

"Yes, ma'am."

"Well then, gentlemen," Agatha commanded, "forward march."

And they did. Agatha was the kind of nurse Dale would want to say no to. She was the kind of nurse even the Joint Chiefs of Staff would not say no to.

When they were halfway down the hall, Fred muttered, "The next time I take a dump, I'm going to do it like a bull."

"How is that?" Jimmu asked under his breath.

"Big and hairy with clouds of steam on a clear fall morning," Fred said under his voice. He had style.

"Why fall?" Dale asked.

"It's the best time for the dewpoint to let you see steam." Fred had lots of style.

An old man sat in his wheelchair in the doorway, playing with himself, apparently for the edification of visitors. Dale always thought they shriveled when you got old.

"Thataway to go," Fred whispered.

"You ought to know," Dale whispered back.

Jimmu chuckled and rolled his eyes like he didn't know these two junior jerkwads.

When they got to the end of the corridor, they hung a left and, in no time, stood outside Suite P7, Uncle Rex's.

Dale knocked. Then waited. Then knocked again. Then realized that Jimmu and Fred were both staring at his head.

"If he's pretending to be in a coma," Fred started.

"He's not going to answer the door," Jimmu finished.

"He has a private-duty nurse," Dale informed them, but I guess it'll be okay if we open the door."

Dale reached out, pushed the handle down, and the door drifted open. He prayed that Uncle Rex would be in bed in a coma. Rex was there in bed, eyes closed, not moving but breathing. A sheet covered him up to about six inches below his neck. Fred closed the door, and they walked over to the bed, Dale and Fred on one side, Jimmu on the other, staring down, as they probably would at the cherished remains of a loved one.

Uncle Rex mumbled some about rats, then went quiet.

Dale had heard him do that even before he got hurt. After a time, Jimmu wandered away and stared out the front window to the right of Uncle Rex's bed. Fred wandered down the little hall on his right. Dale joined Jimmu at the patio doors to see what he was looking at. Over by The John, one man slammed the back of a panel truck closed, while another locked the shed in back. The panel truck pulled out and disappeared. Dale looked up at Jimmu, who frowned and looked around. Fred joined them.

Dale nodded. "I think we better go, guys."

Jimmu nodded, then bent over by the side of the bed for a moment to tie his shoe. He straightened and started for the door, but not before he threw a worried sideways glance that probably meant something, considering that Jimmu was wearing loafers.

Dale suddenly got a hot flash, as though everything was moving faster. He motioned for his friends to leave.

Fred and Jimmu, really Wang Lei Lóng and Liu Wei Lóng, quietly disappeared. At the bed, Dale took Rex's hand.

"Rats," Rex muttered. "Rats. Christmas rats."

"I know you're faking, Dad," Dale said quietly. "I realize that you must have good reasons for doing what you're doing, but whatever is going on, please come back to us. Mom and I need you, and I'm afraid that she will get herself killed trying to investigate this affair on her own."

Rex opened his eyes, turned his head, and grabbed Dale's wrist so tight it hurt. "She mustn't, and who was the little guy with you, Dale?" He sounded frantic.

Chapter 27 - C-15

He didn't scream in pain, of course.

−1−

New York City. Washington Heights. 10:00 AM. Maddie.

In Gretta's Adonis-driven WatStretchEV, Maddie and Angie followed Mrs. Lessix to where? CIA headquarters? A sinister tavern frequented by sinister middle easterners who wanted to do exotic things to your sister? Hell no! They followed her home to Washington Heights.

Full circle and a half.

In New York, Maddie had met a stiff on a toilet. In East 64th Street, she read Angie's research and shared her own for a dangerous and unpublished exposé. In Saratoga, Mad met a lying maid who had now vanished. Now, back in New York, she had helped Angie break into an apartment, then trail a rich-looking broad named Lessix, the real wife of Slag Lessix, from Kennedy Airport back to the apartment they violated to begin with.

"What the hell did we just prove, Angie?"

"Shhh." Angie was watching two men coming out of the building where Mrs. Lessix lived. One was carrying a suitcase remarkably like the one Mrs. Lessix carried off the plane.

Adonis was busily snapping pictures.

The men got into a blue Chevrolet Matisse, and off they went.

"Shouldn't we follow them, Ange?"

"No. They are just returning to Saratoga. We need to see Mrs. Senna."

"We really need to do that, do we," Maddie said.

"Yes, we do. Central Park South, Adonis," she directed to the driver's seat.

"And how do you know where these two bozos are going," Maddie asked.

"They rented the car from a local Saratoga place. I recognized the tag on the windshield. Soooooo, they need to return it there. They probably just came to pick up the package that Ms. Lessix brought from Florida."

"Sometimes you're a trip, Angelica." Maddie meant that.

"And they also knew about Mrs. Lessix's trip because they knew just when to arrive to make the pickup and spend the least time waiting."

"And on top of all that," Adonis said, "I saw those two break into The John Appleseed Cottage. I think they are staying at the Putnam in Saratoga. They have guns."

"Thank you, Adonis. And I really am sorry about your eye," Angie said.

"It wasn't your fault, ma'am. Your son is a good kid despite what he thinks, does, and says."

"It was more my fault than yours, Adonis. I know my son."

"You're not angry that I took him to The John Appleseed Cottage?" Adonis returned.

"I'm sure that in his own quiet little way, he would have allowed nothing else."

"Oh, my God." Maddie had never noticed before. "It runs in the family."

— 2 —

Saratoga, NY. The John. 10:15 AM. Dale.

When they left The Golden Arms with Dale shaking in his socks, Jimmu drove to their regular spot in the woods not far away — they would owe rent soon. They watched The John for signs of life for a few minutes, then crept to the road. For Dale, it was time for sneaking without screwing up.

Fred wanted to see the dead body.

Jim wanted to see if it was still here.

"You need to move fast when we cross," Dale whispered to Fred, as though he hadn't done it before and far better than Dale.

"Thanks for sharing," Fred said. "I would never have guessed that breaking into a house in the middle of an open lawn at 10:00 AM couldn't be done in slow motion."

Jimmu sniggered.

They all got themselves arranged along the road, ready for the dash.

Jimmu whispered, "You go first, Master Dale. And nothing above a whisper."

It didn't take a genius to figure out why Jim and Fred wanted Dale to go first. Occasionally, he experienced a few clumsy moments, so he crouched, hoisted heinie, ran like the Devil, cleared the wall like a pro, and landed with his thigh on a really hard, hard, pointed rock. He didn't scream in pain, of course. Tate kids never screamed in pain, not even the girls. Dale was lying on his back, leg up in the air, massaging his thigh, when Jimmu came sailing over the wall and barely missed him. Fred followed about ten feet to the right of both of them.

"We made it," Dale whispered.

Jimmu looked at Fred, and they both looked at Dale's leg sticking up in his hands. Jimmu reached down into his pants, probably to adjust his cup, before he whispered, "Are you okay, Master Dale?"

"It feels like a little bruise. Anybody wanta kiss it?"

Jimmu and Fred looked again and together said, "Not now."

Jim added, "We had better get into the house before someone sees us. Daytime is dangerous."

They all scrambled along the walls to the back of the house and found the back door still unlocked. The bedroom door where Mrs. Lessix lay dead sat open too, except that she didn't anymore. Dale, Jimmu, and Fred stared at the perfectly made bed.

"You guys are putting me on," Fred said.

"Where did she go?" Jimmu asked.

"Maybe she was late for an appointment?" Fred sounded actually pissed. "I thought we were looking for a dead body."

"We were." Jimmu looked more worried than pissed. "I think we lost it. Dale, look out the living room window so no one surprises us. Fred, you keep your eyes out back. I want to poke around." He headed straight for the armoire.

Fred stationed himself at the back door while Dale sat on the floor by one of the front windows and pushed the drapes open a crack to see out, especially to see the road and driveways. A few cars moseyed by now and then. Most turned in to The Golden Arms. There wasn't much traffic on this road. Dale stared up at the top floor of The Arms. It was too far away to see faces, but he saw someone standing in Uncle Rex's room, looking down. If he had binoculars, Dale could tell if it was Rex, someone else, or just a couple of Mercy Girls looking down from between their candy stripes. He had really already figured out that the tall one was Uncle Rex.

When they had talked, Uncle Rex admitted that he should be able to remember more about Dale but couldn't quite. They did clear up some junk together, and Dale promised to keep Rex's coma act a secret. Rex had promised that he hadn't murdered anybody. Dale half-trusted him again but accepted that his head might still be short-circuiting.

"Let's go," Jimmu said quietly beside him.

Dale jumped. "I think Uncle Rex is staring down at us." He sounded lost even to himself.

"Just a sec, Master Dale." Jimmu left for a moment, then returned and squatted. He was carrying a set of binoculars. He carefully pushed the drapes back, pointed the binocs up at The Golden Arms for more than a second, then handed them and a worried look to Dale.

Dale studied Jimmu's face for a second, then looked. Sure enough, Uncle Rex was standing at the window with a second figure, and they were staring at The John. Dale handed the binoculars back to Jimmu. "Let's get out of here."

"Agreed," Jim said. "You okay, Dale?"

"I'm okay, but let's get out of here."

Jimmu returned the binoculars to the bedroom. He and Dale collected Fred at the back door and slipped out. "Just a sec," Jimmu whispered. He ran to the corner of the house, with Dale and Fred at his heels, picked one of the blue roses climbing up the trellis, then quickly ran to the storage shed behind the house. A Superlock secured the place. Jimmu pulled his keys out. He'd filed two Superlock keys down until only the tips remained.

He fiddled with the lock and finally opened it, then the door. They all stared soundlessly at twenty or so small boxes labeled "C-15," and five labeled "C-15 Detonator Packs."

"Oh, my God," Fred whispered. "That's—"

"Plastic Explosives and detonator packs," Jimmu said. "C-15, the big brother of C-4."

"What is whoever going to do?" Fred asked.

"Yeah." Dale didn't know how but knew that Uncle Rex was involved. What he really wondered about was how they had come to see a dead body but found a shed full of boom-booms. He wondered about Jimmu, too, who was beginning to act like he was investigating and reporting back to someone.

— 3 —

New York City. PMS's Penthouse. 10:50 AM. Angie.

"Hold on, I have to collect myself, Ange." Standing before Paul Michael Senna's building, Maddie looked slightly pale.

"Don't worry, Maddie, it will go okay." Angie let the high facade of the building lift her gaze until her neck couldn't go further. Since success had landed on her head, full-blown and full of excitement, she rarely paid much attention to fancy, elegant, or grand — that was all a pretense, and you could buy it. The Central Park South building beside Maddie's made her want to gag. The ostentatious fake marble and gold looked like the Jolly Green Giant had defecated on it in shades of brown and yellow. Obviously, Paul Michael Senna had redone the entire building, and no one had ever accused him of committing good taste.

"*You're nuts*," Mary Helen said.

"No, I'm not, Mary Helen. Looking at a building can tell you much about the owner."

"So, you think that pile of crap PMS was just being transparent when he refurbished this place?"

"Yes, Mary Helen. It does, though, look like a mastodon with diarrhea let loose on it."

"That it does, Ange."

"I guess I'm ready," Maddie said after she'd gone even paler.

"Forward march, then." Angie led the way, so they would eventually get there.

Of course, they only got about ten feet until the doorman stopped them. You obviously did not get into this building unless the doorman announced you. When the doorman reached up for the house phone, Angie noticed the bulge.

"That ain't a goiter, Ange," Mary Helen commented.

"Heat," Angie answered.

"How quaint."

Armed doormen had become common in Manhattan. This one did seem special, a refined kind of thug.

"Big bastard, isn't he, Ange," Mary Helen said.

It took the doorman only a moment to verify that Mrs. Senna expected them. That seemed to surprise him. "Last elevator on the right, ma'ams." He held the door open for them.

They walked into the main lobby, which was, like the facade, gauche beyond redemption. They followed a regal brown with gold specs carpet to the gold elevator. PMS loved gold.

"Private elevator," Angie said.

"Of course, he has a private elevator." Maddie punched the penthouse button without looking. Evidently, she had ridden up here before. "He owns the place."

The elevator hummed. The ghastly brown and gold wallpaper maintained the fecal motif as Angie whisked up nineteen floors to Senna's three-floor penthouse.

"*Sherlock Holmes*," Mary Helen said.

"*Sherlock Holmes? What are you talking about?*"

"*I'm talking about Sherlock Holmes. He knew nothing about astronomy because he didn't want to clutter his mind with something he seldom used. He maintained that the human mind possessed only so much storage space.*"

"*So? Oh, you mean that even though I have visited here before, I didn't bother to remember anything about this dreary building because I possessed no reason to. Well, now I have a reason.*"

"*You have crap.*"

"*Have it your way.*"

"Are you okay, Maddie?" Angie asked. She had not anticipated Maddie's stoned reaction to this place.

"I guess," Maddie said. "Going to meet one of the other women in my love life has always thrown me. I guess I'm just not that forward."

"*Really?*" Mary Helen said.

"I understand, Mad. And just for clarity, you are the other woman."

The elevator doors opened onto a windowless foyer lit by a clear, domed skylight roughly the size of a school bus.

"They must wash that every day, Mad. It really sparkles. I wonder if that's where the killer got in."

"How could anybody get in through that, Ange? Bent skylights don't open." Maddie sometimes lost her sense of humor.

"And sometimes they do." Angie walked to the carved oak doors and pushed the octagonal brass button. A chime worthy of St. Basil's shook the foyer.

"I read it in the PostNews, Ange."

"You're kidding."

"I never kid."

The door opened, and a huge Afro-American man in white gloves and a pink maid's apron stood there and looked at them. Angie knew him, but if he did not acknowledge their relationship, he probably did not want her to. Marion Kershaw often worked undercover, despite his size. Maddie knew all the Kershaw boys, Marion, Mannie, and Marvin, all cops, and Mannie's adorable eight-year-old son, Mark, who attended Tate.

Marion held a high duster in his hand as he said, "Yes?" He weighed maybe 280 pounds and stood maybe six feet, ten inches—not fat, but very, very well-built. He probably would not appreciate anyone asking about his ruffled apron.

"Where's Adonis," Maddie whispered under her shaking breath.

"On an errand," Angie breathed back at her. Adonis and Marion would have been physical soulmates even though Marion was taller. "I'm Angelica Summers, and this is Madeleine Franck, as in César. Mrs. Senna is expecting us."

The man stared a moment more, then asked, "Ms. Summers, could I have your autograph," and grinned from ear to ear. His deep voice filled the foyer as a Metropolitan Opera bass's might.

"I would be pleased," Angie said.

"You're turning into Little Orphan Annie again, Kid.

"Shut up, Mary Helen."

"Thank you, Ms. Summers. Oh, I'm so sorry. Come in. Please come in." He reminded Angie of three or four Jimmus stuck together and stretched way up, except this strikingly handsome man's voice lilted.

Angie walked into an interior foyer decorated with brown and gold wallpaper. A white shag rug fluffed from the plastic carpet saver as though hair grew along its edges. Maddie stayed close behind her.

"You, too, can have terminal ugly for two thousand dollars a square foot," Mary Helen whispered.

Angie ignored her.

Marion reached under his apron, produced a copy of *Dead Virgin, Live Satan,* and handed it reverentially to Angie.

"Your name is?"

"Marion."

Angie scrawled her compliments and signed the bastard title page.

"More like Marion Stud."

"This time, you're right, Mary Helen."

"Look at that basket."

"Look at what? You're disgusting. You sound like Maddie, Mary Helen."

"I'm not as disgusting as he is hung — it's poofing his apron. Tell him to drop his pants. I want to see what he's got."

"Shut up, Mary Helen."

The door to the suite opened, and a blonde appeared. Her eyes first fastened onto Maddie and then jerked to Angie. Mrs. Senna wore exquisite silver and white lounging pajamas that matched her platinum hair. "How nice of you to drop by, Ms. Summers." Except that it came out, "How nize vyou t'drop eye."

"That broad's smashed. Well, it's almost 11:00 AM."

"A little high, maybe, Mary Helen. No, smashed." Angie glanced at her watch to verify this was not an acceptable time for getting smashed. "It was good of you to see us, Mrs. Senna. Maddie and I wanted to express our deepest sympathy for your loss."

"Please come into the parlor." (Plz cmin t'th parlor). "And please call me Vera-Lamar."

"Do you know Madeleine Franck?"

Vera-Lamar studied Maddie for a moment, then smiled. "Of course. We have ever so much in common, don't we, Ms. Franck, as in César." Remembering Maddie seemed to have cleared Vera-Lamar's diction.

"Mrs. Senna." Maddie sped forward like a skinny Sea Biscuit out of the gate.

"Please call me Vera-Lamar."

"Vera-Lamar, I was so sorry to hear about Mr. Senna." Maddie took Mrs. Senna's hands in hers and, for a moment, looked like she was going to kiss her. "I knew him mainly by reputation, although I did meet him at a few parties. He owned the building that houses *Centered Women*."

"Crap, she's full of it, just like she was of him," Mary Helen commented.

At first, Mrs. Senna looked perplexed. "I do love *Centered Women*. Everyone in it is what I've always wanted to be." Vera-Lamar turned her back to Maddie, walked over to Angie, and took her hands. "Oh, Ms. Summers, I hope you don't think me too forward, but may I have your autograph?"

"I may vomit." Mary Helen gagged.

"Be my guest, Mary Helen."

"Of course, Vera-Lamar."

"Watch out for this one," Mary Helen said. *"She's as artificial as snow at Twentieth Century Fox."*

Angie opened her purse to get her pen and spilled it. The pictures of Rex Caine, John Leech, and Slag Lessix landed on top of the pile, exactly where Angie hoped they would.

— 4 —

Saratoga, NY. Burger King. 11:30 AM. Dale.

They had all ordered triple beef whoppers with double cheese and bottomless fries. Dale had finished his, as had Jimmu. Fred was on his second and still going strong. Dale's mom and Aunt Gretta were always worrying about their weight. He wondered if they might benefit from a piece-of-Fred transplant.

"So, what will you guys do about the boom-booms?" Fred stared at the disappearing burger like he might go for three. "You know something, men? These are the best burgers in the entire world. You do know that, don't you? They're incredibly elegant and shamefully delicious."

"Thanks for the commercial, Master Fred." Jimmu ignored that they were devoted brothers.

"You're welcome. So, what are you guys going to do? I'm the new kid on the block in the spook-sleuthing and nearly-getting-killed scenes."

Without taking his chin off his hands or elbows off the table, Dale rolled his eyes up, then over to Fred. "You got the hang of that when you moved in with me—I'm always on the edge of killing you."

"Too true. So, what are you guys going to do?" Fred asked.

"We've told you everything now, Fred," Dale pointed out, "so it's what are we guys going to do."

"We could steal it." Jimmu seemed deep in thought. "That way, we'd be sure no one would get hurt no matter what happens."

"If we steal it, they'll just get more," Dale said. "We're not messing with amateurs." He made sense, at least to himself.

"Yeah," Jimmu said, "what's in that building is not PlayClay, it's plastic explosives. C-15. They started upgrading C-4 in 2024 or thereabouts, mainly because of the political climate. I loved it when they took out the liberal caucus."

"Yeah, and I loved it when they took out the conservative caucus," Dale put in. "Alfred Nobel invented it back in the 1800s. He did dynamite too."

"So why do you think it's there," Fred asked. "It's not like you'd get a Nobel Prize for blowing something up with it. Does anybody mind if I have another triple? It's the Mona Lisa of burgers, and she'd have three or four if she could."

"Go ahead," Jimmu said. "Live it up, for tomorrow you may die. Besides that, you're my brother. After our pre-Mirtha past, I won't say no to much, Fred. Just remember I can."

"I'm glad you do occasionally. You've saved my life more than once," Fred said.

"Only because you stupidly risked it more than once." Jimmu's serious face had become grimmer than Dale had seen it before.

Without answering, Fred slipped past Dale under the table and trotted merrily toward the counter from which all good came.

"I really like Fred," Dale said.

"Me too. He's a great little guy, but I'm probably prejudiced since he's my little brother, and, as his big brother, can beat him up if he gets out of line. No one would complain. But what about the explosives? We're not talking about Nobel farts here."

Fred had returned to the table and, between mouthfuls, said, "We need to tell you something, Jim."

"You sound serious, Little Brother."

"I am. You tell him, Dale."

"What? Oh, okay. We didn't just see Rex in his windows, we saw him in Congress Park this morning, just snooping around or something. Maybe we should blow Saratoga and go back to New York."

"No. Absolutely not," Jimmu said. "We're all part of this now. What was he doing?" Jimmu asked.

"He was down around the War Memorial," Dale said, "then up around the Canfield Casino. He was out of sight for a time, then he reappeared, got into a Mercury and left."

"He seemed to only be poking around, but we can't be sure," Fred said.

"I saw him too and passed it along," Jimmu said. "That was the reason for the trip to check on Rex and Appleseed. It was an assignment. I work part-time for somebody."

"I don't want to know whom," Dale said. "Maybe we should just ignore the whole fudding thing. This thing is really seeming dangerous." He hadn't told the brothers or anyone else that Rex had talked to him.

"Don't talk dirty, Master Dale. Besides, the most important people in our lives are up here. It's a quo-vadis thing."

"What?" Fred said. "Is that Latin?"

"I made perfect grades in Latin," Jimmu added, "probably because I would have done better in ancient Rome. Live with it."

"Whither goest thou," Dale said. "Where you go, I go. And how come you checked The John Appleseed shed in the first place?"

—5—

New York City. Central Park South. 11:40 AM. Maddie.

Angie had laid the three pictures on the coffee table. Vera-Lamar, in Bob Mackey originals that Maddie would kill for, sat next to Angie on the short sofa, leaving Maddie to fend for herself on the long one. Boffing PMS, Vera-Lamar's husband, had actually been a hobby of Maddie's. He stunk in the bed department but possessed a long fat wallet. Marion had brought Maddie a lovely white wine for lunch. Vera-Lamar retained her hollow-stemmed glass of champagne. Angie dear had set hers on the white marble coffee table with the food.

Champagne, lounging pajamas, and tacky knicky-knackies notwithstanding, Vera-Lamar apparently knew about Maddie's encounters with PMS. "A roll in the hay," Maddie murmured to herself, "is worth two in the grass. Rolls with Paul Senna give you nothing but gas."

"I recognize all three pictures, Mrs. Summers. We hosted a to-dodo for the Police Benevolent Association. I met all three gentlemen, along with fifty thousand other cops. Well, not that many, but ever-so-lots."

Maddie noticed that Mrs. Senna no longer showed signs of drunkenosity and wondered if she had been drinking at all. "We even entertained some representatives from the District Attorney's force." Her drunk, if that was what it was, had vanished, and her voice had become clear and articulate. "Angie, do you think a cop killed my Pauly?" Absent-minded. Almost disinterested.

"I don't know." Angie was in peak diplomacy. "I've been in Saratoga. Do you have any notions about who might have killed him?"

"Well, the detective who investigated the case suspected that whoever did it came in through the skylight in the tub room. Paul always opened the skylight when he soaked and jetted. The bird droppings didn't bother him."

"That might mean the killer was familiar with your apartment layout and your husband's habits," Angie said. "Was Paul consistent?"

"Rigid. Pauly managed his time by the clock."

Maddie watched them carefully. A contest might be developing. Maddie wished that she could look into their minds. Then again, if she could, it would probably scare the hell out of her.

"You're famous for sleuthing, Ms. Summers," Vera-Lamar said.

"Sometimes, I dabble. I really should not, of course. Professionals do the best jobs when it comes to crime. In this case, though, I have a personal interest. The late Mr. Lessix shot a good friend who may never recover." Tears eased down Angie's apple cheeks right on schedule. Few knew that she could cry at will.

"Would you like to see my Whirly, Angie, and you too, Mad?"

"Love to." Angie beamed.

"Great, Vera-Lamar," Maddie said. Ange and PMS's wife had hit it off weirdly, like a spider and fly dirty dancing.

"I hear you like whirlpools as much as Pauly did, Maddie." VL poured another slosh into her glass and led the way toward the back of the condo. She managed to keep her figure despite dropping all the suckers, five to date, and was attractive and well-preserved for a nuclear-powered bimbo on standby.

They paraded through a huge bedroom with a round waterbed and ceiling mirror that Maddie had stared up at so many times. "Perfectly magnificent."

"It is nice, isn't it. Pauly designed it. There's a round skylight above the dropped ceiling, too, but we decided we liked the mirror better. We used to spy on each other all the time. It's why our marriage lasted. No secrets. Pauly had a cute little mole on his buppie. I used to watch it wiggle while we played. No secrets. We shared everything." She glanced at Maddie.

Maddie could testify that it was not that cute and decided VL was no dumb blonde.

A circular glass shower stall stood at one side of the room. A dozen or so shower heads got you from every angle. Water flowed to the nozzles between an outer circle of glass and an inner. The glass wall revolved within a third to form a door that could open into the bathroom or a redwood sauna large enough to accommodate the Donner Party.

On the other side of the room, behind a glass partition, black and gold his-and-her toilets sat adjacent to his-and-her bidets. The centerpiece of this john of the gods was a huge whirlpool bath sunk into the floor under the huge mother of skylights, a domed, crystal-paned masterpiece fifteen feet across, supported by a flawless gold frame that matched all the plumbing fixtures. Diamond-shaped mirror panels circled the skylight. Maddie knew for a fact that it did indeed open. Pigeon poop in her bath, much less her loving place, bothered her. Of course, with this whirlpool, the rotating wake sucked down fecal residue as soon as it rained from heaven.

Angie studied the skylight, then the tub.

"I guess," Vera-Lamar said, "that I really ought to call the whirlpool man to come and clean out the works, hadn't I. There may be blood and bits of Pauly down there somewhere."

"That might be advisable." Angie's eyes went all Little Orphan Annie.

"Yeah, I guess. There was blood, and Pauly let loose at the end. I noticed the recirculation getting cloudy when I bathed last night."

This dumb blonde was not even slightly dumb. "I'd get it flushed if I were you, Vera-Lamar," Maddie put in. "I spilled a gallon of red wine into mine once and ended up with red feet and things."

"Who was in the apartment when Mr. Senna passed?" Angie asked.

"Oh, it was Marion's day off. A cop friend of his was just outside. I think his name was Corset or Goosicks. Pauly preferred to bathe alone unless he had functioning guests. I took the kids to the Great Escape that day as a special treat before they went away to camp, which is where they are now."

"How many can you accommodate in your whirlpool?" Little Orphan Annie asked.

"Oh, ten or so. It depends on what you want to do there. If you only want to jet, you can do anything everywhere if you don't drown easily. That was the day that a llama spit on my bosoms. Isn't that something?"

"In the whirlpool?" That image grabbed Maddie.

"Nooooooo, at the Great Escape. In the Whirly, Pauly used to. I miss that so. Let's return to the living room. This place gives me the creeps if I'm not naked."

"Can you get up to the roof from your apartment?" Angie had been her usual quiet self.

"Certainly. This is the top floor of our condo and is only half inside. Come on. I can show you easier than tell you."

Maddie and Angie followed Vera-Lamar obediently back into the parlor and then into the living room, separated by a glass wall from a magnificent patio with earth-tone ceramic tiles. Vera-Lamar pushed a wall button, and the glass retracted, bringing the outside inside, or vice versa. They walked out onto the patio. The part of the penthouse with the living room, bedroom, parlor, foyer, john-magnifique, Steinway B, and this elegant patio gave the Sennas an additional floor, sometimes called the roof.

For thirty minutes, they sat at a round marble table and talked incessantly about nothing, just a simple CEO, a best-selling writer, and a merry widow who wanted the world to think she was a dumb-blonde baby machine.

Maddie had to give it to Vera-Lamar—she was superb at appearing stupid.

After their tête-à-tête, Maddie and Angie were riding down in the elevator when Angie said, "We're sleeping at your place again tonight, Maddie. So is Adonis."

Chapter 28 - Evening Picnic

A taciturn stud-drudge.

—1—

Saratoga, NY. Crumb House. Backyard. 6:00 PM. Dale.

Sitting at the picnic table with his summer family, Dale said, "Aunt Gretta, I am really enjoying this summer. You're a brick."

Aunt Gretta looked Jimmy in the eye. "Is being a brick good?"

Jimmu and Fred giggled at each other. "Oh sure, Aunt Mirtha," Jimmu said. "It means you're solid, swell, great, and stupendous to Fred and me and our friends."

Aunt Gretta thought about that, then said, "Thank you, boys. I hope I deserve all that, especially that I am solid."

"I agree with Jim and Dale, Aunt Mirthretta. This is all outstandingly superb." Fred was devouring his fourth hamburger of the day.

Besides having a great gazebo, Aunt Gretta had filled the long maple picnic table spread with picnic food. The odd thing was that she was playing hostess but not eating much. Dale had seen her like this before, when she suspected she might be plumping. He guessed that Aunt Gretta had filled out some, though the Hairy Mary had helped, probably by tightening and screwing down.

"Hey, Deac —"

"Fred!" He'd almost called Dale "Deacon," which would have gotten him slapped up beside his little pointed head once they were out of Aunt Gretta's sight. Dale hated that, especially in the school showers, and was grateful to Fred for eliminating the "Deacons" from school. He was small but tough. On the other hand, there was Mary Margaret Pinkham at the Spring Ball — after it, really. She hadn't exactly raped him, he just hadn't planned on more than a kiss.

"Sorry," Fred mouthed to Dale.

"Boys," Gretta asked, "could I interest you in a piece of the apple pie I made this afternoon? We have lemonade to wash it down."

"Oh, my yes, Aunt Gretta," Jimmu said. "You won't have any trouble interesting me in that." He'd been unusually quiet since they found the explosives, but didn't want to do anything until Dale's mom returned.

Dale had told nobody about his talk with Rex.

"Us too," Dale and Fred said together.

"We all love pie, especially yours," Fred added.

"Aunt Gretta, you're a great cook," Dale said. "Did you know that?"

"I notice it far too frequently, Dale. I planned on being a chef until I found something better to do."

"The only problem is," Dale added, "is that if Fred eats more, he'll explode. That would be a mess."

— 2 —

New York City. Central Park South. 7:00 PM. Angie.

The doorbell rang at Maddie's Penthouse at 7:00 PM, an hour later than Angie had anticipated. Maddie was in the shower, so Angie opened the door, and Adonis filled it.

"I've had a really rotten day, Ms. Summers," he said.

Angie smiled. "Bureaucracies are there to help us, Adonis."

"You're getting as cynical as Maddie," Mary Helen said.

"Never."

"I'm sorry, Adonis," Angie said. "We're going to be staying here again tonight."

"Good. I don't think I could walk another step."

"Did you succeed?" They walked into the living room.

"Yes, ma'am. I succeeded." He handed her a thin 11" x 17" manilla envelope. "Jake Slag Lessix was married to Marsha Lessix, the lady we followed this morning, but was having an affair with Henrietta Keeler, her maid, with the promise of marriage. It was the wannabee Mrs. Lessix whom Jimmu saved from assassins. No idea why she pretended to be her boss. The prevailing hypothesis is that assassins targeted Henrietta, not Marsha, but that's just a speculatory scenario."

"She's dead," Angie said.

"Who's dead?"

"Henrietta Keeler, the one who overheard the plan for the Belmont Park affair and claimed that Rex was involved up to his hair. I called Jimmu a little while ago. He found her body in The John Appleseed Cottage, then it disappeared again."

"Ms. Summers," Adonis said, "we can't—"

"We can!" Angie heard her voice turn steely and coarse. "She outed Rex. Now she's dead."

"That doesn't make her a liar." Adonis looked straight into Angie's eyes.

"No, it just makes her dead, and since she did not know about Jimmu coming but did know the real Mrs. Lessix was in Florida, she was probably there looking for something, possibly the lists. Are you sure that The Snow Queens are all in Saratoga?"

"We verified that most were," Adonis confirmed. "What better place for them to get together without arousing suspicion? People come from all over the world to Saratoga during the racing season and the month before, so what better place to have a summit meeting than across the road from a nursing home in one of the most sparsely populated areas of Saratoga?"

"Perhaps. Where does that leave Rex?"

"I don't know, Ms. Summers, apart from in a coma in Saratoga."

"Yes, and he is in Saratoga because of a Living Will he made abruptly and did not tell me about. And the Candy list?"

"The cops? I don't know. I made no headway there." Adonis shook his handsome head.

"Then what do you actually know, Special Agent?"

Adonis stopped cold, his eyes frozen. "When did you figure that out?"

"When you took off your clothes and pretended to be a model. The FBI has a distinctive demeanor that does not support nudity well. You play a taciturn stud-drudge well but, like your brothers-in-arms, have difficulty going into deep cover unless the agency has hired a true actor. Excellent agent-actors are rare."

"That was a considerate insult."

"Yes. Also, you have a birthmark on your left shoulder. I used to change your diapers when I babysat you. I knew Gretta for years before she published me, and only Gretta knows I know about you and your mission, Special Agent. Now you should get some rest. I have another errand for you later, as a pilot. You need to rest, or you'll crash."

"Yes, ma'am." He trotted off to the guestroom to doze, and presumably to wait for Angie's next command.

"You just failed to fully inform a federal agent, Angie," Mary Helen said. *"That's what you have me for. How did you really know his status?"*

"I told the truth. I used to change his diapers. He does not remember it. I pestered Gretta for years before she published me—we're both Saratogans. I was a teenager when I babysat Fritz. The Bureau assigned him to this case because of his ties to the region and background in drug trafficking. Also, he went to high school and college in Vienna and is not well known here."

$$-3-$$

Saratoga, NY. Crumb House. Fred's Room. 9:00 PM. Dale.

Fred stood in the middle of his room and looked silly in one of Dale's black outfits. Dale had rolled up the pants and pinned them in place.

Jimmu was trying not to laugh.

"So go ahead and laugh, you two," Fred said. "Then we can get on with it."

At that, both Dale and Jimmu cracked up. The turtleneck gaped enough to accommodate a second Fred-head. Dale would need to take it in like the rest of his outfit.

"I like being part of this operation, guys," Fred said, "even though it's nuts. Usually, I go nuts only with girls, but you two will do for the moment."

Dale got control of himself. "We need to be quiet. One thing we don't want is Aunt Gretta catching on."

"Too, too true," Jimmu said. "By the way, Master Dale, have you thought about what we will do with the explosives once we steal them."

"We'll hide them."

"Where?" Fred made a funny face. "I know that C-15 is stable and requires an ignition pack to go boom, but I doubt we should tuck it under our pillows, hoping for a dollar. How about the pond in back of The John?"

"Yuk. It smelled." Dale hated smelly junk.

"Agreed." Jimmu abandoned laughing in favor of being thoughtful. "It's close, and it's hidden. And water doesn't hurt C-15. It will still work if we want to get it back and blow somebody up. Agreed?"

"Agreed," Dale said. "Now, let's see if we can alter Fred."

Fred and Jimmu looked at him like he'd farted or something.

"His clothes, guys. We should do a few alterations on Fred, so he doesn't get pricked. I'm afraid he'll come undone and trip on someone when we go over the wall."

DAY EIGHT

Chapter 29 - Boy Wind

Why is it called a root cellar?

−1−

New York City. Central Park South. 1:00 AM. Maddie.

Maddie felt certain she had gone calmly to sleep and that this was some kind of really weird nightmare, by the nuts, for the nuts, and of the nuts.

"I saw no sign of perimeter alarms." Angie's cool and matter-of-fact tone shocked even Maddie. "All I need to do is slip onto the patio, then use the ladder to the shack on the top roof, the one that resembles a room for elevator motors."

"But that's illegal entry!"

"Never mind. It's for a worthy cause." To Angie, any possible evidence for an investigation was for a worthy cause. That covered transgressing boundaries and laws.

"*You tell her, Ange,*" Mary Helen put in. "*It's definitely what I would do.*"

Maddie could not believe her friend was invading Senna's building in the middle of the night. "Angie, I think you're nuts."

"And I think you're thin. Neither thought is pertinent. The problem remains."

"*And what problem is that, Ange? You or the case?*"

"*Shut up, Mary Helen.*"

"Adonis, with note and keys, is on his way to Centered Women to ensure everything is set up. He will wait for us there. If necessary, you can reel him back with a call, Maddie."

Friend Angie had become more aggressive than Maddie had ever seen her. It was as if she were changing into Mary Helen Mack.

"Maddie, I added buds to your Pear Superphone for direct communication. It's traceable to the hyperwave tower but not much more."

—2—

Saratoga, NY. Crumb House. Fred's Room. 1:10 AM. Dale.

"You want me to do what in the dark?" Fred sounded like Dale and Jim had just asked him to poop turkeys. "Why the hell do we have to go down the trellis in the middle of the night? That's what doors are for, you know."

"It's morning," Dale said. "And we want to avoid disturbing Aunt Gretta."

"And to keep me from getting fired by Aunt Gretta," Jimmu added. "Despite all the fun and games, I want to keep my job and life."

"Oh, for damn sake, okay!" Fred said. "I'm not fond of heights, even heights I can't see in the dark. It's not rats, at least—they always look like they want to nibble the goods." Fred cultivated a terrific imagination.

"It's okay, Fred," Dale reassured. "We live on the first floor." This really was the best way out. "Jimmu will go first, and I'll come last. You'll be in the middle in case you freak."

"A Turkish delight?" Fred said. "Gee, thanks, men. Okay, but if I fall, it will be on your heads. And when do I ever freak?"

"On Jimmu's head, actually," Dale said. "I'll be above you. I already told you that. And you freak at Tate quite often. I'm used to it."

"Yeah, but that's mainly to help you, Dale."

"Oh, how simply, simply grand." Jimmu had recovered from the recent shocks and was becoming his old self. "Don't worry, boys. Jimmu will protect you."

−3−

New York City. Central Park South. 1:11 AM. Maddie.

Maddie watched Angie slip effortlessly across the nearly touching roofs to PMS's patio. "Are you okay, Ange?"

"I'm walking over the faux marble patio ten feet from you," Ange whispered. "Of course, I'm okay."

Maddie watched the pilgrim's roof progress, where Angie had crossed to the patio easily.

"Keep your eyes open for any lights from PMS's place, Mad."

"It's still dark. Let's get this done fast," Maddie whispered.

"Not a light. Not an alarm. Good. We're safe."

"You don't know the meaning of that word, Ange."

"Never mind. I have fifteen minutes to replace the memory cards and get out of there."

"What cards? I thought you were just fishing."

"Who ever heard of fishing on a roof?"

−4−

Saratoga, NY. Crumb House. 1:13 AM. Dale.

"I'm down." Jimmu hit land first. "And which of you assholes farted?"

"Both," Dale replied honestly. It had been all he could do to keep from laughing. There was something about crawling down a roughhewn trellis in the middle of the night that made all sorts of things pop out, even from the first floor to the ground, about seven feet. "I apologize for farting on your head, Fred."

"And I apologize for farting on your head, Jim," Fred chimed in, getting into the spirit of things now that he stood on solid ground.

"You two ought to be ashamed of yourselves," Jimmu said, "and you better start looking under your pillow at night." His whisper swished through the dark. "You've made my beautiful Asian hair go all kinky. Now, come on. We'll need to push Adonis's BroncEV out of the driveway before we can start it. I don't want to risk my new Beamer if someone shoots at us, and we must not awaken Aunt Mirthretta."

They all crept around to the front of Crumb House. Dale hoped that no cops dropped by during this part. They would all get busted, which, according to Fred and Jimmu, they had been several times after their parents died but before Gretta took them in and did for them.

Circular Street and Congress Park lay dark and quiet but for a dog barking somewhere. A siren searched someplace in the distance. Jimmu steered while Fred and Dale pushed, and darned if the BroncEV didn't move quietly down the driveway and onto Circular Street exactly as they had planned. Things did go right now and then.

A little past Crumb House, Dale and Fred slipped into the front seat with Jimmu, a bench seat with three belts.

"Let's get going." Dale meant it too. He didn't know if his actions might condemn Uncle Rex, but he was going through with it anyway. He owed it to his mom not to build his life on a fantasy father, but he still loved Rex and needed to know the truth.

— 5 —

New York City. Central Park South. Maddie's Roof. 1:15 AM. Angie.

Angie seemed to have surprised Maddie with her agility and grace. She would make an excellent cat burglar, at least for cats. But when she slipped back over the rail, she had a sinking feeling that her worst fears about Rex might be correct, and her greatest desires might be —

"Dog meat. The situation is sucking you in, Angie."

"Shut up, Mary Helen."

Maddie looked at the box of SD cards that Ange had just put into her hand.

"That shooting wasn't what it seemed, Angie," Mary Helen said. *"Face it. For whatever reason, Rex Caine was in on his own assassination attempt.*

"Shut up, Mary Helen."

"What's on these?" Maddie stared at the small box of memory cards.

"Come on," Angie said. "Let's get over to *Centered Women*. We don't want to miss the plane."

"The plane's waiting for us," Maddie said. "How could we miss it?"

"Adonis could fall asleep and take off without us. Planes do that now."

— 6 —

Saratoga, NY. The John. 1:28 AM. Dale.

Jimmu pulled the BroncEV into their favorite place in the woods, close to The Armpit. The car would stick out like a turd on a doily in any other place. Jimmu went sailing over the wall first, then Fred, then Dale. Well, almost. He did catch his toe on the wall and flipped head over heels, one of which just missed Jimmu's head. He did miss, though.

"Progress!" he whispered.

"Not a word now," Jimmu warned. "We don't know who might be in the house, not to mention outside of it. Follow silently."

Dale and Fred followed, Fred because he would do whatever his brother wanted, and Dale because obeying Jimmu was the right thing to do and held the best odds for success. The three of them peaked over the wall at The John and saw nothing. That was a relief.

Jimmu didn't waste time. They slipped over the wall behind the cottage, intending to drop the plastic explosives into the pond.

At the shed, Jimmu said, "I don't feel anything. I'm going to risk the light." He turned on the little plastic flash with the blue filter. They all stared into the empty shed.

"Oh, shit." Fred always managed to be succinct.

"Oh, my gracious," Jimmu said.

This blew Dale's plan to short-circuit whatever was supposed to happen. "I don't believe it."

Jimmu snapped the light out. "Believe it," he whispered.

— 7 —

PMS Center. Centered Women. Roof WhisperChop Pad. 2:15 AM. Angie.

When they reached PMS Center, the WhisperChop was sitting there waiting for them.

"How about telling me what's going on here, Angie? It is my roof and my WhisperChop. And where did Adonis go? And what's on the memory cards? Tell me something, damn it, or I'll big-time pout."

Maddie was less than happy but Angie knew that she would get over it.

"Remember the mirrors around the skylight in the bathroom and above the bed," Angie said.

"Of course, I do. I'm not blind. Besides, I have looked straight up at them a few times."

"And they were looking back down at you. Do you remember what Mrs. Senna said about her and Mr. Senna sharing everything and spying on each other for sport?"

"Of course. My blood went cold," Maddie snapped.

"Well, above those mirrors—"

"Oh, crap. Senna?"

"The small shack on the roof next door from your condo is likely the nerve center of their personal surveillance system and was where they stored their SD cards, nicely cataloged and labeled, recordings of everything that happened in the condo. PMS probably kept everything up there to keep them from intruders, and possibly to store what PMS did or did not want his wife to see. There are also multiple monitors. I could see the entire house from the roof room. Thank God Rex taught me to pick."

"How did you know that, and how far back do they go?"

"A little birdie told me, and I don't know how far back. We haven't watched them yet."

"*It could have the murder on it,*" MH said.

"If we're in luck, they will show us PMS's murder, Mad. We can watch them on the plane."

– 8 –

Saratoga, NY. The John. 2:15 AM. Dale.

"You two guys are really the limit," Fred said as they stood in the kitchen of Appleseed Cottage, ready to search for the explosives. This was the only building left.

Dale felt perfectly relaxed. "Have you ever done this before, Fred?"

"Of course, I haven't."

"That's a lie," Jimmu put in. "We both have. It's time to trust somebody, little brother, and Aunt Mirtha, Dale, and Ms. Angie are the best somebodies."

"Okay, we have," Fred said softly, "back in Manhattan, up in the Bronx, and a couple of times out at Flushing. We're both crooks."

"We were crooks," Jimmu said. "That scene was necessary for us to survive but is behind us, Dale."

They had found the back door locked this time, but also the key on the ledge above it, so they didn't need to pick. Dale wasn't sure why Jimmu wanted to try this again. He was getting more like Dale's mom every minute, tough and inscrutable, but not because he was Chinese — that would be racist — because he was Jim. Dale's mom was forever doing junk that no one understood, usually wearing her Orphan Annie eyes and half smile to go along with it. Dale called it her Mona Lisa smirk. He had seen the real one in Paris several times. Lots of people didn't know Louis XIII lived there once upon a time. That was before Mona moved in.

So here Dale stood in the kitchen, in the pitch black, wondering who else might be standing here watching him, listening to him, or smelling him.

Jimmu hadn't even tried that little blue flash yet in The John.

"Yes, I think I have it," Jimmu whispered inexplicably.

"By George," Fred said, "she has it. The rain in—"

"Shut up, Fred," Dale whispered."

Fred loved musicals, and sometimes Dale needed to be straight to the point with him about that. "What do you have, Jim? If they haven't used it, where else would they put it? And yes, I can feel the draft. You just opened the cellar door, didn't you."

"Crap," Fred said.

This time Dale agreed with Fred but said, "Great, Jim. You might be right."

"Shhh." Jimmu finally snapped his blue flash on.

The steps leading down to the basement looked old and primitive, like they might have bark on the underside because Alexander Hamilton or someone had built them.

"Be careful, Fred," Jimmu said. "The steps are tall and steep."

"Do we have to go down there?" That seemed a very logical question for Fred to ask. As long as Dale had known him, he'd been skittish about dark, damp, unpeopled places.

"Yes." Jimmu sounded really determined.

"Should Dale and I go with you?" Fred's voice quaked.

"Yes, we need to stay together," Jimmu said. "Besides, I'm not going down alone."

Dale didn't want to stay upstairs without Jimmu, so they followed him slowly, carefully, precisely, down the creaking stairs, not forgetting to shut the door behind them, and not forgetting that they were following Jimmu into real, entirely sheer terror. Nausea would be a great word because the cellar stunk funkily.

"I think I may puke up my whoppers," Fred whispered.

"Too late," Dale said. "In any case, I've seen you naked, and they aren't that big."

Jimmu sounded as though he'd swallowed a giggle. "Quiet, you two. I think we're alone, but I can't be sure." He shined his light around the basement, which was huge and stone and had a couple of doors at the far-left end, likely leading to hell or somewhere.

Jimmu walked to the left door on the end wall and opened it. "Gracious, gracious, a black room." He shined his blue light in.

Staying close to Jimmu, Dale and Fred looked into the small square room.

"It used to be a coal bin," Fred said. "There's one at Crumb House too. One of Aunt Mirtha's dead husbands used to spank their kids there. She uses it for storage now but never forgave him, although she has threatened me with the coalbin several times. I don't know why—I'm a really good kid."

Jimmu growled, "I know why." He shut the door and led the way to the other door. The other door had a huge hasp with a newish-looking Superlock hanging open. Jimmu shined the light down at the floor. The packed dirt looked like concrete. "Door number two," Jimmu said under his breath as he pulled it open by the lock.

Far from going to hell, this door let a blast of cold air out and a heavy dose of the smell that hit them when they came down the stairs. Jimmu flashed the light around the large room. Shelves and bins lined the wall.

"It's an old root cellar," Fred said. "Aunt Mirthretta's got one of those too. It's for fruits and vegetables. She stores stuff there too."

"Why is it called a root cellar?" Dale wanted to know.

"Because," Fred whispered. "They used it to store root and other durable veggies such as squashes, turnips, and rutabagas that can last a good part of the winter. We studied it in American History, Dale. You got an A. I got an A+."

"Oh. That makes sense," Dale whispered.

"Gracious, gracious." Jimmu focused his light on the wire fronts of the bins on the far-left end of the room. "What do we have here?" He walked slowly down the room.

If Dale and Fred stayed any closer, they would be in Jim's pants, so to speak. A few feet from the bins, Dale realized what Jimmu had spotted. The bins contained enough produce and cans for a banquet, probably for the planned meeting upstairs.

"Crap," Jimmu said under his breath. He lowered his light and shined it into the glazed eyes of Mrs. Jake Lessix, who lay sprawled white and half-naked under the bottom row of bins that contained small cartons of C-15.

Dale gasped. "May God—"

"Crap," Fred said.

"Shhh," Jimmu whispered. "I heard something upstairs." He killed his light.

They all drew a breath. Dale heard footsteps moving carefully and slowly upstairs, as though searching, then fading to nothing for at least five minutes before they reappeared. Those feet could belong to someone who belonged here, unlike the invaders in the root cellar. Every second Dale listened, Mrs. Lessix's dead body kept floating through his mind on a bed of explosives powerful enough to blow up the whole—

The cellar door opened. Nothing in the root cellar moved or breathed, not even Fred. The cellar door closed. They exhaled together. The steps moved away toward the back of the house and opened the outside door, the one they came in.

How would they know if the steps and possibly the guns had left the building? Dale figured he would rely on Jimmu for that. This was when following could be great for a guy's peace of mind, as well as pieces of his body that might otherwise self-destruct.

They stood for two more minutes, and then it happened: Dale got an erection that shoved against his fly like a snake in a bag, and Mrs. Lessix turned into Mary Margaret Pinkham, floating naked through the air on a cloud of fall leaves that matched her hair in all four places.

A hand tugged gently on Dale's right arm, urging him toward the main basement room. He figured that he should not talk and didn't, even though he wanted to sound a stout hallelujah to the passing vision of Mary Margaret and her beautiful hair, smooth and moist like the angels around the pearly gates of heaven, even though she was more of a Satanic seductress whom he loved.

The hand pushed Dale back into the main room of the basement. Fred was holding onto Dale's shirt.

"Let's listen for a moment more." Jimmu's mouth was right at Dale's ear, just as Dale's was at Fred's when he passed it on.

They stood still and listened, much better than the uncertainty of moving or breathing.

— 9 —

Maddie's WhisperChop. 2:30 AM. Angie.

Angie had surprised Maddie by having Adonis fly the bird, instead of her usual pilot. Apparently, neither complained. Except for his size, Angie would have had Adonis steal the SD cards, but it needed a woman's touch, like everything else truly important.

Maddie and Angie were relaxing in front of their monitor. PMS's cards contained weeks of coverage. Angie ran it in double-time to save time and paused when it interested her.

"Life in the fast lane, Ange?" Mary Helen said.

"Yes, and shush, Mary Helen."

The recordings started a week before Senna saw his end in the whirlpool. The cameras scanned the entire penthouse.

In the beginning, Mrs. Senna is in bed with PMS, squealing as he plows her roads.

Switch: A huge fat tabby cat drinks from its bowl.

Switch: Mr. Senna is in bed with Mrs. Senna and Marion Kershaw.

Switch: The tabby uses the pan.

Switch: Little Birdie Marion plowed PMS's road. His versatility surprised but didn't offend.

Switch: A gala party stretches throughout the penthouse, including Mayor Quinn and other celebrities.

Switch: The cat relieves itself in the kitchen sink but fails to bury it.

Switch: Mr. Senna shares the sauna with two naked girls who appear to have the bodies of twelve- or thirteen-year-olds but far better skills.

Switch: Tabby relieves himself in the marble bathroom basin.

"The cameras are on motion detectors, Ange. They're not programmed correctly." Mary Helen had hit the truth on the head, and Angie's brain came to life.

"You're right, Mary Helen. Rex taught me about that. Thank you. They may not even be chronological."

"I know what's going on, Maddie. It's a motion detector. If the sensor senses motion, the camera in that room comes on and begins recording. If there are two rooms with motion, it jumps around. It would have worked perfectly if someone had programmed the system to ignore the cat. As it was, we saw Mr. Senna reaching orgasm, then the cat, then a panting Senna — very anticlimactic."

"Well, it's this way, Ange," Mary Helen said, *"you can't just call a repairman to climb onto the roof and fix your dirty movie machine."*

"I suppose not. If you're well known, much less recently murdered, something would get out." Angie realized that she had just spoken to Mary Helen aloud.

"You suppose not what?" Maddie snapped. She was almost panting watching Marion, Vera-Lamar, and Senna in bed together. "Who would have thought that old PMS swung both ways? Maybe that was why he acted so pooped when he got to me."

"What?" Adonis asked.

"It's nothing, Adonis," Maddie said. "I had a passing acquaintanceship with Senna, very passing."

"What she means is a pissing relationship," Mary Helen said.

"Shhh, Mary Helen."

"I wonder why the police didn't discover these recordings, Mad," Angie mused.

"Maybe the cops didn't look too hard, Ange. Senna could buy anybody."

"Anything's possible." On the screen, Senna was sitting in the whirlpool by himself. This could be the

day. It was hard to tell because the index codes in the upper left-hand corner of the screen flew by so fast.

"He didn't have much, did he?"

"Enough, Mary Helen."

Now, PMS was sitting there masturbating. Angie had never realized that the rich and exceedingly well-satisfied spent so much time having a panorama of sex and parties, often simultaneously. In all these recordings, you saw little of the Senna children. Apparently, they spent most of their time away at school and summer camp. Angie saw few of them turn up in scenes of domestic tranquility, which were also scarce, and had not picked up on a single instance of marital or other familial affection or devotion, just marital gymnastics, usually with the assistance of—

Switch: The front door opened. A figure eased in backward and carefully closed the door.

Switch: Senna continued to masturbate. He threw his head back. His mouth opened.

"Thar, she blows," Maddie said, and indeed, he did.

An almost invisible cord encircled PMS's neck.

Switch: With his legs spread in his big pan, the cat strained to force out a fat bowel movement.

"How Turdly," Mary Helen said.

"True," Angie returned.

"Oh, my Christ," Maddie said. "And thar he goes. We just saw PMS murdered."

"About to be murdered," Angie corrected.

Switch: The whirlyroom again. The killer, a black shadow standing above Senna, tightened the garotte. The powerful and famous Michael Paul Senna became a contorted naked thing thrashing in the polluted water. Blood from the garotte had begun to tint the water, in addition to what was exiting Senna's bowels. The body stopped moving. The shadow released it. The corpse disappeared into the murky water of its own waste.

"Murdered," Angie agreed.

Maddie had covered her eyes with her hands.

Switch: The fat tabby scratched in its pan, then hopped out and ran.

Switch: The fat tabby in the living room sharpened its claws on the doorjamb.

Switch: In the whirlyroom, the whirlpool water had turned uniformly light brown.

Switch: The shadow eased out the apartment's front door without showing its face. Angie hit pause. The image flickered. Could that shadow belong to Rex? The build was right, but something about him was not Rex. Whoever killed Senna had lucked out. His face had never made it to the film. He did look shorter than Rex, but Angie could not be sure. She did feel sure that he likely knew about the cameras.

Chapter 30 - Virgil the Virgin

I may be a rich WASP.

— 1 —

Saratoga, NY. The John. 2:32 AM. Dale.

"Have we stood and listened long enough," Dale finally whispered to Jimmu.

"Yeah, Jim, my tiny tootsies are frozen," Fred whispered.

"My big tootsies are frozen too," Jimmu whispered back.

Dale thought that each whisper had gotten a little louder. He wore a size ten shoe, and his feet hadn't gotten cold because he'd vibrated up and down on his toes. But if his friends were going to be victims of their genetic conditions, so was Dale. "I may be a rich WASP, but my stinger's about frozen clean off."

Fred and Jimmu cracked up at that and were a little louder than their whispers had been, but no more sounds came from upstairs. Whoever was there had left.

"If they didn't hear that, they've left," Jimmu whispered.

"Agreed." Fred agreed with Jimmy lots, as a good little brother should.

Fred and Dale had great fun together but rarely agreed about anything.

"So let's get out of here." Dale had been antsy since Mary Margaret floated through—she should have used a broomstick, but not really.

Jimmu turned the flash on, found the steps, then turned it off and led the way. He was still being plenty careful. They had all eased into the kitchen and were on the way to the back door when the lights came on.

"Well, what do we have here." The man grinned like an evil troll and held the longest gun Dale had ever seen. The guy and his purple, chartreuse, and pink plaid jacket were leaning on the arch into the living room as if waiting for a bus. He'd obviously been waiting for them.

"The jig's up, guys." Fred stepped forward in front of Jimmu and Dale like the little trooper he was. "We're really sorry, sir. I'm Tom Destry, and this is my brother Virgil—Virgil the virgin, he's called—and we were looking for a deserted house to bring chicks to, mainly for Virgil, if they'll have him. I guess this house isn't as deserted as it looks."

"No, it isn't. Who's the other one," the man said, gesturing toward Dale, "your brother by another mother?"

"Yeah," Fred didn't blink. "That's Ollie. He's a little slow. My brother by adoption."

"You shut up, kid. You tell me." He waved the gun at Dale, who felt something running down his leg.

"Really and truly, sir," Dale said. "I'm one of their field workers. They own a big dairy farm. Father and son."

"Isn't it lucky," the man said, "that I got here just in time to save the local girls. Were you planning on taking them to the basement with the body? It could hold more, you for inst—"

The blur, grunt, and black streak slammed down against the back of the man's head. A bell rang. The man looked dazed but half-turned and fired twice into the dark living room behind him.

Dale realized that the gun was so long because it had a silencer.

The man staggered and tried to point the gun at them.

Jimmu flew, grabbed the gun arm, swung the man, and brought one hand up under the elbow and the other down on the wrist of the man's arm. Something snapped, and the gun fell. Jimmu shoved the palm of his hand at the man's nose, which changed shapes and started bleeding, then hit the guy in his solar plexus, and when the guy lurched forward, Jim slugged the back of his thick neck with his hand bottoms clasped together, and hit the guy's face with a knee.

That was that. The man flopped onto the floor like a dead crap sack.

Jimmu flipped the living-room light switch and gasped.

Dale and Fred ran and looked.

"Holy crap," Fred said. "Aunt Mirtha!" The decorative cast iron skillet off the living-room wall, with which she'd smashed the back of the man's head, lay on the floor, and so did Aunt Gretta.

Jimmu pulled his jacket off and pressed it against the ragged gash in her left arm while he pressed his hand against the awful-looking wound on her side.

Fred ducked into the bathroom, rushed back, and threw Jimmu towels and a first aid kit.

"You're fired," Aunt Gretta said. "Son-of-a-bitch, I hurt!" In her black pants and overly tight turtleneck, she looked like James Bond's overweight grandmother.

"Aunt Gretta?" Dale could think of nothing more original to say.

"You boys are in so much trouble, all three of you."

"Aunt Gretta?" Dale wailed. "Oh, triple cow!"

"I beg your pardon, Dale Summers!"

"I'm sorry, Aunt Gretta."

—2—

Maddie's WhisperChop. 3:15 AM. Maddie.

"What do you mean you've been shot?" Maddie screamed.

At the word shot, Angie sat up like someone had launched her. "Who's been shot?"

"Gretta, that's who, and she wants to talk to her son."

Angie just pointed at the pilot. "Fritz is her son. He's also a cop, a really big fed, a special agent."

—3—

Saratoga, NY. Crumb House. Fred's Room. 3:17 AM. Dale.

In the dark purple pajamas Aunt Mirthretta had given him, Dale stood alone in Fred's room and looked at himself in the mirror. "Oh God, it was awful." Aunt Gretta proved to have quite a ferocious mouth that he had never experienced before. He supposed that was normal since few writer-editor-publisher CEOs got shot, although Dale's mom often said some should be.

Aunt Gretta was kind of high-strung, and it was probably a very disturbing experience for her, but the things she said were even worse. She was not going to publish Dale's mother's books ever again, was going to burn Tate School, was going to throw Fred and Jimmu back on the street, was going to burn Saratoga, and was going to take multiple contracts out on the SOB who shot her, since Jimmu had failed to adequately kill him.

While everyone was helping Aunt Gretta in The John, the gunman revived and took off, probably limping. The first thing they'd heard from him was his car pulling away from the side of the house.

Jimmu at least kept the man's gun, a Beretta M9, and had urged, "Please, Aunt Mirtha, try to be calm. We all need to be calm."

That was the only time that Dale had ever seen Jimmu truly worried—frantic might be a better word. After he stopped Gretta's bleeding with The John's towels and first aid kit, he went to get the BroncEV. Aunt Gretta had parked at The Golden Arms and had hiked down the hill to The John.

Dale and Fred had struggled to get her onto her feet, which resembled standing up a huge burlap bag filled with rotted watermelons. Despite her elegant appearance, Aunt Gretta weighed a little more than Dale expected. They finally got her onto her feet just as Jimmu arrived with the BroncEV.

Then came the worst near-catastrophe in an evening of disasters. While they were getting Aunt Gretta into the front seat of the BroncEV, Dale tripped Fred, and the poor little kid fell into the front seat with Aunt Gretta smack on top of him. You could only see one foot. Jimmu put his shoulder against Aunt Gretta's back and lifted her enough for Dale to pull Fred out onto the ground before he suffocated. He survived, bent and thinner but alive.

Jimmu had cleaned up Aunt Gretta's blood. Actually, he stole the rag rug she bled on and brought it back to Crumb House to burn. The tidy thug had apparently bled only on himself.

Now, Fred was in the shower, trying to recover his self-respect and body mobility.

Dale didn't look a bit different in the mirror but felt different. He couldn't quite decide exactly how.

The steam from the shower drifted into the bedroom as Fred appeared behind Dale in the mirror, naked as usual, drying himself with a bright green towel that probably belonged to a bruised leprechaun.

"So what happens now, wise roommate and son of the famous crime thriller writer who offered to mentor me but will probably take it back after tonight," Fred asked.

"I don't know," Dale said. "I guess Mom and Aunt Mirthretta will send us back to Tate for the rest of the summer. My mom will not like any of this even a little bit. We just got her publisher shot. I don't think that's supposed to happen in publishing." Dale gave that one some thought, then grinned at Fred in the mirror. "Hey, Freddy, you know what?"

"What?" Bored and dejected.

"I'm fourteen and have never been in any real trouble before."

Fred slapped his head, rolled his eyes up, draped his towel over his head, and walked backward to the bed.

— 4 —

Maddie's WhisperChop. 4:15 AM. Angie.

"Rex is in this up to his eyeballs, Ange," Mary Helen said.

"No, he isn't." Angie was trying to doze. *"That wasn't him on the SD card. I'm sure of it."*

"It was him, big as life. And think about Belmont, Ange. I know you love him but think anyway."

Gretta was okay, just mad as a wet hen, so mad that she had let Adonis's identity slip to Maddie—he was supposed to be undercover, but that did not seem to work well around Angie.

Now she had stumbled onto something that went way past Rex's shooting. Unfortunately, Angie had spirited Adonis away to New York, and Gretta had gotten herself a little bit shot.

"So, what will you do, Ange, lie there and wallow in guilt?" Maddie asked.

"Why not? I got one of my best friends shot and could have gotten her killed. I could even have gotten my own son and his friends killed. I think I'll wallow for a while."

"Why do I think you're not being quite sincere, Ange," Mary Helen said, *"and why do I think you're avoiding what you've already figured out?"*

Down on the ground, tiny pinpoints of light flared.

"You're wrong, Mary Helen. I'm in over my head and have figured nothing out."

"Think about Belmont," Mary Helen said.

"I don't want to think about Belmont."

"You need to."

"I don't need to. Rex drew first, Mary Helen. I know that. He took one look at Jake Lessix, and he drew his weapon. Why would he?"

"You finally stopped avoiding the issue and asked the correct question."

Chapter 31 - Complications

I'll make somebody a good house-person someday.

—1—

Saratoga, NY. Crumb House. Gretta's Room. 10:00 AM. Dale.

Dale fluffed Aunt Gretta's pillow while Jimmu carefully set an enormous wicker basket-tray filled with sausage and Eggs Benedict in front of her on the tray table, and while Fred tried to smooth and tidy her bed with her in it. They nearly got her killed last night and did feel major guilt about it. On the other side of the coin, she may have saved their lives, which felt really sick. And on the other side of that coin, if you could find a three-sided coin, they, Jimmu especially, sort of saved everybody's lives. Dale's mother was still going to be miffed, possibly.

Boy, Dale had blown it. He had even kicked Adonis where it hurt most, and he was Gretta's son. She told them all about it after Doctor Elijah Crumb left last night—this morning, really. Fortunately, her wounds were pretty much near-miss abrasions. The doctor bought the story that she had gotten tangled in barbed wire. Of course, the doctor was a member of the Crumb family.

Dale's mom was Saratogish, too, and one of the Outhouses until she married Dale's dead father, Bernie

Schwartz. Dale's family didn't become Summers until his father went to heaven or somewhere, his mom took on the Summers penname, and then legally changed everybody's name to avoid confusion, including Dale's twin brothers.

When Jimmu took the stainless steel covers off the food, Aunt Gretta finally smiled. "You're unfired, Jimmu, and you and Fred are still my soon-to-be adopted sons. And Dale, I will sacrifice and continue publishing your mother's books despite their making me a ton of money."

"Thanks a bunch, Aunt Gretta." Dale didn't quite know what that all meant.

"Angelica is a wise woman." Gretta beamed like mad. Her hair, usually groomed to plastic perfection, had gone soft-and-wilty and loose-and-pretty. "Fred, I hope I didn't hurt you last night when I landed on you."

"Oh, you didn't." Fred giggled. "I knew it was you, and I learned to survive squishing when I tried to go out for football at school and ended with the jocks on top of me every day. Cow! I almost died at football, but you can sit on me anytime, Aunt Mirthretta." Fred possessed a keen toggle switch for cute.

"I heard about your football problems," Gretta said, "but decided to let you opt-out if you needed or wanted to, which you eventually did. Your coach told me you ended up at the bottom of more piles than Preparation H. He was amazed by how sturdy you were."

Dale wondered how Aunt Gretta could eat Eggs Benedict while she talked about hemorrhoids. Actually, she could probably keep eating no matter what.

"More coffee, Ms. Braun?"

"Indeed, Jimmu." He poured, and Aunt Gretta sipped. "You, my dear, are an excellent cook."

"You, my future Mom, are an excellent teacher. I'll make somebody a good house-person someday."

"No, you will have house persons of your own someday, and thank you for saving my life," Aunt Gretta said with a soft beaming smile that contained love Dale had never noticed in her before. "You could have gotten killed taking on that thug."

Jimmu had probably saved all their lives, and he did it spectacularly, and made Dale not want to even thumb or leg wrestle him anymore. "Yeah, Jim, thanks," Dale said. "I think he might have done us all if you hadn't done him first."

Jimmu took a step back and bowed. "We need to work on your metaphors, Master Dale, but I thank you all. The only thing that bothers me is this." He opened to page three of the Daily Gazette he had put on Aunt Gretta's tray and read, "'Unidentified man in a black Fiero killed in auto accident. Anyone with information about the deceased who was wearing a purple, chartreuse, and pink plaid jacket, should contact the County Sheriff or State Police.'"

"Or the fashion police," Gretta said. "That was him, all right. God could not allow more than one of those jackets every millennium, and I saw a Fiero on my way to The John. What have we gotten ourselves into, boys?"

"And Mrs. Lessix is in the basement of The John," Fred offered. "Dead."

"And somewhere," Jimmu said, "there are cartons of C-15 floating around with detonator packs. They were in the basement of The John, but I'll bet money they aren't there now. Ditto Mrs. Lessix."

"So, do we call the police, boys?" Gretta asked.

"No, Gretta, we don't." The voice came from the door. "The police and feds already know."

Dale didn't need to look to know that his mom had arrived and that he was in deep trouble. Her tone of voice said it all. When he looked toward the door, he saw a stark-serious mother he had never seen before. Grim would be a good word. Behind her stood Adonis and Aunt Maddie, tossing worried looks back and forth as though they had never seen Angie Summers like this before, either. Dale's mom was scaring everyone, especially Dale.

"Dale, please go to your room and wait for me. And while you wait, pack. You will return to Tate shortly, this time with private security."

"Ms. Summers, no," Fred wailed, ready to cry.

"Sorry, Fred," Gretta said, "you're going with him, so you should pack too."

Dale thought about arguing or pleading but gave up on the idea. He and Fred didn't stand a chance with his mom and Aunt Gretta in agreement, and probably Aunt Maddie as a cheerleader, not to mention Adonis's and Jimmu's muscles.

"Oh boy! Crap!" he whisper-breathed through his lips.

—2—

Saratoga, NY. Crumb House. Fred's Room. 11:05 AM. Dale.

Dale, still in PJs, and Fred, in his black underwear, sat on the bed's edge. Dale's mom stood in the middle of the room, her mouth open, tears in her eyes. They had told her the whole entire story, everything. Dale guessed that the most awful thing he'd told her was that he had seen Uncle Rex well and on foot in the window of his room at The Golden Arms. Dale even admitted to having a conversation with him, and that they talked and talked. That was why her mouth was hanging open, and her tears were dribbling out.

"And," he added, "we saw him across the street in Congress Park, too, down around the War Memorial."

"That all can't be true. It simply cannot. Why didn't you tell me this before?" She sounded a little frantic.

"I was planning to tell you, but then we did Jimmu's birthday, and you and Aunt Maddie and Adonis left for New York on the spur. You're a hard mom to keep track of. Besides that, I knew how hard you would take it. I took it hard! Jimmu, Fred, and I went to The Armpit to see him. I looked at him and tried to convince myself I had been wrong, and then he grabbed my wrist. I had sent Jimmu and Fred downstairs then. With the grab, Uncle Rex opened his eyes and looked at me, like he sort of remembered me. At least, he remembered that he should know me and said—"

"Dale," his mom wailed.

"Aw hell. That's a lie. He knew exactly who I was, and you too, Mom."

Fred handed Angie a few Kleenexes, and she took them, blotted her eyes, and dried her cheeks.

"We talked about the Snow Queen meeting," Dale said, "about you, and about a lot of stuff. When I told Fred about our conversation later, he said it sounded like it had been amnesia going into a fugue state or dissociative identity disorder or something like that. A guy hits his head, develops amnesia, and doesn't know who he is. Since he can't find his old life, he makes himself a new one, then begins to return to his old one and, for a while, vaguely remembers both but not always accurately. Fred explained that the new one could vanish as suddenly as it hit him. I think that for a while, Uncle Rex, in his head, was a Candy Trooper or a Snow Queen. Maybe he still thinks so."

"Yes, I know, Dale. I've discussed it with a psychiatrist, Dr. Fry." Dale's mom walked over and sat between Dale and Fred.

"Oh," Dale continued, "the C-15 was in Appleseed's basement along with Henrietta, and we don't know who's going to blow what or whom up. I'm sorry, Mom."

"Me too, Ms. Summers," Fred said. "I'm really sorry." Fred revved his cutes but was probably committing truth too.

Dales's mom didn't seem to know what to say at first, so she just hugged them both. That felt good, but Dale wished that she knew what to say to comfort him. She always knew what to say before this. What had he done to her?

"Dale, it was one thing for you to go sleuthing with Adonis. He has special training and a gun and would not let anything happen to you. It was something else to set out with Jimmu. And all of it was your idea, wasn't it, Dale." Not a question, really.

"Pretty much, Mom. I'll take responsibility for it anyway. I was worried about you and wanted to help. And, like Adonis, Jimmu turned out to be a good protector. First, Aunt Gretta slugged the guy with an iron skillet, then Jimmu literally flew at him, and they had an awful fight, sort of. Jim's a martial arts fury."

"I was in on it too, Ms. Summers," Fred said.

"You could have died, boys. Not that it was all your fault by any means. Jimmu should have refused, but he was doing what I asked, and you guys probably would not have allowed him to do it alone. And Gretta should have stopped you, not followed you to see what you were up to, except that she knew I thought you were up to something, to begin with. Hell, everyone's to blame, especially me."

"Then why are we the only ones getting punished, Mom."

"You aren't. You are merely being kept out of harm's way since you have failed to do a decent job of it yourselves. Also, if Gretta and I know you are both safe, we can stop worrying about you, get on with this case, and reach the end faster, however this mess ends."

"What about Jimmu?" Dale complained.

"He's old enough to make his own decisions and, according to you, is a tremendous asset in a fight. I didn't know his martial arts skills were that advanced." Dale's mom looked bummed.

"Are you still worried that he and I are doing it together, and Adonis too?" Dale finally asked.

"Doing it? It? What gave you that idea?" It was a parental surprised-concerned-curious-disingenuous tone of voice.

"Oh, come on, Mom. I saw it in your face in the window when Adonis tried to pose for us. You thought I might be having sex with Jim and Adonis, and probably Fred, too. That was when I realized that Adonis was almost possibly a fake with muscles."

"You're growing up so fast," his mom whispered.

Dale heard it as a plea not to but didn't think he could put growing up on hold just to please his mother, or Mary Margaret, either.

Softly. "Okay, Dale, I worried about it until I got to know Jimmu better. I do not know if he's gay, but he is an exceptionally responsible man. I decided that even if he wanted to seduce you, he wouldn't push."

"Does that mean you don't know me as well as you should, Mom?" Dale had wanted to ask that long ago but thought he shouldn't.

Her hands tightened and squeezed each other. "No! Yes, you're right. I should have known you better to begin with, but you're an adolescent, like an unbaked cookie. The ingredients are all there and fairly well mixed, but until you bake, no one knows what will come out of the oven. No matter what anyone else does about sexual issues, you are the one who makes the decision for you. I should not have worried. It was just that Jimmu was so much an original, and with the lives he and Fred led before Gretta, I had involuntary questions. I'm sorry."

Dale glanced at Fred, who had squeezed his lips together. Dale's mom was keeping yet something else from them.

"You know his swish mode is a big put-on, don't you?" Dale said. "He's kind of chameleonish."

"I eventually figured that out, too, but aren't we getting off the track, Dale?"

"I'm not sure I've ever found the track, much less gotten on it. I guess I'll figure myself out eventually."

"Oh, Dale." She hugged him even harder. "Couldn't you be mistaken about Rex? I can't believe that—"

"No! At least, I don't think so. I guess I could be wrong. It all happened so fast. He could have been delirious."

"I'm glad you're certain, Summers," Fred said, finally deciding to talk.

"Okay, I'm damned sure!" No matter what Dale said, his mom would find out for herself. "I talked to him, and he isn't completely right in the head, but almost. That's what happened." Dale really wanted to get off the subject.

"Do we really need to go back to Tate, Ms. Summers?" Fred asked. "We love the place, but being here is way better for summer vacations."

"No. Once we stopped being frantic, Gretta and I agreed that you two should stay here but with more supervision. We cannot just throw our kids away because they do something stupid. But for the rest of the summer, you will be brothers. And, as of tomorrow morning, you will have a live-in nanny. It's all arranged. Also, you will be moving to the Tower Suite, but we agree not to lock you in unless necessary, and you two will both agree to Gretta's and my terms or return to school with a dedicated security guard. When the Rex case is over, you can both come to New York together, and we will all have a ball with Gretta and Jimmu. No more spending vacations at Tate."

"Okay, Mom," Dale said, "but I want to help. You do know that, don't you?"

"Yes, but you'll survive taking it easy for a while. Ms. Grub will be here early tomorrow."

"Mable Grub?" Fred asked, obviously horrified. "The Latin and girls' Phys. Ed. teacher at Tate? "

"Yes. Mable was available and needed the money. I've known her for years, and she really knows kids."

Fred turned red but said nothing more.

"You'll survive, Dale," his mom said. "Gretta and I are just trying to protect you both in an uncertain situation, not punish you. I would die if anything happened to either of you. I got us into this mess, and I must finish it without hurting anyone else. And Dale?"

"Yes, Mom."

"I promise that no matter what you saw or heard, Rex has done nothing wrong. He's one of the good guys. He will recover, we will be married, and we will become a marvelous family. And I'm sorry that we must corral you two." She kissed Dale and Fred, then hurried out, closing the door.

After his mom's footsteps faded, Dale turned to Fred on the bed and said, "Yes, Mom, but I didn't promise to stay here." Dale needed to save her whether she approved of it or not. She didn't have Rex's help, so she at least should have Dale's and Fred's. Besides, they knew how to get out of the Tower Suite, even locked, and it was not by going down four floors on the trellis— that option would make them both boom their briefs, Fred especially.

"Dale," Fred said with a deep frown, "there's something I need to tell you, but if you repeat it, we will no longer be friends, and it's kind of a long story."

Chapter 32 - Nurse Maddie

Hallelujah, Deacon!

−1−

Saratoga, NY. Crumb House. Gretta's Room. 11:10 AM. Angie.

When Angie walked into Gretta's room, Maddie, of all people, was fluffing her pillow. "Nurse Madeleine, are you returning to your true calling?" Angie's voice sounded gutted even to herself.

"Buck up, girl," Mary Helen said. *"You'll make this all come out right whether you want to or not."*

"That's what I'm afraid of, Mary Helen."

"Well, what has the senior detective of the Summers family been up to?" Gretta sounded back in form.

"Very little," Angie said truthfully. "How's your nurse, Gretta? Accomplished?"

"Accomplished? Of course, she is. Maddie has spent tons of time dealing with beds. Just read *Climbing Up the Ladder in Bed: A How-To Book with Legs Selectively Spread.* It will be out in December. Besides, I do not need a nurse. I can walk fine. I am merely pampering myself over a couple of boo-boos."

"Wait until the next time you ask for the pan, Grett," Mad said. "I mean, I'm as good as you get, for the moment, but not too much longer than that."

Angie looked at her two best friends. The three of them were so close, not unlike what Jimmu, Fred, and Dale were becoming. Angie needed to include Grett and Mad in this whole mess before they accidentally stepped on a land mine — or jumped up and down on it, more likely. "Mind if I use your entertainment center, Grett? You know about The Snow Queens and The Candy Troops."

Gretta studied Angie, glanced at Maddie, then studied Angie again. "Okay," she said. The entertainment center covered most of the wall at the foot of her bed.

"Where are Jimmu and Adonis, ladies?" Angie walked to the multifaceted entertainment center and pushed in an SD card.

"They're running errands in town. Food and such." Gretta glanced quickly at Maddie. The boys were obviously not running errands.

"They're doing errands, okay, Ange, but they've gone to check on The John again," Mary Helen said. *"But to watch from afar and report. They're also bringing Gretta's precious Cadillac back from The Armpit."*

"It figures, Mary Helen. So long as Dale and Fred are safe."

"Get over it," Mary Helen snapped. *"Dale and Fred are fourteen. Keeping them truly safe ended around eleven. If you don't stop sheltering Dale, he'll just learn from someone else."*

— **2** —

Saratoga, NY. Crumb House. Gretta's Room. 2:45 PM. Maddie.

For some reason that Maddie could not imagine, these PMS surveillance recordings cards were boring her more this time than on the plane. Maybe it was because dear Angie had not shared an inkling of what she was looking for. At the moment, they were watching monied throngs move through the Senna condo during a grand ball, where Senna managed to capture pieces of every boring copulation. Nothing was as excruciating as watching writhing, mindless thongs vibrate.

Angie hit pause, then backward, then forward, one frame at a time. "There he is." She had stopped on a little gathering around the punch bowl. Senna, John Leech, and some dark, Spanish-looking guy stood there.

"There's who," Gretta asked intelligently.

Angie got up, walked to the screen, and pointed. "There."

"There's who?" Maddie added just to be in the conversation.

"There's the man I saw coming from Rex's fire entrance in The Golden Arms and walking over to John Appleseed Cottage."

"Greg Rue?" Gretta sounded like she had just found a dead rat in her bedpan, which Maddie had considered.

"Gregory Rue?" Angie walked over and sat down next to Gretta on the bed. "He was also on the list. Who is he, Gretta?"

"He owns The Golden Arms and worked for PMS until a year ago." Her eyes widened, then focused on Angie.

"Yes," Angie agreed.

Maddie wished Angie would straighten her head and accept that Rex was up to his gorgeous eyeballs in this thing.

"That's what most people thought, anyway," Gretta said. "He scouted, bought properties, everything you would expect a special assistant to a billionaire real estate developer to do. He supposedly returned to Peru."

But Maddie stopped listening, walked up to the television screen, back to the bed to take the remote out of Angie's hand, and back to the TV to replay the moment one frame at a time. Even she almost missed it. The face leaned forward for just an instant.

"Ange, I think you need to see this."

Angie ignored her and kept talking to Gretta about Rue.

"Angie!" Maddie's tone finally cut through the conversation on the bed. "Please come here. Now!"

Angie came.

Maddie pointed to the group that included Senna, Leech, Rue, and the dim but unmistakable face of Inspector Rex Caine.

Angie studied the picture forever, probably trying to make the image disappear or change into anyone else. "We all know he worked security for PMS now and then. Lots of cops did. It doesn't prove anything. Rex was there, and that is all it proves. That's absolutely all."

"Oh, Angie, please." Tears appeared in Gretta's eyes. "He was in their group. We know that you love him, but—"

Angie shook her head frantically, then pursed her lips. "It's time to visit him. Do you want to come, Maddie? Gretta, can you get along without her for a few minutes?"

"You two don't really think you're going without me, do you?" Gretta threw the covers back, hopped to the floor, then the closet. "As soon as Jimmu and Adonis get here to move the boys to the tower, we go. And there's something else. Maddie, there are three packages on the shelf. Get them out, please. I'm fine, just a little sore."

"What now?" Maddie reached up and pulled down two packages. "These are from President Watson's company, WatTechGlobal."

"Technically," Gretta said, "the president's brother, Nat Stag, owns it until he leaves office. The law he got passed while a senator demanded that."

Maddie dumped the packages on Gretta's lap, and Gretta ripped them open and pulled out some kind of long underwear.

"Soft, supportive, and bulletproof," Gretta said. "Two-piece UnderBlocs. Logan and Mike Watson are old friends. I know the kids, too, Nat Stag and President Glen. I would have ordered some for the boys had I known that they would be joining us against our wishes. Three full-body anti-penetration suits. They block bullets and darts. Here, Maddie, wave this at the chest in the bottom of the closet." She handed her a proximity card.

"You're surprising me, Gretta," Angie said.

Maddie opened the chest. "You're scaring me, too." The chest contained enough guns and ammunition to start a war. "XT200s are military weapons."

"It's enough to defend ourselves, and only that," Gretta said. "Fortunately, it's not on sale to just anybody. I just wish they came with some of Nat's Artificials to use them. I must speak to him about that."

"Some of Nat's what?" Maddie shrieked.

"Never mind." Gretta smiled for the first time today.

— 3 —

Saratoga, NY. Crumb House. Fred's Room. 3:00 PM. Dale.
Fred had pulled the covers up for a nap. They hadn't slept much last night and probably wouldn't tonight either.

Dale was on the bed across from Fred and was reading one of Fred's *Playboys*. Dale used to read *Prayboy*, a short-lived competing magazine, but had given up bigotry for the foreseeable future.

Despite himself, his interest in the Playboy pictures stuck out all over. That was more than a little depressing. He should get up and shower but didn't want to shower ever again, much less cold. It was not the sort of thing you did when your mom dumped you so she could get into trouble on her own.

Jimmu and Adonis would be here shortly to move them to the Tower Suite. The three witches had proclaimed it with no chance for an appeal, not that it would have mattered.

"I'm worried about you, Mom. You are not exactly in peak form," he said to nobody. Then Playboy caught his attention again. "Boy, that's a pair! If someone turns up with three of a kind, I'm dead."

"You really want three, Dale?"

Dale tented his book over his underwear and looked around to locate the voice. No one was there except a snoring Fred and curious Dale. "Hello?"

"Hello," the voice said.

"Who are you?"

"I'm Mary Helen Mack. Do you know who you are, or should I give you hints?"

"You're kidding." Mary Helen occasionally popped into Dale's head, but he always figured he was imagining it. She had never before spoken aloud to Dale. How could such a thing even be possible? It wasn't. At least, it shouldn't.

"Not likely. I see you've given up evangelism for sex?"

"I did that with Mary Margret Pinkham. I've decided that sex is a superior sort of evangelism." His holier-than-anybody reputation had pissed Dale off, as well as everybody else. "What do you want me to do? Look at Playboy and yell hallelujah?"

"No. I want you to be yourself and like yourself!" Mary Helen's voice didn't sound happy.

"I'm having a few problems with myself right now, but I'll work it out."

"Why problems? Because you gave up Oral Roberts for oral sex?"

Fred giggled in the other bed.

He could obviously hear Mary Helen too, or Dale was losing his mind. In fact, Dale was pretty sure he was losing his mind, as he couldn't explain actually hearing Mary Helen Mack's voice. Was this some crazy new technology? Some evolutionary leap?

"It's her, Summers," Fred said, "and don't lie to her. Mary Helen Mack be praised!"

"It's a dream," Dale said.

"Then how are we talking to each other, Summers?" Fred said.

"Hey, guys, I only did it once, and Mary Margaret Pinkham forced me, and it was only the appetizer before the main event, even though it lasted way longer than the main event."

"You feel guilty about not telling your mother that you lost your virginity to a wealthy and attractive girl your own age?" Mary Helen asked.

"No, and Mary Margaret Pinkham sort of raped me. And what boy tells his mother he's lost his virginity, much less gotten raped by a girl."

"Summers, a boy has an advantage," Mary Helen said. "If he doesn't want a girl to rape him, he automatically can't do it. So, are you bummed because you lost your virginity, and everyone knew and laughed at you for proving you are as human as any other teen despite the hallelujahs? You already knew Mary Margaret Pinkham would do it with anything, even a Fred."

"Thanks a bunch," Fred said. "I ditched her because of you, Summers."

"My friends all wanted me to get laid but didn't think there was any chance of it. So we made love. Hot duck! I was in love with her way before that. And she's not a slut. Her family is one of the richest in Saratoga. You can't be a slut if you have money."

Fred's head appeared from the blankets. "I didn't know that. I didn't bet on you one way or the other, but I didn't know that."

"If you had voted, Fred," Dale asked, "would you have voted for my clay feet or against them?"

"Clay feet have nothing to do with it," Fred said. "It's more a matter of a concrete middle."

"Being mean to a friend has lots to do with it, too, Fred." It was the only time that Dale ever doubted Fred's friendship

"Everyone kept me out of it," Fred said. "I would have stopped it, but by the time I knew, I couldn't because it'd already happened. Then I decided you really liked her, and I bowed out."

"Afterward, Mary Helen," Dale said, "everyone went around school whispering 'Hallelujah, Deacon!' to me while they grabbed their crotches. Even the girls did it. What started as a romantic rendezvous in Mary Margaret's room turned into a frigging nightmare, until I owned up to myself that I loved her."

"I should have stayed with you that night, Dale. I'm sorry." Fred sounded sorry, and probably was.

"That's okay. You should not need to stay with me, and it would have been embarrassing if you had. I should be able to take care of myself, especially with a girl. By the way, just where were you that night?"

"Well, while you learned to take care of yourself, I was with big Sadie."

"Sadie Ferencyzck? She's two years older and two feet taller than you, Fred.

"Yeah. It worked out well."

"Oh, crap."

"No, it was great."

"You lost your virginity with Sadie the same night I lost mine?"

"No, Summers. He did not!" Mary Helen put in emphatically.

"She's telling you the truth, Summers," Fred said.

"And aren't we getting off the track?" Mary Helen said.

"Oh, yeah. I am. My mom asked me that too. I moved from being worried about her to feeling sorry for myself."

"Yeah, you did," Fred agreed.

"So what are we going to do for her?" Mary Helen asked.

"Well," Dale said, "she did offer a three-way with Fred."

"What!" Fred said.

"No, what are we going to do for your mother?" Mary Helen sounded adultly indignant.

"Maybe pray that when I do it again, no one catches me at it and grabs their crotch. She did apologize and suggest that we go steady: her, Fred, and me."

"What is this, the sixties?" Mary Helen yelled. "What do we do about your mother, Summers?"

"You're nuts, Dale," Fred said. "I vote that we both get some sleep. When we wake up, we'll know what to do, whether by divine guidance or fresh brains—you pick. We'll let you know what we decide, Mary Helen."

"I'm getting worried, Fred," Dale said.

"You were born worried, Summers," Fred said.

"Yeah, I think so."

"Oh, shut up, Summers," Fred said. "And stop agreeing so much and get some sleep. I see a heavy date coming. You know what I've got to do. I explained it to you in detail, Dale. And I'm gonna do it, dangerous or not."

Dale thought about that momentarily. Fred actually had explained it in detail, and sleep did sound like a good idea. "Mary Helen be praised, Fred."

"Mary Helen be praised, Fred said."

"Thanks," Mary Helen said, then added, "I'm administering a preschool."

Chapter 33 - In the Closet

I've botched it, haven't I, Mary Helen?

–1–

Saratoga, NY. Crumb House. 6:00 PM. Angie.

Angie sat in her Rat outside Crumb House and watched. Jimmu had just returned to the house and was moving the boys to the Tower Suite. Adonis needed to orient the Tac Team and others who would participate in the raid tonight.

"I've botched it, haven't I, Mary Helen?"

"God, yes." She could be so God-damned reassuring but also might be the only one who told Angie the unfiltered truth.

"I put Dale and Fred into harm's way and have only marginally increased their safety," Angie blurted.

"Yes. Dale loves you too much to listen to your warnings."

"I'm an adult. They are both little kids." Angie was not so sure.

"Stop telling yourself that, Kid. They may be fourteen but just now are more mature than you and your friends."

"Dale promised to stop playing detective," Angie said.

"If you said that, would you be telling the truth? There's nothing you could use on the boys short of chains to prevent them from protecting and helping you."

"Maybe. Maybe not." Angie would make sure he did, someway, somehow, maybe.

The Rat's trunk opened, and Jimmu loaded Gretta's arms cache. "I hope you ladies know how to use all this."

"It's only for emergencies, Jim," Angie said. "And yes, we've been trained. We learned in Manhattan. Most women there have."

"Boy," Jimmu said, "Dale has got himself a SuperMom, and so do Fred and I. Good luck, Ms. Summers." He pressed the trunk closed.

Five minutes later, the passenger and back doors opened, and Maddie and Gretta climbed into Angie's quad, Gretta in front and Maddie in the rear. "Everything secure in the house, girls?"

"Absolutely," Gretta said," and Jimmu is there to guard our mini-sleuths and, in the process, to keep himself home, which I can't demand but do desire."

"You two are overprotective beasts," Maddie said. "Dale was right—we need a cauldron."

"I hope not." Angie started the car. "I left mine on East 64th Street." She pulled away. "Besides, we are The Fellowship of the Cauldron."

–2–

Saratoga, NY. Crumb House. Tower Suite. 6:30 PM. Dale.

"I wanta go to The Golden Arms," Dale said. He and Fred were lying awake, side-by-side in bed because Jimmu wanted the other Tower Suite bed tonight.

"You're kidding, Summers."

"I never kid."

"Jesus."

"Isn't involved," Dale said. "Will you do it with me?"

"I guess we could call a cab."

"We can't get a cab," Dale corrected, "not with Cindy McGraw's Grand Ball going on across the street. I figured that you might consider driving me."

"Jesus, Summers."

"Jesus didn't ace Driver's Ed, but you did."

"I can, but I don't much want to," Fred said. "Aren't we in enough trouble? And there are too many bad guys and gals around. Besides, Aunt Gretta told me to stay put, and I plan to be good for a few days. And besides that, your mom said —"

"You already told me that too," Dale said. "Now forget what my mom said, and Aunt Gretta too."

"Again?"

"Again. Mom may be a great writer. Okay, I've read all her books more than once, love Mary Helen Mack, and talk to her like you do. By the way, when did she start talking to you too?"

"When I moved in with you," Fred said.

"She'll help. The problem is that Mom's obviously stress-struck, not thinking clearly, and needs our help too. And I don't know how I know, but something is going to go haywire nuts."

"I don't want Aunt Gretta sitting on me again," Fred said.

"You're fourteen, and she's your guardian, soon your mom. You admitted that without Gretta, Mom, Jimmu, and Rex, you would still be a turned-loose slum kid while your brother tried to support you working as a Mail Room Attendant. Aunt Mirthretta will definitely sit on you sometimes. You being you, maybe more than sometimes. Now are you going to drive me, or am I going to drive myself? You do have a key to the EscaladeLectro, don't you?"

"Oh God no, don't drive. And yes, I do know the codes. It doesn't have keys. Aunt Mirthretta was collaborating with me to ensure I would pass Drivers Ed, given my height and everything. You win, Summers. You're a pain in the southern hemisphere but are my best-damned friend. Let's round up some pillows and a disguise."

"Done."

"We'll need to wait until Jimmu leaves," Fred said.

"How do you know he's leaving?"

"Because someone locked the first-floor door, and he's the only one here. Jimmu's on orders from Aunt Mirthretta and will lock our downstairs door for appearances until we get Grim Grub, our nanny. Jim knows we can get out. Gretta knows how too but doesn't know we know. Either way, we can do what we want after Jim leaves."

"How do you know all this stuff?" Dale felt a little left out, even miffed.

"Getting out? I already showed you. The builders intended this as a stop on the underground railroad, for hiding and recuperating before escaping to one of the Adirondack Houses and then to Canada. All the rest sites contained multiple emergency exits. Later, they were popular during prohibition to escape raids. That's why there's more than one way out down there. Jimmu locked the tower door because he was planning to go out. To protect me, he wouldn't tell me where. He just said he needed to meet someone. He's a protective big brother, and I'm a short little brother, but we like each other despite that—lots. We're symbiotic. Like I told you, we have been through big-time troubles and lived to lie about it. What I didn't tell you was that I think I'm the key to this mess, just don't ask how."

"How are you the key?"

"I said don't ask!"

"I suppose," Dale said. "And you and Jimmu are symbiotic? Does that have something to do with sex? It's okay. I can keep your secret. You always seem to know more about the real world than I do."

"Tiny birdies come in threes and often eavesdrop on the Ps—Parents. Besides, Maddie told me. Adonis is an undercover special agent on assignment apart from being Gretta's son and my soon-to-be-adopted brother."

"Does Maddie know she told you?" Dale asked.

"Use your imagination, get up, and look out back. I think I just heard a car." Dale jumped up and ran to the windows with Fred inches behind him. "The Beamer has disappeared. Get dressed, Fred."

"Yeah. Being naked is unnecessary when possibly getting shot at. We better change to our night-stealth blacks—thanks for the alterations. You do know, Summers, that we've bombed out playing detective so far, don't you?"

"And we could again, Wang."

"Yeah. 'Wang.' That makes me feel so much better," Fred said as he picked up his clothes off the floor.

"I wonder where Mom, Maddie, and Gretta went," Dale said, exchanging his pre-ragged teen jeans and green and puce knit shirt hangar in the closet for the all-black casual-dress clothes. "Mom's car is gone, and I haven't heard a Maddie shriek or any other Witch Triumvirate sounds."

"Hey! One of those witches is your mother, who promised to be my writing mentor. The other two promised to help me too. Maddie wants me to write a column called *Climbing Up* and aim it at mothers. It's a big cauldron. Two publishing CEOs and one best-selling author critiquing my writing and helping me with publication when I'm ready—that is major to a little Asian immigrant who not long ago spent time in the dark with only my brother holding a candle. These days, three witches and a ton of money is what you need to have a bestseller."

"Yeah, you're right," Dale reluctantly agreed. "Besides, Mom is my buddy when she's not writing dirty crime thriller bestsellers and sticking me in the attic."

"It's a Tower Suite. Let's get going." Fred walked over to the armoire, reached under, and slipped the latch he'd showed Dale yesterday. The trap door next to the armoire eased up. Fred pushed it the rest of the way and revealed the stairway Henrietta Keeler probably used. "She was too smart for her own good and should have stayed put. She either found the latch or the key down at the bottom of the stairway. I do wonder who killed her. I bet it was the same someone who shot Jimmu's car. I love that car, and as soon as I get my license, he's gonna give it to me. I'll leave the bullet holes. They're friendly conversation topics."

—3—

Saratoga, NY. The Golden Arms. Suite P7. 7:15 PM. Inspector Rex Caine.

"Is everything set, Caine?" They were looking across the road at The John Appleseed Cottage.

Rex had met this man only once before, and he didn't make sense then, either. He could not remember this man, his function in the world, or his dubious right to live there. He seemed to know Rex, though. The guy seemed devoid of trustable atoms. "Yes. Everything." Rex seemed to be regaining his ability to read people.

The man had mentioned the C-15. This was Rex's client. This man wanted them destroyed, the ones down there, The Snow Queens and the infiltrated Candy Troops, who were arriving at John Appleseed while Rex watched. He saw them with his own eyes. He knew some but could not remember their names, just that he once worked with some of them. But this guy wanted more than that. The casino! The Grand Ball. His competitors and enemies were attending.

"I was sorry to hear about Senna," the man said.

"Yes. Some will miss PMS. What about the money?" Until this minute, Caine hadn't remembered the money, but that was part of this.

Something was changing in Rex, pushing out.

The man smiled. His face looked as though it rarely smiled. He nodded, put the catalog onto the bed, and opened it. "It's here—half now, half after. Small bills, as we agreed."

Strange sort of accent. Rex couldn't place it. It seemed a blend of Hebrew and Spanish. At the moment, he doubted that he could place any accent, but it was coming back slowly.

"Okay." Until then, he would fake it. He remembered the little boy he killed, the one the rats ate, thanks to Rex. The greatest defeat of his life.

"The detonator's set for just past midnight here and at the Canfield Casino. The kill switch is in the War Memorial. Of course, you know that because you set it up here and there."

"Yes." He vaguely remembered the C-15 and the body.

"The dealer guests we want are staying late at John Appleseed to expedite side deals. After the event, I'll be

at Congress Park with the money. I want to see the fun."
He tried to smile again.

Rex nodded. "Whatever." He would be there to kill
Rex.

The man studied Rex for a moment. "Are you okay,
Caine? You seem different?"

"It's me, all right." Flat. Even. "I'm just concentrating
on the job."

"Good. I like that. I was worried. One of Zazak's guys
got killed last night. Rego's not too delighted about that."

"How?"

"What?"

"How did he die?"

"Car ran into a tree and burned. Drunk. It happens,
but anything queer raises questions, and Rego can't kill
a tree to resolve the problem. The guy was supposed to
check out Appleseed for the meet and then report back
to Rego. Most of our top guests checked it out. Any
complaints, I call off the meeting. A need for an optional
change often highlights the unexpected."

"Don't call it off." Rex smiled.

The slimy man smiled back. "Wouldn't dream of it."
He turned to go. "Today's Appleseed meeting should
go until 2:00 or 3:00 this afternoon. Most will leave and
then return for the social around 8:00. That's when the
real deals will happen. I won't be there, but I will attend
Cindy Ellen's party at the casino, then slip out in time to
live. The Appleseed Cottage, Canfield Casino, Snow Queens,
and Candy Troops will be history when this is over. My
enemies and competition will be gone. Cindy Ellen
McCraw and her guests will be acceptable casualties for
the greater good, my greater good, anyway."

"Rue?" The name came from nowhere. The dead
part of Rex's brain had become a cesspool of writing

words and images, but one in which he was swimming increasingly better.

"Yeah?"

"Don't be late. I'll be in Congress Park during the blast, not one second more. Reach me by then with the money, or no boom, and you're crap-toast."

"It's going to be quite a show." Rue gloated until Rex wanted to puke. "The blast will go off just after the fireworks start?"

"Yeah. Approximately."

"Wouldn't miss it. I'll leave the casino in time to watch it with you, and I'll have the money."

What he would do was try to kill Rex. No one would hear a shot during the fireworks. This affair was looking like Congress.

Rex whirled, grabbed Rue's throat, rammed him against the wall by the window, and stared into his wet gelatin eyes. "Of course, you will. Neither you nor I will leave before it happens. Think, Rue. Use that beady brain of yours and think. Doublecross me, and you and your son are dead."

Rue raised his trembling hand and pressed down on Caine's gently.

Rex regained himself. He could not afford to let this bastard know the truth, whatever that turned out to be. He could not kill Rue now. Later, he'd kill Rue, or Rue would kill him. "You do your part. I'll do mine."

Rue nodded.

Rex had frightened him and enjoyed doing it. The Candy Troops might have the right idea.

— 4 —

Saratoga, NY. Crumb House. Tower Suite. 7:40 PM. Dale.
"Hey, Dale, where are we going."

"Tate. Our bikes are in the Tate shed but aren't Spielberg models. They don't fly but will do for the ridge if we can get to Tate in the Caddy."

"And Aunt Mirtha's EscaladeLectro has special stuff," Fred said. "I thought about Jimmu's Elantra, but the bullet holes might attract attention, especially since shit drops are falling on our heads anyway. Since I'm driving without supervision and at night, I prefer that no badges pull me over. If that happens, we'll end up in custody, handcuffed to chairs, until someone comes to get us, which, all things considered, they probably won't."

Fred was carrying two taped-together stacks of paperbacks authored by Cagey Magee, one of his favorites, and also a Sleepgram Pillow. Dale carried the other Sleepgrams and Fred's disguise. Fred carried a permit and had aced Drivers' Ed, but Dale didn't want to think about them getting caught. Fred's height was more like an eleven- or twelve-year-old's than the old man of fourteen he really was.

They headed down the stairs to the underground railroad. Dale closed the trap door.

–5–

Saratoga, NY. The Golden Arms. 7:45 PM. Angie.

Angie carefully drove up the long, curved driveway to The Golden Arms, and then around to the side parking lot. From here, they could watch the goings and comings at The Arms, John Appleseed's raucous party, and the private exit from Rex's suite, four floors straight up from them.

Angie got out, propped her binocs on the windshield top, and focused them on The John. They had driven over with the Rat's top down on this glorious evening: warm, slight breeze, full moon. Glorious.

"*I agree,*" Mary Helen said. "*I feel like stripping naked and basking in the moonlight.*"

"*Sharks bask,*" Ange told her.

This was what Angie should do, wasn't it? They all expected her to make a fool of herself playing amateur detective, but she needed to figure out Rex's true state and solve the mess he left, no matter what.

"*And I bask with the sharks,*" Mary Helen whispered.

As far as the dead body and explosives the boys mentioned went, Angie would not even dignify that with a second thought. She reported it but could think about it no more, given the chaos across the road and the expensive cars parked around The John Appleseed Cottage. This resembled the Mafia bosses' meeting at Apalachin. She watched a stretch limo pull up.

Two heavy-set gentlemen got out and looked around, then opened the limo's back door. A well-dressed man and a stunning blonde got out.

"Let me see," Maddie whispered, standing behind her with Gretta. Angie gave her the binocs. "That's Lester Tozzi. He's from Chicago. He likes blondes, takes them with him the way some men carry hip flasks, but he discards them much more easily, but that blonde is Marsha Lessix!"

"*Maddie has been doing her homework, Ange,*" Mary Helen said. "*Tozzi's a disgusting letch. Not too bad in the sack, though. If Marsha is hanging with him, she's in this up to her ingloriously enhanced boobs.*"

"It looks like my exposé hit that one on the nose, Angie," Mad said. "And I would be quite dead if we had published it."

The draft of Maddie's article had been informative. "You're right, Mad," Angie said. "I found pictures of everyone on the list, and they're likely right down there."

"The meeting of The Snow Queens will come to order," Mary Helen said.

"And the Candy Troopers are here too," Angie told her. *"Likely here to slaughter The Snow Queens. I suppose you think this will go off with a bang, Mary Helen."*

"That's the way C-15 works, Ange. You could bust their asses, though. Caches of explosives are illegal. Also, the cops are looking for some of the drugthugs down there, and others are illegals, country-wise. You could buzz the straight fuzz, President Glen Watson, Immigration, Ice, drunk politicians, FritzAdonis, or First Lady Nips... somebody. You're in over your God-damned head, Kid."

"Most of that I already know." Angie knew exactly why she would not call the police. She could not quite believe that Maddie, Gretta, and she were standing here watching another Apalachin-style convention, comprising the most lethal drugthugs in the world and the cops who wanted to kill them, and somewhere the feds and cops who wanted to scoop up the whole bunch.

"How could the police not notice something like this, Mad?"

"You know the answer to that, Ange," Gretta said.

"I do not believe that the NYPD is in on this," Angie said.

"You know the answer to that, too. They're not," Gretta said. "The Candy Troops are a small group of vigilantes. Some may belong to the NYPD, but they're not even an infinitesimal part of the force."

"Including Rex?" Angie asked.

"That we don't know, and you don't either, Ange," Maddie said. "Reason with your evidence, not your gut."

"Don't you use your gut, Mad?" Gretta asked.

"Wrong body part," Maddie said.

"No!" Angie shook her head. "I believe in him. Rex put the honor and integrity of the system above everything."

"How did you learn about the plan details, kid?" Maddie asked. "My exposé mostly touched on generalities, a few names, and pictures."

"The microfilm segment I didn't show anyone, including you two, contained the plan. I thought the plan came from The Candy Troops, but now I believe it was Rex's, or that of whoever he is working for. I have not trusted anyone from the beginning. I'm sorry. I have other sources, too."

"Oh, my God," Gretta said. Another car arrived, a BMW i9, hot-pink in John Appleseed's outdoor lights. A corpulent man with a goatee got out, followed by two boys and a girl, eleven or twelve, and two large companions, probably 300 pounds each, undoubtedly guards.

"*Who's that one?* Mary Helen asked. "*And why's he bringing kids to a summit meeting of criminals?*"

"I think it's Jesus Velazquez," Gretta said.

"According to the source material for Maddie's article," Angie said, "he's often seen with kids but doesn't have any of his own. He borrows them, I guess."

"Rents is more like it," Maddie said.

"*That's sick,*" Mary Helen put in.

"*Rex couldn't be part of this,*" Angie said. "*He just couldn't, Mary Helen.*"

"*Wise up, will you, Kid. Of course, he's in on it,*" Mary Helen snarled.

"*Shut up, Mary Helen,*" Angie murmured. "*Shut up!*"

"I will not shut up. You're making a God-damned fool of yourself. You're looking the other way because you think you love him."

"I do love him." This time, Angie forced Mary Helen out of her mind.

A black EscaladeLectro pulled in and parked in front of The John Appleseed Cottage. Angie recognized Rego Zazak, a Polish weasel who marketed drugs and human beings. He glanced around and walked straight into the front door of The Appleseed Cottage, followed by two companions. He had driven himself.

A man exited from Rex's private entrance, walked to a Hyundai parked next to the road, and drove away toward Saratoga.

"No. Yes. Maybe?" Angie said.

"What the hell does that mean, Angie?" Gretta asked.

"That was Gregory Rue."

Chapter 34 - Wang Lei Lóng

We're not riding Spielberg bikes.

—1—

Saratoga, NY. Crumb House. Back Parking Lot. 9:00 PM. Dale.

At Aunt Gretta's Cadillac EscaladeLectro, Fred punched in a code, opened the driver-side door, then unlocked the passenger-side door for Dale.

It took a while to put on the disguise. Fred stacked the Sleepgram Pillows on the seat, put on a hat and Adonis's chauffer's coat—they had stapled the bottom two feet of it up—then sat on the ground and taped his Cagey Magee paperbacks to his feet, so he could reach the pedals, as Dale had so often seen him do for Driver's Ed. They should have done the feet first, but possibly not, maybe. The main problem was making his head look old or, at least, not too young. Fortunately, Dale had helped with makeup for the Drama Club productions and now with Fred's head.

When they finished, Fred simply said, "Let's go," feisty little best friend and Asian dwarf that he was. He was not really a dwarf—he had just started out small and hadn't reached his growing spurt yet.

Fred climbed into the EscaladeLectro and started the engine. "If you ever tell anybody about the next two things I'm going to show you, I'll divorce you as a roommate."

Dale couldn't imagine how there could be any secrets left between them. "Okay. I hereby promise to forget your past street secrets, devious now secrets, and whatever future secrets you perpetrate." The street history Fred had told him about had fried Dale's gonads. Now, Fred reached to the dash, flipped a switch, and typed something on the little keyboard. The GPS screen disappeared, replaced by a map decorated with colored triangles.

"That's a map of Saratoga and surrounding junk," Dale said. "What are the triangles?"

"Everybody's cars, each a different color triangle. Your mom's Rat is at The Golden Arms. Adonis's BroncEV is on the road to the New York State Police barracks. Jimmu's Beamer is heading toward The Arms or The John, and there we are, sitting in Aunt Mirthretta's precious Cadillac EscaladeLectro, next to the WatStretchEV over there."

"That looks complicated. How did you learn how to use it?"

"Jimmu. Who else? Aunt Mirthretta taught him. All our cars have them, but I think only Aunt Mirthretta, Jim, and I have the password to look at everyone's simultaneously."

"Hey, Fred, why don't you use your Chinese name. You shouldn't need to change your name just because you're an immigrant."

"I didn't, not legally. It's Wang Lei Lóng. You know that."

"Why don't you use it?"

"Chinese surnames come first. You work it out."

"Lóng Wang Lei. What's wrong with Lóng Wang? Oh, but that's whang, not wang. It's in one of my mom's books."

"It's both. So you use Long Dick Dale, and I'll do me." Fred opened the garage door and backed out slowly. The door closed behind them. "Hey, Summers?"

"Yeah."

"Where are we going again?"

"Tate School for bikes, then The Golden Armpit of Rue."

"I know you said that before. I just wanted to make sure you hadn't changed your mind again."

—2—

Saratoga, NY. The Golden Arms. 9:45 PM. Angie.

Angie led Maddie and Gretta up the path to Rex's outside door and picked the lock.

"There's no alarm I can see, Kid," Mary Helen said.

"I know. I checked it when I visited. I also cased the lock."

"Has it occurred to you that we might be the over-the-hill gang?" Maddie put in.

"Speak for yourself," Gretta whisper-snarled.

"I know what's wrong with Rex, ladies." Angie quietly opened the door that led up to P7 and into Rex's suite. The bed looked rumpled, but Rex was nowhere to be seen.

"Watch out, Kid. Something's wrong here."

"Or right, Mary Helen." Angie could feel Maddie's and Gretta's body heat close behind her.

"Four hot women snooping and one hot comatose cop ambulating? What could frigging go wrong, Kid?"

"Shut up, Mary Helen."

The door to the nurse's room opened. Rex appeared from it, naked and pointing a gun at them.

"I told you so," Mary Helen whispered.

— 3 —

Saratoga, NY. Gretta's EscaladeLectro. 10:10 PM. Dale.

Dale and Fred made it out of town without a cop noticing. Tate School was three more miles. Dale was wearing sunglasses on his forehead and the fedora and trench coat he wore in Tate School's Ninth Grade production of *Whose Body Is It, Anyway?*

Fred was a great driver. He stayed in the lane and everything, lots better than Dale ever did in Driver's Ed. Of course, Fred always insisted on getting out of the car when Dale's turn came around.

"Son of a gun, we did it, Summers."

"Yeah. I never doubted it." Dale had doubted a little, but Fred was the most remarkable person Dale ever knew, next to Dale's mom, Jimmu, and Rex. He guessed he could leave Rex out of that now. And his mom was a mom, so she didn't count. And he didn't really know Jimmu well — he was complicated. So really, Fred was the most remarkable, but that didn't count either since they were roommates. "How did you learn to drive, Fred?"

"Before Driver's Ed? Trial and error. I can also hot-wire. Sometimes I practiced driving in the cars that Jimmu and I slept in, before he got a job and a so-so place for us to live until Aunt Mirthretta discovered us. I always put the cars back."

"Oh."

"Thar she blows! The Silver Cup of Tate next door to The Armpit of Rue."

Fred pulled just down the road. His hands were shaking a little. "It's really getting cold, isn't it."

Dale looked at him hard for a minute. His face and hands shined in the light from the dashboard. "You okay, Fred?"

"Sure. I just felt a little chilly or something. A cold breeze, I guess. Or maybe I'm catching Covid or something. Or I'm scared about what I'm going to do later."

"Fred, I know I got you into this and that you've got my back, but please don't get reckless like you sometimes do at school. You're way too big a good habit for me to consider going on in this affair without you."

"Big?"

"Yeah," Dale said. "Big."

"Thanks for the thought, Summers. In case you didn't notice while you were psychoanalyzing me, I just parked behind the Tate School bike shed — that's why I got a chill. Stop and think. If we had gone along with coming back here, your mom or somebody would have driven us, and I would not have needed to steal and illegally drive. The next time, please try to plan ahead."

"Don't mention it. But I'm right. Kids our age are less noticed on bikes than driving Cadillacs."

***

The school owned a million bikes, mostly ten-speed climbers, so small groups could go on trips and junk without using one of the buses. That was one of the neat things about Tate: you got to go places and do things, people, and stuff.

The crash came immediately after Dale boosted Fred through the tiny window into the bicycle shed.

"Are you okay, Freddy," Dale whispered loudly. No answer came from the shed, and Dale started worrying about whether he had a dead Fred on his hands.

A scrambling rattle came, then a hoarse whisper. "Sure, Dale, I'm okay for a four-foot kid who fell six feet and knocked over ten thousand bicycles. And I'll gobble your cob if you stop calling me Freddy. Only Jimmu uses that."

"Just say thanks. Hurry up and open the door. I don't like exposing myself out here."

No answer came until the side door opened. "You've never exposed yourself anywhere," Fred said.

"Mary Margaret would disagree." Dale slipped in, closed, and locked the door behind him. It took a moment for his eyes to adjust, but pretty soon, he saw Fred standing five or six feet away, his hair ruffled up like a tornado had caressed him, a bleeding gash on his forehead — well, more of a little nick with the runs. The top two buttons of his dress shirt had disappeared, exposing his smooth little chest. "Are you hurt?"

Fred shook his head very slowly and pointed to the long row of bikes that had toppled with, on, or under him.

Dale thought it best not to linger on spilled Fred and plowed ahead. "So pick which one you want, and let's get going."

Fred nodded. "As you said, this isn't *ET,* and we're not riding Spielberg bikes — or did I say that already."

Once Dale picked two bicycles, wiped and mounted Fred, they eased outside and slowly rode up the Tate Road to the ridge bike path, and got on with it. They stopped a little above their crushed grass parking plot in the woods, hid their bikes, then crept down the hill.

They would be able to see everything from there. Dale was using The Armpit lights to keep them on the straight and narrow — actually bent and on a hill. When Dale heard low voices, he grabbed Fred's shoulder to stop him.

After they crept closer, Fred whispered, "Holy crap," which kind of covered the thing. "Will you look at that?"

They were just above their secret parking place. Two figures stood by a black car. Dale couldn't tell what kind. At The John Appleseed Cottage across the road, raucous music blurted into the evening. Outside lighting reflected off the windshields of the many parked cars, as well as a bunch of large attendant types.

It looked like maybe a Beamer in their private parking spot, and it was not alone. Two guys were standing there, not Jimmu or Adonis, with their pants down. One of the guys was a female woman—you could tell by the silhouettes. Dale and Fred shushed each other and crept down through the trees until they were on their bellies in the underbrush about ten feet away.

"What was that?" The man spoke with a foreign accent.

Dale and Fred froze.

"Probably nothing," the woman said. "Maybe somebody hunting. Sound carries next to a ridge." The woman's voice had a tough sound to it, like what Dale always thought Mary Helen's should sound like.

"Maybe we ought to wait and see who," the man said.

"I suppose, but I don't want to wait," the woman said.

The man laughed softly, leaned down, and kissed her, tongue first. Dale vaguely considered that he had moved from housebreaking to peep-tomming. He could feel Fred take a deep breath. Of course, they really should not be seeing what was going on here, but they were here and wanted to.

It didn't take the her and him long to get going. That probably meant they were part of the huge gang across the street at The John. He pulled her blouse and bra off over her head and got her to step out of her pants. Her nipple tips glinted in the light from The John. The man silhouette pushed her back against the car, then nearly lifted her off the ground with the force of the thing.

"Hallelujah!" Dale whispered.

"Come on," Fred whispered. "We can get away now without their noticing us."

"Hallelujah," Dale whispered again but followed Fred as they slid back, walked on their knees, then ran on tippy toes toward the huge Armpit lawn.

They slipped over the lawn and up the path to Rex's fire exit/private entrance. The Arms stuck out like a golden castle on a hill while the party was going full blast across the road at The John.

"Hey, Fred, I wonder if they're all doing it across the street. Naw. That would be an orgy."

According to Fred, grownups' recovery time couldn't match Dale's and Fred's automatics. Also, being adults, the bunch across the road didn't care how much noise they made because they were Teflon and not afraid of getting caught.

"There's your mom's Rat." Fred pointed to the end of The Arms, to the top of the private driveway to Rex's room.

They found the entrance door that led up to Rex's suite unlocked, which was super. Dale couldn't stand anything else going wrong. His mother was here somewhere, and Dale intended to find and protect her. She was not up to her hyper-alert self, and her up-and-around Uncle Rex might not even know her and might decide she was his enemy.

They started the long four-story climb. "Why couldn't your Uncle Rex have rented a ground-floor room," Fred said.

When they reached the fourth floor, Dale opened his fly and pulled out a short crowbar.

"Where did you carry that?"

"On my thigh. Where else? I can't pick locks like my mom can."

"I can pick some," Fred said. "Besides, the door is unlocked."

Fred held the door open and ushered Dale through. Inside, the bed stood empty except for three Berettas, and the air seemed hot, heavy, and maybe a little damp.

"Let's try the nurse's room," Fred said. "It's down that hall. I snooped there the last time. Take the guns. They belong to the Witch Triumvirate."

Dale eased the nurse's door open. The bed lay tumbled over. Torn panties lay on the floor. They weren't Rex's—he wore Calvin Kleins. A pile of used condoms lay on the bedside table, some ossified. Dale didn't know what kind of condoms Rex used—that was private—but whoever fornicated here was obviously counting.

"What the hell went on here," Fred said. "Why would someone attack Rex?"

"For one," Jimmu said behind them, "because he's not one of The Candy Troops. I think that he's still on the right side, except that he may not know it or how to do it, and no one knows what he will do next, so consider him dangerous. Come on, guys, we need to get out of here. Also, what took you so long. "

"My mom's here," Dale complained, "and I'm not leaving until I find her." Jimmu's popping up out of nowhere no longer surprised Dale.

"You're not kidding me, Dale?" Jimmu asked.

"Where did you park, Jim?" Fred asked.

"At our spot in the woods, but I came in the front door."

"Mom's Rat is around the end from Uncle Rex's entrance," Dale said. "She has to be here."

"He's not crapping you, Jim," Fred said. "We borrowed Aunt Mirtha's EscaladeLectro and used the tracking device, then came here from school by bike. Your Beamer is over in our space?"

"Yes."

"When we were on foot, we saw a couple from the party fornicating on your car. I guess you locked it."

"You're playing with fire, guys," Jim snapped.

Dale heard a wooden thud.

"Stay behind me," Jim added. "I may be twenty now, but I'm close enough to a kid that I can still smack you two silly and—"

"Shhh," Dale interrupted. He sniffed. "That's Aunt Gretta's perfume, and there's scratching somewhere." He walked to the nurse's room closet and opened it.

Jimmu stepped into the closet, tapped around, then pulled open a plywood panel in the back wall. They saw a little storage space eight feet by eight feet that opened into the closet on the near side, and then into the hall beyond. The outside plywood was down too.

"What are those curly yellow things," Dale asked.

"Tac restraints," Jimmu said, "and they've been cut."

"My God, we were all in that little space." Aunt Maddie's voice behind them in the closet.

"Good job, Jim." Aunt Gretta's voice.

A third said, "Hi, Dale." Dale's mom's voice. She, Aunt Gretta, and Aunt Maddie had just appeared behind them, rubbing their wrists, when Mark Kershaw pushed past the ladies, Dale and Fred's tough little eight-year-old mentoree at Tate.

"Shit. What's going on, guys?"

Not far behind him, Marion, Marvin, and Mannie Kershaw thundered in, probably trying to corral Mannie's Mark. Together, the Kershaws weighed a ton and a half and worked for the NYPD, all crowded into the closet behind Dale, Fred, Jimmu, the Publishing Coven, and little Mark. Because Dale and Fred mentored the kid, the big Kershaws often stopped to ask how the little guy was doing at Tate.

"Hi, Dale," Mannie said. "The raid will start in forty-five minutes, Ms. Summers."

"Are you involved, Officer Mannie?" Dale asked.

"No," Marvin said. "This is a Fed and State party, but we're piped in and can help on request."

"Mannie," Dale's mom said, "according to Jimmu, there's a load of explosives around somewhere. I don't know where or why. I reported it, but I think the dispatcher thought I was a queer crank."

"Have you actually seen them, Ms. Summers?" Mannie asked.

"No, but Dale, Fred, and Jimmu have."

"Cartons of C-15," Jimmu said, "with detonator packs. They were in the shed behind The John but moved to the basement. I suspect they're not there anymore, but that's a guess."

"That's good enough for us," Mannie said. "I'll send an alert. Where's Rex?"

"I don't know," Angie said. "Wherever he is, he is in a dissociative fugue, in and out of probably two life realities, possibly even remembering things that never happened—not the way he thinks, anyway. He might see you or us as friend or enemy, and he is armed."

"How do you know that, Ms. Summers," Jimmu blurted.

"A little birdie and two different psychiatrists. I have not been exactly idle. Also, he pointed a gun at us when he tied us up and herded us into the closet's secret compartment."

"Me," Gretta blurted. "I'm the birdie."

"I may know where he's going," Fred said. "And Aunt Mirtha, I need to tell you something that may slightly gruff you."

"It's not like you often admit when you're wrong, Fred, so out with it. I promise to forgive you if you deserve it." Gretta glared down at poor dead Fred.

"Dale and I kinda drove your EscaladeLectro from Crumb House to Tate School." He shrugged and turned his mouth down. "We took bikes from there to here." Fred eased behind Marion Kershaw, the biggest thing in the room apart from the floor.

"Forget the car!" Aunt Gretta gasped. "You. You. The two of you could have died." She turned from red grape to purple grape. "Why the hell didn't somebody arrest you?"

"We wanted to go where you guys went," Dale volunteered. "I figured that here would possibly be a good place to start, maybe, probably," Dale lied so as not to condemn Fred more by letting Aunt Gretta know that Fred had revealed the car-tracking thing to him. "We were right. You are here."

"Hey, Aunt Mirtha," Fred bitched, "I made top grades in Drivers Ed, and in addition, you taught me, and on top of that, Jimmu taught me before I even met you."

"That's true." Jimmu shrugged.

"How did you reach the pedals," Angie asked.

"Cagey Magee paperbacks?" Grett asked. Her face was barely under control and was blackish-purple with mild discontent.

"Yeah. Foot Magee's as usual," Fred said.

"And what's in your boys' pants," Gretta said, studying.

"Your guy's guns. They were on the bed when we came." Fred pulled two Berettas out of the front of his pants and handed one to Maddie and the other to Gretta.

"How did you keep your pants up?" Gretta's scowl could have turned dirt to stone.

"Tight bikinis," Fred whispered with a shrug.

"This one," Gretta said, "is cocked."

Dale carefully whipped his mom's gun out and handed it to her.

"Maybe you should forgive Lóng Wang some, Ms. Gretta," Mannie said. "We spotted the boys parking at Tate and then leaving on bikes in this direction. Fred did an excellent job—I couldn't have parked better. We guessed where they were going. We're keeping Mark with us until the affair across the street finishes. Fred and Dale took off along the ridge trail in the back of here. They didn't come by the road or go past The Appleseed Cottage. They showed good sense. There was little danger, but I'm sure Marion will spank Lóng Wang if you really want him to."

Fred slipped from behind Marion to behind Dale's mom. "You're not safe there either, Fred," she said quietly. "Dale was with you. You two are going to Tate now and staying there with a guard."

"No, damn it!" Dale stomped his foot, turned on his heel, and faced his mom. "Enough of this! I *talked* to Uncle Rex just like I told you, and Fred and I saw him leaving Congress Park. You dissed me with a 'you couldn't have' then diddled the lead away, woman!"

Everyone looked at Dale as though his nose had dropped off.

Fred eased away from Ms. Summers's backside to rejoin Dale's.

Jimmu had been quietly taking this all in but finally blurted, "Hell, I'll spank Fred myself. I told him to go to bed and stay out of this." Then he turned his swish on. "I was his substitute father until Aunt Mirtha sent him to Tate, and I knew perfectly well that all this fecal residue was heading for a scrumptiously huge fan with him probably in the middle of it—that's Fred." Then he turned it off. "I didn't want Freddy even near this mess, and I'm lividly pissed up one side and down the other that he's here."

Mark looked up. "Uncle Marion, do you really spank kids?"

"Definitely!"

"Cow!" Mark whispered.

"Jimmu," Aunt Gretta said, "take them back to Tate with you and tell Headmaster Fessin to keep them there, in chains in his office, if necessary."

Those were the words that Dale most did not want to hear again.

"If they go to Tate, Mom, and ma'ams," Jimmu said sincerely, "they'll just find a way out and risk their lives worse. They should stay with us because it's probably the safest place to be tonight. The boys can stay with me, and I will definitely control them."

"Oh, jeez, Dale," Fred said. "He means it. I can tell."

Chapter 35 - The Kershaw Boys

Does that surprise you, Ange?

—1—

Saratoga, NY. Tate School. 10:35 PM. Angie.

Angie pulled her Rat into the Tate School campus and went straight to the bike shed. "No EscaladeLectro!"

"Does that surprise you, Ange," Mary Helen whispered. *"Fred promised to return to Crumb House, not to refrain from driving, and not to remain in any particular place. He's such a boy after my own heart."*

"Where is he?"

"Somewhere over that way."

"Great!" Gretta snarled. "I didn't punish him for illegally driving my car, so he drove it again." She loved her cars almost as much as she loved Spencer and Sons.

"Fred is such a sweet child," Maddie said. "He reminds me of myself."

"Fred likely drove the EscaladeLectro back to Crumb House, Gretta," Angie said, "to undo what he did and make everything right."

"I've never spanked Freddy," Gretta replied in her sweetest tone of teeth-clenched fury, "but the razor strop and coal bin are looking better and better, even if he is fourteen. And I suspect that he now knows how to track us. The EscaladeLectro contains the master controls for all the car bugs."

"You bugged my car?" Angie tried to sound annoyed despite having known right along. "How dare you?"

"Yes," Maddie said, "how dare you!"

"I dared, girls. I dared. I bugged the BroncEV and Jim's new Beamer too."

As Angie neared the bottom of the Tate driveway heading back to Crumb House, Marion and Mannie were waiting for her next to their black van.

"You have an entourage, Angie," Mary Helen growled. *"Some things never change."*

"You're jealous?"

"Why? I'm more famous than you are, and Stud's more famous than either of us. She makes Lassie look like a cow chip."

"Twice in an hour, Mannie?" Angie was not surprised. "You gentlemen are watching us, aren't you."

"Have been since we came up for our summer vacation with Mark, but he can stay at school at least another day. Marvin is staying with him in case Rue or Mark get any bright ideas. This should be over tonight."

"You've been talking to Adonis Fritz," Maddie said.

Angie corrected her. "No, you've been talking to Rex."

"Yeah," Marion said. "Before the Belmont accident, Rex told us to keep you ladies safe when tonight's operation went down. He thought you and Dale might interfere and might need protection when the Feds and State closed in on The Candy Troops and Snow Queens. Rex also made sure that we would have intelligence pipelines. Only a couple of hours ago, we learned about his true medical condition—it was supposed to be fake—and friend-or-foe unpredictability."

Angie had also calculated that she and Dale might be targeted. Her relationship with Rex had often made social columns on the Net and in what few newspapers remained. Rue might well fear her knowledge of this affair.

"And since we were coming up from the city to see Mark anyway, we decided to kill two stones with one brick," Marion said.

Marion's spectacular performance on the PMS recordings while undercover, so to speak, darted through Angie's mind.

"We're also looking for Kossick," Mannie said. "Have you seen him?" He passed a picture to Angie.

"No," Angie said, "and I already recognize him. He was at Rex's apartment after we found Leech. What's he doing out of his jurisdiction?"

"He's wanted for killing Paul Michael Senna, Henrietta Keeler, and Hooker," Mannie added. "Henrietta's body turned up this morning in a dumpster. Kossick just walked off the force and disappeared but was seen in Saratoga. Originally, he was PMS's hitman before he switched to Rue. He was possibly even working for both at the same time. We can't prove all that, though."

"Kossick, like Leech," Marion said, "was a Candy Trooper but also a gun for hire. Now, he's just a wanted hoodlum."

"We need to fly," Maddie said.

"The boys could be anywhere by now, possibly even Cambodia," Gretta said. "We do need to scoot, gentlemen."

"We're going to Beast — sorry, Gretta — Crumb House, then Congress Park, boys," Angie said as she pulled out.

Once on the main road, Angie asked, "Are the Kershaw boys behind us, Gretta?"

"Of course they are," Maddie said.

—2—

Saratoga, NY. Crumb House. 11:00 PM. Dale.

Dale and Jimmu pulled up the Crumb House driveway, parked near the back door, and waited for Fred. He drove beautifully, though he'd have difficulty passing a driver's test with Cagey Magee taped to his feet and Sleepgram Pillows beneath his behind. Jimmu had promised to help him with that, something about shoe lifts and an elevating car seat. Tonight, Fred was being extra careful to avoid a cop catching him and had fallen behind.

"We may as well go in," Dale said.

Dale and Jimmu hurried into the back door of Crumb House and down the hall.

Jimmu fished a gun out of his underwear drawer in his room, slipped it into a holster on his left ankle, and looked at Dale. "I wonder where my Beretta M9 is. It's my favorite now, but I still like my USP."

"Jimmu, aren't we going off the deep end here?" Dale knew where Jim's Beretta was.

"Well," Jim said, "at the moment, we have a group of drug criminals gathered together at The John for purposes other than playing bridge, doing their hair, trading salacious gossip, or having a picnic. Close and among, we have a small but deadly contingent of bad cops who consider it good practice to assassinate said debutants. Past them, we have the Feds and State, armed to the teeth, intending to scoop up all the above and toss them into the can while they sort out who should stay there."

"That's nothing new for Saratoga," Dale said. "Shoot, Dutch Schultz, Myer Lansky, Arnold Rothstein, Legs Diamond, and Lucky Luciano practically lived here once upon a time, not to mention made a ton of money here. We studied prohibition in Local History, and it's all over the place on the web."

"True," Jimmu said. "Then we have Señor Gregory Rue, who wants the Candies and Snows both dead, and also wishes to abruptly end Cindy McGraw's Grand Ball in the legendary Canfield Casino in Congress Park with a bang."

"Why don't they evacuate the place?"

"Because no one believes it could happen, much less would, and, anyway, all the cops are at The John. Local cops did search for any sign of explosives, then declared it safe, and maybe it is. Remember that all those folks whom you mentioned who once visited there, not far from our front porch, also visited here—it's part of the legend. It's a thrill getting drunk and having sex in a historical setting, and it draws a crowd. Unfortunately, Señor Rue's richest competitors and his enemies' bankrollers attend The Grand Ball. Rue wants to become The Once and Future Drug King simply by wiping everyone else out. I submit that under these circumstances, carrying a weapon might be prudent."

"How do you know all that?"

"I have connections. More importantly, you and Fred are connected to me at the hip until this is over."

"Okay. Do you have a gun for me, and where is Fred?"

"Fred told me about your exceptional markspersonship in the now sadly wounded Tate Gun Club, although you reportedly did occasionally hit what you aimed for." Jim tossed Dale a switchblade fishing knife. "Use that if you absolutely must, just not on Fred, me, or anyone we know. And Fred should be back by now. You're right. Where is he?"

"And how about Rex? He's lost too." Dale heard himself say it aloud for the first time.

"I don't know about Rex, but there's more there than meets the eye. At the moment, I'm more concerned about my cantankerously cute, stupid little brother. I would kill or die for him, but he always keeps me in the dark and taunts me with his intelligence. And I have the feeling he just did it again." Jimmu hurried down the hall to look out the back door with Dale just behind.

The EscaladeLectro was sitting there in the back parking lot. They ran out and opened the driver's door. No Fred, but his Cagey Magee bundles were on the seat, on top of his ridiculous disguise that worked perfectly. On the floor were dirty tissues he used to wipe off his makeup.

"Okay," Dale said. "Fred has to be here somewhere. He told me that he was the key to this mess."

"What? That's crazy! Why does he think he's the key?" For once, Jimmu looked flummoxed, discombobulated, swishless, and seriously worried.

"He wouldn't say, Jim. He never told me the truth about his scars, either, not until recently."

"It is kind of a secret."

"Could his being the key have something to do with the scars?" Dale asked.

"You could say that. In addition to accidents, Fred has always impulsively taken chances and has often gotten himself hurt, usually with good intentions. My little brother has a conscience as big as New York City.

It's just that he sometimes chooses to go with that rather than his survival sense. Freddy will become an exceptionally good man if he survives adolescence. And he's not stupid, not even close. He just acts it sometimes."

Dale felt ashamed because of his Fred-loyalty and Jimmu-deceit—he'd only recently learned how to do that. "Let's search the house, Jim. I'm worried too."

They began walking around the house to see if they could find the little guy, even though Dale knew he was not there. This was a big house and would take time to search, and time was what Dale needed to buy for Fred.

Chapter 36 - Mary Helen Mack

I wiggled. They nibbled.

—1—

Saratoga, NY. Congress Park. 11:05 PM. Inspector Rex Caine.

The Barbara Party Orchestra in Canfield Casino twanged the night air. Lightning danced in the sky, an approaching storm. A thunder dome rumbled, merged with the orchestra, and ricocheted down Congress Park from Cindy McGraw's Grand Ball.

Rex slipped down toward the War Memorial. He needed to retrieve the kill switch and defeat the blast, or the party would end abruptly simply because Gregory Rue wanted it. Rex barely remembered planting the C-15 but was sure he'd done it. The Candy Troops were gathering at Appleseed for the kill, and the FBI Tac team, with help from the New York State Police, was preparing to apprehend the whole bunch.

Rex needed to stop the casino blast.

He had regained most of his memory about the plan. The Bureau would manage, and state cops would support. He also knew that his nurse, whatever her name was, considered him a resident stud. He was lost between two independent worlds but horny in both. He vaguely knew who Angie and her friends were and had apologized for locking them in the closet—he wanted to protect them because he knew they meddled and would end up in the wrong place at the wrong time. The US and NY Attorneys General wanted no civilian casualties and exclusively good press from this operation. Nothing new in that.

Then there was Dale. He had talked to Rex like the trusting little kid he had always been, sometime, somewhere. Dale and his little friend, whom Rex should remember but couldn't quite, had triggered memories that expanded after the boys left his suite. Rex believed that everything was possible, even more than Angie did. Nothing was certain except what he wanted to happen, and just now, that was to earn Dale and his friend's trust.

Dale now knew that Rex was no longer comatose. That didn't matter. During their conversation, the boy had cleared up much and seemed likely to keep Rex's secret. He must protect the boys, not kill them. Rex might take out druggies who ruined the streets, but not innocent kids. It didn't matter that The State now executed kids for capital offenses.

Rex did not take out druggies that way, The Candy Troops did that, and it was wrong! Without unbiased due process, the sanity principle vanished.

Rex's identity confusion for self and others was his biggest problem now, that and discerning which memories were genuine, if any. He knew he'd killed John Leech when Leech tried to kill him. He told Leech he wanted no part of The Candy Troops. Slag Lessix was John's backup, inept as usual. He ran rather than face Rex. Trying a second time at Belmont was stupid.

Rex thought he'd stayed true to his assignment but was unsure of the details. Belmont had hurt his head. It still hurt. No one would notice him here in Congress Park, not with the approaching thunderstorm, The Grand Ball, and the distractions he was counting on, but he'd need to be careful. Rue was here somewhere, and he would not be alone. At some point, Rex alerted the Kershaw boys but couldn't remember when. He could remember planning the operation and then submitting it for approval. Gregory Rue was the monster. Above all the others, he needed to die before Rex forgot his face too. Rue planned to kill Rex. Rex planned to kill Rue.

The grass felt dry under Rex's boots. The park needed rain, and would receive some, judging from the flashing sky. All the better for Rex. Streetlights lined the deserted walks that snaked through the park and points of interest. Saratoga's Congress Park was bordered by civilization on all sides, an oasis with a big history. By day, the park was a pristine historic sanctuary, but by night, she was a menacing giant who guarded her treasures and night walkers.

– 2 –

Saratoga, NY. Crumb House. 11:10 PM. Dale

"That's your mom's Maserati Hydro-Quad," Jimmu said.

They both heard Dale's mom's Rat purring up the driveway to the back of Crumb House.

"Front door, Dale. Out!"

Dale didn't ask but knew. If the palace queens detected Fred's absence, Jimmu and Dale would die or possibly lose parental respect.

Outside, the air smelled cool and fresh despite the cigarette smoke drifting over from the back of the Canfield Casino. Finally, he couldn't hold it in. "Fred's going to confront Rex about something back in New York. I think he intended to be in Congress Park by now, somewhere near the War Memorial where he and I saw Rex."

"He's what?" Jimmu ducked into the rhododendron by the front porch and dragged Dale after him. Gunfire broke out behind Crumb House but was nearly inaudible over the din in the Casino.

"Go help Fred, Dale, and be careful, or you'll answer to me," Jimmu loud-whispered. "Stay at a safe distance, whatever you do." Jimmu pulled his gun and fired twice into the air. That was probably a help signal. "I'll go help the cauldron sisters."

Dale saw shadows moving toward him. A bullet hit the mailbox just above his head.

"Don't move," Jim hissed. "Change of plans, and don't you dare move."

— 3 —

Congress Park War Memorial. 11:20 PM. Inspector Rex Caine.

When Rex approached the dark War Memorial where he'd hidden the remote, a light flared deep inside, a small flame. Rex pulled his M9 out and walked toward the light. If this were Rue, he'd soon be dead, but only a small hand held the flame, soon replaced by a cigarette cherry.

A lightning strike shook the path to the Memorial. Thunder followed. Lightning jumped from cloud to cloud, stretching across the sky like fingers. C-15 could take down an entire building if you correctly placed it and the detonator packs.

***

Looking at the sky, Rex remembered that night a year ago when the sky raged like this, that awful night on Manhattan's Upper West Side.

He had pulled the sheet metal back from the deserted tenement door, stepped inside, and smelled bowel—Manhattan perfume. Benji could have had an accident. You couldn't blame the kid. This place scared Rex too. All he wanted was to turn Benji loose and get the hell out of here. The little pusher had maintained his rep for telling the truth: his sister and her friends were dead before Rex reached them. Now Rex would keep his word and release the kid.

Rex knew Benji well from his arrests. The boy was a few notches above the average street-kid pusher. He kept himself clean, got good grades in school, and never played hooky. He avoided suspicious characters, except maybe his product suppliers and dead sister. He sold drugs but did not use. Apparently, small miracles did happen. The boy had obviously set his sights on something better. Rex wondered if he could possibly give the kid a hand. His teachers all agreed that any kid as smart and pragmatic as Benji might be able to graduate to a decent life, especially with his big brother Jimmu at his back.

The smell here grew from annoying to overbearing as Rex crept forward. Something in the dark tenement warned him not to turn his light on. Something. His shoes squished on the sticky floor. He didn't remember that sound and feel being there when he'd tied Benji on the pile of abandoned clothes to keep him from running. A sound, not faint but thin and gentle, licked through the air—a cheerful sound lapping and rustling.

Rex froze and listened. He whiffed and smelled rat droppings. He snapped the flash on. Three more steps, and he would have tripped over the boy. Still tied, Benji lay face down now. He'd turned himself onto him stomach and tried to reach the front door, but his desperate thrashing had not deterred the rats.

Even now, in the circle of light, the rats rustled around the boy in a tight little cluster, nibbling an arm and a string of intestines. They had severed a vein. Rex was walking through blood and fleshy bits, smelling the boy's guts that the rats had dragged out onto the floor. Benji's open, sideways-looking eyes fixed his death agony in Rex's mind forever. He could see every futile moment, frantic effort, and snarl of anguish and disbelief that he saw in his brother Emory's eyes when Benji's sister and her friends finished with him.

"Noooo!" The sound of his scream radiated up the stairwell of the tenement.

Benji's rats eyed Rex inquisitively, as though they wondered if he were one of them.

"Noooooo!" Rex heard his second scream from far away, echoing through the sprawling spiraling labyrinth of tenement night horrors, muffled by the butt of the flash he'd jammed into his mouth so he could aim his gun.

He fell onto his knees by Benji's body and dropped his light. "Get away, God damn you."

The rats scattered in an explosion of chuckling chatters. Rex rolled the little boy onto his back. The neat incision in his abdomen gaped. Rats had threaded an intestine string out. He frantically pried the boy's little mouth open and did mouth to mouth. He pounded on the chest and tried to breathe air into Benji's lungs.

"Nothing! There's nothing I can do." He closed his eyes. "Dear God, there's nothing left of him. No life. Please help me. Please. There's no life left."

Rex's flash lay on the floor. The light lit the boy's right hip and outlined the rest of his body in shadow halos. Behind the body, the red eyes of the rat congregation waited. Rex stared at his blood-painted hands and at the rats. They stared back. Survivors, like rats, druggies, pushers, and dealers, multiplied faster than you could kill them, but if you didn't, what good were you? "No, not Leech's way," he moaned.

The rats surged toward Rex, an army that could put him on the floor with the boy. The red eyes beckoned.

Someone knocked Rex out of the way. "Benji," the boy yelled and dropped to his knees.

"Rex! Put away your gun," Angie yelled. "Help us. We've got to get him to a hospital, Jimmu."

"He's dead, Ange!" Rex moaned.

"I'm a nurse, and he's not dead!" Maddie snarled. "Now help me, damn it! Gretta, get in here."

He was dead. Rex had killed him.

—4—

Saratoga, NY. Crumb House. 11:30 PM. Dale.

While Jimmu searched West Circular Street for the gunman who fired at them, Dale slipped through the rhododendron toward the back of the house. His mom was an excellent shot, but the entire neighborhood had come alive with lightning, music, and gunfire. He peeked around the back corner of Crumb House.

His mom had parked her Rat parallel to the house. She and Aunt Gretta were pinned down behind the car, his mom with her Beretta and Gretta with a WatTech XT200. Aunt Maddie didn't need a gun because she was face down on the ground next to the car, her head hidden in her hands.

Dale saw a clown approach the Maserati Hydro-Quad from the far side of the driveway. Cindy McGraw always hired clowns for The Grand Ball. She called it comic relief from propriety. Mary Margaret Pinkham was part clown, too—Dale so loved her. This clown, though, carried a gun aimed at Dale's mom. Without thinking, planning, aiming, peeing, or breathing, Dale reached for his sock holster, grabbed Jimmu's M9, stood, and fired.

The clown fell backward without his hair and part of his head. Dale had missed the chest. An instant later, Aunt Maddie reared up with her XT200 and sprayed the bushes on Dale's right. Two voices screamed, then went plop in the jewelweed just as a wall moved in behind Dale, and he looked up into the eyes of Marion Kershaw, the hugest of the three Kershaw man mountains.

"Gun in pants, small of your back, Dale," Marion whispered. "Crawl out of here on your belly toward the park."

Dale obeyed. Near the street, he saw the shadows of Jimmu hand-to-hand fighting a small group of attackers. Even with only shadows, it was obvious that the attackers didn't stand a chance. Jim flung one guy down the walk that bordered the front of the Canfield Casino.

—5—

Saratoga, NY. Congress Park. The War Memorial. 11:45 PM. Inspector Rex Caine.

"No choice," Rex murmured to the boy standing in the War Memorial. It was wishful thinking in the end. It couldn't be, but—

Rex stood on the brick walkway that led into the War Memorial. Benji was dead, but he stood there waiting for Rex. His small face seemed to float in the street light. He waited for revenge, for Rex, for the kill.

"From what Dale told me," Benji's trembling voice said, "you needed to do it." He sounded scared but determined. "Somebody's making you, or your fugue state is. Dale says that you are important in the Department and was participating in a big bust when you fell on your head and misplaced your brain. Cow, no one knew you were really in a coma."

Rex stared at the boy. "Benji?"

"You know, Rex, Dale really loves you. And I'm not Benji, I'm Fred, Dale's best friend."

"I killed you, Benji."

"Do I look killed?"

"I killed you!"

"I don't feel killed and kinda want to keep it that way."

Rex shined his light on the boy standing there, a little more than four feet tall, with neatly combed black hair, slight body, clean jeans, and a clean white T-shirt with a picture of Gandhi — way cleaner than most street kids. He probably planned on graduating to a higher class of drug clients.

"Get away, Benji!"

"Hey, Rex, you sat with me in the hospital, you and Angie and Maddie and Gretta and Jimmu and Dakota Jefferson — you hardly ever left me, Rex.

"Just get away. You've tortured me since the night at the tenement. I did not want to kill you then, but now I need to, boy. I really need to. It's the only way you'll go away once and for all." Rex heard his voice plead.

The boy backed away a step.

"I don't want to hurt you again." But Rex saw his hand raise the Beretta M9 and aim at the small target who looked as he had under the streetlight that awful night, the night that Rex and the rats took the boy. Such a happy, rosy little fellow for a schoolyard pusher. "You know where it is, don't you? You know. You found where I hid it. The remote. You're torturing me again."

"Yeah. Dale and I saw you hide it, and we moved it. It's still here. And I don't want you to hurt me even more than you don't want to, which is worrisome. Killing me? I guess I could live with that since I wouldn't know, but I don't think you'll do it, and I can't let you kill everyone at the party. I know about that too. You don't look like a killer except maybe if somebody's trying to kill you, which I'm not. You don't look like a killer or a hurter. What you are is my best friend's dad. That's how he feels about you, anyway."

The blank expression on Benji's face was that of a canny liar. Rex was a cop and knew a liar when he saw one. Cops could tell, and this kid was snowing him and pissing him off. "You're lying, Benji. There's not much time." Voices screamed from the street above, from two figures, three, four, running toward them from somewhere. "You need to give me the remote."

"To blow everyone to hell?"

"No!" Rex walked toward the boy. "To stop it from happening." Benji's cheery chutzpah kept him right where he was, not backing down. "It started with you, Benji. I wanted to kill Emory's killers, your sister and her friends, but they were already dead—you warned me. It started with you." Faint steps ran at Rex from inside the park, down away somewhere. Rue's men? The triumvirate? Someone was firing.

Benji shook his head. "Naw, it started with you, Rex. Everyone's problems start with themselves. Dale taught me that, and I taught him to practice what he damned preached."

"The rats ate your guts out."

"Really? Maybe that's how I got so short."

"I killed you by accidentally leaving you for the rats."

Benji shrugged, tilted his head, and held his hands out sideways, palms up. "You didn't know. Besides, I like rats, and your mother's a suitcase. Hey, why don't you knock it off, Rex? Dale ratted you out. He told me everything he knew about what a great guy you are, what a kidder, and what a great father you will make. But you're beginning to scare me."

"You're a pusher."

"I was a seller," Benji corrected, "to make ends meet, to help Jimmu feed us before he got the job with Aunt Mirthretta. I know it was wrong, but I never pushed anybody to buy, and Jim would have killed me painfully if I ever used, and he almost did when he found out I was dealing. The night you grabbed me was my last buffet."

"The rats got you."

"Yeah, a little." Benji lifted Ghandhi. "It hurt too." A trail of faint bite scars trailed across his stomach with a stitched-looking healed place in the middle. "I wiggled. They nibbled. After all, I was in their territory. But I'm not Benji anymore. I'm Fred now, Fred the Small, first of his name—no kids are named Fred in China. The rats would have killed me if you and everybody hadn't rescued me and gotten me to the hospital, and Aunt Mirthretta hadn't pretty much adopted Jimmu and me. That will be official soon, if I live that long. Jim misplaced me the night of the rats and asked Gretta and Angie for help. We even lived in our own apartment by then. And you didn't mean to hurt me. You just wanted me to stay in one place until you got back. It's not like you knew the rats personally. And I'm talking way too much."

Rex stood ten feet away from Benji now. The kid couldn't move back any farther. He could not run. Rex glanced back. From his left, shadows appeared, running down from West Circular Street. The streetlights flashed on their faces. Out on the streets, sirens sparked into the night.

"I'm a hired killer, nothing more, nothing less, Benji."

"Naw. You're a neat guy, Inspector Rex Caine. You just have some problems that messed with your head, and I turned into part of it, maybe even led it. I didn't mean to, but I figured it out when Dale and I visited you. You went pale when you saw me, and as soon as I left the room, you started talking about rats—I eavesdrop lots. Honestly, I didn't mean to cause you a problem. Is this what you're looking for? I think I believe you now. Are you sure I should push it?"

Benji's speech was accelerating as he waved the remote at Rex. He would bolt soon. Even though there was no place for him to bolt to except the water that surrounded the War Memorial, the kid would bolt.

"You hid this, then planted something in the Casino's foundation. You don't really want to kill me or blow up the Casino with the explosives from The John Appleseed Cottage, do you?"

"I don't remember," Rex said, "except I came here twice before today."

"From what I've heard, I can't say that I blame Dale and Ms. Summers for loving you like mad. I don't buy that you're a killer, either." Benji finished the cigarette and flicked the butt over his shoulder into the water.

"Push it, Fred. Please! Push the 'OKAY' in the remote. It will stop the blast. It's a kill switch!"

"Angie and Dale wouldn't love a killer, Rex. Maybe you are a little confused, but so am I. Even short people and konked-on-the-noggin people can get over that, can't they?"

Rex spotted the triumvirate running down from Crumb House: Angie, Maddie, Gretta. He knew them, and Dale.

"It's almost midnight. For God's sake, push it, Fred. It's the kill switch to stop the blast."

"Fred, get away." A familiar voice.

"Dale?" Rex called. "Push, Fred! Please!"

Fred pushed.

Blinding lights flared. Magentas, greens, blues, and gold lit the sky above Congress Park. South of town, a blast lit the rest of the sky and shook the park and city.

"Oh my God, I forgot them," Rex screamed.

The guests were leaving the Canfield Casino to see the midnight fireworks display that always ended Cindy McGraw's Grand Balls.

"No. The well." Rex drew a breath and smiled. "The Golden Arms well."

"Rex," someone called closer.

"Angie?" The name warmed Rex.

"I guess maybe you did get hit in the head, Rex," Fred yelled.

"Angie, get back here!" Gretta's voice.

"Angie!" Maddie's voice.

"Fred, Dale, get away from there." Gretta's voice again.

Dots of light punctuated the dark. Gunfire splattered.

"Drop your weapon, Rex." Mannie Kershaw's voice.

"I guess you did lose track of yourself some," Fred screamed over the fireworks explosions. "I heard about it from Adonis and Dale and Jimmu. It was supposed to be play-acting to get you into The Golden Arms without suspicion, so you could help take down The Snow Queens across the road. Your head injury at Belmont was the mistake."

"No." The memory panicked Caine. "Slag needed to die. He tried to kill me."

"Fred, get away from there," Dale shouted. "Jump into the water."

Benji's small body cringed. Fear blazed in his eyes as it had that night in the tenement.

"Okay, I was Benji Shinker. Now, I'm Fred Styles or Lóng Wang Lei. Dale, I'd appreciate some help with this!"

"Uncle Rex," the familiar voice, the closest, on the hill down from the Casino. "Please put your gun down. Please, Uncle Rex. Dad, it's Dale." The voice sounded out of breath. Dale needed to exercise more.

"Get away, Dale. Get away."

Dale, the puppy who sat on Rex's knee. The puppy with big eyes, the one who fell down a lot. Dale. Angie's Dale. Rex's Dale.

"I don't know who I am," Rex screamed to the sky.

"Caine, you son-of-a-bitch!" A familiar voice.

Rex turned, saw Dale running toward him, raised his weapon, and ordered, "Get away from here, Dale." Dale seemed bigger than the little puppy, his voice deeper. "Back off Kossick." The world was changing around Rex like a revolving stage. Leech. The Snow Queens, The Candy Troops. Benji, the one face he couldn't free himself from.

Rex lifted his head, lifted his Beretta, screamed, "Stop or I'll shoot," at the man closing in behind Dale.

The park shifted into clear focus: Circular Street, monuments, lightning, Dale running toward Rex.

"Stop where you are, Kossick!"

Kossick stopped in his tracks, but lifted his forty-five and point it at Dale.

Dale twisted.

Rex aimed, but Fred lurched forward, grabbed his hand, and diverted the shot.

Kossick fired straight at Dale, who flew off the walk onto the grass.

Kossick and Rex fired as a black shadow flew from the walk and landed on Kossick with a loud snap. Gunfire exploded from all over. Rex felt nothing but realized he had fallen and now lay on the floor of the War Memorial in his own blood.

— 6 —

Saratoga, NY. Congress Park. 12:27 AM. Dale.

Something had knocked Dale out of the way. The partiers at the Canfield Casino had scattered as gunfire replaced the fireworks.

Then, everything stopped.

A man with a gun lay bleeding on the path, his head at a crazy angle, Dale's fishing knife protruding from his chest.

Jimmu lay not far away in splatters of blood. Mannie and Marion Kershaw were there tending to him.

Dale dragged himself up and ran toward the War Memorial, then froze. Uncle Rex lay on his back, a ragged hole near his shoulder. Blood trickled off the Memorial into the cracks in the brick path.

Rex was conscious. "Dale, help Fred."

Fred was slumped, holding himself up by the back monument of the War Memorial with his left hand as his right tried to stop the bleeding.

"Oh, Fred." Dale pulled off his T-shirt, lowered Fred to the Memorial floor, then dropped to his knees, crammed the shirt against Fred's chest, and pushed like mad. "Hold on, Fred. They're coming."

"Rex was going to shoot you," Fred whispered.

"No, Fred. I realized that Kossick was close behind me. I couldn't reach my gun, so I opened my knife. Rex was aiming at Kossick. Kossick fired at me, but someone grabbed my knife and then tossed me to the grass out of the way. At least, that was what it felt like. I guess you couldn't see over my head. I think Rex killed Kossick, or Jimmu did, or one of the Kershaws, or Mom or somebody. The whole bunch was toting and shooting. I don't really know who shot whom. Sometimes I think there are too many guns in the world."

"I really thought Rex was aiming at you," Fred gasped with a smile. "No shit. Well, that's one on me. I think Rex figured out he was wrong and maybe remembered that he helped me that night. He and Dakota Dong even sat with me in the hospital. I told you about Dakota." Fred clenched his fists. "Jeez, Summers, I did lots of stuff I never want to tell you about 'cause I can't forget it if I do, but getting shot really hurts." Fred's eyes closed. His clenched fists relaxed.

Dale's mom, Aunt Maddie, and Gretta were there now, all with XT200s, Berettas, or something.

The ambulance guys took over and started working on Jimmu, who got shot and was bleeding, but he'd snapped Kossick's neck on the fly.

A couple of ambulance attendants were trying to help poor Fred, who really was the key. Without him, Rex may never have come around. Maybe fugue states could help you fly away to a new life, but they could also cause lots of damage. Dale's mom had carefully explained that.

After the ambulances hurried away, Dale, shirtless and covered in Fred's blood, hugged his mom. He wanted to hug her forever.

"You guys are heroes, Marion," Dale's mom said.

At ten feet tall or something, Marion Kershaw towered over them all. "No, ma'am, Rex, Jimmu, and Dale are the heroes. We didn't have a shot because Kossick was too close to Dale, and Rue's guys were firing at us, though Rue himself wasn't here. Dale jumped out of the way. We think Jimmu flew, broke Kossick's neck, and took Rex's bullet. Kossick got hit at least six times once Dale was out of the way. Rex was always the best shot of any of us, but Jimmu and Dale are really fast.

"Rex came through," Marion said. "Despite his confusion, he planted the C-15, the detonator packs, and a remote detonator in the old stone well that sat in the middle of the field next to The Golden Arms, across from The John Appleseed Cottage. Fred set it off. Where the well was, there's now a crater. The fireworks here were planned for the end of Mrs. McGraw's party. If it hadn't been for Jim and Rex, Kossick would have fired and kept firing, a good cop once, a lethal son-of-a-bitch now, like most bad cops."

"How did Kossick miss me?" Dale asked.

"Involuntarily fast response, son. Adrenalin," Mannie said. "It happens. Involuntary response. Like Jimmu, you're really fast when you want to be, kid."

Dale knew that was bull but decided to drop it. He knew who saved him.

"Take me to the hospital, Mom," Dale demanded. "Take me now!"

Epilogue

Hallelujah, Mary Helen, and thanks.
Saratoga, NY. Greenridge Cemetery. 2:00 PM. Dale Summers.

With the cheerful sun shining on him, Dale felt even worse. Considering who lay at his feet, nothing matched anything anymore. Nothing made sense.

Dale smudged a tear off his right cheek as he lowered himself to the ground and crossed his legs, as he used to in the middle of his dorm bed back at posh old Tate Prep, where he'd return soon. Autumn already tinged the leaves.

He supposed you could think of the Greenridge Cemetery as a big bed, but the damp ground felt as cold as if he were under it, and the monuments, mausoleums, and stone angels kept whispering, "Dead."

Of course, some people here possessed only little stones, this one only a few inches off the ground, even at the high side of the polished top.

"It shouldn't be small," a hollow voice said behind him. "It should be huge. After what happened, it should be tremendous."

"This should never have happened. Never ever." Dale was part of it too, and God was, and by rights, neither God nor Dale could look into the mirror and still feel comfortable with themselves.

Dale stared at the stone. His tears got the best of him and started dribbling down his cheeks again. He wished the sun would go away and dry up and blow to Hell.

"It's okay, Dale," Jimmu said, still behind him, his arm hung in a sling around his neck.

"I know I'm being silly, Jim."

"Not really. At least you're still here, healthy and alive."

Jimmu was one of the heroes of this story, and Gretta gave him what he wanted. Today he would return to New York to get ready to enter Columbia University, one of the best universities in the world. Everyone was going with him to get him settled, like the family they had all sort of become. Gretta had even given him his own apartment on the Upper West Side.

Dale had sat here at the cemetery for a long time, but he couldn't leave. His whole life had come unglued and fallen into the dirt. The sun glared down on the tall old monuments and the mausoleum that shaded the marker before him.

Somewhere, a car door closed—Aunt Gretta's WatStretchEV. Dale heard his mom's brisk quick steps punctuating the wind easing through the ancient oaks dotting the cemetery. For a moment, Dale smelled wintergreen.

"Dale?"

"Yeah, Mom."

"Are you ready to go yet?"

"I don't know."

"We've got to get back to New York to get Jimmu ready for Columbia. We can visit again."

They had made a pact to work hard to repair each other's damaged lives. They wanted to let the past stay past and forget as much of it as they could. "Okay, but I really want to visit again before school. There are some things I don't want to forget ever."

Dale dragged himself up, and his mother put her arms around him and squeezed. He leaned his head over until it rested on her shoulder. He could feel that she was sad too and, apart from Dale, alone.

The smell of wintergreen grew stronger now. Dale reached out and pulled Fred in for a three-way hug, carefully because Fred was still bandaged. The sun had moved some and was shining straight at the stone now. It missed Fred. He was little, you know, but not in ways that counted. Jimmu and Fred were, after all, the real heroes of the story.

Dale cried harder when his mom finally got him turned around and headed back to the WatStretchEV with Fred helping her and Jimmu bringing up the rear. "Are we going to visit Uncle Rex before we leave?"

"No, I don't think so, Dale." Gently. Almost a caress or a smile.

"Will he ever get better, Mom? Will he ever get to know what went on and what's happening now?"

"I think he just might." Her voice kind of smiled a little. "Actually, I'm sure of it."

"Like on the moon's dark side, past the Terminator Line, like you said in Aunt Gretta's gazebo?" Dale lifted his head off her shoulder and looked into her eyes.

She was nursing her own tears. "I guess," she agreed.

"Just throw it all onto the frigging wall," Fred whispered. "If you're lucky, what sticks will be the good stuff, and we're going to have a wonderful time in New York."

"I guess." Dale reached over to give Fred another man hug.

They all climbed into the WatStretchEV. The window opened, and a big woman, Dale guessed

Gretta's new chauffeur, Margaret, asked, "Are we ready back there?"

"Yes," Aunt Gretta said. "Are we ready up there?"

"Oh, yes," Margaret said. "We're fine up here."

As they took off, Fred asked, "Can I tell him, Ms. Summers?"

"I think you should."

"I have a surprise for you, Dale," Fred said. "Please don't cry, faint, puke, or crap your knickers."

"Okay," Dale said, "I'll try."

"Definitely," Aunt Maddie said. "Margaret, turn on the air conditioning."

Fred slipped open the window behind the front passenger seat. Rex turned around and waved, pretty much looking like his old self, plus a few bruises, eye bags, and bandages.

Dale looked at his mom, and she showed Dale her hand. She was close to her old self, too, despite the engagement ring.

After Dale regained consciousness with Mom, Aunt Maddie, Aunt Gretta, Jimmu, and Fred fanning him, he murmured, "I'm so happy." And he was.

Only Mary Helen Mack was missing. She had saved Dale's life when she pushed him off the path and used his knife to stab Kossick's heart. She did not exactly die—she was just a character in a book—but she also didn't seem to be here anymore.

Aunt Gretta bought her a headstone and gave her a couple of feet on the site of the Crumb Mausoleum. His mom may have dropped Mary Helen for now—she was not in his mom's newest novel, *Saratoga Cauldron*, but if Dale and Gretta got their way, there would soon be a bright resurrection. She had, after all, saved Dale's life.

Don't worry, Dale," Mary Helen whispered, *"I'm still here. You can't really kill an idea. I'm glad my shove and stab saved you.*

"Your mother doesn't need me anymore, I guess, so I'll stay with you guys for a while, Fred and you. Just don't tell anyone. Uncle Stud and I like a low profile."

"Hallelujah," Dale whispered. *"Hallelujah and thanks, Mary Helen."*

About the Author

Author, editor, teacher, virtuoso, Mr. Cagey Magee, graduated from modestly bookish, obnoxious kid to obsessive young-adult reader at around the age of eleven. He lived not far from an excellent library filled with novels that led him to faraway universes and fascinating people. He devoured them — the novels, not the people — and soon became obsessed with writing his own horror, young adult, mystery-thriller, and coming-of-age stories.

Cagey's first novel came in at the size of two long books. He quickly learned the error of his ways when he needed to print the thing out and carry it. His current novels are more compact but still a little offbeat. He inevitably falls in love with his characters and really hates to kill them. For Cagey, the near future holds infinite marvels. No one is all good or all bad. He loves them for who they are and where they go next, and hopes his readers will hang in there for the bumpy ride.

For more, please visit Mr. Cagey Magee online at:
Website: www.EvolvedPub.com/CMagee
Facebook: @Cagey Magee

More from Cagey Magee

Be sure to check out the complete "NorthWatch" series of near-future young adult thrillers.

Cass and Wat (Book 1):
Cass discovers an intricate pattern of betrayal as she protects her family and her father's presidential campaign.

Cass and Logan (Book 2):
Cass is counting down to her father's inauguration when she realizes that Mac Beverly may be alive. Her 2036 kidnapping now seems a lovely vacation.

Cass and Nat (Book 3):
After basking momentarily in her father's inauguration and midnight marriage, Cass must race to Boston Children's Hospital to save Little Mac. She's beginning to suspect that she can no longer feast without at least two disasters for dessert. When Little Mac's wheelchair explodes, she's certain.

Cass and Keith (Book 4):
Nearly 15-year-old Cass senses that more violence will come, and she wants no part of it. She abandons her presidential aspirations in favor of becoming the next Stephen King — higher bar but nobler pursuit.

More from Evolved Publishing

We offer great books across multiple genres, featuring high-quality editing (which we believe is second-to-none) and fantastic covers.

As a hybrid small press, your support as loyal readers is so important to us, and we have strived, with tireless dedication and sheer determination, to deliver on the promise of our motto:
QUALITY IS PRIORITY #1!

Please check out all of our great books, which you can find at this link:
www.EvolvedPub.com/Catalog/

Thank you!